Y0-BQE-366

Soap Bubbles

Soap Bubbles

Denise Dietz

FIVE STAR
A part of Gale, Cengage Learning

Detroit • New York • San Francisco • New Haven, Conn • Waterville, Maine • London

Scripture quotation is taken from the King James Version of the Bible; Job 38:7.

Five Star Publishing, a part of Gale, Cengage Learning.

Set in 11 pt. Plantin.

Printed on permanent paper.

LIBRARY OF CONGRESS CATALOGING-IN-PUBLICATION DATA

Dietz, Denise.
Soap bubbles / Denise Dietz. — 1st ed.
p. cm.
ISBN-13: 978-1-59414-875-0 (alk. paper)
ISBN-10: 1-59414-875-9 (alk. paper)
1. Television soap operas—Fiction. I. Title.
PS3554.I368S63 2010
813′.54—dc22 2009050612

First Edition. First Printing: April 2010.
Published in 2010 in conjunction with Tekno Books.

Printed in the United States of America
1 2 3 4 5 6 7 14 13 12 11 10

This book is for Eileen Dietz,
who played "Sarah" on *General Hospital*

Overture

August 25, 1985

A ghetto blaster blasted Blood, Sweat and Tears.

Delly Diamond covered her ears, but her palms couldn't block out the music that coursed through her body like the throb from a stubbed toe.

"I give it five for the words and nine for the beat," she whispered.

Once upon a long time ago, she had prayed on her knees. Prayed every night. Prayed to appear on *American Bandstand.* God, how she wanted to shake, rattle and roll. Maybe even shake Dick Clark's hand. "Hi Dick, I'm Delly from Bayside, New York," she would have said, "and I give it five for the words and nine for the beat."

Instead, her twin sister had appeared on *Bandstand.* The TV cameras honed in on Samantha during every dance. Sami, a professional amateur, didn't even wave.

The kid with the ghetto blaster headed for an exit door. Delly freed her hands from her ears and switched her tote from one shoulder to the other. Bloomingdale's buzzed like a payphone's busy signal. Stationed near the cosmetics counter, a mime squirted sample perfume. Before she could object, Delly was engulfed by a cloud of disgusting musk. The mime patted his heart and held up the bottle. Delly squelched the impulse to gesture with her middle finger. Samantha would have blown him a fingertip kiss. Or blown him for free perfume.

Delly's throat clogged and her heart slammed against her ribs. She squeezed her eyes shut then opened them again because her shrink said that stage curtains only momentarily hid the sets and actors.

She found a table with sample cosmetics. She stared into a magnifying mirror as she applied eye shadow, mascara and lip gloss. Then she smeared thick goop beneath her eyes. What a difference! Without the raccoon smudges she looked ten years younger—twenty-two rather than thirty-two.

Her dress helped, too. The lilac silk whispered against her bare legs. Could a dress whisper? Okay, so it *swooshed.* But it *swooshed* seductively. That was important because she had to show Judith Pendergraft that Delly Diamond could still look young and sexy.

Her sneakers ruined the effect, somewhat. She'd hoped to find the perfect pair of sandals on sale and had: an adorable pair with fake gemstones, size five-and-a-half. But she'd forgotten that her credit cards were maxed out.

"I'm just an ugly duckling," she sang, "with feathers all silky and puce."

A woman with a babushka and a baby stared.

"So I'm not Blood, Sweat and Tears, so sue me," Delly said to the Babushka Woman, who continued staring—*how rude*—as Delly pushed open the doors that led to Lexington Avenue.

Hot. Very hot. Above Lego-stacked buildings, the sky was filtered with canary-yellow sunshine. New York City shimmered and Delly felt dizzy.

Maybe her dizziness wasn't caused by the sun. Maybe she was hungry. She'd spent last night inside the bus station, dozing, using her tote as a pillow. Supper had been a bag of peanuts from a vending machine.

Running her tongue across her lips, she thought about what she'd order at the luncheon meeting. Less than an hour to go before she was due to dine with Judith Pendergraft. After lunch she'd join Anissa Cartier and Maryl Bradley for a matinee at the Winter Garden. Delly hadn't seen her two best friends in ages and she felt a happy twinge when she pictured the reunion. Then, dismay. Anissa played the lead on a popular soap. Although Maryl was a mom, she could still easily grace the cover of *Seventeen.* What would they talk about? Delly nudged a curbside candy wrapper. She'd invent something plausible. Was the lead in a new Neil Simon play plausible?

Mentally totaling the money in her wallet, she decided it wasn't enough to justify a cab. Even a bus ride across town would deplete her resources. She had a few subway tokens, but she'd traveled to Bloomingdale's via the subway and she shuddered at the thought of re-submerging herself underground.

Until a few years ago she had gaily traipsed through the subterranean grottos, heading east side, west side, all around the town, rarely giving her surroundings a second glance. But this morning she'd focused on the dirt, the obscene graffiti, and the bright posters advertising movies. A new movie co-starred Amy Irving. Furtively, Delly had slashed through Amy Irving's name and printed DELLY DIAMOND with a black felt-tip pen.

Panting like a woman giving birth, Delly trudged block after block, finally reaching the street with the scriptwriter's apartment building. She walked past it, retraced her steps, and stood under a small burgundy-and-white striped entrance awning. The building was nondescript, sandwiched between a luggage store and a shoe boutique. At seven thousand a month, she had expected at least one naked fountain Cupid, its sculpted penis urinating mineral water. But she'd been in Hollywood too long, forgotten how Manhattan grows up.

Walking through the entrance, she caught her reflection in the mirrored wall that deceptively enlarged the tiny entrance foyer. God, she looked pale. But suntans were for tourists and she was an ersatz-native Californian who had lost any trace of a New York accent.

Long bangs curtained her forehead and shaded the corners of her green eyes. Her thirteen freckles gleamed beneath her sample makeup. She'd never counted her freckles until the night Jon played connect-the-dots on her nose, his abacus a lipstick pencil.

She found the name Pendergraft on the call-board and pressed a button. A carved wooden door buzzed back and the hallway expanded briefly, ending with a tiny wrought-iron elevator. Its wrought-iron arrow quivered—*one-two-three*—and the lift slowed to a bumpy halt. Delly stepped into a green and gold vestibule. It smelled musty, like the inside of Mom's old attic trunk, the stupid trunk where Samantha had found Mom's music. If Sami hadn't found Mom's music—

"Hello, Delly, how are you?"

"Fine. You look great, Judith."

"Yes. New York agrees with me. But I've kept my house in Malibu, the one on the beach. Remember how Drew called it the house on the bitch? Something to do with the friggin' Wizard of friggin' Oz."

Following Judith, Delly stepped into an enormous living room and blinked at the brightness. The walls and ceilings were pure yellow, the floor a highly glossed parquet. An eclectic mixture of paintings crowded the walls. Delly recognized Andy Warhol, Peter Max, and Renoir. Her gaze lingered on the Renoir, and she wished she could step into the painting. In a Renoir there were no cameras panning for a close-up, no directors screaming for another take, no rejection. *Renoir's flowers have no smell, but they don't die. Renoir's people have no smell, but they live forever.*

Once she had believed that actors lived forever.

Opposite the entrance were recessed windows with open

drapes. The city skyline looked exactly like the picture postcard she'd sent Jon this morning. She'd written no message; they'd said it all before her . . . pilgrimage.

In the middle of the living room, denting a couch cushion, sat a chubby man, a pencil threaded through his thinning hair. Delly didn't catch the quick introduction, issued just before Judith grabbed her purse and ushered Delly back into the musty hallway.

"Wish I had time to show you the whole layout," Judith said. "Both floors. But time flies when you're having fun."

"Define fun."

"Success."

Delly had expected a sexual innuendo so she swallowed her next words, which would have been something about how soap operas turn back the clock. After all, the director counted backwards. Ready, action, three-two-one.

Crossing the lobby, both women instinctively checked their reflections. Although Judith was four inches taller and thirty-five pounds heavier than Delly, the contrast went beyond that. Judith's short blonde hair looked like a lacquered bathing cap. Delly's shoulder-length, chestnut-colored hair suffered from terminal humidity. Judith wore lime green slacks, a white blouse with a lace collar, and high-heeled sandals. Her blood-red fingernails were un-chipped. Delly's ragged nails showed the remnants of subway grime, and Magic Marker marred her thumb. Once upon a long time ago, the cops had blotted her fingertips with ink, blotting out her life.

With that remembrance, she felt her eyes blur. Bad memories, like bad onions, brought on tears.

Forget the past. Turn back the clock. Three-two-one.

Judith recommended a restaurant five blocks away. Her heels clicked rhythmically along the sidewalk's pavement. Slanted store awnings interrupted the sun's spotlight. Judith looked cool as a cucumber but Delly felt sweat dot her brow. Worse, perspiration began to shape half-moons beneath her armpits.

Blessed air conditioning orbited the restaurant's plants and wicker chairs. Several caged parrots fluttered their wings, and diners had the slick appearance of highly glossed antique furniture. *I shouldn't be caged inside a fancy restaurant with parrots,* Delly thought. *I should be feeding pigeons in Central Park.*

After the two women were seated, Judith ordered a vodka gimlet. Delly hesitated. Should she drink on an empty stomach? So much depended on this meeting. "Club soda," she said.

Drinks delivered, the waiter stood, pen poised. Judith ordered her "usual." Delly ordered chicken and artichokes in a vinaigrette sauce, trying not to be obvious as she reached into a cloth-covered basket. With sensual satisfaction, she spread unsalted butter across a slice of warm, seeded rye bread. She took a big bite and chewed slowly, savoring every seed, every crumb, every glob of melted butter. Then she quenched her thirst, downing the club soda, sucking on the lime as if she were a tequila addict.

"I didn't have time for breakfast this morning," she said, retrieving another slice of rye.

"Don't start skipping meals, sweetie pie. Your breasts look like pancakes."

Delly resisted the impulse to glance down and verify the older woman's statement. Thin was in; pancakes were not.

Finishing her cocktail, Judith talked about her move from the coast—"the only coast, my dear"—and the friggin' hassles from network officials when her *Morning Star* contract had run out. She'd negotiated a new contract to become head writer for *Chantilly Lace,* and, with Judith at the helm, that New York based daytime drama had recently surpassed the ratings for *Morning Star.* Fixing her gaze on Delly's flushed face, she said, "What's going on in your life, sweetie pie?"

Delly watched the waiter place Judith's pink jelled salmon and her own chicken dish on the table. "Nothing much, Judith. Things are pretty slow right now. Summer. They're talking about another directors' strike and—"

"Bullshit! Don't con a pro, my dear. You haven't worked in how long now?"

"A long time."

"And how old are you?"

"Twenty-seven. And a half."

"Very good, Delly. Most actresses would say twenty-nine. Why, may I ask, are you trying to look like Mia Farrow as Rosemary's baby?"

"Mia was Rosemary, not the baby."

"Forget Mia. Why are you trying to look like Pandora?"

"What makes you think—?"

"Your hair, your makeup, your friggin' socks and sneakers."

"Maybe I wanted to play Pandora because you knew me that way, loved me that way."

Judith swallowed a carefully chewed portion of salmon and a crisp lettuce leaf. "I still care for you, Delly. If I didn't, I wouldn't waste my valuable time."

"What do you mean?"

"Killing time isn't murder, it's suicide."

"Cute, Judith, but I still don't understand."

"Hours and flowers soon fade away. The moment Peter finished taping your last scene, you ceased to exist."

"Wrong! Fans stop me for autographs all the time. Why only this morning a woman in a babushka—"

"Delly, Delly, Delly." Judith wagged her first finger. "Pandora was a role. An actress can't spend her whole life living off the memories of one small part."

"It wasn't small!"

"That's because the writers made you important. We built

the part. We gave birth to Pandora."

Delly nudged the pungent chicken with her fork. "Do you think what happened . . . the fire . . . is that why I can't get past my first interview with casting directors? Do they still believe I had something to do with Maxine's death? Is that why I couldn't get another part?"

"No. Producers adore publicity and you were the victim in that sordid . . . installment. The reason you couldn't get another part right away was because Pandora had become too distinctive, too unforgettable. Remember, Delly, patience is the art of concealing your impatience."

"It's been two years, Judith."

"And look at you, still playing Pandora, dressed like a thrift shop slob. Do you know who dimpled my couch with his fat tush? An associate producer. I was ashamed to introduce you. I know how talented you are, but you look like shit."

"Would there be a part for me on your show?" Delly's chest thumped so hard she feared her heart would fall out onto her plate and mingle with the artichokes.

"Impossible. As you're undoubtedly aware, Anissa plays Chantilly. That's one of the reasons *Morning Star* plunged downhill in the ratings. Like an avalanche," Judith added smugly.

Sipping her melted ice cubes, Delly had trouble swallowing. Impossible? Why? Nothing was impossible when you slid down Alice's rabbit hole and entered a world where some genius dreamed up a soap called *Chantilly Lace,* set it during the frigid fifties, gave each female performer a wiggle when she walked, and scored a huge hit. Delly twisted the napkin in her lap. "Anissa and I have always worked well together, Judith."

"That's the point. We can't have Pandora and Charl on the same show. You're not eating, sweetie pie."

"Restroom, excuse me." Delly's sneakers found the floor. Weaving around tables, entering a lounge, assaulted by the smell of an ammonia deodorant, she bent her head over the sink. Then she turned on the water and watched her shrink, her shrinking shrink, go down the drain. She had opened her eyes and raised the curtain, only to find that Judith had changed all the lines. It simply wasn't the performance Delly had mentally rehearsed.

Suddenly aware of background music, she raised her face, sniffing as though the melody had a gaseous odor too.

From hidden speakers she heard the lovely ballad "Daddy's Coming Home." The music grew louder.

"Turn it off!" she screamed. There were three toilets and she flushed each to drown out the sound, before she fled and returned to the table.

"You have to look like a star every minute, every second," Judith continued, as if Delly had never left. "I'm over fifty and it's taken me almost thirty years to reach the top. But I've learned one thing. Success breeds success. I don't even take a dump in the morning until I've applied my makeup. I figure somebody important might parachute through my bathroom window. Do you understand?"

"Yes."

"I hate to harp on your appearance, Delly, but you look so defeated, so frightened. A vicious animal can detect fear in humans and attack. A casting director who senses desperation will react the same way. Those are the vibes you're sending out. Desperation. Are you going to cry?"

"No. Jon says the same thing." *Except Jon doesn't use the word desperation. He tells me to relax and pats me on the head. Sit Delly, stay Delly, roll over and play dead, Pandora.*

Judith said, "How's Jon?"

"Fine. Paramount just bought his new screenplay."

"Really!" Her carefully tweezed eyebrows arched. "It's none of my business, of course, but you look so destitute. Did my favorite lovebirds finally split?"

"What do you mean, destitute?"

"Your dress. It's what? A garage sale special, right? In any case, it's much too long and needs a belt. Let's be honest, sweetie pie, it's not you."

"If it's not me, who is it?"

"Oh, dear. I hurt your feelings."

"Come on, Judith. Who? Anissa? Maryl?" Delly stood. "Thanks for lunch. Have a nice day."

"Sit down! That's better. Now answer me. Did you and Griffin sever the sacred bonds of palimony?"

"Sort of. We argued."

"About what?"

"You."

"Of course."

"I called Anissa. She had your unlisted number so I called you."

"Collect."

"Yes. Collect. I'll pay you back."

"Sorry. That was thorny."

"You wear sackcloth and ashes like a mink cape."

"Some people wear mink like sackcloth. Please go on."

"My credit cards were maxed out, but I managed to scrape together enough cash for a bus ticket. Then I grabbed my tote and ran because . . ."

"Because?"

"Jon would have changed my mind."

Reaching inside her purse, Judith retrieved a small pad and a slim pen. "I've decided to help you, Delly. First, get that shaggy mop shaped and conditioned. Then a facial, a manicure—"

"I've got twelve bucks and three subway tokens!"

"Shut up and listen. I'll call my hair salon, tell them to charge the makeover to me. Next, an outfit at my consignment shop.

No labels but it'll be in mint condition, culled from a celeb's wardrobe. I'll call the shop, too." The pen bobbed as she scribbled madly. "Did you pack a recent photo?"

"Yes." Delly handed Judith an eight-by-ten glossy, retrieved from the tote beneath her wicker chair.

"Shit, you look like an over-the-hill Pandora. Did you happen to bring the negative?"

"Yes."

"Okay. I'm putting you in a cab as soon as we leave here. There's a studio at Broadway and West Forty-sixth. Seedy looking building, but they do the best work in the city. Remind them to air-brush those shadows under your eyes." She tossed Delly three hundred-dollar bills.

"Thanks, Judith, but I can't accept—"

"Sure you can. It's a loan. You need money for photos, transportation, shoes. You've got to look successful when you meet Vance Booker, and that means no sneakers."

"Vance is here? In his Manhattan office?"

"He's here, casting a new show, very hush-hush, hasn't even made the trades yet. I'll set up an interview for Friday, eleven sharp, don't be late. If you give a halfway decent reading, the part will be yours."

"What's the part?"

"What's the difference?"

They exited the restaurant. Judith flagged a taxi, handed the driver money, and cited the photo studio's address. Before closing the cab's door, she leaned forward. "I'll expect a return on my investment. Do you understand?"

"Yes."

She ran her palm lightly over Delly's arm, then cupped her chin. "Sunday night, my apartment, seven o'clock. By the way, that perfume you're wearing stinks to high heaven. It's much too strong for Pandora."

"Yes, I know."

"Until Sunday then."

"Yes. Bye, Judith." As the taxi pulled away from the curb, Delly covered her face with her hands and began to sob.

She finished her crying on the sidewalk at West Forty-sixth, then followed the smell of chemicals up a staircase. Leaving her negative, she returned to the street, walked inside a corner souvenir shop, and bought postcards. She would send one to Jon, but this time she'd write a message. *Dear Jonny,* she mentally composed, exiting the shop. *Everything is great, even better than I expected. Wish—*

"Dell-eeee! Delly Diamond!"

She glanced across the street. Clothed in white slacks and a sequin-studded Daisy Duck T-shirt, Anissa Cartier carried a rope-handled shopping bag. Beside her, Maryl Bradley waved. She wore black slacks and a red silk blouse. They both looked so cosmopolitan. You'd never guess that they had once been ugly ducklings.

Three ugly ducklings—Delly, Anissa, Maryl. During their childhoods they'd been connected by a cord no thicker than a spider's single thread.

"Don't move," Delly shouted. "I'll cross over."

"No, we'll come to you," Anissa shouted back, her voice so confident, so distinct, so Anissa.

Delly's gloom evaporated. This was her city, there stood her two best friends, and the theatre district was nearby. To hell with thorny Judith Pendergraft. Once upon a long time ago, Delly had found success on Broadway, just like Streisand. Barbra Streisand. B. S. Great initials. Delly laughed and felt pretty again. Pretty wasn't beautiful, but it could be different, and different was pretty damn good. She yelled, "Ready or not, here I come!"

Ready, action, three-two-one.

She met Anissa and Maryl in the middle of the street. The three women formed a football huddle as they giggled, hugged, and kissed the air. Then, as though choreographed, they parted, arms stretched, children playing ring-a-rosy.

A yellow cab braked for the stoplight. A rusty orange Volkswagen swung around the cab.

There was the sound of a loud *thunk.*

"Oh, my God!" A woman elbowed her way through curbside voyeurs. "Look at all that blood! Is she dead?"

Three-two-one . . .

Act One
Chapter One

Bayside, New York

Delly Gold looked down at her clown-shaped birthday cake, where DELILAH & SAMANTHA were printed across the icing. Delly had been named for her grandmother, Sami for a man. Their middle names were Olivia and Vivian. Mommy said Olivia and Vivian were the stars of a movie called *Gone with the Wind.*

"Your 'nitials spell dog," Samantha said. She pulled out the sixteen melted candles, eight for each twin. She had wished out loud to grow up fast.

Delly had wished for cherry-vanilla ice cream. "When I'm older," she said, "I'll change my middle name to Judy, for Judy Garland. Then everyone can call me DJ like the man on the radio." She plowed her index finger through the clown's smile. "Happy birthday, Sami."

"Happy birthday, Dog."

Third grade had started three weeks ago, but today was Saturday, the best day. Earlier, Delly had watched a man on a ladder and imagined he was Jack and the Beanstalk, only older. "Jack" had changed the tall black letters from last night's movie to this afternoon's movie and the marquee shouted:

HANS CHRISTIAN ANDERSEN
STARRING DANNY KAYE

Bouncing her ball, Delly hopped on her left foot and swung her right leg in a semicircle. "A, my name is *Alice,* and my husband's name is *Adam,* we live in *Alabama,* and in our baskets we carry *apples.*"

On the last word, apples, Delly missed. Her right leg was suspended and the pink rubber ball hit smack in the middle of her undies. Ouch! The ball veered away, rolled down the sidewalk, then stopped, subdued by the theater's red bricks.

She retrieved the ball and stuffed it inside the pocket of her blue jumper. The theater's display glass reflected her round face and straight hair, cut like Buster Brown who lived in her shoe.

Standing on tiptoe, she pressed her freckled nose against the glass. It misted from her whiff-puff, but she could still see the black and white photos advertising the Bayside Theater's double bill, a retro-something starring Robert Mitchum. Delly had learned to read before she began kindergarten so the words weren't hard. Tonight Robert Mitchum was appearing in THE SUNDOWNERS, followed by a movie called RACHEL AND THE STRANGER, starring Loretta Young.

"Lor-et-ta." Delly tasted the name. She captured it with the tip of her tongue, ran it over her teeth, and tapped the last syllable against the roof of her mouth. "Lor-et-ta."

Someday she'd be an actress. De-li-lah. Loretta Young. Delilah Gold. Delilah *Old.* She giggled, her green eyes crinkling at the corners. Delilah *Old.* She wanted to tell her sister the name-joke.

Where *was* Sami? Mommy had given them money for snacks, but Sami said she didn't like the stuff at the theater's candy counter so she'd gone to the corner drugstore to buy Sugar Daddies. Yum. If you sucked carefully, making dents with your front teeth and wiggling the caramel back and forth, a Sugar Daddy might last the whole movie.

Delly strolled through the theater's double doors. Brightly

colored posters decorated the lobby. Hans Christian singing to a bunch of children. Delly had a sudden thought. Hadn't Daddy once mentioned Jewish actors? Wasn't Danny Kaye Jewish? Outside again, she squinted up at the marquee. *Hans Jewish Andersen starring Danny Kaye and Delilah Old.*

She wanted to share her second joke with Sami, or anybody else, but the sidewalk was empty. Other kids were already seated inside. Gee whiz, where was Sami? Delly didn't want to miss the cartoons. On Saturday they always showed Tom and Jerry, Bugs Bunny and Elmer Fudd, Mr. Magoo and—.

Fumbling through her pocket, Delly reached around the ball until she fingered her ticket stub. Should she go in and find a seat, or run to the drugstore and see if Sami waited in line?

Just inside the drugstore, above the door, were bells that could have been attached to a horse-drawn sleigh. The store smelled of Johnson's baby powder and sick people. Rows of shelves led to Mr. Hailey, who looked like Santa Claus on diet pills. Most of him was skinny but his tummy was fat. He wore a white shirt rolled up to his elbows and black pants with suspenders and he had a witch's-wart to the left of his nose. The big kids said Mr. Hailey drank cough medicine and stole glue from shelves filled with school supplies. Sami said Mr. Hailey sniffed the glue, which was a big fat lie. Why would anyone sniff glue? Alongside Mr. Hailey's hairy elbows were bins of candy. Delly walked toward him. "Have you seen my sister, sir?"

"Seen lots of kids today," he said. "She look like you, little girl?"

"No, sir. We're twins but Samantha's got yellow hair while mine's brown. And she's taller."

"What's your name? How old are you?"

Delly hesitated. Mommy always said don't-talk-to-strangers. Mr. Hailey wasn't a stranger but it couldn't hurt to pretend.

"My name's Lor-et-ta. I'm eight and a half."

"Have some candy, Miss Loretta."

"I've only got a nickel."

"Who said anything about money? Help yourself."

Delly glanced around the vacant store, studied the selection, and wolfed down a Three Musketeers.

"Here, have some kisses." Mr. Hailey laughed, scooped up a handful of Hershey's Kisses, and stuffed them down the front of Delly's belted jumper. "You want some Bazooka bubble gum, Loretta?"

"No, sir. I have crooked teeth and Mommy says gum's bad for me. But my sister Samantha can blow the biggest bubbles in the whole world."

"I remember when you bought gum for the baseball pictures. I collected 'em all, 'specially Joe DiMaggio. He married Marilyn Monroe. Talk 'bout bazookas. I get a hard-on when I picture them in bed."

"Yeah, me too," said Delly, even though she had no idea what he meant.

She walked a few paces backwards, picturing the house in Hansel and Gretel and the witch with the wart on her nose. Mr. Hailey's eyes looked a little crazy, but boy-oh-boy, free candy. Wait till she told Samantha. Sami would say you-lucky-stiff.

"Eat," Mr. Hailey said, unwrapping another Musketeers.

Delly finished the bar in six bites. "My sister's waiting for me outside the movies," she said. "Thanks for the candy."

"Your sister got yella' hair?"

"Yes, sir."

"Her name's Samantha, right?"

"Uh-huh. How'd you know?"

"She's in the back of the store."

"Why?"

"She had to go to the toilet, said she couldn't hold it in no more."

"Oh."

"You wanna wait near the toilet, Loretta?"

"I guess."

Mr. Hailey clasped Delly's hand and led her into a dimly lit storeroom filled with boxes. Lifting her onto a huge carton, he patted the top of her jumper. He said, "Got enough kisses, little girl?" and laughed again.

Delly didn't get it, but before she could say yes-thank-you, he thrust his hand into his pants pocket, pulled out an Almond Joy, and stripped the wrapper. "Here, Loretta, eat. There's plenty more where this comes from and soon I'll let you suck a great big lollipop."

Oh boy, thought Delly, *a Sugar Daddy. Yum.*

It took her ten bites to finish the Almond Joy because it was getting harder to swallow. "Where's Samantha?" she asked, licking chocolate from her fingers.

"She'll be here soon. Can't you hear the toilet flush?"

Delly didn't hear anything. Mr. Hailey handed her a bag of peanuts.

Sleigh bells sounded and Mr. Hailey winced. "Damn," he said. "Wait here, Loretta. I'll be back before you can finish them peanuts."

Delly chewed, cracking nuts between her front teeth. The salt made her thirsty and her tummy felt funny and beneath her bangs her forehead began to perspire. Climbing down from the carton, she walked toward where she thought the bathroom might be. "Samantha? Sami?"

No answer.

Delly's tears merged with the sweat on her face. She didn't know what to do. An adult had told her to eat. He had said Sami was in the bathroom and she wasn't. Maybe Mr. Hailey fed children candy, then put them inside a cage until they grew big and he could cook them.

Hearing footsteps, she ducked behind a carton.

"Where are you, Loretta? Playing hard to get? Hide and seek? I'll count to ten. One, two, three, ten. Come out, come out, wherever you are."

Delly heard squeaks.

A mouse?

A rat?

Something furry brushed against her legs.

A cat?

A *giant* rat?

Daddy said Manhattan had giant rats but not Bayside.

Glancing down, she saw a big, hairy spider. With a scream, she stood and shook her foot, then her body, as if she played put your whole self in, put your whole self out, put your whole self in and shake it all about.

"Here you are," Mr. Hailey said. "I found you. Ollie, ollie, income tax."

It's ollie, ollie, income free.

Mr. Hailey placed one hand between Delly's legs and lifted her up until she reached his whiskered chin. She felt his hand squeeze, like she sometimes did to herself when she had to go to the bathroom real bad. She smelled cherry cough medicine on Mr. Hailey's breath and felt her tummy lurch. "Let me go," she said. "I don't feel good."

"We can play Marilyn Monroe and Joe DiMaggio."

Delly felt him press his mouth against hers. His tummy jiggled like a bowl full of jelly. Her tummy jiggled, too. "Put me down! I'm gonna throw up!"

As soon as she said the words, candy and nuts spewed onto Mr. Hailey's beard like chocolate-covered BBs shot from a gun. With a muffled oath, he dropped her to the floor.

Delly finished throwing up on Mr. Hailey's socks and shoes. Then she ran through the drugstore, skidded along the sidewalk, entered the theater, and washed her mouth at the drinking fountain. The warm water tasted like toothpaste.

Thank goodness the movie hadn't started yet. After her eyes had adjusted to the darkness, she found her sister.

"Too bad you missed the cartoons," said Samantha. "They had your favorite, Elmer Fuddy-Duddy. I bought popcorn. What's in your jumper?"

"Kisses," said Delly, wriggling onto the empty seat next to Sami.

"Huh?"

"Chocolate kisses. Someone gave 'em to me." She waited for Sami to say you-lucky-stiff.

Sami scrunched up her nose. "Throw them away. They might be poisoned."

Delly fished the kisses from her jumper and dropped them behind her seat. "Why didn't you tell me you were going inside, Sami?"

"Gosh, Dell, you were having so much fun playing with your ball. A, my name is Aretha and—"

"Alice. I said Alice."

"Well, I like Aretha better, so there."

Even in the dark, Delly could see Samantha's tongue slip between her lips like a fat pink garden snake. Samantha wore dungarees and a yellow T-shirt. Her hair was clustered in two long bunches, secured by Scottie Dog barrettes. She ignored the movie, chatting with her friends and hurling popcorn at the screen.

Delly watched Danny Kaye sing about Thumbelina and the Ugly Duckling and fall in love with a ballerina. The ballerina looked like her mother, Carolyn Ann, only Mommy played the piano.

Delly knew that her mother had been born in Chicago, not Copenhagen. Her father, William, was a photographer, not a person who fixed shoes and made up stories like Hans Christian Andersen did. And Daddy was Jewish, not Christian. Mommy had been engaged to a man named Samuel Curtis. Then she went to a party with Samuel, met Daddy, and fell head over heels in love. "Whoopsie-do, what a somersault," said Daddy. They got married and lived happily ever after, first in Chicago, then Bayside, Queens, New York, the World, the Universe.

Someday Delly would fall head over heels in love and live happily ever after, whoopsie-do.

The sisters waited for their ride home near the pictures of Robert Mitchum. Delly said she had a tummy ache and stretched out on the back seat of Mommy's station wagon. Should she mention Mr. Hailey? No. She'd been a bad girl, eating all that candy. When she thought about it, she felt like throwing up again, so she concentrated on the movie. Her favorite part was the ugly duckling.

Softly, she began to sing the ugly duckling song.

Sami said, "What are you singing?"

"A song from the movie. The one about the duck who becomes a swan. I remember the whole thing. Listen."

"Sometimes you're such a baby." Sami turned on the car radio and the Marcels drowned out Delly's song like a siren overpowering a cricket.

Delly didn't know why, but she was glad she hadn't said anything to Sami about Loretta Young and Delilah Old.

Tonight, after supper, she'd make a wish. *Star light, star bright, first star I see tonight, I wish I may, I wish I might, grow up to be an actress.*

Whoopsie-do. Whoopsie . . .

★ ★ ★ ★ ★

"Doodah, doodah." Eleven-year-old Delly Gold sang the words under her breath. "Bet my money on de boom-tail nag . . . dang! *Bob*-tail nag. Bob, not boom."

She scanned the school auditorium. There, right there in the first row, sat Mike Bleich, the cutest boy in school, who didn't even know she was alive. After she sang, he'd know who she was. Maybe Mike would say, "You sounded best, Delly, and you looked good enough to eat." Daddy always told Mom she looked good enough to eat.

Seated on a chair, center-stage, Delly balanced a guitar on her lap. Her fifth grade's Salute to Stephen Foster was in progress. At first Delly had a non-singing part. She was supposed to stand near the piano and pose as Jeannie with the light brown hair, even though Delly had a feeling Stephen Foster's Jeannie didn't look like a short fat Dutch kid.

Teacher had loaned her guitar to Sami for "Camptown Races." Then Sami caught the chicken pox.

"Can you learn the music in three days, Delilah?" Teacher had said. "Or perhaps," she'd added, her face hopeful, "your sister will be better in time for our show."

Delly practiced and practiced until Daddy, wearing earmuffs, walked into the living room. "That's enough, Smarty-Pants," he said. "You sound scrunch-delly-iscious."

Daddy had to photograph a jockey named Willie Shoemaker and his horse, Candy Spots, so Daddy was at a race called the Preakness. Mom was taking care of Sami, who kept screaming that at age eleven-almost-twelve she was too old for chicken pox.

Would Daddy be here if Sami sang? Sure he would. Sami was his favorite. Daddy called Delly Smarty-Pants, but he'd nicknamed Sami Princess Pretty.

Sami's jockey costume didn't fit—too tight—so Delly wore a

red plaid shirt over jeans. Blackface hid her flushed cheeks and made her feel like a real actress.

From the corner of her eye, she saw Mary Sue limp toward the piano. Mary Sue had once caught polio. She wore a leg brace and refused to sing with the chorus because, she said, everybody would stare at her leg. Sami said she wouldn't sing if Mary Sue played the piano but when Sami got sick, Teacher put Mary Sue back in the show. Delly didn't care. *Poor crippled girl.*

Clutching her guitar pick with sweaty fingers, Delly took a deep breath, then nodded at Mary Sue. "De Camptown ladies sing dis song, doodah . . ."

Something's wrong, she thought. *Oh, no. Teacher forgot to tune my guitar with the piano.*

Mary Sue had already finished the intro. Hair wild, eyes feral, her fingers raced up and down the black-and-white keys. Delly tried to catch up. "I bet my money on de boomtail . . . I mean bobtail . . . slow down, Mary Sue!"

There was a gasp from the audience as Mary Sue burst into tears and limped away. At the same time, Samantha's face appeared, peeking 'round the side curtain. She pranced center stage, her chicken pox scars covered by makeup, her body clothed in silky pants and shirt, her hair hidden by a jockey's cap.

Jockey's cap? Delly focused on the audience. Daddy stood in back of the auditorium. Mom, too.

"What are you doing here?" Delly whispered.

"Candy Spots won the race and Daddy came home and I felt better, thank goodness. You almost ruined everything."

"You're too late."

"That's what you think, Smarty-Pants." Sami winked toward the first row. "My name's Samantha Gold," she announced in a loud voice, "and I'm Delilah Gold's twin sister."

The audience laughed because the Gold twins didn't look

anything alike, except for their dark makeup.

"No, really." Sami grinned. "Delilah's the smart one. She gets all the good report cards. I'm the singer in the family, but I caught the stupid chicken pox so I told Delilah the show must go on. Then I figured I was *chickening* out . . ." She paused for another wave of laughter. "So here I am."

During the applause that followed, Samantha hissed, "Sing my doodahs, Delly-Dog."

The audience hushed.

"De Camptown ladies sing dis song . . ."

"Doodah, doodah," Delly warbled tremulously.

"De Camptown race track five miles long . . ."

"Oh, doodah-day."

"I come down dah wid my hat caved in . . ."

Grasping the brim, Samantha removed her cap and curls tumbled down past her shoulders. Delly saw Mike Bleich lean forward. His mouth was open and he looked as if he wanted to eat Sami for dessert.

"Your turn," Samantha whispered. "What's the matter?"

"Doodah," Delly said. Then she shouted, "Doodah!"

Samantha's eyes blazed. Walking to the very edge of the stage, she smiled at the audience, *her* audience and sang the next line.

"Oh, doodah-day," they responded and began to clap.

The sound hurt Delly's ears. She wished she could limp away like Sarah, but her tush seemed stuck to her chair. Tears filled her eyes and trickled down her black face, leaving a trail of streaks. She felt hot and feverish. Gee whiz, she'd probably caught Sami's stupid chicken pox.

Later, Daddy said, "I can't tell the difference between your spots and freckles, Smarty-Pants." Focusing his camera, he snapped her picture three times.

"Don't," she said. "I look like an ugly duckling. Please, Daddy, shoot Sami."

After Daddy closed the door behind him, Delly balanced a pad of lined paper against her drawn-up knees. Her school's *Weekly Reader* printed the names and addresses of kids who wanted to be pen pals. Delly had waved her pencil over the newspaper, shut her eyes, then thrust. The pencil's sharp point had landed on a Milwaukee girl, Anissa Stern.

Dear Anissa, Delly scribbled. *Today I played the guitar and sang Camptown Races. Everyone clapped and Mike Bleich said I looked good enough to eat.*

Delly had memorized the soundtrack from Gershwin's *Porgy and Bess.* Today she sang "Summertime"—a song about easy living and fish jumping and cotton growing high.

She paused, thinking how bizarre she sounded. Because cotton didn't grow between the cracks of a paved cul-de-sac and the only aquatic jumper around was Samantha's goldfish, Scarlett O'Hara the Fifth. Scarlett the First, Second, Third and Fourth had been flushed down the toilet, and Delly suspected that Scarlett Five had already written her estate disposition, which consisted of one miniature Neptune statue, one strand of fake seaweed and one algae-infested bowl.

Summertime . . . August 1, 1966 . . . and the living was lazy. Standing by an open window, Delly watched a Good Humor truck cruise her street. Suddenly, a telephone echoed the truck's ding-a-ling summons.

Samantha heard the phone ring, but ignored it. If the caller was a boy, Delly would shout Sa-*man*-tha, their special code. If it wasn't a boy, who gave a rat's spit? She preferred to daydream about the Hollywood home she would someday occupy. A heart-shaped swimming pool and maid's quarters and a special room for screening the latest Paul Newman movies.

Her parents' white-shingled, two-story house was okay. Nestled behind clipped bushes, it faced a lawn anchored at both corners by weeping willows. But there was no—what was Delly-Dog's favorite word?—oh, yeah, ambiance.

Samantha Vivian Gold had ambiance. Didn't her new dress prove it? Mom would freak. Carolyn Ann, not Mom. When a girl became a woman, even went through her stupid bas mitzvah, for Christ's sake, she shouldn't have to call her mother Mom. Where was Carolyn Ann? Still in the backyard?

"Delly," Samantha yelled. "Carolyn Ann. Answer the phone!"

Carolyn Ann Gold didn't hear the phone. Wearing jeans and her husband William's Chicago White Sox T-shirt, she stood in front of a barbecue grill at the end of a long cobblestone driveway. Clouds drifted overhead. One looked like a sheep. As she watched, it dissipated into a prone woman. No. A woman lying on her back wouldn't have rounded breasts. In a prone position, breasts flattened, unless William played brassiere with his hands.

Her whimsical meditation was interrupted by an alto yowl that sounded like gargled mouthwash, and she shifted her gaze toward a three-legged cat.

Southern Comfort, the family's Siamese, was a pain in the tush. Samantha adored the crippled cat while Delly teased him, a distinct personality reversal. When had Delly begun to poke fun at Comfort? Three years ago, following the Stephen Foster recital. But why? Never mind. It was too hot for psychoanalysis.

Carolyn Ann inhaled nature's perfume, thankful that the aroma of sizzling beef juice was disguised by the scent of overripe grapes. *I should put up grape jelly,* she thought, shading her eyes from the sun, admiring her purple arbor and the myriad of colors that flashed from her flower beds. Pink, red and white roses climbed toward the clouds, then tripped over the top slats of a wooden fence. Squeezing her eyes shut, Carolyn Ann pictured her husband pruning the roses and heard her mother's indignant screams: "It's just as easy to fall in love with a rich man as a poor man. Samuel Curtis will inherit his father's real estate and brokerage firms."

"I love Samuel, Mom, but I'm *in love* with William."

"What about your career?"

"So I won't be a concert pianist. William and I make beautiful music together."

"Oh, my God! Are you pregnant?"

"Not yet."

Carolyn Ann's father, an insurance salesman, had given his only daughter term-life policies for every anniversary, all fifteen of them, despite Mom's objections. Mom was unforgiving, stubborn as a mule . . .

"You're an ungrateful brat," her mom had said in 1951, after Carolyn Ann eloped. At the time, William Goldstein was a young struggling "shutterbug." They enjoyed blissful poverty until 1956, when William was invited to photograph a Brooklyn cousin's wedding. Afterward, he attended a baseball game between the Yankees and the Dodgers. Aiming his camera toward Don Larsen, who had just pitched the first perfect game in the history of the World Series, William sold the result to a sports magazine. The magazine chopped the "stein" off his name. Photo by W. Gold.

A year later, "W. Gold" drove to Little Rock, Arkansas, where Federal troops were trying to enforce the Supreme Court's school integration edict. His freelance photos accompanied front page headlines.

In 1958 the Golds moved to New York. That same year, the New York Giants played the first overtime game in the history of a National Football League championship. They were beaten by the Baltimore Colts, but William's photo of the two opposing quarterbacks, Johnny Unitas and Y. A. Tittle, became a poster that was sold in novelty shops. Although W. Gold wasn't exactly a household name, his poster eventually graced thousands of walls and could be found in sports taverns throughout the United States.

During 1961 he toured the deep South with busloads of freedom riders. He also produced a poster of Roger Maris after the baseball star had whacked his sixty-first home run.

When Shoemaker rode Candy Spots to victory in the Preakness, ruining Chateaugay's bid for a triple crown, W. Gold's photo decorated the cover of *Sports Illustrated.*

His camera captured James Meredith being admitted into Mississippi University, then recorded marches from Selma to Montgomery and the five-day Watts riot. He even did a layout for *Playboy,* a sports theme, and one lovely lady, shown with a horse nuzzling her bosom, went on to fame and fortune. That led to a slew of celebrity portraits. Carolyn Ann wasn't jealous or anything, but she did tactfully suggest that William stay home and put together a book of sports personalities, perhaps even a volume of the Civil Rights movement.

Three days ago her husband had received a call from the University of Texas. An alumnus offered W. Gold big bucks to photograph Longhorn football players. With a deep sigh of resignation, Carolyn Ann watched William pack a bag and catch the first available flight.

Now Carolyn Ann opened her eyes and smiled fondly. Her husband hadn't even kissed her good-bye, too busy munching a peanut butter and jelly sandwich. Homemade jelly from their own grape vines.

"I'll bottle some more tomorrow. Oh, damn," she swore, scooping up a hamburger patty with her spatula. Too late. Adding the meaty lump to the charcoal it resembled, she wished William would call and let her know what time he'd return. Samuel Curtis was in New York on business. William and Samuel had become close friends, despite the fact that Samuel admitted he still carried a torch for Carolyn Ann and had never married.

She heard a loud belch and directed her gaze toward a redwood bench, attached to a picnic table.

"I've never been so stuffed in my life," said Samuel, unbuttoning the waistband of his slacks and drawing a deep breath. "Delly insisted I eat a hamburger with coleslaw, her favorite combination. Samantha practically force fed me two wieners. Then I had to taste the potato salad and—"

"Deviled eggs." Carolyn Ann returned his grin. She was short, barely five feet, but Samuel topped her by only four inches. His brown hair had cute David Niven crinkles. "Look down at your feet. No, closer to the table. When William poured the cement for our patio, before it dried, he printed a message."

" 'Eat at your own risk,' " Samuel quoted.

"That was Delly's idea. Samantha wanted 'good-looking boys welcome.' "

"Are you absolutely certain they're twins?"

"You were at the hospital with William when they arrived. The doctor insisted they were identical."

"Is he near-sighted or far-sighted?"

"Both. I think he had a buxom nurse on his mind. In any case, when the egg split a few genes got mixed up. Here comes your favorite now."

"Hush. I don't have a favorite. You're still my best girl. When are you going to leave William and run away with me?"

"Oh, in about fifty years." With slender fingers, she brushed her dark hair back from her forehead. "Better yet, we'll all perform a *ménage a trois* at the old folks' retirement home."

"William will never retire."

"I know." Carolyn Ann sighed then watched her daughter, Samuel's namesake, dance down the cobblestones.

Samantha had a voluptuous figure, stretched over five feet,

four and a half inches. Her low-cut party dress barely covered her fully developed breasts. Hazel eyes with golden glints were rimmed by black lashes and black liner. Her long blonde hair had often been compared to Trigger, Roy Rogers' horse.

"Look at my new dress, Uncle Sam," she said. "Isn't it divine?"

"Where's the rest? The bottom, for instance?"

"In case you haven't noticed, skirts are getting shorter."

"So am I." He stood, stretched, and attached his waistband buttons.

"I think you're the handsomest person in the whole world," said Samantha, "except maybe Mike Bleich."

"Who's Mike Bleich? A movie star?"

"Mike is the young man escorting Samantha to the pool party tonight," Carolyn Ann said. "It's a sock-hop. Music from the early fifties. Remember our favorite song? Darn, it was on the tip of my tongue. Something by Jo Stafford."

" 'You Belong to Me.' Stafford sang you belong to me and I asked you to marry me. You said sure-why-not and we became engaged. Then three weeks later—"

"Samuel, please." Carolyn Ann flushed beneath her tan. "Are you planning to wear that dress, Samantha?"

"What's wrong with it?"

"Thirteen-year-old girls shouldn't wear black."

"I'm fourteen, Carolyn Ann."

"Don't argue, Samantha, and stop with the Carolyn Ann already."

"Aw, Mom, it's a present from Uncle Sam."

"Wait a minute. I plead innocent. I gave you the money for a new dress but I didn't pick it out."

Hands on hips, Carolyn Ann said, "What are the other girls wearing?"

"Junk from the fifties. Poodle skirts and stupid ponytails. I told all my friends about Uncle Sam's present. Do you want me to sound like a liar? Daddy would say it's okay."

"Daddy's in Texas."

"Can I ask him when he calls?"

"May I."

"May I, Mom? If he says okay, can . . . may I wear it?"

"We'll see," she said. William would never say no to Princess Pretty so why continue the argument?

Samantha blew Samuel a kiss, the tips of her fingers traveling through the air like bright scarlet stars. Then she danced up the cobblestones, toward the house. "Thanks, Carolyn Ann," she called over her shoulder.

Moments later Delly skimmed the bumpy cobblestones with her bare feet, and Carolyn Ann recalled Samuel's remark about the visually impaired obstetrician. Delly wore braces to correct an overbite while the dentist had never found one cavity in Samantha's smile. An inch shorter than her sister, Delly had tiny, budding breasts, and checked each morning for evidence of her first period. With menstruation, Samantha's chest had bloomed while the rest of her body slenderized. Delly was heavy, and the long felt skirt over a full slip and several petticoats looked unflattering.

"How does my skirt look, Mom?" Delly twirled. "Sami says it has ambiance, but I feel like a jerk. I look like a jerk, don't I? Be honest."

"A blouse and shoes would help the overall effect," Carolyn Ann said. "Why are you holding your hands behind your back?"

"I can't get the button to close."

"Move it over. There's a needle and thread in my kitchen what-not drawer."

"If I hold my breath, you can fasten it."

"Darling, it would just pop open with the first dance."

"Biff Garfunkle can't dance."

"Delly's been invited by a very nice boy," Carolyn Ann told Samuel. "The son of my mah-jongg partner."

"I wasn't invited. I was inveigled."

"By whom?"

"You. Mrs. Garfunkle. Can't I just forget the party, Mom?"

"Don't be silly. Would that be fair to Biff?"

"He wouldn't care. Besides, he drools."

"Biff wears braces."

"I wear braces and I don't drool. Do I? Oh, gosh. Do I?"

"No. You don't drool. Listen, darling, if we can't do something with your button, I think there's an old cinch belt hidden away inside my bureau."

"I'll look like the fat lady in the circus. Won't I, Uncle Sam?"

Samuel glanced helplessly at Carolyn Ann. Then, turning toward Delly, he said, "Let's drive to the store. I'll buy you a bigger skirt, the sky's the limit. You can even choose the same style dress as your sister. Although," he added quickly, "you'll have to get permission."

Delly's bottom lip quivered. "I don't want a bigger skirt."

"At least say thank you, child."

"I was going to . . . oh, gosh, Mom, I'm sorry. You have a phone call, person-to-person, long distance. It was a terrible connection and the operator had to call back three times. I hope she didn't hang up. Rats!"

Samuel put his arm around Delly's shoulder as they watched mother and ex-fiancée scamper, like a teenager, up the cobblestones.

Inside the cozy kitchen, a wall receiver dangled to the floor. "I told Sami to hold on while I got you," Delly said. "I'm really sorry, Mom."

"That's okay." Carolyn Ann reeled in the receiver by its cord. "Hello? Yes, this is Mrs. Gold. Hello? William?"

Samuel had turned to smile at his namesake, still in her black dress, posing at the kitchen archway.

Delly saw her mother's face lose every stitch of color. "Mom? Mommy? What's wrong?"

Startled by the panic in Delly's voice, Samuel ran to Carolyn Ann's side, pried the phone from her fingers, led her to a captain's chair, then retrieved the receiver. "This is Samuel Curtis, a close friend of the family." He listened, said "Thank you very much," and hung up. "Your dad's been shot, kids. That was a man from the police department. Your dad's on his way to the hospital."

"Shot?" Delly and Samantha said together.

"There was this crazy guy, Charles Whitman. They think he killed his folks. Then he went up into a tower at the University of Texas and sniped at people with his gun. Your father decided to take pictures for the newspapers."

"I have to go to William, Samuel."

"Of course. We'll both go. You sit there while I make the arrange—"

The phone's strident ring interrupted his words and all four faces turned toward the wall. Samuel identified himself again, listened, then replaced the receiver.

"Carolyn Ann," he said, "you've got to be very brave. William's gone. He died a few minutes ago."

"That's a big fat lie!"

Samuel knelt by her chair and clasped her hands in his. "I'm so sorry."

"It can't be true. I didn't kiss him goodbye. I'll make more grape jelly, I swear. Don't you see? It's a mistake, someone else with a camera, someone who stole William's wallet. He's on a plane right now, flying home . . . shut up, Mother!"

Samuel straightened and stared at the twins, who were standing in silent shock. "Girls, I need your help. Delly, can you call the doctor?"

"Yes."

"Good. Call your grandparents, too. Tell them I'll have tickets waiting at O'Hare."

"Yes, Uncle Sam," said Delly, a small forlorn figure with a brown felt skirt, unbuttoned, hanging halfway down her hips.

Samantha hid her face against Samuel's neck. "This is . . . the worst thing . . . that's ever happened," she sobbed.

"I know, I know. Uncle Sam's here." He led Samantha toward a chair near her mother's, watched the broken-hearted girl bury her face in her arms, then gently tilted Carolyn Ann's chin with his finger. "I'm going to help you upstairs and put you to bed now, darling."

"No. I've got to wait for William." Rising, Carolyn Ann walked through the connecting archway and sat down at a piano. "This was my fifteenth wedding anniversary present," she said, as if speaking to a stranger. "William loves to hear me play."

Delly cradled the phone's receiver between her chin and shoulder. Her spit tasted like bittersweet chocolate and she knew that nothing would ever be the same again. Actors got killed in one movie then starred in another. That wouldn't happen with her daddy. *Actors live forever, even when they die. If I become an actress, I'll live forever.*

Samantha couldn't stop crying. What a lousy break. Now she couldn't go to the party and Mike Bleich would dance all night with Peggy Adler, and Samantha Vivian Gold, oozing with ambiance, wouldn't get a chance to show off her new dress.

Yes, I will, she thought. *It's black. I'll wear it to Daddy's funeral.*

Chapter Two

Delly tossed her school books on top of the counter and reached for the clay cookie jar she had kilned last year.

Samantha's voice: "Thanks for walking me home. Oops, I tripped on a cobblestone. Wow, you're so strong. Ummm . . ."

Sami and some boy were kissing, right outside the kitchen window. Delly heard a meow that sounded like a cross between a Swiss yodel and a scratchy record.

"Jim, I'd like you to meet Southern Comfort," Sami said. "My pussy."

A male murmur, then Sami said, "I don't like boys who talk dirty, Mr. Marks."

Jim Marks, thought Delly. New kid at school. Skinny. Ugly. Pimples all over his face and body. What was Sami doing with *him?*

"My uncle knows Dick Clark personally," Jim said. "So what do you say, Samantha?"

"I don't date just anybody."

True, thought Delly. Unless *anybody* was a jock or very popular, Sami turned him down with vague promises. Gosh, Dick Clark. *American Bandstand.* Delly would give *anything* to appear on *Bandstand.*

"Let's try a movie," said Samantha, "and see how it goes. *Rosemary's Baby* is at the Bayside this weekend. If you find my sister a date, we can double."

Delly couldn't hear Jim's response, but Sami's voice was loud and clear. "So what? It's only a movie."

School books thudded against the cobblestones; they were kissing again. Ugh! Sami would kiss a shark if she thought it might lead to buried treasure.

Furtively, Delly peeked through the window. Good grief, they weren't just kissing. Jim had maneuvered his hands underneath Sami's sweater.

"Dick Clark'll introduce us to the Fifth Dimension," he said, breathing hard.

Sami was up, up, and away, as she wedged one knee between Jim's thighs. He continued pressing his fingers against Sami's bra and Delly felt her own breasts tingle. With a sigh, she grabbed a handful of cookies and walked through the kitchen, into the living room. Mom sat at her piano.

"Bayside . . . um . . . High . . ." Delly cleared her throat and crossed her arms over her breasts. "School's holding auditions for *South Pacific.* Can I try out?"

"May I."

"May I?"

"Me too, Mom." Sami entered the room.

"Except for math, Delly's grades are fine. But you're barely passing, Samantha."

"I really want to be in the show, Mom. Dell and me together. The Gold sisters, da-dum."

"You have cheerleading practice and your grades—"

"Grades, grades, grades! That's all you ever talk about. If Daddy was alive, he'd let me audition."

"Sami!"

"You know he would, Dell."

"I'll think about it," Carolyn Ann said.

"I'll study real hard, Mom, and Delly can help me with my homework. Please? I'll never ask for anything again. Well, maybe one thing. You see, this new boy at school invited me to dance with him on *American Bandstand.* I said okay because he's just moved here and he doesn't have any friends yet and I thought you'd want me to be nice to him. He has pimples and he's not all that cute. But if I go out with him, the other kids—"

"Will you help your sister study, Delly?"

"Sure, Mom."

Sami rained kisses all over her mother's flushed cheeks. "I'll tutor Delly for the audition. She has a sweet voice, but it takes more than that to be a star."

The twins tried out together, singing a duet. Samantha Gold won the show's lead, Nellie Forbush. Still chunky and undeveloped, Delly was given a part in the chorus. Eventually she doubled as a sailor since there weren't enough boys in the show.

"I feel goofy singing there's nothing like a dame," she told Samantha. "After all, I'm a dame."

"What should I wear to *Bandstand,* Del? Maybe Uncle Sam'll send me money for a new sweater. Why are you looking like that?"

"Like what?"

"Like Southern Comfort on a bad-weather day. Sad and gimpy. Gosh, I'm so stupid. You've always loved that show. Why don't I tell Jim to take you, instead?"

"He wouldn't want to go with me."

"I'll call at the last minute and say I'm sick. Then he'll have no choice."

"No, Sami, thanks anyway."

"Well, all right, if you insist."

The play scheduled after *South Pacific* was *Macbeth.*

"Me try out?" Samantha grimaced. Sprawled across her bed, she was underlining passages from the latest Harold Robbins bestseller. "Are you serious, Dell? I hate Shakespeare. Except for *West Side Story.*"

"*Romeo and Juliet,* not *West Side Story.* Will you come to the audition with me, Sami? I won't be nervous if you're there."

"When is it?"

"Monday and Tuesday, three-thirty. I'm reading on Monday."

"Monday I've got glee club rehearsal. Don't worry, you'll be great."

The list, posted Wednesday afternoon, cast Samantha Gold as Lady Macbeth. Delly didn't get a part.

"You said you weren't going to try out." Delly slammed her books on top of her bedroom desk. "You said you hated Shakespeare."

"I do. But Mike Bleich said I couldn't perform a serious role. He called me an airhead and double-dared me."

"You don't even date Mike anymore. You're dating that guy from Great Neck, the one you won't tell Mom about because he's so old."

"Older, Dell, not old. Drew Florentino has the most gorgeous bod I've ever seen."

"Did you . . . have you gone all the way with him?"

"Of course not. I promised I'd wait until you found somebody. I was tempted, though. God, can he kiss."

Delly, who'd never kissed a boy, felt her lips tingle. "Did you open your mouth?"

"Sure. I even touched his tongue with mine."

"Did you touch his you know?"

"His penis? Yes. I'd been drinking and—"

"Sami!"

"Just one drink, a Tom Collins, tastes like lemonade. If you tattle—"

"Did you let him touch your bra?"

"Nope." Sami giggled. "I took it off."

"Did he touch your undies? Or did you take them off?"

"Off. It was only fair. Drew took his off."

"But you said you didn't go all the way."

"Maybe I wanted to go all the way." Her eyes blazed. "Maybe Drew stopped because he said there were rules about taking advantage of a girl who'd had too much to drink."

"What happened to one Tom Collings?"

"Tom *Collins.* Maybe I had more than one. Maybe I got dizzy and couldn't sit up. Maybe Drew put me on the back seat of his Thunderbird. Maybe he sucked my breasts and licked me between my legs. Maybe he kneeled above my face. Maybe I did more than touch his *you-know.*"

"Gosh, you're such a liar."

"I am not."

"You lied about *Macbeth.*"

"I didn't lie. Mike Bleich double-dared me, I swear to God. Don't be mad, Dell. I'll tell them to give the part to you."

"Okay."

"I'll phone John Gibbs right now."

"Sami, wait. Don't call Mr. Gibbs."

"Well, all right, if you insist. Would you help me learn my lines, Dell? Nellie was easy. Lady Macbeth's hard. Is there a special trick to learning Shakespeare?"

"Sing the words first, until you learn them by heart. Pretend they're rock lyrics."

"Rock lyrics. Damn, that's brilliant. C'mon, we'll do the Lady like she's never been done before . . . with ambiance."

"Okay, toss me your script," Delly said, somewhat mollified by Sami's praise. "I guess we can't have a school play without a Gold star."

"Gold star, that's a good one. Remember the stupid stars Teacher pasted on your grade school compositions?" Samantha scowled. "I haven't finished my history homework. I wish we really were identical twins. Then you could take my exams, too. Only kidding, Dell. You wouldn't want to look like me."

Oh, wouldn't I? Mr. Gibbs cast you because of your big boobs. You could say out damn spot in Pig Latin and Mr. Gibbs would ooldray like an ogday.

Seated at her desk, Delly pulled a piece of stationary from her middle drawer.

Dear Anissa, she scribbled. *Today I was offered the part of Lady Macbeth, but I said no because I'd have to cut down on cheerleading and glee club and I only auditioned because Mike Bleich double-dared me. I think he's mad because I don't date him anymore. I'm dating this older boy, Drew Florentino. He lives in Great Neck, not far from Bayside, and God, can he kiss. I drank something called a Tom Collings and almost went all the way. I took my undies off and Drew kissed me between my legs.*

"Are you nuts?" Samantha squealed.

"I merely asked if you two had filled out your college applications yet."

Delly grinned. Mom was the only person she knew who could knit a sweater, watch *Mission Impossible* on TV, and talk seriously, all at the same time.

"College," Samantha said with a sneer. "We're the Gold sisters. We're going to star in movies, TV."

"Delly?"

"I don't mind college, Mom, if that's what you want."

"What do you want?"

"I sort of want to be an actress."

"Sort of? What does that mean?"

"I do want to be an actress. Like Sami says, we're the Gold sisters, da-dum. We've starred in every school play. Well, at least Samanth—"

"High school isn't the real world," Carolyn Ann cut in. "The real world is the Poor People's March on Washington and President Johnson's Civil Rights Act. The real world is the Democratic convention in Chicago next summer. I'm tempted to spend a week with Gramps and Nana, join the planned protests."

"You just want an excuse to visit Uncle Sam," Delly teased.

"I know all about the real world, Mom," Samantha said. "It's Bobby Gentry winning her Grammy for 'Ode to Billie Jo.' It's Warren Beatty as Clyde and Bonnie's fabulous clothes." She shivered. "If I could date Warren Beatty just once, I'd never ask for anything again."

"I'll make a deal with you," said Caroline Ann, ignoring Samantha's prattle. "Attend college, Carnage Tech or Goodman's in Chicago, where you can learn to be an actress and take other courses at the same time. That's fair."

"It's not fair. Delly's good at school. She likes it. I don't. If Daddy was alive—"

"He'd agree with me. You need a solid educational background, and I'm not going to discuss this any further."

"Hey, no, wait. You can't force me to go to college, Mom."

"I wouldn't call it force. More like persuasion. If you want to strike out on your own, fine. But you'd better learn how to wait tables or run a switchboard."

"If you hadn't given Daddy's insurance money away, I could get my own apartment and—"

"I didn't give it away, Samantha. I invested it."

"In what?"

"The future. Your father believed very strongly in civil rights."

"He also photographed movie stars and athletes. Why didn't you invest in a movie or buy a football team?"

"Sami! She's only kidding, Mom."

"There's money in a trust fund for you kids, which you may collect when you turn twenty-one. Meanwhile, Samantha, it's college or nothing. Not one red cent. Do you understand?"

"How can you be so mean?" Samantha squeezed her eyes until tears brimmed.

Carolyn Ann handed her daughter a tissue. "Blow your nose, Princess Pretty. That nonsense won't work with me."

"I'll call Uncle Sam. He'll talk to you and—"

"Samuel Curtis may give you expensive presents, young lady, but . . ." Carolyn Anne took a deep breath. "Go to your room and don't come down until I say you can."

Later, Samantha said, "You were a big help, Delly-Dog. Why didn't you stick by me?"

"It wouldn't have changed anything. Mom says she's sorry she didn't attend college. She says Daddy always wanted to go but couldn't afford it."

"I think Mom married Daddy so she wouldn't have to go to college."

"Get real, Sami. Would you marry to avoid school?"

"Maybe. It all depends. I'd marry Drew Florentino."

"But you said Drew's stuck on himself and—"

"He is. I was only kidding."

"No, you weren't. Drew ditched you, right?"

"Maybe we broke up because I wouldn't go all the way. Maybe I told him I wanted to wait until my sister found somebody. Maybe he thought that was stupid."

"It is stupid."

"A promise is a promise, Delly. I'm gonna stay a virgin till you fall in love."

Delly wanted to hug her twin. Sami was into gratification, not self-sacrifice, and refusing Drew Florentino must have been a huge sacrifice. Delly had never met him. Sami had never brought him home because, she said, Mom would ground her for life.

Samantha tossed her mane of thick, palomino hair. "I'll call Uncle Sam, reverse the charges."

Samuel did talk to Carolyn Ann, but couldn't change her mind. "Enjoy high school," he told his namesake, "and worry about college later."

During their senior year, Samantha played Kim in *Bye, Bye, Birdie,* Eliza in *My Fair Lady,* and Emily in *Our Town.* Delly was cast as "chorus" in the first two and as "townsperson" in the last one, even though, writing her Anissa-letters, she starred in them all.

I guess I will be Delilah Old before I get a leading role, she thought. But she was wrong.

"I'm finally going to star in a school production, Uncle Sam," Delly said over the phone. "And with Jules Perry. Jules is a guard on the basketball team, president of the senior class, editor of the school yearbook, and he picked me to write the senior play with him and gave me the best part, just because we did that English assignment on Chaucer together. He even asked me to the prom. I must be dreaming. Pinch me, Uncle Sam."

"I can't reach you from Chicago, sweetheart. Right now, this very minute, I'm writing a check for your prom dress."

Samantha suggested they shop together.

"No, thanks, I vant to be alone," Delly said, mimicking Garbo. She selected a pastel-green strapless gown in an empire style. It hid her chunky waist and hips, exposed her creamy shoulders, and gave her small breasts additional cleavage. The color even turned her eyes a darker green. She thought about cutting her hair, but Sami had once said that boys liked long hair, so she simply brushed the red-brown strands till they were static-crisp.

I look pretty, she thought, wishing Mom hadn't flown to Chicago. An emergency. Nana had caught pneumonia. *Gosh, Mom would have kittens if she could see Sami's dress.*

As usual, Samantha had chosen to be daringly different. Her gown was an orange marmalade taffeta sheath. Tiny ruffles flared at the bottom. A built-in bra pushed her breasts up, almost, but not quite above the fitted bodice. The gown wasn't cheap, and didn't look cheap, but Samantha Gold shimmered like a fiery sun in the midst of the other girls' pastel-cloud dresses.

Through the magic of lighting and crepe paper, the old gym enhanced the theme OVER THE RAINBOW.

Jules looked handsome in a black tux with red silk lining. Despite his grace on the basketball court, he was an awkward dancer and preferred to mingle with his friends at the punch bowl. Delly dismissed the nagging notion that Jules had invited her so he could be near Sami.

Sami's date, Neely McIntyre, another guard on the basketball team, wore a dark blue tux with a light blue ruffled shirt. Neely's real name was Cornelius, which he hated. Some kids called him Corny, but not to his face.

Neely's a fabulous dancer, thought Delly, switching partners with Sami.

"I'm pretty," Delly whispered, gazing at her reflection in the restroom mirror. "How far should I let Jules go tonight? A French kiss? First base? Second base?"

Her reflection nodded.

"Have you seen your sister?" Neely asked, after Delly emerged from the bathroom.

He looked angry, and Neely angry wasn't a pretty sight. She swallowed and said, "I thought Sami was with you."

"She was, but I had to take a whiz and now I can't find her."

"Where's Jules?"

"I don't know. Do you think they're together?"

Neely and Delly checked the dance floor, then the parking lot. Jules's Corvette was missing.

"Maybe Sami felt sick and Jules drove her home," Delly suggested.

"I'll bet they went on ahead to Artie Ruben's party, a joke on us. C'mon, Delly. My car ain't no 'Vette but it runs good."

Artie Ruben's finished basement overflowed with cast-off furniture, folding chairs, and kids. The ceilings and walls were covered with the same crepe paper used at the gym; Artie had been on the decorating committee. Bottles of beer and empty glasses had already left wet stains on tabletops. An entire wall of stereo equipment blasted out Simon and Garfunkle's "Bridge Over Troubled Waters." Delly's stomach hurt from the thundering of too much bass and the fact that Sami and Jules did not appear in the crowded basement. Or the small cubicle with furnace and water heater. Or the laundry room.

"What the hell," said Neely. "Let's have some fun. Want to dance?"

Wish I could leave, Delly thought later. She had phoned the house twice but no one answered. Maybe Sami really was sick. Maybe she'd passed out.

I don't like this party. My corsage fell off and got trampled. Neely will think I'm a baby if I ask him to take me home. What if Sami and Jules got into an accident on the way to the party? Should I call the police? The hospitals? The house again?

"Here, Delly, try this," Neely said, handing her a glass filled with a light amber liquid. He had removed his tux jacket and unbuttoned his shirt to the waist. "Tastes like iced tea."

"It's strong."

"That's the idea. How do you feel?"

"Fine."

"You should get a rush soon. Here, drink mine. How do you feel?"

"I think I got a rush," she said, eager to please him.

Leading her into the laundry room, he seated her on top of the washing machine. *I'll let him do what I planned to let Jules do,* she thought. Neely looked a little like Warren Beatty and he danced better than Jules and he'd scored more during basketball season.

She felt Neely's hands work the zipper at the back of her gown. He fondled her breasts. *That feels sort of good,* she thought, suddenly dizzy from the drinks and the touch of his fingers on her nipples.

He eased her down so that her head hung over one side of the machine. Uncomfortable, she struggled to rise.

"Don't move, this'll only take a minute," Neely mumbled, unzipping his fly.

Rolling sideways, Delly slid off the washer and zipped up her dress.

Neely said, "What's wrong?"

"Nothing. That's as far as I go. Touching my, you know, first base."

"I haven't heard it called first base since P.S. 41."

"I don't care if you make fun of me," Delly said—a big fat lie.

"Goddamn tease."

"I want to go home. I don't feel good."

"Aw, Delly." Neely looked confused. How come the ball didn't fall through the hoop? "Oh, I get it. You ain't on the pill, right? Look, you can go down on me." He grabbed a clean undershirt from a folded pile of laundry. "I'll come in this, not your mouth, I promise."

"You're disgusting, Neely McIntyre."

"Your sister don't think I'm disgusting."

"You're a big fat liar!"

"Am I? The only reason I took Samantha to the prom was because she promised she'd blow me afterwards."

"The only reason? You've been dating for weeks."

"Yeah, but we broke up. Samantha wanted to get married."

"Now I know you're lying. We're both enrolled at Hofstra College."

"Listen, Delly, your sister thought I was real good. If you

ain't on the pill I'll pull out before—"

"No. Take me home."

"Take yourself home. You're a charity case, you fat bitch. Jules felt sorry for you. He said so, and—"

"Your fly's open, *Cornelius.*" Delly fled from the laundry room, ran across the basement, found a door, and stumbled outside. Leaning against a red Chevy, she began to cry.

"Delly, what's the matter?" Artie Ruben approached from the direction of the vibrating party room.

"I want to go home."

"I'll drive you home. That's my car you're crying on."

"Can't drive, it's your party."

"Nobody'll miss me."

Artie pulled her into the circle of his arms, lifted her gown, cupped her buttocks, and ran his first finger beneath her panty girdle's elastic.

"Stop it, Artie," she protested. "That tickles."

As he continued exploring, he laughed, and Delly, still a tad woozy, thought she heard the echo of his laughter, which sounded like the Oz Munchkins. Then she was consumed by a shameful sensation that blocked out all sound. Her legs felt weak, her nipples felt taut, and her heart slammed against her chest.

"Give me a kiss, beautiful," Artie said, licking her earlobe then the inside of her ear.

Beautiful? Artie was so nice. It would be easy to fall in love with him. She leaned into his tongue, which had practically reached her tympanic membrane. Her legs began to buckle, so she disconnected her ear from his tongue and gave him a French kiss, which was kind of germy when you thought about it, and who wanted to think about it?

He opened the Chevy's door, guided her inside, and fumbled at her dress until her bodice fell down about her waist. Then, easing her across the back seat, he tugged at her panty girdle.

"I'm think I'm sort of drunk," she cried.

"Don't puke in my car, Delly. It's brand new, a graduation present."

She wished he'd say something a little more romantic.

"Are you ready?" he shouted.

"Don't yell, Artie, you're making my head spin."

"Sorry," he said, unzipping his fly.

After Artie drove her home and said he'd call, she entered the house and checked the bedroom she shared with her sister.

Empty.

Shedding her rumpled prom dress, she filled the tub with steamy water and pink bubble bath. Southern Comfort perched on the sink. "I don't feel any different," she told the cat. "A little sore. Okay, a lot sore. It took ten minutes. First base, second base, third base, home plate. Big deal."

Naked, she sat at her desk and began to compose a letter to Anissa.

Tonight I went to the prom with the most popular boy in school, got sort of drunk, ~~and did it~~ and ~~screw~~

She hesitated, then crumpled the piece of stationary. She wanted to keep "it" a secret, and anyway she had a feeling her pen-pal days were over. Why write to Anissa when she had Artie? Why spend her time on a long-distance girlfriend when she'd finally found a boyfriend?

With that last thought, she curled up on her bed and fell asleep.

An insistent telephone woke her. Sunlight streamed through her bedroom window. She smelled her mother's roses as she stumbled down the hallway, reached for the phone's extension, and remembered the seemingly innocent ring-a-ling four years ago. The day her daddy died. The day the music died. Was Mom dead? Nana? Sami?

She said hello, listened, and made the Western Union operator repeat the message twice.

"Do you want the telegram delivered, Miss?"

"D-liver D-letter D-sooner D-better," Delly chanted. "D my name is Ugly *Duckling* and my sister's name is *Dirt.* We come from the devil and in our baskets we carry diarrhea."

"I beg your pardon?"

"Yes, I want it delivered. I'll paste it inside my scrapbook, next to Sami's collection of Robert Wagner movie magazine pictures."

After the operator hung up, Delly struck a cheerleader's pose. "If I could sleep with Robert Wagner just once, I'd never ask for anything again," she said, her voice accurately mimicking Sami's. "I've already slept with Drew Florentino and Neely McIntyre, Mom, because I thought you'd want me to be *nice* to them."

An hour later Delly stared down at the beige-yellow piece of paper. Slowly, she traced the black print with her index finger. There were ten words, no more, no less. Sami had developed a sudden sense of frugality. The telegram read: GO TO COLLEGE FOR BOTH OF US. ELOPED WITH JULES.

Chapter Three

Horse sense is what keeps horses from betting on what people will do.

Delly's daddy had said that, just before he lost the biggest gamble of his life by pitting his camera against a sniper's gun.

On the other hand, Artie Ruben won fifteen dollars by screwing Samantha Gold's dumpy sister. How could he prove it? Easy. Several kids listened to his are-you-ready and her sharp, pain-filled cry, and the news spread faster than an epidemic of teenage mononucleosis.

Delly wanted to die. But first she wanted revenge. She had read Mario Puzo's *The Godfather.* Her godfather, Samuel Curtis, was Jewish rather than Italian. However, he had enough money to hire an assassin. Did she really want to see Artie assassinated? *You bet!* Would jail be worth killing him herself? *Yes!* But it might upset Mom.

It was smarter to bide her time until she could make Artie an offer he couldn't refuse. Revenge, she decided, tasted sweeter than dessert.

So she dieted. With Sami gone, Delly found it easy to follow a balanced food program. She cultivated a golden tan, cut her hair just below her shoulder blades, and brushed the thick strands three hundred strokes every night. And she began to lather daily with an expensive, lemon-scented soap.

She hated exercise but loved to swim, so she added pool laps to her summer regime, trimming inches of "baby fat" from her thighs and rib cage.

After weeks of procrastination, she visited Sami, who was sallow with early morning nausea. Sami's palomino mane looked brittle and her large breasts sagged.

The sisters made awkward small talk. Then Sami said, "You look terrible, Dell, thin as a stick."

"I know. Pregnancy must be fun, Sami. You don't have to worry about what you eat. Can . . . may I borrow your prom dress?"

"Are you kidding? I'm two inches taller."

"One and a half. I'll cut the ruffles off the bottom. The dress can't possibly fit you and after childbirth they say your figure changes. There's a pool club party next week and I don't have a thing to wear."

Samantha's eyes sparked. "Might as well have fun while you can, Delly-Dog. Don't you start college soon? Study, study, study. Do you honestly believe you'll star in college plays? Without me, you might not even be cast."

"You're probably right, but it doesn't matter. Mom and I reached a compromise. I'm attending college part time, at night. During the day I'll commute to the city and take acting lessons. I don't have your natural talent for pretending, Sami, but I can learn. Gee, you look upset. Settle down. It's not good for Jules Junior. Or is it Neely Junior? Now you look pale. Was it something I said?"

August arrived. Hurricane Celia swept across the Gulf Coast and New York commiserated with rainy days. At long last, the weather cleared, settling into the somnolence of late summer. The pool would close after Labor Day, so Delly took advantage of the few remaining afternoons of sunshine. Her arms cut through the turquoise-tinted water while the lifeguard, on a break, nibbled at her toes like a piranha.

Her one-piece bathing suit had looked conservative in the department store. With a deep slit down the front, its shimmering white material became almost transparent when wet. Delly escaped from the lifeguard, toweled her body, moisturized her face, wriggled onto a cushioned chaise lounge, then twisted her hair into a knot and covered it with a Mets baseball cap.

A shadow hid the sun and somebody said, "Delly Gold? Is that you?"

"Artie Ruben. Hi."

"You look great."

"Thanks." Delly studied her prom-night lover from beneath her cap's visor. Inside his tight stretchy bathing trunks, his *you-know* was practically saluting her. Grinning wickedly, she turned sideways so that her suit's front slit revealed more than it concealed.

Artie hunkered down. "I meant to call, Delly, honest, but I worked all summer at a camp in Pennsylvania and I just got back. Did anybody say, I mean, did the kids say anything about—"

"Your graduation party? Gosh, there was so much excitement after my sister's elopement I sort of lost track. Did you leave for camp right away?" At his nod, she said, "I did hear one thing."

"What? What did you hear?"

"Neely McIntyre gave Micki Bloch a few drinks before he practically carried her into the laundry room. Someone said Neely promised not to come in her mouth. Micki was almost comatose, but she gagged and threw up on Neely. His tux was ruined."

"Yeah. Poor Neely." Artie mopped his brow with his wrist. "You sure look great, Delly."

"Did I look so un-great before?"

"No. Just different. You've lost—"

"My suntan lotion. There it is, near your foot." Scooping up the bottle, she slathered lotion between her thighs.

"I really had a good time," said Artie, watching her hands. "I think about it a lot. Did you?"

"Did I what?"

"Have a good time at my party."

"Artie, I was upset. I cried."

"Yeah, but later, inside the car."

"Whose car?"

"Mine. The back seat."

"You must be talking about my sister."

"Your sister and I never did it in a car."

"Where," Delly asked softly, "did you do it?"

"Backstage. During *My Fair Lady.*"

She burst out laughing.

Artie looked bemused. "What's so funny?"

"Nothing."

"Don't you remember my red Chevy Impala?"

"Vaguely. I was sort of drunk. I remember standing in your driveway and crying, just before you drove me home."

"Yeah. But first we—"

"Wait a sec. Hold that thought." Delly stood, then submerged her body in the water, up to her chin. "It's hot, isn't it?" She stretched out on the chaise again. "If you don't mind, you're blocking my sun."

He sat on the cushion's edge. "Can I take you out?"

"May I?"

"What?"

"Never mind. When?"

"Tonight?"

"Sorry. Busy."

"Tomorrow night?"

"Busy."

"How about the Labor Day pool party?"

"The lifeguard invited me weeks ago."

"Are you booked for New Year's Eve?" he asked, sarcastically.

"Silly Artie." Turning sideways on the lounger, she slathered lotion between her thighs again.

Two weeks later, they dined at an expensive restaurant. Delly nibbled a couple of appetizers and an entree flamed table-side by a waiter with a fake French accent. "I can't decide," she told Artie, then selected an éclair and chocolate cheesecake from a strolling cart. She took three small bites and finished her second glass of Sterling Chardonnay, poured from a bottle that cooled inside an ice bucket. Artie didn't like wine so he drank a beer, wolfed down her desserts, then excused himself and headed toward the restrooms.

"Would you care for a doggie bag?" asked the waiter.

Who just happened to be the best looking man Delly had ever seen. "I don't have a dog."

"Do you have a boyfriend?"

"Seven. One for each night of the week."

"Anybody special?"

"Nope. What about you?"

"They call me The Monk."

"Doesn't a monk swing?"

"This monk swings through vines." He nodded toward the bottle. "Your vine was sour, *liebchen?*"

"I thought you were supposed to be French?"

"That wasn't French?"

"The *vin* tasted *merveilleux, mon cher monsieur,*" she said, thankful for her good memory and her A in high school French. "It's just that this dinner date's the result of a bet. I'm not a swinger."

He winked. "Tarzan swings. So does Jane."

"So does Cheetah."

"Cheetah's what you do when you play solitaire."

"I never cheat," said Delly. "I scheme. Doesn't solitaire mean alone? A recluse, like Tarzan was before he met Jane? If he hadn't been raised by solitary monks, Tarz might have become a swinger."

"*Touché*. God, you're smart. What's your name?"

"Smarty-Pants."

"No, really."

"Jane."

"Of course." He quirked one eyebrow. "Where's Boy?"

"Here he comes now. How much was dinner?"

"A hundred dollars, more or less."

Artie glanced down at the tab, then placed some bills on the table. "Keep the change."

"Don't be so stingy," said Delly, gesturing toward the tip tray.

"Christ, baby, I left him five bucks."

"Cheapskate."

"Cheapskate's what you do in a public park, on thin ice," said the waiter.

"Ice," said Delly, "is what some people call a diamond solitaire." She looked at Artie. "You'd better add another ten or I'll phone for a cab."

"That's fifteen bucks!"

"That's fifteen percent. Goodbye, Artie."

"Okay, okay." He reached for his wallet.

"Mercy, sir," said the waiter, surreptitiously pressing something against Delly's palm.

"Merci, mon cher monsieur," she said.

While Artie retrieved his Impala, Delly opened her clenched fingers and sneaked a peek at the piece of paper. Jon Griffin, followed by a telephone number. Wow! Samantha was the one who collected phone numbers. And the waiter was gorgeous. A sexy Tyrone Power, except his hair was lighter than Tyrone's and his eyes—what color were his eyes? Cobalt? Smoke? The Impala's horn tooted. Startled, Delly dropped her small slip of paper down the gutter's grate. Rats!

Artie parked on top of a wooded hill overlooking Little Neck Bay, then turned the radio's dial to an all-music station.

"I love listening to music," Delly said. "It puts me in the, you know, mood. Could we keep the radio on while we . . ." She paused, lowering her lashes.

"Sure. You look beautiful tonight, baby."

"This old thing? It's a hand-me-down, Samantha's prom dress. Orange isn't really my color."

"Well, I think you look beautiful." Artie shed his jacket and tie. Leaving his keys in the ignition, he extricated a blanket from the back seat.

Delly gazed at the starry sky, where a sliver of pale moon smiled sideways. Stepping from the car, she said, "Gosh, Artie, all that food made me sleepy."

"All what food? You hardly ate a thing."

Yeah, but I ordered enough to make the fifteen-dollar tip legit. Bet you won't bet again, buster.

She stretched out on the blanket, unbuckled Artie's belt, and removed his shoes, socks, slacks, shirt and underwear.

He fumbled at the small buttons on the back of her gown.

"Here, let me help you." She wriggled free from the clinging orange taffeta. Standing, wearing panties and high heels, she carried her dress and Artie's clothes toward the car.

"What are you doing, Delly?"

"I'll be right back. The radio's playing my favorite song and I want to turn up the volume." She slid onto the front seat, hit the lock, gunned the motor, and leaned her head out the window. "It's a new song by the Carpenters," she said, releasing the emergency brake. " 'We've Only Just Begun.' "

"Wait! What the hell are you doing? You can't leave. My clothes! I'm naked!"

"I'll park the car in your driveway, Artie. You remember your driveway, don't you? I remember your driveway. It has an echo that sounds like Munchkin laughter. It's not a long walk home, only seven, maybe eight miles. Gosh, seven and eight equals fifteen. What a coincidence. I called Micki Bloch, Patsy Lash, Peggy Adler, and a whole bunch of other kids. I told them to watch out for you, just in case you got lost or something."

Unfortunately, Cornelius McIntyre had already left for Notre Dame on a basketball scholarship. Delly thought about traveling to South Bend but dismissed the notion as impractical. Instead, she fervently prayed that Neely would get bitten by a rabid dog.

Oh, yeah, she thought, *we've only just begun.*

"Keep your tongue in your pocketbook," Delly said, and burst out laughing.

"All right, all right." Madame Sourdellia scowled. "What's the problem, Augustias?"

"Nothing, Madame." Delly tried to control her giggles. "I had an image of a tongue poking around in a pocketbook. Mine is so filled with junk . . . my purse, not my tongue . . . rats!"

"It's a literal translation, Miss Gold. *The House of Bernarda Alba* is by Frederico Garcia Lorca." The name ran smoothly from Madame's mouth, perfectly accented. "Your line is translated from Spanish and means—"

"I know what it means. I'm sorry, Madame."

"You are always sorry, Miss Gold. If you cannot treat my class seriously, you will be dismissed. Take it again from your entrance."

Two hours later, Delly turned her face toward Jon Griffin. "I really pissed off Madame this morning," she said. "Do you think she'll drop me from class?"

"What month is it?"

"February. Why?"

"In a few short weeks, Madame does her taxes. She won't

drop you, Delly, not if you keep paying her for lessons."

"I wasn't joking."

"Neither am I. If Madame took students for their acting ability alone, I wouldn't be allowed in her class."

"Are you saying I don't have ability?"

"No. You're very talented. But you won't treat Madame's class seriously. For instance, take your clothes."

"Off? Inside a Manhattan coffee shop? Well, okay, if you insist." She tugged at the bottom of her T-shirt, lettered SUPERSTAR. The musical, *Jesus Christ, Superstar,* had been attracting large audiences and Delly knew a member of the chorus.

"Take your clothes," Jon repeated. "Madame has a dress code which you blatantly ignore."

"Everybody wears jeans."

"Everybody does not wear old, faded jeans, especially when they're shredded up the thighs to the crotch."

"You said my jeans were a turn-on."

"Not to Madame. You're purposely defying her."

"I know. I've been doing that for months now, ever since graduation. Testing people. Trying to make them accept me despite my flaws."

"Floss? You don't floss in public, honey. You floss at night when you brush your teeth."

"*Flaws,* you nut. Imperfections, shortcomings, cavities."

"That's my point. If you floss, you won't get cavities."

"What were we talking about?"

"Jeans. Listen, Delly, if you want to wear faded jeans to class, why don't you audition for the Actors Studio?"

"I'm not good enough."

"Sure you are."

"No, I'm not. I've been to hundreds of auditions, practically made it over to Jersey, but I've never gotten one call-back."

"You have to crawl before you can walk."

"Oh, that's good, Jon, really original. It must be your writer's creative mind. Crawl before walk. I'll have to remember that, write it down."

There, I paid him back, she thought. *Paid him back for what?*

Jon shrugged. "I give up. Speaking of giving up, I don't know how long I can stay with Madame. I'm running out of money."

"Why stay? You don't want to be an actor."

"A script writer should be involved with actors, learn by watching them perform."

"You're involved with me."

"I meant the classroom."

"What classroom? It's a loft. Truthfully, Jonny, you're a lot better than some of those Marlon Brando clones."

"Not really, except when I perform love scenes with you."

She felt her cheeks bake. "How's your play coming along?"

"*Duck Pond Sonata*'s coming along fine, just fine. All I have to do is figure out how to finish Act Three without killing everybody off."

"What do you mean?"

"Like an opera. When things get sticky, characters die." He sipped his coffee. "This stuff's cold. Where's the waitress?"

Delly studied Jon above her open menu. He was a shade under six feet, with a muscular body. His eyes were a smoky bluish-green. Natural streaks of blonde mingled with the brown strands of his hair.

He was even better looking than Tyrone Power.

They had finally met again three months ago, when he'd signed up for Madame's class. He didn't remember the girl in the marmalade gown, the dopey kid who insisted "Boy" tip him fifteen bucks, but Delly immediately recognized her handsome waiter and chased him shamelessly.

After their first night together, ten hours rather than ten minutes, she finally learned what home plate meant.

"Is there a part in your play for me?" she asked, placing her menu on the table.

"The part is you. I'm writing it for you."

"Then why can't I read it?"

"*Duck Pond*'s not 'flossed' yet," he said, "and maybe I'm afraid you'll laugh at the dialogue."

"You have lines like keep your tongue in your pocketbook?"

"It wasn't all that funny, Delly."

"Can't you visualize a better use for a tongue?"

"I suppose. How about licking ice-cream cones?"

"Too fattening."

"Stamps?"

"Okay. While I'm licking stamps, you can lick envelopes. Gosh, I'm getting hot. Visualization is the one thing I *have* learned from Madame Sourdellia. Let's vamoose to your apartment, Jonny."

"A vamoose is an antlered mammal, a member of the deer family, probably the Hispanic branch of the family."

"I'm serious."

"You said you were hungry."

"I am." She tried a leer. "But if I eat one more bowl of cottage cheese, I'll turn into a curd."

"Don't you mean turd?"

"Turd is what you've done when you finish a vacation in Europe."

"Europe," said Jon, "is what they yell during baseball games."

"Very good, smarty-pants. C'mon, let's watch the soaps on your TV."

"Since when do you like soap operas?"

"I don't." She tried another leer. "But if we stop watching, it won't matter."

"We can't watch soaps. We have the rest of Madame's class, and afterwards we're supposed to find you a new name, although Delly Gold would fit great across a marquee."

"I know. But my twin, Samantha, always called us the Gold sisters. How does Delilah Griffin sound?"

"Perfect. I thought you didn't want to get married."

"I don't. Not yet. I just want to borrow your name."

"The word Griffin means a fabulous creature with an eagle's head and a lion's body."

"What's wrong with my body?"

"Why do you always take everything I say as a negative? You have a lovely body. Sinuous. Sensuous. Even, to a certain extent, carnivorous."

"Aw, it's not that great," she mumbled. "What do you mean, carnivorous?"

"You don't have an eagle's head, thank God. I don't hanker to kiss an eagle, ma'am." Leaning sideways, he pried her lips apart with his tongue. At the same time, he ran his hands underneath her T-shirt. "Where's your bra?"

"Country boy! In Manhattan a lady never wears a bra with shredded jeans. Rats! Until you touched me, you didn't even notice, and my nipples have been puckering all morning."

"Isn't Puckering a character in a Shakespeare play?"

"Enough already."

"More than a mouthful is a waste," he teased, staring at her T-shirt, giving her an honest-to-God leer.

"Speaking of mouthfuls, let's explore new name possibilities while we lick stamps and envelopes."

They paid for their coffee and exited the restaurant. Delly peered through the window of the jewelry shop next door. "If we really did get married, which one would you choose?" She pointed to a display of engagement rings surrounded by Valentine hearts.

"The biggest one, Jane, right there in the middle. The *solitaire* we could never afford."

Delly grinned like an idiot. He did remember the marmalade kid. "We'll afford it someday, Tarz, when the movies buy your play and I'm starring in my umpteenth Broadway smash."

"Nothing like being positive. Where are you going?"

"To reserve my ring. I'll tell the jeweler to put a sign next to it. Delly's diamond. Jon, that's it! My new name. Delly Diamond."

"I don't know, honey. Diamonds are hard. They cut glass."

"Let's cut *class.*"

"Wasn't it Marilyn Monroe who said something about diamonds being tacky for a woman under forty?"

"No. Audrey Hepburn. *Breakfast at Tiffany's.* Audrey doesn't have big breasts either, so maybe I can be a superstar."

"Let's christen your new name while we lick stamps and envelopes."

"You want to waste your tongue on envelopes?" Had she possessed bushy eyebrows, Delly would have Groucho'd them.

Samantha's kitchen smelled of garlic.

"Was that Jules on the phone?" asked Delly, thinking how a vampire wouldn't be caught dead lurking outside the Perry residence.

"Yes. He should be home soon." Samantha nursed six-week old Samuel William, nicknamed Will. "Jules and his father kept the store open late. Valentine's Day is the best time of the year to buy furs retail, except maybe Christmas. Did I show you the mink jacket Jules gave me for my birthday?"

"Yes. It's lovely. Wow, it must be fun breast feeding."

"Not really, but they say you get your figure back quicker. Damn, my milk's just about dried up. I think I might be preggers again."

"You're kidding."

"I wish." Samantha burst into tears, joining her new son's

wails. "Jules is gonna kill me."

"Why? You didn't do it alone."

"I know, but I haven't taken off the weight from Will and now I'll get even fatter. I'm so tired all the time. I can't cook worth a damn and—"

"Dinner was fine."

"Canned spaghetti, and you hardly ate a thing, even though you're so skinny you could give Olive Oyl a run for her money." Samantha wiped her nose on her sleeve. "Mom says you spend most of your time in the city. Do you have a boyfriend?"

"Yup. His name's Popeye."

"Seriously."

"I sort of have a boyfriend."

Samantha smiled through the last of her tears. "I remember when you said you sort of wanted to be an actress. You know, Delly, you should think about getting married and having kids. It's really the best thing. I mean, you wouldn't have to sweat all that acting crap. Rejection, rejection, rejection. I hear Jules. Hold Will." She ran to the door, threw her arms around her husband's neck, and rubbed her body against his.

He pushed her away.

While Jules ate his spaghetti, Delly bathed the baby and put him down in his crib for the night. Samantha sang a lullaby.

She may have lost her figure, thought Delly, *but she sure hasn't lost her voice.*

They watched TV for a while, then Delly said she'd call a cab and leave for the train station.

Jules said, "I'll drive you."

Sami said, "Why the train station?"

"I'm spending the night in Manhattan." Delly winked. "With Popeye."

The sky was starry and clear but smelled like snow. They were too early for the train so Delly waited inside the car with

Jules, who had traded in his Corvette for a station wagon. An uncomfortable silence ensued before he said, "I'm sorry about the prom."

"That's okay. Ancient history."

"One minute I was dancing with Sami, the next we were in the 'Vette and she was kissing me and promising all kinds of things. We had a lot to drink and I was horny and—"

"Please, Jules, I don't want to hear this."

"It was a mistake. I ended up with the wrong twin. It was you I wanted. I was in love with you, not your sister."

"You're crazy. Sami was the most popular girl in school and we were never anything more than friends. Neely said you took me to the prom because you felt sorry for me."

"That's a lie." He sidled closer. "See that box on the floor mat? It's for you, Delly, a mink teddy bear. Sami says you collect stuffed animals. She says you have a bear named Measles."

"Mumpsy. And I have a polka-dot bear named Chicken Pox."

"Sami was laughing about your collection but I think it's cute, just like you. Gimme a kiss."

"Don't be stupid. I have a boyfriend and—"

"Popeye?"

"That was a joke, Jules, just like you."

"C'mon, Delly, gimme one kiss and I'll let you go."

She pecked his cheek.

"You call that a kiss, bitch?"

Pinning her against the door, he raised her jacket, then her sweater, until the dashboard heater blew warm air across her nipples and she felt the cold window glass chill her spine.

"Jules, stop it!" Wrenching one arm free, she slapped his face. He collapsed and she felt his hot breath singe her rib cage. His hand nudged her ankle. What on earth was he doing now? "Let me go!" she screamed. "Let me out!"

"Okay. Relax. Here it is."

Lifting the mink teddy bear from its box, Jules stuffed its nose into her mouth and pushed hard. She tasted fur, choked on fur, while he unzipped her jeans with one hand. "You don't wear underpants," he said.

Delly's vision blurred. She tried not to swallow. The bear's nose had a button. The button tickled her tonsils. She spasmed and bitter bile crept up her throat. Her legs trembled and her stomach convulsed, but the bear was wedged tighter than a champagne cork. Tears streamed from her eyes. She spasmed for the third time.

"Yes." Jules moaned. "Oh, yes."

She felt his fingers unzip his fly, momentarily felt his erection against her navel. Then, just as Delly thought she might pass out, he removed the bear, pulled her jeans down below her hips, and crushed the mink against her vagina.

"Jules," she rasped. "Jules, don't."

Ramming his penis into the bear, he moaned and writhed, then went limp.

With shaky fingers, Delly fastened her jeans. At the same time, she choked out great, gulping sobs.

"Stop crying," Jules said. "Sami loves it when I do that. Stop crying, Delly. I didn't rape you."

She heard the train's strident whistle. With one last desperate twist, she managed to grasp the door's handle, open it, and propel herself outside, landing butt-first on the ground.

Jules tossed the bear at her and drove away. Instinctively, Delly grabbed the bear, staggered to her feet, and ran toward the station. Seated inside the Long Island Railroad car, she pressed her nose against the window pane.

Once upon a long time ago, she had pressed her nose against a movie theater's showcase. Then Mr. Hailey offered her candy rather than a teddy bear because mink was tacky for a woman who was only eight years old.

Damn, another secret. Mr. Hailey and Jules. Had she been raped by Jules? Technically, no. Violated? Yes.

Outside, it began to snow. Diamond-shaped flakes pelted the window, mingling with her tears.

For the first, last, and only time in her life, Delly thought: *Poor Samantha.*

"Mom, I have something important to tell you." Delly crumpled a chopped liver hors d'oeuvre between her thumb and first finger. Avoiding her mother's eyes, Delly stared at the spray of pussy-willow that nodded from the sun room's windowsill.

"By the look on your face, it's serious."

"*Very* serious, Mom."

"Is it college? Do you want to quit and devote full time to your acting career?"

"Yes. But first we have to talk about Sam—"

"Your sister? What's she done now?"

"No, Mom. Samuel Curtis."

"Oh, sorry, what about him?"

"We've been chatting on the phone and he took me out to dinner last night, just the two of us, and . . ." Delly paused, then blurted, "We've decided to get married."

Carolyn Ann's face paled. "You want to marry my Samuel? Uncle Sam?"

"Obviously, I don't call him Uncle Sam anymore. And he's not *your* Samuel. Good grief, he's asked you to marry him a dozen times since Daddy died."

"But Samuel's old enough to be your father. In fact, he almost was your father. If I hadn't met William—"

"I love him, Mom."

"Not the way I love him."

"Gosh, Mom, I want to marry Samuel Curtis and you suddenly develop this great—"

"I've adored Samuel since I was a little girl."

"Then why wouldn't you say yes after Daddy died?"

"Because . . . because . . . I don't know."

"You really, truly love him?"

"Yes."

"And you'd marry him right now if he asked you?"

"Yes!"

"She's all yours," said Delly, as Samuel entered the room.

"Thanks, kiddo." He embraced both women.

"What's that smell?" asked Delly.

Samuel grinned. "Happiness."

"Duplicity," said Carolyn Ann.

"I don't think duplicity smells like scorched pot roast."

"I was supposed to keep my eye on the stove," Samuel said ruefully. "Should I treat both my girls to a restaurant?"

"No." Delly retrieved her jacket from the closet. "I'll borrow your car and buy some Chinese take-out. I should be gone at least an hour."

After the last bites of Szechuan chicken and fried rice had been eaten, Carolyn Ann turned to Delly. "Do you really want to quit college?"

"Yes. It's a hassle traveling back and forth between the city and Long Island, and I know what I want to do with my life."

"I'll call your parents, Carolyn Ann," Samuel said. With a goofy grin, he disappeared, heading toward the kitchen phone.

"I have no doubts about your talent, Delly," said Carolyn Ann. "You sure had me fooled."

"Uncle Sam put me up to it, during dinner last night."

"Oh, so now he's *Uncle* Sam?"

"Of course. What did you decide?"

"We're getting married right away. I'll live in Chicago, but I'll let Samantha and Jules have the house. You can stay here, too. There's plenty of room and—"

"No! No thanks, Mom. I'll move to Manhattan."

"Okay, but I hate the idea of your living alone."

"I won't be alone. I'll have a roommate."

"Who is she? What's her name?"

"Jon Griffin."

"Why, you little devil. Marry Samuel Curtis, indeed!"

"I promise, Mom, no more pretending—except on the stage."

"I once considered the stage. I wanted to be a famous pianist. Now I just doodle." She smiled wistfully. "Your father would be so proud of you."

"Samantha was always Daddy's gold star." Delly walked over to the window and caressed a pussy willow. Gazing up at the sky, she saw her favorite wishing star. But instead of making a wish she whispered, "Up above the world so tough, like a diamond in the rough."

Dear Anissa, she mentally composed, even though she hadn't written her pen-pal a letter since her metamorphosis. *Dear Anissa, I got bas mitzvahed at thirteen, my first period at fourteen, and screwed at eighteen. But tonight I think I finally became a woman—and an actress.*

Chapter Four

Madison, Wisconsin

Anissa Stern said, "Why'd the Kaiser have to die?"

"Bury him in the backyard," said Helene Stern, focusing on her daughter. "Put his body inside one of your papa's shoe boxes and ask the gardener to dig a hole."

By the age of five, Anissa knew that it was 1957, Tammy was a girl in a song about an owl, the Russians had something called Spitnik or Sputnik (a sat-a-lite), and she was an evil juju. Having overheard a colored servant say the words, Anissa pestered until Black Pearl explained. But, said Pearl, she'd meant that the West African chauffeur was an evil juju, not little Nissa.

Black Pearl fibbed. After all, flowers died when Anissa picked them. Her kitten, Kaiser, had been squished under the tires of Papa's Cad-a-lack. And Mama kept saying how she almost died when her only child was born.

Anissa wondered how a person could die by making babies. Cook said God made babies. Before she was fired, Nanny said a stork brought them.

A stork?

Bobby Hoffman said a boy stuck peanuts into where a girl peed. Maybe, before she was born, Anissa had been a peanut.

Susan Hoffman, Bobby's mother and Mama's nurse, said that a man had something between his legs called a pee-nis.

Oh, pee-nis, Anissa thought, *not peanuts.*

And a pee-nis made babies. Anissa hadn't been a nut, but a feet-us.

What?

With a teensy head and body and ten fingers and toes.

Oh, okay, a feet-us with toes.

And now Anissa was a pretty little girl who shouldn't worry about where babies came from.

But Anissa worried anyway. Because after she was born and had almost killed her mama, Helene stayed in bed night and day, an in-va-lid, propped up on pillows, watching tel-a-vision. Mama had been skinny, said Cook, but illness and lack of exercise made her fat.

I'm not fat but I'm not pretty, thought Anissa.

Pretty was Kathy on *Father Knows Best.* Kathy had dark hair. Anissa's hair was yellow. Kathy had dark eyes. Anissa's eyes were a funny color. "Rabbit fur gray rimmed with black," said Susan.

Kathy Anderson had a papa who loved her.

On the afternoon of her sixth birthday, Anissa sat next to her mother and watched *Search For Tomorrow.* Waiting until the sad music signaled the soap opera's finish, she said, "Mama, do I have one papa or two?"

"One." Helene fluffed the lace at her chin, then straightened her bed covers. "Your papa's a senator and most of the time he lives in a city called Washington, working for President Eisenhower. Do you like my Mamie Eisenhower bangs? Susan cut them."

"Yes, Mama," said Anissa, thinking how the new bangs made Mama's face look like Mr. Moon with fringe on his forehead.

"Why'd you ask about your papa?" Reluctantly, Helene turned her face away from the television.

"On the show today the little boy had two papas and they both want him very much. They yelled at his mama and the big man tried to steal him."

"The word is kidnap, Anissa. That little boy doesn't have two papas, just one. You see, his mama got pregnant and kept it a secret and we don't know which man is his real papa. That's why we have to tune in tomorrow."

"Why can't both men be his papa?"

"A person can only have one."

"Why?"

"Because."

"Because why?"

"Because I said so."

Anissa, disappointed, held back tears. Yesterday Susan had taken her to the movies and they'd watched a man named Troy who wore red sweaters and had yellow hair like hers, and she had begun to hope that Troy was her real papa.

"How come my Washington papa don't have yellow hair?" she asked.

"Doesn't have. He did, but it turned silver."

"Silver's the name of the Lone Ranger's horse. Is Papa a horse?" Anissa waited for Mama to laugh at her joke.

"Are you being naughty on purpose, missy?"

"I'm sorry." Mama didn't say how she almost died when Anissa was born, but it was in her voice just the same.

Mama closed her eyes. Beneath the short bangs, her brow puckered like a wrinkled handkerchief. "I have an awful headache," she said. "Be a good girl and fetch Susan. Maybe Cook will make you a hot fudge sundae."

"I don't want ice cream, Mama." *I want a birthday cake, Mama. I want to blow out six candles and make a wish, just like Kitten does on* Father Knows Best.

"Tell Cook to fix a sundae for me," Helene said. "Tell her not to be so stingy with the chocolate sauce. Tell her to put lots of whipped cream on top. Cream is healthy. It has calcium, which makes your fingernails grow long."

I hate cream. I don't want long fingernails. I wish Troy what'cha'macallit was my real papa.

"Quick like a bunny, Anissa. I'm starving."

"Yes, Mama." She slid off the bed, crossed the room, hesitated at the doorway. "Does Bobby have a papa?"

"Bobby's papa is dead, and don't start that Juicy Fruit thing again. Mr. Hoffman died a long time ago."

"It's juju, Mama. Is Bobby an orphan?"

"No. He has Susan. But you must be especially nice to him, dear."

"Why?"

"Because."

"Because why?"

"Because I said so."

Anissa lowered her lashes. It was hard being nice to Bobby. Maybe if she juju-ed enough, Bobby would die. Except she had a feeling that if Bobby died, he'd come back from the grave. Cook called him a spawn-of-the-lord-of-the-flies.

Anissa didn't know what lord-of-the-flies meant, but she'd been inside a spawn shop when Nanny spawned Mama's diamond bracelet. Nanny said, "It's a secret, don't tell." Anissa hadn't tattled, but Bobby found out and told Mama and Mama said "what a good boy." The spawn shop man gave Nanny some money and said she could have the bracelet back if she "claimed it within thirty days."

Which meant, thought Anissa, that—even dead—Bobby would come back in thirty days, that lord-of-the-flies was very strong, stronger than God maybe, and that she should have spawned Kaiser before he got squished by Papa's Cad-a-lack.

Ten-year-old Bobby Hoffman didn't die. Instead, he continued to live at Anissa's Wisconsin estate, Hillhouse, and no one liked him except Mama.

Bobby was nasty. Bobby was the meanest boy in the whole world. He was 'specially mean to Anissa. He put caterpillars in her food and garter snakes under her sheets. Once he hid a warty toad in her coat pocket and she got in big trouble 'cause she screamed at church.

He said that Anissa was Susan's daughter, not Helene's, and that he belonged to her papa, Jacob, who worked for President Eisenhower. Jacob didn't want her, Bobby said, because she wasn't a boy.

"You're fibbing," she said, poking at her spaghetti with a fork, looking for caterpillars. "Papa stuck his pee-nis inside Mama and I was born. Mama almost died. She told me so."

"Jacob and your mama weren't married yet, so they gave me to Susan 'cause my daddy was killed in Korea and couldn't tell nobody nothing different. Ain't you seen how much your mama likes me, Nissa?"

"That's 'cause you tattle," she said.

"When Susan had you, she traded back. Remember when your father traded in his Cadillac for a new car? It's the same thing."

"I don't believe you," said Anissa. But she did.

Bobby hid behind furniture. Then he'd pounce, pinching Anissa's arms and behind. He said she'd be sorry if she tattled because he'd break every bone in her body, and anyway Jacob and Helene would side with their own son.

By the age of seven, Anissa knew that she could catch a falling star and put it in her pocket, like Perry Como did. But she couldn't swallow her food or sleep through the night. She grew very thin. Dark circles shadowed her eyes and she began to stutter.

Helene believed her daughter's strange behavior was due to Jacob, who had wanted a male heir. Jacob treated Anissa with indifference. Well, to be perfectly honest, hostility might be a better word.

Thank God I had a daughter, thought Helene. *I'm glad Jacob didn't get everything he schemed for, only my money.*

She recalled their wedding night when Jacob had stifled her screams with his hand. Later, she had stifled her sobs with a pillow.

Why wasn't her husband more like the men on her soap operas? They were tall and handsome, just like Jacob, but they didn't rape their wives.

Dr. Dietrich couldn't find a cause or cure for Helene's illness, so she resigned herself to permanent invalidism. Too bad, so sad. Too bad her mysterious ailment prevented Jacob from demanding his conjugal rights. So sad that Anissa, a *girl,* would be his only child.

One summer morning Anissa sat on Mama's bedroom floor and played with her Toni doll. A tall bureau hid her from sight. The room smelled of butterscotch candy, Joy perfume, and rubbing alcohol. On the bed were several new nighties 'cause Mama shopped from a cat-a-log.

Mama and Susan don't know I'm here, thought Anissa, which didn't surprise her. Lately she'd been slipping into Mama's bedroom, hoping to learn more about Papa, Bobby Hoffman, and switching babies. Was Papa really Bobby's father?

Suddenly she felt her ears rise, as if she'd turned into a puppet and someone was pulling ear-strings. Her silent visits had paid off because Mama was rem-in-iss-ing.

Mama told Susan that Jacob had been a struggling Madison, Wisconsin, lawyer when they met. Mama had been Helene Deutsch way back then, the only child of a department store mogul.

What's a mow-gull? Anissa wondered. *A bird? A sea gull?*

After their marriage, Jacob had launched a successful campaign for Republican State Senator.

Re-pub-lick-can. Birds again. Pel-lick-can?

Jacob would have been happy if his wife had died in childbirth, but she hadn't. Those were the facts, as Joe Friday liked to say.

Who was Mr. Friday? How did he fit into Mama's story? What a funny name. Maybe she'd call her doll Toni Saturday.

After Hedrich Deutsch passed away, after she inherited Hillhouse and the Chicago department stores, Jacob couldn't find himself another wife and produce the desired heir, said Mama. Those were the facts.

"I've been thinking about sending Anissa to my Aunt Theresa in Milwaukee," Helene said, following a stretch of silence. "Have you noticed how thin and sick she's been looking lately? And that stuttering. Damn Jacob!"

"Good idea," said Susan. "Hillhouse is too big for one little girl. In Milwaukee Anissa will have other children to play with and she can come home for the holidays."

"To tell the truth, I've already called Theresa and she said yes. Jacob doesn't care."

Papa doesn't care, thought Anissa, playing he loves me, he loves me not with her doll's eyelashes. *He loves me not.*

Surrounded by suitcases, Anissa stood in the vestibule.

Bobby sneaked up behind and pinched her hard above her elbow. "I told you they don't want you," he said. "They don't even want you to live with them no more. They want a boy, not some fucking girl."

Anissa hung her head, trying to control her tears. From Mama's bedroom on the second floor, she heard, "Kiss Bobby goodbye, dear. He'll miss you so much."

"Cook says your aunt's a bitch," Bobby sneered.

"How does Cook know th-that? What's a b-bitch?"

Anissa's heart thumped painfully. She considered running away, but where would she go?

The word spread faster than a gospel sermon by Aimee Semple McPherson. *Theresa Deutsch was a you-know-what—rhymed with witch.* Some women even said it to her face.

Truthfully, Terry inspired jealousy because she was so beautiful. But she hid her hurt feelings and set out to prove everyone right. To that end, she wore tight skirts and rolled-down stockings, smoked brown cigarettes, and slept with any man who looked like Ronald Coleman. Her gents had to be Jewish because they treated women nice and didn't talk marriage with non-Jewish girls. Surprisingly, there were numerous men in Chicago who looked like Semitic movie stars.

Her own parents called her Jezebel, strumpet, floozy, tart, or in more generous moments, a woman of easy virtue.

Terry had inherited a large trust fund from her dead grandfather, doled out quarterly. Kissing her brother and new niece Helene goodbye, she took off for Europe. There, she wed an impoverished Italian count who looked like a Catholic Ronald Coleman. Terry attempted, with little success, to avoid her husband's sadistic sexual abuse. The count had gambling debts. He decided to poison his young wife for full control of her money. Drunk, he mixed up their wine goblets and died in agony.

The count had been unpopular and the Italian police were sympathetic. Returning to the United States in 1930, Terry stood on the upper deck of the *Queen Mary.* As she stared into the dark, swirling water, she thought about the mess she'd made of her life. The moon's glow shed its reflection on the ocean's surface, a rippling spotlight. With a sigh, Terry lifted her leg up over the railing.

"You are planning to fly to the stars, yes?"

She turned and looked down at the man in his wheelchair. "Please go away."

"You are German like me, yes?"

"I'm American, but my parents came from Germany. How'd you know?"

"How did I know, she asks. The rosy cheeks, blonde hair, blue eyes—"

"My eyes are gray."

"Come closer so I can see. Yes, gray like smoke."

"You tricked me. I was going to jump."

"You cannot reach the stars by jumping, *liebchen.*"

"I was going to jump into the ocean!"

"The ocean . . . *ach,* that is different."

"You won't stop me?"

He nodded toward the wheels of his chair. "How could I stop you? It's a nice warm night for a swim, yes?"

"A swim?" Terry glanced out over the vast expanse of dark water. Then she smiled. Then she laughed.

Albert was a Lutheran minister who had been wounded during the Great War. He was paralyzed from the waist down, but that didn't stop him from playing shuffleboard, skeet-shooting, or joining Terry inside the glittering ballroom.

She'd sit on his lap while his strong hands maneuvered the wheels of his chair. A blur of motion, they would speed down the long deck, causing other passengers to scurry for safety. Terry fell in love with Albert's strong hands, his craggy face, and his sense of humor.

"Can a Lutheran minister wed?" she asked. They were sharing a sumptuous meal in the ship's opulent dining room.

"Of course, *liebchen.*"

"Will you marry me, Albert?"

"You swore you would never marry again."

"I've changed my mind."

"I do not look like your Mr. Coleman."

"You look like Barrymore. That's even better. Won't you please marry me?"

"No."

"Don't you love me?"

"Of course I do, smoke-eyes."

"Is it your legs? I don't care, Albert, truly."

"I know that," he said with a sad smile.

"Then why?"

"Because I am dying. In a few short months I must take your journey to the stars."

"You're dying?" Terry stared at him with horror, hoping he was teasing, knowing he wasn't.

"My body is wasting away."

"But that's not fair. Why would your God do that to you?"

"He is your God as well, Theresa."

Terry's half-nibbled chicken Cordon Bleu blurred. Blinking away her tears, she said, "May I stay with you until the end?"

"I do not consider my death an end. Would it make any difference if I said no?"

"No."

Eighteen months later, standing over Albert's grave, Terry vowed to immerse herself in church work. Throughout the years she carefully hid her emotions, believing she could achieve more positive results that way.

Eventually, her facade became reality.

Anissa had once overheard her father and mother discussing Aunt Theresa.

"Affairs? Marriage to an Italian count? You're kidding," Papa said.

"It's true. My parents told me when I was little."

"You must have misunderstood, Helene."

"I didn't misunderstand. Since she never remarried, her title is still Countess, even though she doesn't use it."

"Well, I'll be damned. I never thought that dried up leaf could make it with any man, much less a dago aristocrat."

"Hush! Lower your voice. Anissa might hear you and she remembers everything. What do you mean by dried up leaf?"

"Brittle, Helene. Theresa looks like she'd crumble at a touch. Anyway, she's much too religious for my taste."

"I didn't know anyone could be too anything for your taste, Senator Stud."

"Hush, Helene, your *daughter* might hear."

Arriving in Milwaukee, Anissa was afraid to hug her great-aunt, afraid Theresa might crumble like a leaf.

Theresa was strict but fair. Although never openly demonstrative, she truly loved her sad-eyed niece.

Anissa followed every structured rule, afraid she'd upset her aunt and be sent home. Attending a Lutheran all-girl school, she maintained a straight A average and formed no real friendships, possibly because of her stuttering, probably because of her outstanding beauty. Anissa's gray eyes matched the color of her school uniform's jumper, and her blonde hair swung down her back in braids that were as thick as a rope. She was both vulnerable and self-sufficient.

Just like me, thought Theresa, although there were no problems concerning her niece's moral attitude. Could the child be unaware of her beauty?

"Now I lay me down to sleep," prayed Anissa. "Please, God, let me wake up tomorrow morning with black hair and Elizabeth Taylor eyes. Amen."

Anissa wasn't sexually naive, her knowledge honed by movies, books, and the inevitable gossip of her peers. She formed crushes on Rock Hudson, Robert Redford and Jon Voight. Once she even fantasized a love affair with the minister who preached every Sunday from the pulpit of Aunt Theresa's church.

The stupid boys who clustered outside her school's iron fence made fun of her stutter. Had Anissa lingered with the rest of her classmates to strut and flirt, verbal torments would have ceased. She didn't know this and treated every boy as a potential Bobby Hoffman.

She spent the generous allowance Jacob sent on volumes of poetry and movie matinees. Every Saturday afternoon she would lose herself in the action on the big screen. Later, she'd re-run the film in her head, playing all the roles. When she repeated the lines before her mirror, she never stuttered, never.

If Bobby was Anissa's nemesis at Hillhouse, her Milwaukee enemy turned out to be a large white cat with a furry fringe of black directly beneath its nose. Aunt Theresa had named him Adolf, but Anissa nicknamed him Dolf. Anissa loved animals. Dogs, cats, even the friendly sparrows who nested outside her bedroom window, keeping their tiny heads cocked for the sound of Dolf. The cat, like Bobby, would hide behind furniture and pounce. Anissa became adept at avoiding Dolf's needle-claws.

After years of scratches and hisses, an elderly Dolf clawed his way up Anissa's cotton bedspread and mewed until she awoke. Then he rested his shaggy head on her arm, licked with his sandpaper tongue, gazed into her eyes, and died.

I'm a juju, thought Anissa, even while she understood that the cat had been very old. Was it better to die loved? Or to live lonely?

" 'And youth is cruel, and has no remorse,' " Anissa quoted to her reflection in the mirror.

T.S. Eliot's words were apt, and although Anissa didn't know it, her loneliness was about to end. Not with a whimper. More like a bang.

★ ★ ★ ★ ★

Thirty days hath September, April, June, and November . . .

"Happy Thanksgiving, Anissa. I'm sorry you couldn't go home, but your mother has a mysterious virus and your father is spending the holidays in Chicago."

"That's okay, Aunt Theresa."

"Would you like the turkey leg? I miss Adolf. He always nibbled my giblets."

"Only s-seven more m-months of school before I graduate. I'll m-miss you s-so much, Aunt Theresa."

All the rest have thirty-one, except February . . .

"Anissa, did you remember to send your parents a Valentine's card?"

"Yes, b-but they didn't s-send m-me one."

"Nonsense. There was a lovely card in today's mail."

"Do you honestly think I can't recognize your handwriting, Aunt Theresa?"

Anissa graduated from high school with honors. Jacob made arrangements for her homecoming to Madison and registered her for classes at the University of Wisconsin. She returned to discover that Bobby, now twenty-six and a garage mechanic, had his own apartment across town. Bobby's room at Hillhouse was occupied by Joseph Weiss, a pre-law student who attended the University on a Deutsch-Stern scholarship and worked part time for Jacob. Anissa thought Joe was a physical composite of her teenage crushes, Robert Redford and Jon Voight.

Other things had changed, as well. No longer active in politics, Jacob had established a Wisconsin branch of Deutsch Department Store. Warmer toward Anissa, he called her "daughter" and hinted that it was time for her to start thinking about a husband.

"The man you marry must agree to hyphenate his last name,

daughter. You may select your son's first name, but his birth certificate will be registered as Stern-whatever."

"Yes, Papa."

Anissa Weiss. Mrs. Joseph Stern-Weiss. She wrote the names over and over on lined paper, then shredded the paper before Joe could find it.

He liked her but did he love her?

Roberta Flack was heading the music charts with a song about the first time ever I saw your face. The first time Anissa saw Joe's face, she knew he was the man she wanted to marry. He was handsome and nice and her father's protégé. If she married Joe and had a baby, Papa would be so proud of her. She fantasized walking into Joe's bedroom and sliding beneath his sheets.

She had seen *Klute,* starring Jane Fonda. Jane played a prostitute. Anissa practiced walking and talking like Jane, then decided to forget the whole thing. Joe wouldn't react to the prostitute bit, especially from Jacob's daughter. Besides, who in his right mind would respond to a stuttering prostitute? By the time she enticed him with sexy words, Joe would be sound asleep.

December twenty-fourth arrived. Overloaded with ornaments, an eight-foot tree struggled to wave its branches toward the vaulted living room ceiling. The angel on top resembled Anissa, who wore a white blouse and skirt above blue suede boots. Her entire outfit was a gift from Jacob, although the little To/From tag included Helene's signature.

Beneath bristling pine needles, wrapping paper littered the carpet. Anissa's open boxes included sweaters, accessories, and a soft brown faux-beaver coat. One small square Cartier box held diamond ear drops, sparking like tiny stars. The earrings, said Jacob, were a double-event present since Anissa would celebrate her twentieth birthday in thirteen days.

Wedged into a wheelchair, Helene had descended via a new electric staircase contraption, and she now presided over the assembled Christmas Eve guests—Dr. and Mrs. Karl Dietrich, their son, Karl Jr., Susan and Bobby Hoffman.

Anissa had selected her gifts with care. Proudly, she gave her mother a hand-knit pink shawl. With a rare show of defiant humor, she gave Joe and Bobby the newest recording by Helen Reddy, which included the feminist-inspired title song "I Am Woman." Shopping for her father had been the hardest. Anissa finally settled on a gold tie clip with the engraved word SENATOR.

One unopened gift remained: a crudely wrapped box bound by what appeared to be an entire roll of tape. Small holes had been punched into the top. The tag read "From Joseph/To Anissa," and she broke a fingernail trying to remove the tape.

Inside, a tiny white kitten slept, its head a little larger than the catnip mouse resting between its paws. Directly beneath its pink nose was a furry black mustache. "Oh, Joe, th-thank you," said Anissa, awed. "Is it male or female?"

"Male."

Anissa smiled at Joe. She had told him about Aunt Theresa's cat, especially the part about Dolf eating her aunt's giblets. "I guess I'll call him Adolf, t-too. Do you believe in reincarnation?"

"Only if you do good deeds. Adopt homeless kittens or homeless students."

"You earn your scholarship, Weiss," Jacob muttered, puffing on a thick Cuban cigar.

Helene said good night, turning her cheek for Jacob's quick company kiss. She was wheeled from the room by Susan. The Dietrich family left, then Jacob retired.

Lighting a cigar, Bobby plopped his wiry body into Jacob's

abandoned armchair.

"Papa won't like that, Bobby," Anissa said. "Those cigars were a g-gift from Dr. Dietrich, and very expensive."

Bobby peered at her through brown eyes set close together, then grinned around a chipped front tooth. "Mind your own business, Nissa. Jacob don't care. Did you see the tools he got me? Must be five hundred dollars' worth." Draining a full glass of whiskey, running a comb through his shoulder-length hair, he added, "Joe got a lousy jacket. Guess that's because Jews don't believe in Christmas."

"Haven't you heard, Bobby? Santa Claus converted to Judaism last summer. He's now called Santa Claustein." Joe winked at Anissa and turned on the radio.

She placed her hands over her ears. "Change the station, please. If I hear one more Christmas carol, I'll b-barf."

"How's this? Better?"

The radio now played the top hits of the week. Joe had cut in at number ten, "I'd Love You To Want Me." With an exaggerated bow, he asked Anissa to dance, and they glided around the tree. She was tall, but her head fit perfectly into the curve of Joe's neck. She pressed closer and felt his response. If he didn't love her yet, he wanted her. She stifled the urge to rub her breasts against his shirt, aware that Bobby watched.

"I'm stayin' over," Bobby mumbled. He poured himself another drink and left the living room.

"Do you need help cleaning up?" Joe yawned and flicked off the radio. "Today was a big day at the store."

"No, thanks." Anissa nodded toward the kitten. "First, I want to feed Charlie Chaplin."

"Charlie Chaplin? What happened to Adolf?"

"Naming a sweet little kitten for Hitler seems a tad perverse, don't you think? Wait a sec. I'll call him Tramp. You said he was homeless, and Chaplin played the little tramp."

"Tramp. I like that."

"He's so precious. Thank you, Joe."

Anissa Stern kissed Joseph Weiss. He tasted like cinnamon. Her legs felt like the jelled cranberries served at their Christmas Eve dinner. Wow!

"Wow!" Joe stepped backwards. "Next year I'm going to give you three kittens."

"Papa would have a fit. He's always wanted a large family, but I don't think kitties are what he had in mind."

"Anissa, have you noticed that when we talk you hardly ever stutter?"

"That's because you're so easy to talk to. Want to hear a secret, Joe? When I quote poetry or movie dialogue, I never stutter. It's almost as if, inside my head, there's an iron pressing out wrinkles."

"Too bad real life isn't movie dialogue." He yawned again. "Sweet dreams, Christmas angel."

After Joe had left the room, Anissa tossed her new fur jacket toward a chair, placed Tramp inside the large, puff-papered box, and carried her kitten into the warm kitchen. She filled a bowl with milk, then walked through the downstairs, turning off lights until only the tree glowed. "Have yourself a merry little Christmas," she sang, "kiss-ing Joseph Weiss."

At the bottom of the staircase, Bobby Hoffman appeared, and Anissa was instantly transported back to childhood. "What d-do you w-want, Bobby?"

"I want to dance with you, Nissa."

"But everything's tur-turned off now."

"You danced with Joe. I'm as good as that Jew-boy."

"You're dr-drunk!"

"I'm shit-faced. I've been drinkin' all night, didn't you notice? Or were you too busy dancin' with *him*. Dance with me, Nissa."

Bobby grabbed her about the waist, grinding his body against hers. He maneuvered her toward the hall closet, guided her roughly inside, kicked the door shut, and yanked the string on a hanging light bulb. "Are you cherry, Nissa? Shit, 'course you are. Never had me no virgin before." He unzipped his fly. "I got a special Christmas present for you. You can name it Dick." With a swift motion, he ripped her blouse down the front and lifted her breasts from her strapless bra. "In'creble tits," he said, and reached out with his thumb and first finger.

The familiar pinching gesture broke Anissa's paralysis. Stepping back, she felt wire hangers press against her bare shoulders. "Leave m-me alone, Bobby, or I'll scream."

"Go ahead and scream. Do you think Jacob gives a shit? All he wants is a grandson and we're gonna give him one. He don't care nothin' 'bout you, Nissa."

"You're wr-wrong," she said, but even to her own ears her voice sounded uncertain.

Bobby pushed her to the floor, covering her mouth when she let out an instinctive scream. Impeded by her long skirt, pantyhose and boots, he tried to control her flailing arms and remove her clothes at the same time. So he didn't see the closet door opening and he didn't see the tall figure whose head was on a level with the light bulb. He did, however, feel the hand that grabbed his long hair and yanked him upright. He felt the slap on the side of his face and he tasted the blood that spilled from the corner of his split lip.

"Get out of here, Jew-boy," he snarled. "This is none of your business."

"You maniac!" Furious, Joe slapped Bobby's face back and forth. "If you hurt that sweet kid . . ."

"Stop it," Anissa whimpered. "Bobby'll tell my mother and she'll tell Papa and you'll get in trouble. You might even lose your scholarship."

"I don't care," said Joe. Pulling Bobby from the closet, he

added, "If I catch you near her again, this Jew-boy will slice off your puny Christian prick."

Bobby fled while Joe helped Anissa to her feet. "Are you all right, honey? I could have sworn I heard you scream. Did Bobby do anything, um, bad?"

"I fought him off. For the first time in my life I fought back." She tried to maintain her new-found maturity, but suddenly felt six years old. "Bobby ripped my new blouse. Papa will be so m-mad."

"Aw, don't cry. I'll invade the store tomorrow and get you another blouse. Jacob will never know the difference."

"You c-can't. Tomorrow's Christmas and the store is cl-closed."

"Then the day after. Your blouse will probably be on sale."

At that, she managed a small smile, even took a few steps forward. "Joe, I feel funny . . . dizzy."

Easing Anissa to the floor, he bent her head between her legs. "Take a deep breath. Good. That's my girl."

Looking up, she saw his worried blue eyes probing her face. His thick hair, the same color as hers, fell across his forehead. Bare-chested, he wore beige pajama bottoms, tied at the waist with a drawstring. "Thanks," she said. "I'm feeling much better now, almost human. Oh, I forgot. I'm an angel, a human angel. But I don't have any wings so I can't fly and . . ." She swallowed the rest of her words, aware that she was babbling.

"Can you make it to your bedroom, Anissa? You don't weigh all that much, but you're so tall I don't know if I can carry you up the stairs."

"I'm okay, Joe." Rising, she enjoyed the gentle touch of his arm about her waist as they climbed the staircase and entered her bedroom. "Can you stay a while? I think you scared Bobby, but I'd feel so much safer if you stayed."

"What would your father say if he found me in your bedroom?"

"Please? I'll set the alarm for very early."

"I'll stay until you fall asleep." Joe stretched his long body on top of the canopy bed.

Anissa walked into her bathroom. Discarding her clothes, she slipped a flannel nightgown over her head, braided her hair, and brushed her teeth. When she returned, Joe was asleep. An hour later, she blinked open her eyes. She had mistakenly set the alarm for twelve-thirty rather than six, and a local station played "It Never Rains In Southern California."

Her head rested on Joe's chest. He felt warm, safe, so different from Bobby. Bobby was abrasive. Joe was persuasive. Bobby's voice mocked. Joe's voice rocked—like a cradle.

She would never let Bobby Hoffman frighten her again.

Anissa turned off the radio. Then she untied the drawstring to Joe's pajamas.

"Scoot over," he whispered. "Stay on your side of the bed."

What would Jane Fonda say? "I want to make love." *That's not what Jane would say, you dumbbell.* "Don't you want me, Joe?" *Better!*

"You're still upset over Bobby, right?"

"Bobby has nothing to do with this. I'm a nineteen year old virgin, almost twenty. I'm the only almost-twenty-virgin left in Wisconsin, possibly the whole world."

"That's no reason to have sex. Wait until you find someone you love."

Mrs. Joseph Weiss. "I love you, Joe."

"You're confusing love with gratitude."

"Gratitude doesn't make a person feel all wet and thumpy. I want to be a part of you. I want you inside me." *Much better!*

"You've been watching your mother's soap operas."

She giggled. "They don't use words like wet and thumpy on

Mama's soaps. I know you feel something for me, Joey. I couldn't be wrong. I love you. I love—"

"I'm leaving! Even if we made love, I have nothing to keep you from getting pregnant."

"You can't get pregnant the first time."

"Sure you can."

She pushed her nightie down so that her breasts were revealed. *Good move, Jane would approve.* Wriggling free from her gown, she instinctively nuzzled his chest, following the trail of emphatic body hair.

Joe stifled a moan. Her long lashes fluttered like the wings of a butterfly. The wispy strands of her braids tickled. Her lashes tickled. Her soft, moist lips tickled. Slowly, he guided her face toward the open slit in his pajamas.

What would Jane do now? Anissa's mind went blank. "I think I'm scared," she murmured, as Joe kicked his pajama bottoms free.

"We can stop. We should stop. We—"

"No. I trust you. I love you. I want to learn."

His hands reached out and pulled her up the length of his body until her gray eyes were on a level with his blue. "I'll teach you," he said. "We'll start with kisses."

Anissa shivered, intrigued by the wetness that accumulated, unbidden, between her thighs. Wet and thumpy, hell! She was soaked and throbbing. " 'The anatomical juxtaposition of two orbicularis oris muscles in a state of contraction,' " she chanted nervously, thinking how even Jane would have stuttered over that particular quote. "Dr. Henry Gibbons. 'Definition of a Kiss.' "

Joe kneeled above her prone body and spread her legs wide. He ached to bury his face and taste the protruding bud that lay hidden within the triangle of her golden mound. She was a virgin. He must stimulate moisture enough to ease the inevitable stab of pain that would occur when he severed her gauzy membranes. But he didn't want to frighten her.

If he could only control his own body. Desperate, he tried to remember the score of the last Wisconsin-Purdue football game. Twenty-eight to twelve? Wisconsin-Michigan State: thirty-five to six . . . no, thirty-five to nine. Damn! It wasn't working. Definitions . . . he had a brilliant legal mind . . . everybody said so, his friends, his professors.

"The anatomical juxtaposition of my fleshy muscular organ, attached to the bottom of my mouth," he managed.

"Your tongue," she said with a smile.

"The main organ of taste, used to facilitate an easy entrance leading to the vulva in the female angel."

"Kissing's fun," she gasped, plowing the mattress with her heels, propelling herself closer to the maddening thrust of his flickering tongue.

"Soon we'll try my other muscular organ. But first I want you to come painlessly."

"Come where?"

"You may not have wings, angel, but I can teach you how to fly. There's a wonderful galaxy called Orgasm."

"Orgasm," she repeated, her voice a caress. Then, as she felt Joe's tongue plunge deeper and deeper, she reached for the vault of heaven, beyond her ceiling sky-light. Her vision was filled with exploding stars. And yet, beyond the stars, high above Orgasm, she saw a new constellation: Jane Fonda winking.

Chapter Five

On March 27, 1973, Oscars were presented to Joel Gray and Liza Minnelli.

As Anissa watched the televised Academy Awards, she decided she wanted three children—a couple of Lizas and one Joel. *Papa, I'd like you to meet Joseph Stern-Weiss, Jr. We plan to call him Joel for short. If he has my eyes, we'll call him Joel Gray.*

The Godfather won for best picture, and, out of the blue, Anissa remembered her last letter from her pen-pal, Delly Gold. The letter had been written when Anissa was still living in Milwaukee. Delly had said something about making some boy an offer he couldn't refuse.

The day after the Awards show was unseasonably hot. Joe and Anissa took advantage of the weather by sunning themselves from a bench next to a fountain in the University's courtyard. Pranksters had poured a box of Tide into the fountain's machinery and bubbles foamed, looking like Disney-inspired sea monsters. Throughout the yard, art students held an impromptu sale. Joe bought Anissa a miniature, silk-screened angel.

"Do you believe in tutelary saints?" she asked, admiring the exquisite print.

"Earth angel, earth angel, will you be ma-hine?" he sang.

"Okay, Joey, I'm yours."

"Give me that old time religion, honey. The Bible's a very sexy book."

"Don't let my Aunt Theresa hear you say that. Speaking of old time religion, do you want me to turn Jewish?"

"Nobody turns Jewish, angel. They convert."

"Like Santa Claus?" Anissa placed her print on the bench, jostling their stack of texts and notebooks. A blue-covered script fell, and Joe bent forward to retrieve his copy of *A Streetcar Named Desire*.

"I wish you'd audition," he said.

"Oh, sure. I could stutter with a Southern accent. Blanche DuBois with a speech impediment."

"You once said you didn't stammer over memorized passages."

"Clarence Darrow Weiss, the defense attorney who remembers every—"

"Don't get defensive. Your stutter has just about disappeared, except when you're nervous."

"And auditioning is such a *non-nervous* event."

"I'd love to have you play Blanche to my Stanley."

"You don't have the part yet."

"I'll get it. Hey, if you try out for Blanche, I'll marry you."

"You're going to marry me anyway. After graduation we'll tell Papa."

"First there's law school."

"Which Papa's paying for. He'll be thrilled to support my husband, keep it in the family. After all, you're supposed to join his store's legal department."

"I don't know, angel. I've considered criminal law. It has a lot in common with the stage."

She winked. "We won't tell Papa until you pass the Bar. And we'll give him a grandson, Joey, like lunch ordered through a McDonald's drive-up window. One double cheeseburger, secret sauce, fries, a grandson, and a Coke." Anissa kept her hand from straying toward her belly. She hadn't told Joe yet, wouldn't confess until she was absolutely certain. She'd never been late with her period before, but that didn't mean she was pregnant. "Now I'm hungry," she said.

"Audition with me and I'll buy you *two* double cheeseburgers, secret sauce, *large* fries, and a Coke. Such a deal!"

In the end, just to shut Joe up, Anissa auditioned. She had always been able to memorize things quickly and she learned Blanche's lines while waiting for her name to be called. Laying aside her script, forgetting her stutter, she illuminated the bare boards with a charismatic radiance. The other Blanche hopefuls immediately clamored to read for the part of Stella.

On opening night Jacob pushed his way through the crowds backstage and entered Anissa's dressing room. "You're a chip off the old block, daughter," he said. "You should have heard me on the Senate floor."

"I've considered switching my major to drama, Papa."

"That's fine by me, though I do wish you'd major in finding a husband and starting a family."

"I've been working on that, too," she said, making a sudden decision. "You see, I've—"

"Darling Blanche," her director interrupted, brushing Jacob aside, "I'd like you to meet Daniel J. Travanti."

Anissa stared up at a handsome face with soul-filled eyes.

Travanti grasped her hand in his. "I once belonged to the Wisconsin Players. We did Tennessee Williams' *Cat on a Hot Tin Roof.*"

"Yes, I know. You played Brick. I hear you were so good they retired your crutch. What are you doing now, Mr. Travanti?"

"Dan. I'm still acting. You were wonderful tonight, Anissa. But," he added somewhat bitterly, "if you plan to act professionally, you'd better learn how to deal with rejection."

"I've learned." She flashed him a brilliant smile. "The first three letters of rejection are r-e-j, which are also the first three letters of rejoice." She turned to her father and said, "Let's talk tomorrow, okay?"

During the cast party, Joe said, "Why don't we elope? Right now. Tonight."

"Are you crazy? Drunk?"

"Neither. It's just that I love you so much."

"Me, too, you. But I want a church wedding. I want a white gown and champagne and rice. I want kiss-the-bride and, *oh, God,* how I want Papa to escort me down the aisle and give me away."

His gaze probed her face. "Why that fervent last want, Anissa?"

"If Papa gives me away, I'll finally belong to him. Do you understand?"

"Not really, but we'll wait." Forcing anguish into his voice, he said, "Anisssaaa, Anisssaaa."

"Damn," said a cast member. "Brando can't hold a freaking candle to Weiss."

For some dumb reason, Anissa's heart fluttered fearfully and she felt like a tiny firefly trapped inside a clenched fist.

Rejoice, not rejection, she reminded herself.

"Did you see the reviews, Papa?"

Anissa shifted from one foot to the other. Why was she so fidgety? Papa would burst his buttons when he heard about Joe and the baby, especially the baby. She'd missed another period.

"I've read all the reviews, daughter. 'Last night a new star rose above Madison's Capital building. Astrologers have named it Anissa Stern.' I plan to frame that one and add it to my collection."

Jacob sat in a padded leather chair behind a huge desk. Above his silver pompadour, the wall of his office held photos autographed by politicians—his "collection." Eisenhower grinned with all his teeth, as if he'd just clubbed a hole-in-one. Nixon smirked enigmatically. Even the democratic Kennedy brothers shared the cluttered wall space.

"You'll be so happy when I tell you my news, Papa." Anissa took a deep breath. "I want to get married. I'm in love, Papa."

"Bless you, daughter. Who's the lucky man?"

"Joseph."

"Joseph who?"

"Your Joseph, Papa. Joseph Weiss."

Anissa saw her father puff on his cigar. His eyes were cold, and she recalled childhood vacations when he had expressed displeasure with her stuttering. And the fact that she was, as Bobby Hoffman had so delicately put it, a fucking girl.

"You cannot marry Joseph Weiss," Jacob finally said.

"Why not?"

"Because I won't allow it."

"I don't think you understand, Papa. I love Joey."

"And how long have you loved this boy?"

"From the very beginning. Why do you say loved in that horribly sarcastic way? Why do you call him 'this boy'? We're talking about Joe, who has lived in your house and—"

"Seduced my daughter."

"Seduced? That's a joke. It was me. I seduced him. I d-don't understand. Is it because he's Jewish and p-poor? You were p-poor once, Papa. Joey's planning to become a lawyer, just like you, and probably a sen-senator t-too."

"Stop stuttering, Anissa. You didn't last night, although as far as I'm concerned this discussion is finished. Kaput!"

"But I d-d-don't understand." She swallowed both her stupefaction and stammer. "Why can't I marry Joey, Papa?"

"Because I have said no. Did you hear me? No!"

"Papa, I'm over eighteen. I don't need your permission. Joey and I will get married, with or without your approval. I wanted him to keep your support for law school, but I'll work and we'll manage. Would it make any difference if I told you I'm going to have his baby?"

"You're pregnant?"

"Yes."

"You're sure?"

"I'm sure."

"How many months?"

"Eight, maybe ten."

"Ten months?"

"No, Papa, weeks."

"You'll have an abortion as soon as I can arrange it."

"Are you insane? You've always wanted a grandson."

"I'll find a good doctor and—"

"Papa, I'm going to marry Joey. Kill my b-baby? You'll have to kill me, first."

"You cannot marry Joseph Weiss, Anissa. He's your brother."

"What did you say?"

"Joseph is your half-brother, close enough. That's why you must agree to this operation."

"My brother? But . . . but that's impossible."

"Grow up, daughter. Must I explain how one conceives a child?"

Why was Eisenhower grinning like a dirty old man with a naked mistress hidden inside his rotunda? Anissa wanted to turn Ike's picture so that he faced the wall. Instead, she stared at her father, focusing on the brownish-gray mustache he called a soup-strainer. Then, clearing her throat, she said, "Does Joey know? What a stupid question. Of course he doesn't know. How could he not know?"

"She was well paid, his mother. Joseph was told his father died in Germany, an American soldier. I decided to put my son through school. It was a mistake, bringing him here, but I wanted to see . . . I never thought . . . it was a big mistake."

"Please don't tell him, Papa. He'd be so hurt. He doesn't even suspect." She felt her eyes widen. "Mama's illness. Is that the reason? Did she find out?"

"No." Jacob chomped on his dead cigar. At the same time, he reached for a box of matches. "My father fought for Hitler, died for Hitler. My mother did things to survive, and I was born fifteen months after my father died."

Papa's a bastard, Anissa thought. No wonder he wanted a legitimate son so badly. And now, a legitimate grandson. Stern-whatever, not Stern-Weiss, which would be Stern-Stern. *Oh, God!*

"I don't blame my mother," Jacob continued. "Sometimes you have to weather the storm, no matter what it might cost. The ends justify the means."

Anissa blinked her tears away. "Did you love Joe's mother?"

"I suppose I did. But I couldn't marry her."

"Why? Because she was Jewish?"

"No. Because she didn't have any money. Politics require lots of money."

"Joe must never find out. You should see his mother's grave. All he talks about is making her proud of him. You must never tell him, Papa."

"Then you will forget this plan to marry?"

"No." Anissa dabbed at her tears with the back of her hand. "We can still be married. After all, he's only my half brother. You just said the ends justify the means. I'll have my tubes tied when I get the abortion."

Jacob jumped up, overturning his chair. "You will not have your tubes tied. If you are foolish enough to attempt it, I will tell Joseph that he is my son."

Stupid, thought Anissa. *Tubes tied. What a stupid thing to say.*

"I will describe every moment I spent with his mother, in

detail. Then I will remove him from my house."

We should have eloped last night.

"If you run away together," Jacob continued, reading her mind, "I'll hire a private eye." Rising, he walked around the desk and extended his arms. "You're so white, daughter. Are you going to faint?"

"Don't touch me. And don't call me daughter."

"But you are my daughter. Because you are, and because I care for you, I will make the arrangements for your future."

"What does that mean?"

"I'll find you a husband. Once you're married, Joseph will leave you alone. You will honor your marriage vows. You could not have lived all those years with Theresa and learned deceit. You'll be wed after the abortion, but we need to find someone who will keep the abortion secret. *Mein Gott!* I loaned Dr. Dietrich the funds for his medical center. Did you know that?"

I know what a thirsty flower feels like.

Maybe Joey's love was stronger than mere illegitimacy, stronger than their half-brother, half-sister relationship. If only Bobby Hoffman had told the truth about switching babies. Anissa remembered how she'd felt when Bobby insisted he was Jacob's son and she was Susan's bastard.

Joey might be consolatory today, next month, next year. He might even forgive his mother's sin. But eventually he'd grow to hate Anissa because she had caused his hurt and because she was Jacob's legitimate child. Child. Children. What about children? She and Joey could adopt. But wouldn't Joey, like Jacob, desperately desire a legitimate heir?

It was hopeless, a Tennessee Williams script.

Jacob re-lit his cigar. Mesmerized by the flaming match, Anissa remembered last night, when she had felt like a firefly trapped inside a fist.

"Do you promise to obey me, daughter? Do I have your word?"

"Yes, Senator."

Reject. Rejection. Screw rejoice!

Anissa planned her confrontation carefully. Waiting for Joe to join her in the library courtyard, she pretended the situation was a Biblical play titled "The Denouncement of Joseph."

Clouds had dimmed the day, so she wore a red University of Wisconsin sweatshirt whose black badger eyed her breasts. Beneath a short plaid skirt she wore knee-socks and sneakers. She had plaited her hair in two braids, then wound them on top of her head like a crown; a regal *Christian* image.

She had even blocked the play in her head—Joey sitting at her feet, a subject playing homage to his sovereign.

Unfortunately, he hadn't studied her secret script. Sliding his body close to hers on the bench, he said, "It's about to rain. Let's scurry to the Rathskeller for coffee." His eyes probed her face. "Anissa, what's wrong?"

"I've made a decision and I don't think you'll like it."

She had already written the play, figured out which lines would occur, memorized her responses. Act one, scene one followed her script, with a few inconsequential adlibs. Anissa said she was marrying Karl Dietrich Jr. because Jacob didn't approve of Joe, at least not for a husband. Yes, she had told Jacob last week, following *Streetcar*'s opening night, and the Senator had threatened to cancel all financial support, probably because Joe was poor and Jewish.

Anissa kept her shoulders straight and her head high, made it sound as if she would miss Jacob's department store generosity, for example her pretty clothes. Then there was her new Mustang convertible—damn, she'd hate to lose that. She cued Joe but cut his lines when he replied. She never stepped out of character and she could see that he believed her dialogue.

Act one, scene two, Joey threw her a zinger.

"What about the baby, Anissa?"

"Baby?"

"I'm not dense, or blind, and I can count. You haven't had your period since February. I've noticed a look in your eyes and I've seen you stroke your stomach when you thought I wasn't watching."

She pressed her hands against her flat belly. Her mind raced, revising the script, forming a desperate lie. *Dear God, help me. I've got to give the best performance of my life.*

"There is no baby," she said.

"What did you do? Oh my God! You had an abortion." Anguish clouded his blue eyes. "We could have made it without your father, angel. Did you think I'd be upset? You know me better than that. I must have done something to make you lose your trust." Gathering her into his arms, he massaged the rigid muscles in her neck and shoulders.

She pulled away. "I had to have an abortion," she said, her voice sincere, bitter. "I had no choice."

"Why? Was there something wrong with the baby?"

"Yes. It wasn't your child."

"What are you talking about? We've been together since Christmas. There's no one else. There couldn't be."

"Yes, there is. Was. Remember the week you and Jacob went to Chicago for that Deutsch staff meeting? The stock thing?"

"March," Joe said, "around St. Patrick's Day."

"Susan had Bobby over for dinner and I drove him home. His car wasn't working. Isn't that fuh-funny? He fixes cars for a living and his wasn't working."

"Very funny."

"We stopped for some drinks. Piña coladas with little umbrellas. I got sloshed. The umbrellas were so cute and they served the drinks in co-coconut shells."

"Go on."

"Bobby started to m-make love and I had never had sex with anyone but you and I was curious and I . . . I . . . it was only that one night."

"How was he?"

"What?"

"Am I speaking a foreign language? Read my lips. How was he?"

She winced. "He was okay."

"Did you do all the things we do together? Or did you just let him have his way with you?"

"I . . . we . . ."

"You said you were sloshed. He took advantage of that. You couldn't fight back and I wasn't there this time to stop—"

"Together. We did it together."

"Shut up!" Joe jumped to his feet and clenched his fists. "I'll have a talk with that stupid shit. Bobby's face will look like a strawberry piña colada when I'm finished."

"Typical. Beating up a man to protect your honor."

"Why are you protecting him? Bobby did something, threatened you. He must have."

"No, Joey. I wanted it. Remember Christmas Eve when you said I was reacting to my mother's soap operas? Bobby believed every word, especially the wet and thumpy part. It was me. I got down on my knees and—"

"Shut up! Shut up!" Blinded by tears, Joe staggered to the bench, bent his head, and covered his face with his hands. "I don't understand why you're telling me all this." Tightening his fingers again, he pounded on the bench slats.

Anissa flinched.

"It might have been my child," Joe said. "If it was only that one night with Bobby, it probably was mine. Did you think

Bobby would brag about it? I wouldn't have believed him."

I have to tell the truth. She pictured Joey kneeling beside his mother's grave. "Mom would have adored you, angel," he had said. "We'll name one of our babies after her, okay?"

I have to tell the truth. Dizzy from indecision, she heard Aunt Theresa quoting from the New Testament, something about how a fool, when he holds his peace, is counted wise.

I can't tell the truth.

"It doesn't matter," she said. "I'm engaged to Karl."

"He plans to become a doctor like his father, doesn't he? Second generation butcher of babies. Are you going to cheat on Karl, too?"

"Not if he keeps me satisfied," she said, wanting to end her painful play. No applause for this performance.

"You remind me of your father, Anissa. He had quite a reputation. They called him Senator Stud."

It began to rain. Anissa felt as though God held a piña colada umbrella over her head. She patted her crown of wet, regal braids. "Jacob says I'm a chip off the old block," she said, remembering her father's backstage compliment.

"Go to hell, angel."

"Yes," she whispered, her reply lost in a sudden burst of thunder. "Yes, that's a good idea. Oh, Joey, my love, my only love, the devil can't compare to Papa."

It was the last time Anissa ever called her father Papa.

The lounge on State Street was filled to bursting with students. Some celebrated the end of finals while others avoided studying for tomorrow's exams. Joe focused on a Budweiser clock. Tick-tock. Clip-clop. Chip-block. What the hell were the Budweiser horses called?

Tick. Tock. Clop. Chip. Anissa was a chip off the old block.

"You okay, Weiss?" asked a pre-law buddy.

"Bet your fuckin' A."

It's almost over, thought Joe. He wondered if Anissa expected him to attend her wedding farce. Strange how Jacob didn't object when Joe gave some lame excuse about exam fatigue. Anissa's confession outside the library was strange, too. She wouldn't sleep with Bobby Hoffman and she didn't care that much about money.

Something else was very strange, almost bizarre. In that whole discussion she never once said Papa. She sounded as if she hated him and called him Jacob or Senator. The Senator doesn't approve, Joey. The Senator will cancel my allowance. Jacob wants me to marry Karl.

Joe shook his head. *Christ, I'm drunk. Can't think straight. Maybe she did call him Papa. No, she didn't.*

Gulping down a full stein of beer, he added the empty mug to the others lined up along the table's edge, then swallowed a shot of whiskey.

"It's almost over," he said.

"What's almost over, Weiss?" asked his pre-law buddy. "School? Exams?"

"The contest, you asshole. Place your bets. Bet your fuckin' A."

Nickels, dimes, quarters and dollar bills rained down upon the table. Across from Joe, an overweight student named Howard finished his eighth mug of beer, although most of it trickled from the corners of his mouth, toward his double chin. Howard stared hypnotically at his shot glass; they'd added the whiskey after mug number five. "Chugalug," he finally mumbled.

"Chugalug," several voices chanted. The contest had attracted a large crowd. One woman—had Joe brought her?—rubbed her pointy breasts against his shoulder. Her sweater was so tight, he could see the outline of her bra. Christ, she was drunk too. He couldn't remember her name.

"Your turn to chug, darlin'," she said with a pretty pout. "Then maybe we can leave. I don't want to spend all night in this crummy joint."

"Objection sustained. Chugalug." Joe downed his mug of dark brew and swallowed his shot of whiskey.

"Chuggy-lug," mumbled Howard. He lifted his mug, gulped half, belched it all up, then slid from his chair to the floor. He started spouting beer, like a whale. His face turned as green as the Jolly Green Giant. In another moment, less than a moment, he'd puke. Six students carried him toward the restrooms.

Joe remembered. The girl with the pointy breasts was Sharon—Sharon The Homecoming Queen. She hailed from Georgia, belonged to Sigma Delta Tau sorority, and was engaged to a Harvard Med student. Queen Sharon had bumped into Joe, agreed to help him celebrate finals, but warned him that she was "savin' it for the weddin' night." Now Joe watched her drink her own gin and tonic, then Howard's neglected shot. Scrambling up onto the table, she tugged at her sweater. "Itchy," she said.

"Take it off, take it off," chanted the crowd.

Queen Sharon shed her sweater, reached for her bra, and pitched forward, straight into the arms of an All-American tight end. Black and beautiful, he wore a gray sweatshirt with sawed-off sleeves.

"On Wisconsin," he sang, hefting her across one broad shoulder and staggering toward the exit. "A touchdown sure this time."

Queen Sharon's legs dangled down his chest like a turkey's wishbone. Her skirt had hiked all the way up and the jock was fondling the crotch of her silk panties. She looked as if she was about to orgasm. Eyes shut, she chugged like the little engine who could, but her face was almost as green as Howard's, and

Joe didn't hold out much hope for the back of the jock's sweatshirt.

Neither did anybody else. People scurried out of the way, aware that projectile vomiting wasn't uncommon—especially among sorority girls.

Joe wondered if he should object. After all, he had brought Sharon to this "crummy joint."

Objection overruled. God, he was such a bastard. He tried to focus on the Bud horse-clock. Numbers solidified. "Ish over," he slurred. "I made it."

"You sure did, pal," said Joe's pre-law buddy. "We just won fifty bucks."

"Sharon?"

"Gone."

"Where?"

"The moon? The pavement? Who cares?"

"I should 'scort her home."

"Why? You couldn't get it up."

"No, no, she's engaged to a *doctor.*" Joe glanced at the clock again. "Wrong. She's married. Oh, God! Anisssaaa."

"C'mon, numb-nuts, I'll 'scort *you* home."

"Shit, man, I can drive."

"You can't even walk, you asshole."

Anissa made all the correct responses at her wedding. Karl was the one who stammered. He even forgot to lift her veil after the minister's kiss-the-bride.

Through the wispy shroud that covered her face, Karl's breath tasted like cherry Lifesavers. Anissa endured the sloppy kiss. She would be a good wife but she'd never give Jacob his grandson. On her way to the church she'd picked up a full wheel of birth control pills.

Dry-eyed, she clutched Karl's sweaty hand and walked back

down the aisle. Jacob had given her away, but now she belonged to him completely.

Last week, after Joey had abruptly raced from the courtyard, the curtain of rain had continued descending on her original one-act drama, mingling with the tears on her face. She hadn't cried since.

I'll never cry again, never feel anything again. Tears don't wash away sorrow. They just make your eyes puffy.

During the reception, Anissa drank champagne, hoping it would blur the evening. Instead, it gave her a throbbing headache.

The moon was full when she and Karl finally left, escorted to her dark green Mustang by the cheering guests. While Anissa drove toward the small house that Jacob had leased for the "happy couple," tin cans played a discordant tune. She turned on the radio, hoping to drown out the sound. The radio played Harry Nilsson's "Without You." She turned it off.

She parked, navigated three porch steps, and hesitated at the doorway, wondering if Karl planned to carry her across the threshold. But he brushed past her and disappeared into the bathroom. When he sauntered out, he had put on white pajamas with red hearts and chubby-winged Cupids. Anissa shook the rice from her long hair. Karl probably couldn't lift her anyway. He was exactly her height and looked like the Cupids on his pajamas, minus their wings. During football season he wore a fuzzy badger costume and led the cheering squad.

"Hey, get ready *Mrs.* Dietrich," he said. "Why are you just standing there? Hey, if you need to use the can, I'm finished. If it smells, light a match. Hey, do you want a drink first? There's champagne. Damn, I left the bottle in the car. Hey, do you want me to fetch it?"

"No, thanks. I've had enough, more than enough. In fact, if you don't mind, Karl, I'd rather go straight to bed. We can consummate our marriage tomorrow night. I've got this stupid headache and—"

"I don't want to wait, Anissa. The sooner you get pregnant, the better."

"Pregnant? I didn't know you wanted a baby. You have med school and I want to get my degree. That's why we postponed the honeymoon, remember? Finals."

"Anissa, we have to make a baby right away."

"Why?"

Karl's excitement was palpable. "During the reception your father gave me a check for ten thousand dollars, and he promised ten more if we have a son. I'm not shitting you, Anissa, he really did. Isn't that great?"

She stumbled backwards, as though her husband had suddenly developed a Ben Hurian case of leprosy. "Jacob did what?"

"I just told you. He gave us ten thou—"

"The Senator paid you to marry me?"

"No. To get you pregnant."

"Dear God, he paid you to stud for him."

"It was a gift."

"It was a bribe."

"What's the difference? You can still get your degree, even if you're preg—hey, where do you think you're going?"

"Out." She snatched up her car keys.

"But it's our wedding night. You can't just—"

Anissa slammed the door on his words. Afraid he'd follow, chase her down the street in his red and white pajamas, she drove to the first gas station. Tin cans rattled, but this time it sounded like a Halloween graveyard.

Parked near a pump, she yanked at the bumper strings, cutting her palms and fingers. Then she wiped the bloody scratches on her white wedding gown, took off the gown, and stuffed it into a trash receptacle that was already filled with grimy paper towels. If the gas station attendant saw her, he didn't venture outside his safe cubicle.

Back inside her Mustang, she found the champagne bottle, popped its cork, and washed down a birth control pill.

She parked three blocks away. Wearing a bra, panties and half-slip, she approached Hillhouse. Clouds hid the moon but she needed no light to wriggle through a side window, climb the winding staircase, and enter Joe's room.

His stereo needle was stuck on Helen Reddy.

I am woman, I am woman, I am

Taking off her underwear, she crept into Joe's bed.

"Sorry, Sharon, can't," he mumbled, and began to cry. "Oh, God. You smell like my angel."

"Hush, darling."

"Anissa?"

"Quiet, my love." She straddled his body.

At first he tried to push her away. Then his hands caressed the velvety skin of her back while his lips nuzzled her breasts. She rocked back and forth. The bed bounced, the floor boards shook, and the stereo needle scratched forward.

I am woman, hear me

Roaring with primitive passion, Anissa consummated her marriage.

Chapter Six

During the day Anissa performed by rote. She arrived early for her final exams and stared at the lined pages between the covers of her bluebooks. If the room had a clock, she stared at the clock. When the proctor warned, "Five minutes, boys and girls," she answered multiple choice questions with "all of the above." And every night she visited Hillhouse.

"Why are you doing this?" Joe groaned.

"Because, my love, I'm lost without you."

Afterwards, she returned to her new husband. She bathed and powdered and perfumed, but she couldn't lose Joe's scent. It was in her eyes, her nose, her mouth, her fingers, even her feet.

Sometimes she felt Karl's gaze boring a hole through the bridge of her nose, so she attempted polite conversation. "Please pass the butter. Wisconsin is known as the Dairy State. That's why we use lots of butter. Did you know that the butterwort, an herb of the bladderwort family, produces a secretion to capture and digest insects? Yesterday I flunked botany. Today I'll flunk English lit."

"Anissa, why are you doing this?"

"Doing what? Flunking? Never mind the butter. My toast is cold."

If Anissa treated Karl like a familiar stranger, she answered Joe's questions with endearments, silenced his words with kisses, and halted his refusals with her pliant body.

All he understood for certain was that she had lied about Bobby. But why?

Every evening Joe swore he'd visit the lounge on State Street, the library stacks, the Rathskeller. Instead, he remained at Hillhouse, listening for Anissa's ballerina-soft footsteps. She was a drug. He was stoned on lust. There was no panacea for narcotized passion, no anti-lude for love. Vaguely, he wondered if Karl knew what was happening.

Karl didn't but Jacob did. One week after the wedding ceremony, Anissa entered Joe's bedroom and Jacob turned on the lights. Following a moment of temporary blindness, she glanced toward the empty closet. "You told him."

"I warned you, daughter."

"You really told him. How did he take it?"

"Very well, considering. He said to let you know he forgave your performance." Jacob heaved a deep sigh. "You disappointed me, Anissa. So much for a strict upbringing. I did not remove Joseph from my life, merely my house."

"Mama's house," she snapped.

"I'll continue my support while he attends law school in Chicago. If you join him there, I'll cancel his funds immediately. I still maintain a certain amount of political clout, Anissa, so if Joseph disobeys my orders his career is kaput. In other words, don't tempt him. Do you understand?"

"Yes."

"Return to your husband. I'll ring up young Karl tomorrow and garner a full report."

"Garner? My body isn't a granary and my bedroom isn't the senate. Karl doesn't have to take minutes."

"Hopefully, he'll take more than minutes."

"You're such a bastard, Jacob," she said, enjoying his instinctive wince. "When I was a little girl, I wished with all my heart that Troy Donahue was my real father."

"Who the hell is Troy Donahue?"

"I hate you," Anissa said softly. Then she turned and ran from Hillhouse.

Karl was asleep, snoring. On the bedside table, a bottle of Wild Turkey lay on its side, the remaining liquid dripping like a leaky water faucet.

Anissa packed her suitcases, hesitating when she came to her diamond earrings. Then, with a shrug, she put the small box inside her makeup case.

On tiptoe, she walked across the room to a wooden desk, opened a bottom drawer, pulled out a cigar box filled with wedding-gift cash, and separated the money into two equal piles. Finding Jacob's check, she methodically ripped and flushed until ten thousand dollars' worth of shredded paper vanished down the toilet bowl.

"Good-bye Wisconsin, farewell my only love," she whispered, walking toward her Mustang.

The Mumm Napa Cuvee bottle from her wedding lay on the back seat. Re-corked, it tasted flat, but she drank some anyway. The night was filled with stars. Convertible top down, her blonde strands tangling like Medusa, Anissa sang "I'm Forever Blowing Bubbles."

Then, since the champagne had lost its bubbles, she changed her tune.

"California, here I come . . ."

California was beaches and freeway, tacos and truffles.

In Hollywood, thought Anissa, the Age of Aquarius will always let the sun shine in. The Age of Twiggy, however, had finished its long run and women were growing their breasts again.

She met Buzzy Beeson while sight-seeing outside Universal Studio, and spent her first weekend at his hotel. A famous comedian during the nineteen fifties, Buzzy had emerged from self-induced, drug-related exile, and wowed the public with a guest appearance on *Saturday Night Live.*

Inspired by the small script on her earrings box, Anissa changed her last name to Cartier. Yet it took Jacob's private "eye" only five days to find her lodgings, a small room in a boarding house run by a Mrs. Kathleen Kaye.

The certified letter from Jacob included annulment papers and an allowance check. Anissa signed the papers but destroyed the check.

Decent jobs were scarcer than hens' teeth. She tried waiting tables, which looked easy but wasn't, and found she didn't have the temperament. Every minuscule tip became a personal rejection, every generous gratuity a covert invitation. Exactly one month later, Jacob's money order arrived, with double the amount of the first check.

He's keeping the door open, she thought. *Karl didn't work out but he still wants a grandson. Shit, I don't care. I'll cash the damn bribe.*

Soon she was spending her days like her mother, watching soap operas on her tiny black and white TV. Evenings she hung out at a local bar called The Polka-Dot Unicorn, often picking up a partner to make the long nights less lonely.

She celebrated her twenty-first birthday at the Unicorn, eyeing its decor through the oversized glass of her margarita. The walls were filled with paintings of wizards, unicorns and dragons. Several suits of armor guarded tables. The regulars, mostly daytime TV personalities, could design their own blazons. Since she was a steady customer, Anissa had chosen the anise plant, a yellow-white flower with licorice-flavored seeds. "I flunked botany," she told the artist who painted her shield on the mirror behind the bar, right next to Randy McNeal's kangaroo Coat-of-Arms.

Randy was tall and muscular, with the relaxed good looks of a California beach boy. Born in Australia, he had a delightful accent, and he was one of the minor characters on a soap called *Children of the Night.* Anissa greeted him warmly.

"G'day, love," he replied, swiveling his bar stool around and raising his wine glass.

A bearded man introduced himself as The Duke. Clothed in cords, boots, and molded Stetson, he sat on the stool next to Anissa's and casually placed his arm across her lacy white chemise top. His other hand stroked her legs in their faded denim until she trapped his fingers between her thighs.

"Let's get out of here," he mumbled.

She shook her head and last year's birthday earrings glittered. "I want four shots, straight tequila," she said. It was her favorite test. One drink, two drinks, three drinks, four; all of the above. If this duke person objected, it meant that he was rinky-dink schlock and she'd find somebody else.

"You'll pass out cold, honey buns," he said, nodding toward the bartender.

"You're big enough to carry me home." Anissa gulped down all four shots. Then slowly, emphatically, she licked salt from the back of her hand.

"I'm big all over," The Duke promised. He appeared mesmerized by her tongue.

She felt his fingers searching and wriggled closer. He wasn't handsome, but his cowboy clothes intrigued her, he smelled okay, and the alcohol had made her dizzy, tingly, which usually occurred before total oblivion. Fortunately, due to her Teutonic drink-and-plunder-without-consequence bloodline, she never got sick. Fortunately, inspired by her generous gratuities, the bartender tended to ignore her under-age status. Now she was legit. If she were a dog, she'd be one hundred and forty-seven years old.

"I can drink tequila all night long," she slurred. "It's 'cause I'm Mexican."

"No shit. I could have sworn you was a kraut."

"Kraut*ess*. I was raised by a countess. My father's a bastard."

"Mine's a Baptist minister." The Duke nodded toward the bartender again.

Glancing down the bar, Anissa met Randy McNeal's gaze. His blue eyes were filled with . . . condemnation? Defiantly, she downed the first shot, licked her knuckles, squinted toward The Duke, and felt her vision blur. "Where's Joey? You're not Joey."

"Who's Joey?"

"The father of my baby."

"You got a baby?"

"No. Jacob got the baby."

"Who's Jacob?"

"He's not Troy Donahue," she said mournfully.

"Finish your drinks and I'll take you home." The Duke pressed his hand against her crotch.

"Stop it, Bobby!"

"Who's Bobby?"

"The father of my child."

"But I thought you said somebody named Joey—"

"Shut up. Go 'way."

"You must be kidding. I gotta pay the bartender for your drinks and I've already given Kath—"

"Are you ready to leave, Anissa?" Randy McNeal placed a wad of bills on top of the bar's surface.

"Get outta here," The Duke growled.

"This young lady is leaving with me," Randy told the smaller, heavier man.

"The hell she is. Find your own girl. Don't screw with mine."

"I won't, cowboy. Anissa's my sister."

"You're full of shit. She don't have no accent."

"I'm his half-sister," Anissa said. "I've got half-brothers all over the place. They seem to pop out of the woodwork when I least expect it."

The Duke vacated his stool. "Shit, man, I didn't know."

"Are you ready to leave, love?" Randy placed his hand on her shoulder.

"Nope." She shrugged him off and reached for the second shot glass. It spilled on the way to her mouth. So did the third and fourth. "Damn! Order me four more shots, Randy. It's a test," she added slyly.

"You've had enough, more than enough."

"So I'm sloshed. It's my birthday, Ran-man. I can get shit-faced if I wanna."

"Yes. You're definitely ready to leave."

"One more," she pleaded, "and then we'll celebrate my birthday. I'm one-hundred-and-forty-seven. You won't be sorry, cross my heart." She crossed her heart with Randy's first finger. "See? I don't wear a bra, Ran-man. I'm lib'rated. I'm woman, hear me roar. Hap' birthday to me, hap' birth—whoa, wha'cha' doin'?"

Placing his hands about her waist, he lifted her from the stool and supported her through the crowded room because her legs didn't work too good. "Meow, meow, meow, Ran-man," she chanted. She halted. On tiptoe, she rubbed against the front of his tight jeans. At the same time, she squinted past his shoulder, toward a sign that read: NO SHIRT, NO SHOES, NO SERVICE.

"Never saw *that* before." Pulling the chemise up over her head, she stepped from a pair of sandals. The bar patrons whistled and cheered.

Randy picked up her sandals, pushed her out the door, and shoved her into a Volkswagen convertible. "Put your gear back on, nit," he said.

She ducked her head through the chemise straps and gathered the material under her chin. "I've got incredible tits, Ran-man. That's what Bobby Hoffman said. Bobby duced . . . uh, *see*-duced me with a piña colada umbrella, only he didn't know it, the dumb slob."

"Belt up, Anissa."

"What?"

"Shut up."

"Where we goin'?"

"My duplex."

"You don't wanna visit my room?"

"No."

"Are you mad?"

"No."

"You sound mad. Hap' birthday to me?" she asked, her gray eyes huge, tear-bright, uncertain. "Don't be mad, Ran-man."

Silently, he drove and parked, then helped Anissa climb a short flight of steps. He led her through his living room, down a hallway, into the bathroom. Scooping her off her feet, he deposited her in a claw-legged tub and turned on the shower.

"What are you do-doing?" she sputtered.

"Sobering you up."

"Let me out of here, you Aussie bastard!"

"No." Randy rotated the faucet so that only cold water poured from the shower head.

"Stop it! What's the matter with you? Are you kinky or something? Do you plan to screw me under ice-cold water?"

"I don't plan to screw you at all, darlin'. I'm gay."

"You are? I didn't know. Then why'd you take me home with you? I want a drink, Ran-man." She fumbled for the faucet and turned it off.

"Anissa, you have a bloody problem."

"I have a problem? You're gay and I have a problem? I want a drink. Now!"

"Okay. Wait here and I'll bring you one." He returned, holding a tall glass filled with a white liquid.

"Is that a White Russian?" Defiantly, she gulped every drop, then gave a surprised little urp and vomited down the front of her chemise.

"I blended a special grog called a White Australian," he said, handing her a wet washcloth. "Cream, vinegar, Milk of Magnesia and raw eggs. It's my home-made remedy for too many sleeping pills. Sometimes gay leading men find their closets claustrophobic."

"Who do you think you are? My real brother? God?"

"Neither. But I've had problems and my mates have been there for me. Please, Anissa, I can't just stand by and watch you poison yourself. Are you finished being sick?"

"I never get sick. I pass out first."

"Right. Are you finished *not* being sick?"

"Yes. No." This time Randy bent her forward, toward the commode, and pressed the washcloth against her brow.

How convenient to plumb a toilet next to the shower, she thought. That way one can bathe and puke at the same time.

Randy's hand was above her rib cage, instinctively cupping her breast, and she felt an orgasm build, her first since leaving Wisconsin. But the throb went away when tiny hummingbird wings fluttered inside her throat. *Please, God, not again.* Despite her fervent prayer, she issued forth a desperate moan, clearing a path for the liquid that gushed through her open mouth.

"I'm going to d-die, Randy," she cried. "You've killed me with your damn grog."

"It's not my damn grog anymore." He removed the cloth from her brow and cleansed her mouth. "It's your damn tequila. Hold on, darlin', here we go again. Don't fight it, baby. Okay, good, you've got the dry heaves. That's the last of it."

She leaned weakly against the tiled wall as Randy stripped off her clothes. He rinsed and draped them across the shower rod, then helped her stand under warm water, wrapped her in a fluffy pink towel, and half-carried her to the living room. "Sit down," he said. "We have to talk."

"I want a drink," she rasped, "a real drink."

"After what just happened you want more grog? You're bonkers."

"I'm getting out of here. Lend me something to wear."

"Are you serious? How tall are you? I'm six-three."

"Give me a shirt, you Aussie rat. The bar sign says shirts and shoes. It doesn't say anything about pants. I'm gonna' find my Duke."

"That's what we have to talk about. Sit down, Anissa. Coffee or tea?"

"Tequila."

"Coffee or tea?"

"I don't care!"

Randy returned from the kitchen with a tray that contained Brie cheese, summer sausage, and two steaming mugs. Huddled against the couch cushion, Anissa glared at him.

"Listen carefully," he said, "and if you still want to find your cowboy after I'm finished, I'll lend you some gear. Okay?"

"Do I have a choice?"

"Not really. You're going to bloody well listen, even if I have to toss you back into the shower like some damn boomerang. Anissa, that Duke person paid Kathleen Kaye to sleep with you. She's a high-class pimp."

"Kathleen? My landlady? You're crazy."

"I didn't think you knew."

"Are you saying I'm a whore?"

"No. But Kathleen runs a kind of whorehouse. She finds some poor lost soul and rents her a room."

"You're out of your mind! I've never been introduced to anybody by Kath—"

"That's not the way it works. You choose your partners, but Kathleen tells them where to find you. She collects a non-refundable deposit, plus more money afterwards. 'First you get laid, then Kathleen gets paid.' It's the worst kept, best known secret in town."

"I don't believe you," Anissa said.

Yes, I do, she thought. *It must be true. Why would Randy make it up?*

She recalled the last few months. Her partners had always found her at the Unicorn. There'd been very little verbal sparring, no tentative body language. The men bought her drinks and took her back to her room, never theirs. She suddenly realized that most of them hadn't even asked her address.

"It's true," she said. "I'm so stupid."

"No, darlin'. It's not your fault. Kathleen usually rents to kids who hope to star in movies. She keeps the rent very low."

"True. Once I told her I was thinking about leaving because Jacob . . . because the Senator . . . she chopped thirty dollars off my rent. I couldn't leave."

"She doesn't need rent money. That's a bonus. She bails up the men."

Between bursts of uncontrollable laughter, Anissa said, "It's so fuh-funny, Randy. Jacob . . . Aunt Theresa . . . strict upbringing. I feel like I'm stuck inside some Looney-Tunes cartoon."

"Calm down or you'll get sick again."

"I c-can't. You d-don't understand." Abruptly, her wild laughter ended on a painful sob. Randy pulled her into his lap and held her tight. "I swore I'd never cry again," she wailed.

"We all make promises we can't keep."

Anissa gave him a tremulous smile, then quoted a long passage about broken vows.

"Those are Crissy's lines! You not only watch *Children of the Night,* you memorize the alfy dialogue."

"I watch all the soaps. It's hereditary. Why does everyone call you Randy? Children's credits list you as Stuart McNeal."

"It's a long story. I'll confess if you eat your tucker and spend the rest of the night here. You can't go back to Kathleen's. Your cowboy might be lurking. I did promise I'd drive you to the Unicorn."

"No, thanks." Anissa shuddered. "Look, I'm drinking my tea. Why are you called Randy?"

"I was born in Queensland. My dad was a fair-dinkum Ocker, what you'd call a hillbilly, or maybe a redneck. When I was thirteen we moved here." Randy inflected his voice with a deeper accent. "Dad would introduce me to his drinking mates. 'This is my son Stuart,' he would say, 'a randy little bugger if ever I saw one.' The name stuck. My dad's not a violent man but he beat the hell out of me once. He was crying and calling me a drongo—a born loser. He couldn't call me a fag, you see. In his part of the world, fag is another word for cigarette."

"Randy, I'm so sorry."

"Well, we all have our problems. I didn't mean to grizzle . . . complain. I've learned to deal with Dad and he likes to watch me on the telly. Mum brags about me to her friends. Have you finished your tucker?"

"Yes."

"Do you want to go to bed now?"

"Yes, please."

"Good on yer," said Randy, taking her by the hand. "This is my bedroom. You already know where the loo is." He tossed her a black silk pajama top. Stepping from his jeans, he donned the bottoms. "Do you really watch my soap every day?" he asked, crawling into bed, staking a claim on the left side.

While she buttoned her pajama top, Anissa responded with

one of Randy's monologues, accurately mimicking his accent.

He whistled. "Can you always pull lines out of a hat like that?"

"I have a great memory, like a sponge. Test me. Give me a movie. One of your favorites."

"Casablanca."

"That's too easy," she said, plumping a pillow and joining him on the bed. "What lines do you want? Ingrid says, 'Kiss me, kiss me, as if it were the last time.' If that doesn't turn you on, you randy bugger, there's the part where Bogey says, 'Remember, this gun is pointed at your heart,' and Claude Rains says, 'That is my least vulnerable spot.' "

"Amazing. I thought you were going to quote the famous play-it-again-Sam line."

"Actually, Bogart never says that."

"You *are* incredible, Anissa, and I'm not talking tits. I think I'll introduce you to Maxine Graham. She's a bitch, but a very powerful bitch."

"Who's Maxine Graham?"

"I thought you read the soap credits. She's my bloody producer. Maxine would flog her own mother for higher ratings."

"She'd beat up her mother?"

"Sorry. In Australia, flog means sell or hock. I'll have to make you a list."

"Flog. Loo. Tucker. Drongo. I won't flunk this foreign language course, I promise." Playfully, she ruffled his tawny, sun-streaked hair. "Are you saying that I can get a part on a soap opera?"

"Absolutely. You're a beaut, Anissa. Do you know how much you sounded like Bergman, Bogart and Claude Rains, when you did their lines? And with that retentive memory you could learn pages of dialogue overnight. You'd be a ripper, as we used to say in the Outback."

"Me on a soap opera? What an incongruous twist of fate."

"How so?"

"It's a long story and all that 'tucker' made me sleepy. Take my word for it, okay?"

"Okay. Good-night, angel."

She caught her breath at the pet nickname. *If Randy can deal with his problems,* she thought, *I can deal with mine. I'm not going to be a loser—a drongo.*

"Come closer," he murmured. "I can't have sex with women but I sure like to cuddle 'em."

She nestled against his warm chest and smiled at the irony of Anissa Stern Cartier performing on a soap opera. She heard the echo of her mother's words: *That's why you have to tune in tomorrow.*

Chapter Seven

Flushing, New York

No matter which way she turned her head, Valerie Florentino could hear a man singing in her ears.

"Turn off the radio!" she screamed.

"It's a record," said the nurse, cradling Valerie's shoulders with one arm. "*Kismet.* And it's the third time we've heard it. I wish Doc had given you a Caesar salad. Come on, Miz Florentino, huff and puff like the big bad wolf."

"A lady doesn't huff and puff." From her new vantage point, Valerie could see her sheet-draped toes. "What do you mean, Caesar salad?"

"That's what we nurses call a Cesarean section."

"Why won't the doctor just knock me out, like he did last time?"

"Because you went into early labor and it's safer for the baby. You want a healthy baby, don't you?"

At this point, Valerie didn't give a rat's ass if she produced a healthy baby, a healthy watermelon, a healthy bowling ball, or Mickey-fucking-Mouse.

The record came to an end. Then it began again.

"Pant like a thirsty dog," said the nurse.

"A lady doesn't pant."

"Push, dearie," the obstetrician said. Other doctors might enjoy listening to classical music. He preferred show tunes.

"If I push," Valerie wailed, "I'll soil my undies and a lady doesn't soil—"

"You're not wearing undies." Through his mouth-mask the doctor sang about a stranger in paradise.

"Shut the fuck up!" Valerie screamed.

Baby Girl Florentino was born on June 1, 1954. She huffed, puffed, panted, and wept at the injustice of entering the world prematurely. Then she sucked her thumb.

"I'm calling her Marilyn Monroe Bradley Florentino," Valerie told the nurse. "My movie magazine says today is Marilyn Monroe's birthday. If Andrew doesn't like it, he can lump it."

The nurse held up the tiny infant. "Little Maryl sure has herself a full head of red hair. You probably had gas the whole eight months you were pregnant."

Valerie squeezed her eyes shut, unwilling to admit that the nurse was right. A lady didn't have gas. And even if she did, she didn't discharge it. Then she remembered the news that had sent her into early labor.

Gas! Fumes! Explosion! Dear Jesus!

While Marilyn Monroe Bradley Florentino's newborn bottom was being spanked, her father hurried home. Not wanting Val to become suspicious, he hadn't packed a suitcase. Stupidly, idiotically, he had left his bus ticket where he'd hidden it—in the pocket of his ratty brown bathrobe.

"Stupid idiot," he muttered, unlocking the door and stepping into a brief hallway. He and Val leased an apartment within walking distance of Flushing's IRT subway. Partially subsidized by Val's parents, the apartment had high ceilings, low rent, and cockroaches.

Val and Andrew Jr. were gone. Shopping for groceries?

Tonight was Hamburger Delight—chopped meat, lumpy mashed potatoes and canned peas. Tomorrow they'd dine on leftover burgers, disguised as tacos. The next day, chicken. The day after, leftover chicken with "oodles of noodles." The next day, Tuna Delight. The day after that, soup; a big pot, filled with leftovers from the previous five days—hamburger, chicken, tuna, noodles, and in all likelihood, roaches. Val usually dumped beans into the soup, and beans, especially baked beans, bore a striking resemblance to roaches.

On the seventh day, God created Val's parents. Andrew never *could* remember what he ate at the Bradley residence since every week his father-in-law would say, "You a famous artist yet, son?" But the way he said "son," it sounded like asshole.

The roaches must have sensed his arrival because Andrew didn't hear the sound of their scratchy skitters. They were playing hide-and-seek, search-and-stomp.

He halted to admire his hand-painted mural, on the wall of what their landlord had the nerve to call a second bedroom. Above the crib and tiny dresser, Mickey, Minnie, Goofy and Pluto scampered through a field of smiling daisies and daffodils. Andrew joked that Disney spies would discover his mural and sue the shit out of him for infringement of copyright laws. Well, they could sue till doomsday but they'd never collect anything except Val, Andrew Jr., second-hand furniture and roaches.

Maybe after they discovered his talent, he'd be hired as a Disney animator.

Andrew's laugh was mostly snort. Up until today he had worked as a proof-reader for *Candid Confessions,* a magazine he privately called "Spill Your Guts." The head honcho had promised that Andrew would eventually rise to the position of illustrator. Sooner or later, he'd draw men kissing women and men screwing women, even though they didn't actually show that, but everybody knew.

Sooner or later meant when hell froze over or the Pope turned Jewish.

Impatient with unfulfilled promises, bored with his marriage,

Andrew had given two weeks' notice and bought his one-way bus ticket.

As Andrew focused on Minnie Mouse, he pictured his wife. She'd been an eager virgin rather than a reluctant virgin. First they'd necked and petted on the front seat of her daddy's car. Then, wet and woozy, she'd screamed, "Do it, do it, do it now, Andy!"

"Don't call me Andy," he'd said.

Afterwards, she'd puked cheap wine all over her daddy's dashboard and he had fled. Any other red-blooded American boy would have done the same, right?

"You're a bad boy, Andy," his mother had crooned, swinging a broom handle like a baseball bat.

Andrew heard a phlegm-filled *harrumph.*

Cops? Had Disney sicced the cops on him?

Cigarette smoke overpowered the scent of roach spray. Following his nose, Andrew saw his neighbor sitting at the spindly-legged kitchen table.

"Hi, Bud." Andrew always called his neighbors Bud and Hon because he never *could* remember their names. Hon looked like Dagwood's Blondie while Bud looked like Buffalo Bob on that Howdy Doody puppet show.

"Good evening, Florentino. Your wife's at the hospital. She had a phone call. *Harrumph.*" Bud cleared his throat and lit another Camel. "Her father's car was smashed to smithereens by a moving van. Her parents are dead."

Andrew assumed an expression of pious solemnity, but his heart soared. No more famous artist bullshit.

"Your wife went into early labor," Bud continued, "so I called an ambulance. My missus has your little boy at our place. She gave him milk and cookies and now they're watching that puppet show on our new television set. When your children get bigger, they can join the Peanut Gallery." Bud blew smoke rings toward an empty roach trap.

Jesus! Children! This morning Andrew had one wife, one son, and two in-laws. Now he had one wife, two kids, and a couple of dead in-laws.

Thank God he had left his bus ticket in the pocket of his ratty bathrobe. An agnostic, Andrew had never really believed in a benevolent God. But he did now.

Mr. and Mrs. Bradley's last will and testament left Valerie a Great Neck, Long Island house, mortgage paid, and an insurance policy that totaled fifty thousand dollars. Valerie inherited her mother's diamond ring, too, but they couldn't find Mrs. Bradley's finger in the wreck.

Witnesses claimed the Bradley's Chevy had run a stop sign. Andrew wanted to sue the moving company anyway.

"That won't bring Momma and Daddy back," Val said. "A million dollars won't bring them back from the dead."

Andrew wondered if that was really true.

Val wasted three thousand dollars on a funeral. Andrew had the feeling she was pissed because it was a beautiful summer day, not one hint of rain. At the gravesite, the minister kept pressing a handkerchief against his nose, probably because Drew had dirtied his diaper.

"Your son is sitting in his own shit," Andrew whispered. "Change him."

"I'll do it after the service."

"What kind of mother are you?" Andrew wheeled Drew's stroller toward a waiting limousine, retrieved a diaper bag, handed the driver ten bucks, then returned in time to hear the minister's amen and catch Val before she hit the ground.

"How can you say shit at a funeral?" Still in his arms, Valerie sagged against Andrew's chest, squeezed her eyes shut, and panted like a thirsty dog.

It was their last intimate moment.

The Florentinos moved to Great Neck. Andrew burned his bus ticket. He bought art supplies and a drafting table, then cleared out the downstairs sewing room. There, he created his own original comic strip, which he called *Chien.* The main character was a shaggy, unclipped poodle. Mingling with a cast of animals, Chien strutted through panel after panel, barking philosophical "dogma."

For six years—from 1954 to 1960—the Florentinos lived off the Bradley's insurance policy. And for the first time in his life, Andrew didn't need sex. All his get-up-and-go went into creating *Chien.*

A few newspapers bought his strip and he soon attracted a cult following. Chien was a "left-pawed liberal" who opposed his right-winged friend, an ostrich named Barry Silverwater.

Screw Disney!

Viva la Chien!

Marilyn Monroe Bradley Florentino was not a beautiful child. Her hair was unmanageable—a curly, carroty flame that her mother tried to subdue into a couple of Pipi Longstocking braids. Maryl's eyes tilted at the corners but were a plain brown. Not dark or golden or greenish-brown. Just brown—like mud.

Her brother's eyes were black—two perfect chips of polished onyx.

Maryl's pointy-chinned face had the look of a scruffy cat trying to hide behind a blade of grass.

Her brother was beautiful.

From early childhood strangers were always touching Drew to determine if he was real, not some life-size doll, and as a result he grew painfully shy. Only thirteen months separated brother and sister. Since Maryl's hyperactivity and Drew's diffidence alienated playmates, they became best friends.

Naturally, Andrew gave them boxes of crayons.

Maryl loved the slick sticks that smelled like candles. Daddy handed Drew a coloring book filled with the outlines of Mickey and Minnie Mouse, then handed her Donald, Daisy, Huey, Louie, and what's-his-name.

"Soon you kids will be coloring Chien and sleeping on Barry Silverwater sheets," Daddy said. "Anything's possible. After all, Kennedy promised to put a man on the moon—if he can get the Pope to volunteer, ha-ha."

Maryl's fingers flew across the pages, creating free-form blotches. "Jackson Pollock on Mary-wanna," said Daddy.

Drew stayed within the lines.

"Andrew's son has inherited his father's art talent," Valerie told her friends, silently thanking God that Drew had inherited something of Andrew's. Because she had a feeling Andrew Junior wasn't her husband's son. Furthermore, she could have sold her 1952 diary to *Candid Confessions.*

In one short week, Valerie Bradley lost her virginity twice. First to Andrew Florentino, then to Buzzy Beeson. Andrew was a fluke, a chance encounter at the Flushing Meadows Ice Rink. They had ended that memorable evening on the front seat of her father's Chevy, sharing a bottle of cheap Chianti. Wet and woozy, Valerie had shouted, "No! Don't!" But Andrew had penetrated anyway, the louse.

Hours later, when Valerie opened her eyes, Andrew was gone. Her mouth was dry, her undies wet, and before passing out she had thrown up all over the car's dash. Weeping into a wad of tissues, she fervently hoped that some of her throw-up had landed on the dashing Mr. Florentino.

Valerie had once been described as "the spittin' image of Shirley Temple, only older and taller." She worked as a receptionist for a Manhattan-based talent agency, and she *adored* being employed by a company that created properties for the fledgling television industry. Her agency handled writers, directors, and a dozen rising stars. The brightest star was Buzzy Beeson, a poodle-haired comedian who wore checkered pants, plaid jackets, and polka-dot bow ties. Buzzy established the popular expression "So what'cha' say, bootsie?" The public wasn't sure what bootsie meant, exactly, but from the way Buzzy said it they figured it was something dirty.

A few days after Valerie's horrible experience with Andrew, Buzzy invited her to a party. A dazzled Valerie accepted and actually met Eddie Fisher, her favorite singer. And Lucille Ball with her handsome Cuban, Desi Arnaz. And the prizefighter, Rocky Marciano. And—

Buzzy insisted she drink glass after glass of bubbly until she was practically falling-down drunk. At one point, she batted her false eyelashes at Eddie Fisher. "I'm Shirley Temple," she slurred, but Eddie wasn't fooled. God, how embarrassing. Tearfully, she let Buzzy guide her upstairs and propel her into a guest room. He tossed her on top of the bed, unsnapped her garter belt, peeled off her stockings and cotton underpants. "Nice bootsie," he proclaimed. "So what'cha' say?"

This time she said yes, because she was drunk and he was a star and one didn't screw around with stars.

Several weeks later, when Valerie told Buzzy she was pregnant, he suggested a discreet operation. "No way," she said. Abortions were illegal and she had seen movies where the doctors had dirty fingernails and talked in foreign gibberish. Did he want her to die of an infection?

Buzzy had her fired.

Valerie haunted the ice rink until she found Andrew again. The artist, recently transplanted from Detroit, accepted responsibility. Thank God he had played on his high school hockey team. Thank God he owned a pair of skates and grooved on gliding around the ice, looking for girls to seduce.

"It was all so romantic," Valerie told her friends. "Andrew skated straight into my heart."

Thank God Drew didn't look like his other father.

Maryl had just finished her best picture yet. She'd crayoned a piece of paper with every color of the rainbow and covered the whole thing with black India ink. Then she'd fingernail-scratched a doggie that looked like Chien. Maybe his eyes were lopsided and one shaggy ear longer than the other, but a person could hardly tell the difference.

Securing a pencil between her ink-stained fingers, she printed her name and the date across the paper's white border: MARILYN MONROE BRADLEY FLORENTINO 1962. There! Now it could be hanged on the wall, right next to her brother's neat pictures.

Bursting with pride, she wanted to show somebody. But Mommy was at the dentist with Drew. Daddy was in his studio, and he said to stay out when his door was closed.

"Shit," Maryl swore, then glanced around to make sure she hadn't been overheard. Was she nuts? She was alone. Even Colleen, their twice-a-week-maid, had disappeared.

Maryl sighed. Colleen was young and spoke with what Mommy called "a Maureen O'Hara singsong lilt." Colleen would appreciate Maryl's hard work, maybe even thumbtack it on the wall.

Wait. If Maryl hurt herself, she could ask Daddy for help. That was the rule. Placing her beautiful drawing on the kitchen table, she eyeballed a sharp knife. Then she opened the refrigerator and grabbed a clump of carrots.

A few minutes later her thumb bled nicely. Now all she had to do was tell Daddy she wanted to surprise Mommy by fixing a salad for dinner, and—oh, gosh, Daddy—the knife slipped.

Carefully grasping her picture with her uninjured hand,

Maryl tiptoed toward Daddy's studio door.

The door wasn't locked. Maryl inched it open and sneaked inside, expecting to see Daddy scrunched over his drafting table.

Instead, he sprawled across the studio couch, looking just like an octopus. Four arms, four legs, two heads—

Two heads?

Daddy's head and Colleen's head.

Maryl felt a giggle ripple through her. She dropped her picture and covered her mouth with both hands because she had a feeling Daddy might be mad if he saw her standing in the doorway. Because Daddy was naked. Colleen, too.

Bending down to pick up her Chien drawing, slinking through the doorway again, Maryl saw that she held her pretty picture between her bloody thumb and her first finger. Which was probably why she cried and cried.

When she finished crying, she fainted.

1967 waved good-bye, and Andrew Florentino, laughing all the way to the bank, developed a line of greeting cards, posters, clothing, sheets, towels, and stuffed animals.

Chien ran for President. His platform included bringing the "dog soldiers" home from Vietnam, National Veterinarian Care, and the legalization of drugs, starting with catnip. Chien promised to stop all bugging by the F.B.I.S.—the Federal Bureau of Iguanas and Spiders. Then, just for grins, Andrew created another cartoon character, Mary-wanna, a promiscuous spaniel who looked like Disney's cocker spaniel, Lady. Disney protested. The Catholic Church protested. And the strip's popularity soared to new heights.

By the time Maryl entered high school she was five feet, ten inches tall, and except for the basketball team, she towered above her classmates. Her mud-brown eyes hid behind thick eyeglasses while braces fortified her perpetual scowl.

She was intelligent, but could hardly sit still long enough to concentrate. Valerie called her daughter a Jackie-in-the-box with batteries that never wore out.

But Maryl knew damn well her batteries atrophied, because she fainted at the drop of a hat.

One doctor called it a "temporary suspension of respiration and circulation due to cerebral ischemia." Another doctor claimed it was all in her head and suggested a psychiatrist.

"I'll play shrink," said Drew, sitting at the kitchen table and sharing a box of Girl Scout cookies. "Tell me, Maryl, do you hate your mother?"

"No. I think she's great."

"Do you want to sleep with your father?"

"God, no."

"Okay. You're cured."

"I could cheerfully kill Daddy," Maryl said.

"Why?"

"He just introduced a peacock named Monroe."

"So what?"

"Look at me, Drew. Peacock?"

"How do you know the peacock's supposed to be you?"

"Because Daddy's peacock, Monroe, faints at the drop of a hat. May I have another cookie, please? Where are you going?"

"Out." His cheeks reddened. "This cheerleader saw me at a basketball game and invited me to the movies. She cheers for Bayside High and her name is Samantha Gold."

"I'll bet *she* looks like a peacock."

"It's just a date, Maryl."

"Right. And the fainting is all in my head. Do you hate your father, Drew?"

"No. I think he's great."

"Do you want to sleep with your mother?"

"God, no. I want to sleep with Samantha Gold."

"I could never win the Miss America title," Maryl said. She and Drew were curled up on the sofa, watching TV.

"Why not?" Drew grinned. "You're tall enough."

"Thanks a lot. I couldn't win because I have four names. Marilyn Monroe Bradley Florentino. The winner can only have three names."

"Terry Anne Meeuwsen," said the TV reporter, "is 1972's Miss America. She's twenty-three years old and she hails from Wisconsin."

"Speaking of Miss America," said Maryl, "I heard a joke but it's kind of dirty."

"I'll try not to blush."

"What's the difference between a slut and a bitch?"

Drew said, "A slut screws everybody. A bitch screws everybody but you."

"The person who told me the joke used the F-word."

"They mean the same thing, Maryl. But," he added, "a nice girl makes love."

"What about a nice boy? Do you make love, Drew?"

"Ever hear of Mike Nichols?"

"Of course. *The Graduate*. Why?"

"Nichols once said, 'A movie is like a person. Either you trust it or you don't.' "

"How'd we suddenly go from dirty jokes to movies?"

"I'm thinking about an acting career, Maryl. Want to hear a secret? I believe that a successful actor thinks of his audience as one person, one *woman*, whose sexual appetite he'll whet and whose fantasies he'll satisfy."

"Like Miss America does with men?"

"Yup. That's the real difference between a slut and a bitch, between a nice guy and a bastard. You see, Maryl, an amateur nice guy hopes for success while a bastard works at it. That's why Dad's a true bastard."

"Oh my gosh! Did you know about Colleen?"

"Sure. How'd you know?"

"Long story." She pushed her glasses up the bridge of her nose. "Are you a true bastard, Drew?"

"Yeah. But don't let my girlfriends find out. They think I'm romantic."

"It was so romantic." Maryl braced herself against the passenger seat while Drew's Thunderbird screeched to a halt. The stoplight, momentarily yellow, had suddenly turned the same color as her new Cashmere sweater.

"Alice is at the diner," Maryl continued, adjusting her backbone. "All of a sudden Kris walks inside. Now remember, she's had bad luck with her husband dying, even though he was a stinker, and she wants to be a singer, and she had this really horrible experience with another guy. Anyway, Kris says he'll give up his ranch because he loves Alice and—"

"Enough," Drew said.

"You could have played the Kris part."

"What a memory. Three years ago I mentioned something about wanting to be a movie star."

"And fulfilling fantasies."

"A person can change, Maryl. Now I just watch movies."

"You'll never watch *Alice Doesn't Live Here Anymore.* You're twenty-three years old and you outgrew every romantic bone in your body, along with your Little League uniform. Besides, why should you pay to watch love when you can get screwed for free?"

"Screwed, Maryl? Thanks a lot."

"Would you prefer the F-word? You once said they meant the same thing."

Drew pressed his pedal to the metal. "Why do we always end up talking about sex?"

"Who else can I discuss it with? Dad? Mom? Dear Abby? By the time you were a senior in high school, you'd become a legend. The eleventh commandment. Thou shalt honor thy basketball jock. Kids swore that Florentino could F-word the hall monitor and still make home room by the third bell."

"Knock it off!" Drew turned on the radio. Barry sang about writing songs that made the whole world sing.

"Whatever happened to the shy little boy who used to stay within the lines?"

Drew turned off the radio. "Miss Rodale happened."

"That skinny math teacher who looked like Miss Grundy?"

"Yup. Beneath those shapeless polka-dot dresses, Jean Anne Rodale wore silk bikinis. And she had breasts, Maryl, breasts a kid only dreams about during football, basketball and ejaculation season. If you recall, math was my only decent grade. I wanted to sew new letters across the back of my jock jacket. J-A-R."

"Jar?"

"Jean Anne Rodale, you nut."

"The kids used to call her Miss Rodent."

"Nibble, nibble, little mouse."

"Oh my gosh! You didn't do it inside the classroom, did you?"

"I'll always love the smell of chalk dust." Drew sighed theatrically. "I'll always picture George Washington, Abe Lincoln, and Richard M. Nixon gazing down at us from above the blackboard. The idea of discovery turned Jean Anne on, but it scared me to death."

"Speaking of scared, I'm shaking like a leaf."

"Why?"

"The audition."

"*I'm* the one auditioning." He considered a yellow light,

glanced around for cops, downshifted.

"Are you nervous, Drew?"

"Yes. My mouth is full of . . . shit!" He slammed on the brakes.

"That's true," Maryl said, adjusting her backbone again.

"Crackers. My mouth is full of crackers and dry as dust. No spit." He tried a whistle. "See? Damn! I don't know how I let Deborah talk me into this."

"Poor baby. You probably promised her in your sleep."

"No. I was awake. Don't ever make promises while you're having sex, Maryl."

"I know what you mean, Drew. Last night I was in bed with Dustin, or was it Pacino? It's so hard to keep them straight. Definitely Pacino. He used the F-word a lot. Anyway, I found myself promising—"

"Shut up, you nut. I wouldn't trust Al Pacino for one moment with my favorite sister."

"Favorite? I'm your only sister."

"Thank God." Drew skidded to a stop. "Why are all the lights red tonight? Here's an idea. Let's skip the audition and grab a pizza."

"No way. You talked me into going with you and I can't wait to see my favorite brother make a fool out of himself."

To Maryl's secret delight, Drew performed flawlessly and was awarded a leading role in the next production.

"You said you were nervous," she teased later. "No spit, you said." Discarding the mushrooms and olives from her slice of pizza, she winked. "You stalked that stage like a wild panther."

"The girl in the front row kept crossing and uncrossing her legs. She wasn't wearing underpants."

"How could you see that? You were growling lines like Pacino on an F-word rampage."

Drew drained his mug and signaled their waitress. "The

redhead in the second row kept fiddling with the buttons on her blouse. No bra. Deborah was painting sets. The chick with the long braid—"

"I give up. And here I thought you were focused."

"I was. Maryl, why'd we order olives and mushrooms?"

"I adore olives and mushrooms."

"Why don't you eat them?"

"I'm afraid they'll get stuck in my braces."

"You don't wear braces anymore."

"I know. Habit."

"When you blush like that . . ." Drew grinned. "When your face turns the same color as your sweater, you're a very colorful personality. Why didn't you audition tonight?"

"Me? You're kidding, right?"

"No. Community theatre is a great place to meet members of the opposite sex."

"Puh-leeze! I have no intention of becoming involved with an F-word actor. No writers, either. There's this guy at Dad's office who thinks up Chien dialogue—"

"Aha! A secret love. Why didn't you tell me?"

"He's married, Drew. Besides, I said no writers. No actors, stars, celebs of any kind. They all have egos bigger than King Kong."

"I have a big ego, and as of tonight I'm an actor. I'm hurt, Maryl. You've hurt me to the quick."

"Your 'quick' will recover, probably get you in big trouble some day."

"Why'd you mention the guy in Dad's office? Do I know him?"

"I guess you work with him sometimes. Ed Vega wants to write historical romance novels. I promised to edit his manuscripts, even suggested he write a Maryl series. 'Maryl Almost Loses Her Virginity.' That's the first book, where she's married off to a wealthy leper who, beneath his hideous scars, is really a hunk. He discovers a cure for leprosy but before they can consummate, he's guillotined. 'Maryl on the High Seas.' She's captured by a pirate, who's really her husband in disguise, miraculously brought back to life, only she doesn't know it. Before they can consummate, there's this Bermuda Triangle disaster. 'Maryl Reaches Mid-life Crisis Still a Virgin,' followed by 'Maryl has a Hysterectomy.' "

"You nut."

"I'm up here in the nuthouse," she sang. "My mind is in a rut—"

"My keeper thinks I'm crazy," Drew cut in. "Christ, Maryl, camp songs? A million years ago."

"Is this a private chorus or can anybody join?" Deborah, a tiny divorced blonde with Siamese-cat-eyes, leaned across Drew's shoulder, captured his hands, and raised his beer mug to her own lips. Then she gave him a wet kiss somewhere to the left of his right ear.

"Excuse me, pit stop." Maryl stood and brushed crumbs from her jeans.

"Nice sweater." Deborah eyeballed Maryl's small breasts.

F-word you, Maryl swore silently. *I'm gonna wed a hunky leper and get captured by a pirate.*

On her way back to the table, she ducked behind the restaurant's attempt to create Italy—a white trellis covered with green plastic vines and fake purple grapes. Through slats of plywood she watched Playhouse cast and crew members converge upon her brother. A gorgeous British model named Jasmine Cresswell pushed Deborah aside and draped her own body across Drew's broad shoulders. The woman from the second row, the one with no bra, slid into his lap. Others spread out like flower petals.

Romantic bastard, thought Maryl.

"Too bad an actor can't get himself elected President of the United States," she murmured. "If he could, Drew would win in a landslide. Goodbye, Deborah, you dumb jerk."

Maryl adopted two stray cats. One she named Quasimodo, the other Maureen O'Hara.

Drew adopted strays, as well. Community theatre, he discovered, was dominated by neophyte actresses, rich divorcees, and bored housewives.

His tall form strutted across the stage in a variety of leading roles. Dark brown hair fell forward into his onyx eyes. He smiled often, his mouth creating a couple of deep dimples.

When the heavy ruby curtains opened, he fulfilled his fantasies on stage. When the curtains closed, he eased his hard-on from the enthusiastic applause with a succession of backstage performances. Maryl had compared him to a wild panther. The prop or costume alcoves became his lairs.

Twice he accommodated his leading lady beneath a sawhorse in the room where lumber and tools were stored.

Women offered the panther pussy. Soft pussy. Curly pussy. Crinkled pussy. Shaved pussy. They purred, yowled, rubbed, licked and scratched.

Drew began to associate the smell of stage makeup, powder, cold cream, even sawdust, with a woman's climactic scream.

Despite his advice to Maryl, he promised his partners everything. Except fidelity.

Chapter Eight

"After all," Maryl paraphrased, "tomorrow is another damn day."

She wondered if tomorrow would bring rain. Outside the kitchen window, thunderclouds gathered. But they had gathered yesterday and the day before and the day before that.

As she watched, the clouds became wisps of cotton candy.

God was sweeping the sky with His universal broom, she thought. Why couldn't God water the earth with His universal garden hose?

Clenching her fist in a classic Scarlett-O'Hara-I'll-never-be-hungry-again pose, she knocked on her brother's door. "Are you decent, Drew?"

"I'm never decent," he replied, "but I'm clothed. At least as clothed as I plan to get in this god-awful weather. I think I'll market a T-shirt that says something about surviving the heat wave of 1978. Come in, Maryl."

Drew's walls were filled with posters—five years worth of starring roles at the Great Neck Community Playhouse. In its place of honor, above an unmade bed's headboard, hung a framed reproduction: Andy Warhol's print masterpiece of Marilyn Monroe, autographed by Maryl. Once a sewing room, then an artist's studio, the small chamber now belonged to Drew, who preferred his own side entrance to the Florentino house.

Barefoot, wearing a pair of faded cut-offs, he had just finished hefting weights, and the muscles in his bronzed arms convexed.

His rich brown hair, darkened even more by perspiration, flopped into his dark eyes. Around his neck, above his naked chest, was a Chien-Silverwater bath towel.

"It's a sauna in here," he said. "Let's escape to the kitchen."

"Good idea." Maryl pushed her wide-framed glasses up the bridge of her sweaty nose. "It's the coolest room in the house. I've been sitting there reading *Gone with the Wind.*"

"Again?"

"It helps me proof Ed's historical romance manuscripts."

"Bullshit. You have this thing for Rhett Butler. That's why you won't date mere mortals." Drew glanced around the kitchen, as if searching for the source of the bacon-coffee smell. "Where's Mom?"

"I drove her to the train station forty-five minutes ago." Sluggishly, Maryl placed her paperback on the counter, next to an unplugged waffle iron. "Mom's gone with the wind."

"Again?"

"You sound like an old song, Drew. Sha-boom, sha-boom, again, again, again, again."

"It's just that she's never home anymore," he grumbled. "Why does she go to the city every day?"

Because she's having an affair, you dope.

That sounded like such a cliché, but Valerie Florentino wasn't very good at deception. Health club, new haircut, new attitude, new clothes, phone calls. Maryl had answered one call and immediately recognized the voice of the "insurance salesman." Any TV addict would recognize that voice. Buzzy Beeson. Mom's lover had to *bee* Buzzy, ha-ha, else why would he call and lie through his teeth?

"She's visiting Picasso at the Museum of Modern Art," Maryl fibbed, because boys tended to forgive their dad's extra curricular activities but not their mom's. "She left a magnetized refrigerator note that says she's taped a week's worth of soaps."

"I can't believe you're hooked on that trash."

"I've seen you sneak an avid peek at *General Hospital.*"

"I peek avidly at the girl who plays Sarah. Eileen something or other."

"There's a fresh glass of iced tea on the table, waiting for your fingerprints."

"What's up?" Drew crunched ice cubes between his straight, white teeth.

"You. It's after twelve. I thought you'd sleep all day. What time did you get in last night?"

"Late."

"One of your co-stars?" The family referred to Drew's dates as his co-stars, even if they weren't.

"Nope. I went to the movies. Alone."

"Why didn't you invite your favorite sister?"

"No time. It was a last minute impulse. I decided to waste my hard-earned money on *Ordinary People,* which just received rave reviews."

"How was it?"

"I don't know. While waiting in line, I saw that girl I used to date. Samantha Gold."

"So?"

"She flirted, Maryl. It was embarrassing."

"Why?"

"She wasn't exactly subtle. She wore a wedding ring and she looked pregnant, or else she's gained fifty pounds. Christ! There was a time when I believed myself madly in love with her."

"But you broke it off."

He nodded. "Samantha was too eager, too passionate, too . . . exhausting. I suggested we cool it and she became hysterical, swore a blue streak, even threatened to sever a certain portion of my anatomy."

"Did you ever F-word her?"

"Nope. We did everything but."

"So she was a bitch, huh? Like in that old joke?"

"No. Samantha wanted me, and that's not bragging. She was a high-class slut." Drew shook his head. "Last night I said something about hating to stand in line. Then I caught a revival of Milland's classic, *The Lost Weekend.*"

"I hate weekends."

"Me, too. I'm not real fond of weekdays either. The only good thing about Dad's office is his air-conditioning."

"Listen to us." Maryl sat across from Drew at the kitchen table. "We're a fine pair. Both members of the proverbial family dynasty, working for Dad. Both living at home, even though we're twenty-five and twenty-four. Never engaged, never married, never even divorced."

"Is that the reason for this Sunday interview? Meet the press. Stop the presses. Maryl Florentino plans to wed."

"Are you kidding? Who on earth would marry me?"

"Your romance historian. Isn't he divorced?"

"Yikes, Drew. Ed's six inches shorter than I am, even though he writes about ten-feet-tall heroes, not to mention heroines with alabaster breasts named Gweneth and Heather."

"He names their breasts?"

"Maybe if Ed was taller or my breasts were whiter, I'd consider it. Nope. It would never work. Ed's heroines all have golden hair. I mean, tendrils."

"He names their breasts, Maryl?"

"Yup. That's probably why he isn't published yet." She fiddled with the drawstring on her blue halter top and contemplated a seam in her white sailor shorts. "Drew, are you satisfied with your life? Happy?"

"I'm not *un* happy. Bored, maybe. The art department at Chien, Ink. runs itself. Dad employs artists with ten times the ability I have. I'm dead-ended."

"Dad doesn't think so. He plans for you to take over the business some day."

"Dad's fifty-one. He has years left to play with his strip, not to mention the second, *huge* office he's opening in California for animated features. The contest to name Chien's illegitimate puppies was Dad's idea. Besides, if anyone inherits the business it should be you."

"Me? I answer the phone, read the mail, interview aspiring artists, and send 'autographed' Chien photos to his fans. Anyway, I've never been able to stay within the lines. Did Dad select winning names for the pups?"

"He sure did. Buzzy and Bootsie."

"The poodle hair. I love it."

Maryl grinned. Curly-topped Buzzy Beeson (her mother's lover) starred in an ABC sitcom, portraying a jovial W. C. Fields child-hater who hosted a children's show called *Kiddie Korner.* Recently, Buzzy's TV character had been written into three weeks' worth of summer scripts, televised on the popular soap opera *Morning Star.* Buzzy, Milton Berle, and George Burns had appeared on the *Jonah Wiggins Show,* where they entertained with old burlesque-style routines. Both the daytime drama and late-night talk show were based in Manhattan, and Beeson had visited Dad's studio after Andrew had created a week-long comic strip about Chien invading the conservative, segregated *Kitty Korner*—no dogs or black cats allowed.

Maryl brought her attention back to Drew. "What were we talking about? Oh, yes, boredom. Are you bored with the Playhouse, too?"

"I've got to take a shower."

"Great. Then you'll skedaddle out the back door and we'll never finish this discussion."

"I don't skedaddle, Maryl. I 'swagger' and 'stalk' and 'dominate the stage.' Don't you read the reviews?"

"Okay, Drew, what's wrong?"

"I *am* bored with the Playhouse. I don't think the audience even listens anymore. They're so used to me starring in every play, I could recite from the phone book and they'd give me a standing ovation."

"But you have so much talent."

"Yeah. Right. I've developed this huge talent for screwing up school, work, my life."

"Oops. I've opened Pandora's box. Self-pity isn't your style, Drew."

"Let's ride to Montauk Point in my 'Bird. I'll put the top down. Maybe the breeze'll clear cobwebs, or at least dry our sweat. I'll even spring for lobster."

"First, tell me what's wrong."

"You wouldn't understand."

"Try me."

Drew walked over to the kitchen sink, rotated the faucet, and ducked his head beneath the cold water. Face dripping, he stared out the window. "When we were kids, Mom would turn on the sprinkler and we'd run through, trying to get wet and not get wet at the same time. Remember, Maryl?"

"Sure."

"Well, that's how I feel. Life's a fucking sprinkler. I'm running back and forth, going nowhere. I'm Jack be nimble, jumping over the candlestick, burning my balls. Christ, I've been screwing around for thirteen years . . ." He paused to catch his breath.

Drew's impotent, she thought, hiding her instinctive gasp within a discreet cough. *The rumors I heard are true.*

"Did you ever wonder why Jack jumped over the candlestick, Maryl? Maybe he had this thing for fire, like Miss Muffet had this affinity for spiders."

"She didn't have an affinity for spiders, Drew. She had an affinity for tuffets and lactose."

"Aw, forget it. You're right. I've developed a terminal case of self-pity." He snapped his towel at a mosquito. "James Stewart once said that the great thing about movies was giving people tiny pieces of time they never forget."

"Is that what you want? To star in movies?"

"Movies, TV. I want to be an actor, a real actor, a superstar. It's the only thing I know how to do well. All my other performances are . . . forgettable."

"You want immortality, a chance to give people a piece of yourself they'll never forget."

"Shit, Maryl, you're attaching a more profound meaning to a base instinct. I merely want to perform before a camera rather than an audience."

"Then go for it."

"I can't. It's too late."

"Read the trades. Audition."

"No. I'm tired. And burned out."

She studied his tall form, still standing by the sink. Drew could put any number of actors in the shade, assuming God ever offered up shade again.

"Okay," she said. "Let's drive to Montauk and watch a couple of beady-eyed devils get boiled alive. Is there a lobster heaven where lobsters select people from a tank? How long does it take to boil away your life?"

"Christ, Maryl, we're both so damn morbid."

"I wonder if lobsters go to heaven."

"Nope. Hell. Hell is heaven's junk yard."

"Who said that?"

"Me."

"Smartass," she murmured.

There was so much tenderness in her voice, Drew felt an overwhelming urge to cry. But if he did, he'd ultimately confess that, after years of screwing around, Andrew Florentino's son had become an impotent nice guy. He didn't know if it was medical or psychological, but he definitely knew one thing.

His romantic bastard image was a sham.

"I'll miss you so much," Maryl said.

"Be brave. In a pinch, you can start a Drew Flory fan club. You can even tell folks you've seen my quick through our shower curtain."

"Your quick?"

"Boy oh boy, old age sure destroys memory cells. You once said that my quick was bigger than King Kong's."

"There's nothing wrong with my memory. I said an actor's *ego* was bigger than King Kong. By the way, I like your new name, Flory. It sounds like kitchen linoleum."

"Want to hear something funny? When Maxine Graham insisted I change my name, Buzzy Beeson suggested I use his."

"Drew Beeson? That's awful. Damn! Why'd they move the show to California, after your interview, audition and contract? I'll tell you why. They did it just to piss me off. It's not fair."

"Who said life is fair? Maryl, come with me. I've asked you a hundred times. We'll get a two-bedroom—"

"Yeah, right. I can see you bringing your co-stars home to meet your little sister." She smiled, anticipating a wisecrack. After all, she had never been considered little, not by any stretch of the imagination.

Drew merged his dark eyebrows. "Haven't you noticed? I don't have 'co-stars' anymore. I'm too busy developing the character of Caleb on my soap."

"Temporary, big brother. Wait until you hit Hollywood." Prudently changing the subject, she said, "Why are they called soaps?"

"In the early days, serial dramas were sponsored by soap

manufacturers. Why are you changing the subject? Share an apartment with me and help Dad with his California division."

"I appreciate the offer, Drew, but my life here is settled and I'm happy."

"What life? You work, watch TV, and proof your friend Ed's manuscripts. That's not life, Maryl. That's merely existing."

"Don't start playing philosopher again. You once said that soap operas were trash. Does that mean they end up in heaven's junk pile?" When he didn't reply, she said, "You wouldn't understand."

He grinned. "Try me."

"Well, I'm waiting, biding my time. I have this strong feeling that something special will happen soon."

"Don't give me that *que serra* shit. If you hadn't told Mom about our self-pity discussion, if she hadn't known Buzzy Beeson from the old days at her agency, I wouldn't be starring on TV, achieving immortality from a distance."

"You're wrong, Drew. It was fate. Buzzy just happened to be in New York. Maxine Graham just happened to owe Buzzy a favor for his guest stint on *Morning Star.* So she watched you at the Playhouse and cast you in her soap."

"Maybe your *que serra* is moving to L.A. with me."

"I don't think so, but if I change my mind you'll be the first to know. I'll write often. Is everything packed? Your posters? The picture of my namesake?"

"Yes. Do you want a lift to the city in my 'Bird?"

"No, thanks. I have to leave now. In fact, I should have left thirty minutes ago."

"Maryl, the sun's barely risen."

"I know, but there's this photographer coming in today. He's from *People* magazine. Bryan Edwards. They're doing a feature story on all the characters from the strip, including Buzzy, Bootsie, Mary-wanna, and Chien's new poodle girlfriend, Streisand. Dad put me in charge."

"I guess this is it, then." Drew kissed her on the tip of her nose. "Go get ready for your photographer. Maybe he'll look like Clark Gable."

Bryan Edwards was young, the same height as Maryl, and he didn't look like Clark Gable. His light brown hair was much too long and he had pure green eyes above an aquiline nose. His nose sheltered a trimmed mustache and beard. After a brief introduction to Maryl, he began clicking his camera at everything, wasting rolls of film.

I guess the magazine can afford it, she thought, doodling on her pad of telephone messages. Maybe Drew was right and she should change her life. How? Move to California? No. She was depressed over Drew's leaving, plain and simple. It would pass.

It didn't pass. Three days later Maryl sat in the same position, scribbling on the same pad. The phone rang. "Chien, Ink. This is Maryl. How may I help you?"

"Bryan Edwards here. Remember me?"

"Sure."

"Can we meet for lunch?"

"Lunch?"

"You eat lunch, don't you?"

"Usually at my desk." She glanced down at her yellow shirt and black slacks. Circling the slacks was a tooled-leather belt that Drew had made for her in summer camp—a million years ago.

"Eat with me today," Bryan said. "Please?"

"All right. But I only have an hour."

Bryan greeted her at La Seine restaurant. The bar was roomy, decorated in Wedgwood greens and blues. Between deep drags on his cigarette, he chewed a swizzle stick. Staring at Maryl, he said, "It's amazing."

"What's amazing?"

"Later, after we eat. Would you care for a drink?"

"White wine, very dry. Why can't you tell me now?"

"Relax, Maryl, it's a surprise."

A waiter who looked like a pregnant penguin led them up a marble balustrade, toward a red-walled dining room. Bryan sat her at a banquette, lightened by white pilasters. "You said you only had an hour, Maryl, so I've already ordered."

"How could you possibly know what I like to eat?"

"Trust me."

"I don't trust people who say trust me," she said. But the *quenelles* in a rice sauce were delicious, the *poularde au champagne* exquisite.

"I've lived in New York my whole life and never been here before," she said, wondering if she'd gross Bryan out by loosening her belt a notch.

"La Seine is my favorite restaurant." Bryan shook a Pall Mall free from his cigarette pack, then began to tell her anecdotes about celebrities he had photographed. Elizabeth Taylor, the most beautiful woman he'd ever met. Jonah Wiggins, the talk show host, standing against a montage of spouting whales. The gorgeous Candy Bergen, who had spilled a bottle of Cie perfume down Bryan's pants.

Instinctively glancing at his lap, Maryl blushed.

After the soufflé dessert dishes had been cleared, Bryan leaned against his padded cushion. "Are you ready for the surprise, Maryl?"

"I don't have time. I'll have to taxi back to the office."

"Not until you look at these." He spilled the contents from a manila envelope across the table's surface. "What do you see?"

Maryl studied Bryan's photos. One showed her sitting behind her desk, swinging her glasses by their frames, her eyes staring dreamily into space. In another, the phone was cradled on her shoulder while she nibbled at the end of a long quill pen. A third picture showed her drinking coffee, the steam creating an almost three-dimensional effect. "I knew you were wasting film," she said.

"Aren't these amazing? I took them while I waited for your father. I didn't even know exactly what I had until I developed the roll."

"Bryan, I don't understand."

"Are you blind?"

"Technically, yes," she said, pushing her glasses up the bridge of her nose.

"Study the pictures."

"You're a good photographer. You make me look good."

"No. You make you look good. I had nothing to do with it. I was just testing the camera, setting the light meter."

"What's your point?"

"Damn it, Maryl. Focus on the pictures!"

She focused. Was that really her? No way. Bryan had shot a total stranger who resembled Marilyn Monroe Bradley Florentino. Her body appeared slender and secure—a sexy piece of art work. All the uncertain elements of her face came together in a smooth, impeccable mixture. Her mop of auburn hair looked like a lion's mane. Tilted eyes, upturned nose, full lower lip and pointy chin were all defined by the unbiased lens of Bryan's camera.

Glancing up at him, then down at the photos again, Maryl realized she hadn't had a picture taken since her braces were removed. Even her graduation yearbook had been lettered CAMERA SHY. "I wish I looked like this woman," she said.

"You do."

"Are *you* blind? I do not."

"Maryl, the camera sees things the eyes miss. It's magic. I don't know how to explain it better than that, but I'd like to take some more."

"Some more what?"

"Pictures, you nut. Can you get the afternoon off?"

"I guess. Why?"

"I want to photograph you in Central Park, no artificial lighting, a natural setting. I'd like to shoot a close-up of your face resting on top of the lions outside the New York Public Library. Your hair reminds me of their manes."

"What for?"

"A composite," said Bryan, his jade eyes gleaming. "All the important modeling agencies are right here in Manhattan. I'll peddle the finished product. I don't want you walking inside one office until they've seen my proofs. I'll be your manager. This isn't a come-on, Maryl. I've been dying to freelance." He tweaked her nose. "For the record, I think you're cute even when you're not in my photos."

"Cute? I've never been called cute in my life. The ducks in Central Park are cute. Chien is cute. Me? Cute?"

"You're adorable. Please say yes," he urged. "What have you got to lose?"

Maryl's mind raced. She remembered her words to Drew: *I have this strong feeling that something special will happen soon.* And his response: *Don't give me that* que serra *shit.*

Bryan was right. What did she have to lose?

Six months later, Maryl graced the cover of *Vogue.*

Chapter Nine

The operator had a marvelous Brooklyn brogue.

"Poi-son to poi-son, for Drew Florintina," she said. "Is this the potty called? Are you by any chance him?"

"Yes, operator. But I've got an unlisted num—"

"Hi, big brother."

"Who's this? I don't recognize the voice."

"It's Maryl, smartass."

"I don't know any Maryl Smartass. You must have reached the wrong potty, Miss Smartass."

"Knock it off, Drew, or Chien will bite your butt."

"Oh, *that* Maryl. Are you by any chance her?"

"Okay, so I promised I'd write. Honest, I never have time. Last week Bryan shot a complete layout of me in a school playground. Monkey bars, swings, a wall filled with graffiti. It was for lingerie. Can you believe that?"

"Sure. Bryan Edwards has a great imagination. Your *People* cover is hanging on my wall, right next to your Monroe namesake."

"Isn't Bryan brilliant? Superimposing Dad's cartoons of Chien and Streisand dancing on my desk while I crunch a quill pen between my once irregular, now perfect teeth."

"Jesus, Maryl, you have this thing about your braces."

"Wrong! I have a thing about spiders, lactose and Alfred Hitchcock birds. Anyway, Bryan thought the cover was 'cute.' But that was before I metamorphosed into Maryl Bradley, drudge and slave."

"Welcome to the club. How are Mom and Dad?"

"Fine. Better than fine. All of a sudden Dad's in love with Mom. He even sends her flowers. Mom looks ten years younger and giggles all the time. I'm moving out. They don't need a chaperone. Besides . . ."

"Besides what?"

"Nothing. What the heck are you drinking?"

"Mineral water. I've gone Hollywood."

"Me, too. You should see my wardrobe. And I don't wear glasses anymore. Bryan insisted on contacts. By the way, have you collected any new co-stars?"

"Nope. Caleb collects enough for both of us. If Caleb's heart ever fails from over-stimulation, they should donate his quick to medical science. Damn, it's good to hear from you. Call any time, day or night. You can even call collect."

"Collect for Kris from Alice. That's Kris with a K."

"Alice doesn't live here anymore."

"The call is *from* Alice, sir."

"Oh, that's different. I'll accept the charges, operator. Hi, Maryl."

"Drew, I'm borrowing a neighbor's phone. She's walking her dog. They installed mine but it's dead."

"They installed your dog and it's dead?"

"No. My phone. It doesn't like me."

"Your phone doesn't like you?"

"No. The neighbor's dog. I have to talk fast, before they get back."

"Okay. How are you?"

"Fine. Not so fine. Drew, what's wrong with me?"

"Well, for one thing you've never named your breasts."

"I'm serious."

"So am I. Why do you think there's something wrong?"

"I'm still a virgin."

"That's not wrong, Maryl. It's smart."

"If you weren't my brother, would you F-word me?"

"In a minute. Maybe Bryan's gay. That's what this is all about, isn't it?"

"He's not. Honest. I don't know what to do. I declared my independence, leased an apartment, and bought such a humongous waterbed I have to gulp down Dramamine every night. Next, I invited Bryan to an intimate dinner. He said yes, and there was lust in his heart, Drew, I swear. Things were heating up nicely when a bunch of people knocked on my door. 'Surprise, happy housewarming,' they yelled. By morning there were so many empty liquor bottles, I'm sure my neighbors think I'm an alcoholic, and Bryan left sometime during the party. He just . . . chickened out."

"Maybe Bryan doesn't want to mix business with pleasure, Maryl. Maybe he doesn't want to establish a reputation as a photographer who screws his clients."

"Then I'll fire him."

"No, you won't."

"I fired Bryan, Drew. Actually, we fired each other."

"I'm sorry, Maryl. Would you like to come out here for a couple of weeks?"

"I wish I could squeeze myself through the phone wires. Don't you want to know what happened?"

"Only if you want to tell me."

"In brief, my platonic love affair with Bryan came to an end three days ago. We decided to use the loft in my new apartment for a fashion layout—winter resort swimsuits. We set up a backdrop of ocean and sunrise, painted no less by Salvador

Dali. Bryan imported a bunch of parrots, cockatoos and love birds."

"I can *hear* you shuddering, Maryl. I guess Hitchcock is responsible for more than one phobia over feathery critters."

"Bryan had nearly finished the shoot when one of the parrots lost his cool and flew around the room, bouncing off the backdrop, squawking obscenities. I freaked out, raced into my bedroom. The bird's wings had touched my body, like a bat, and all I could think about was shedding my swimsuit. Bryan followed me. There I stood, naked and shivering. I ran into his arms and we sank down onto my waterbed. I could hear the crew through the closed door. They were soothing birds, complaining about how the parrot's beak had slashed our backdrop. Brian kissed me and—"

"Please, Maryl, skip the details."

"There *are* no details. All of a sudden, this golden-haired Scarlett O'Hara opens the bedroom door. Have you ever seen anyone try to rise quickly from a waterbed?"

"No, but I can imagine. Was she his wife?"

"Yes. She'd been 'down South with Mumsie and Fathah.' Bryan had neglected to mention her. This diminutive, *cute* Civil War apparition had long flaxen hair and a Rhett or Scarlett Junior hidden beneath her maternity jeans and pantalets."

"Good-bye love, hello reality."

"Reality is turning twenty-six, still a virgin, and lighting a special candle for Marilyn Monroe, who would have celebrated age fifty-four. Reality is my brand new manager, who looks like Disney's Dopey Dwarf, only taller and smarter. Reality is signing an exclusive contract with Rosebud Cosmetics. Reality is . . . reality is . . ."

"Aw, don't cry."

"Reality sucks. Three days ago I felt like Cinderella. Now I feel like Sleeping Ugly."

"Jesus! You're not into sleeping pills, are you?"

"Of course not. God, you *have* gone Hollywood."

"It's just that Marilyn Monroe killed herself and—"

"No, she didn't. I'd bet my Rosebud contract that Marilyn Monroe was murdered."

Maryl blotted her Rosebud lipstick and applied Rosebud mascara. Then she auditioned a smile in the mirror.

I'm putting on makeup for a phone call, she thought. *Am I nuts?* She dialed, disconnected, dialed again.

"Hello, Drew? Can you hear me? Is this a bad connection?"

"What's wrong? Why do you sound so strange?"

"For one thing, the smell of Rosebud's Petal Perfume makes me nauseous. And their new line of nail polish—give me a break! Thorny Red, Thorny Pink, Thorny Orange. Isn't it a coincidence that Rosebud has become your biggest sponsor? They can call *Morning Star* a cosmetics opera rather than a soap opera. Damn! I just chipped my pinkie's thorn."

"You're all shook up over nail polish?"

"No. Of course not." Clutching the receiver tightly, she took a deep breath. "I'm scared to death."

"Why? Did Dopey Dwarf lock you inside a room filled with parrots?"

"Don't joke."

"Sorry. What's the matter?"

"Dopey Dwarf booked me on the *Jonah Wiggins Show.*"

"Yes?"

"That's it. I'm scheduled for an 'in-depth interview.' Don't laugh, you beast. As a model I act unnaturally natural and the cameras click. Even TV commercials are rehearsed and shot a million times. I couldn't possibly screw up. Stop laughing! Please, Drew, you've done talk shows. What do I talk about? My Marilyn Monroe theory? My thing about braces? My thing about birds? I'm scared, Drew, abso-fuckin-lutely scared."

As Maryl paced the carpeted floor of the studio's Green Room, she wondered why they called it green when the walls were painted beige.

Tempted to kill Dopey Dwarf, she scratched the rash that had mysteriously cropped up on both wrists. Why had she eaten lunch? The cottage cheese and avocado salad were swirling, undigested, midway between her stomach and throat.

"Doesn't Mr. Wiggins usually greet his guests before the show?" she asked, turning toward Michelle, her fellow Green Room companion.

Michelle No-Last-Name possessed a flawless complexion, the color of milk chocolate. She wore a short leather skirt, stiletto heels, and a motorcycle jacket.

"I heard Jonah got caught in a traffic jam on his way to the studio. The makeup girl said he was late and cranky." Michelle hugged her jacket's shoulder pads. "Lord, lord, I can't do this. I used to be part of a group and now I've gone solo. I can't sing tonight. You've got to tell them, Mary."

"Maryl."

"Lord, I've lost my voice. Oh, lord . . ." She bolted for the bathroom.

Maryl wondered if there was room for two. Her wrist hives had multiplied. Scratching, she tried not to chew her nails. She had applied the newest Rosebud polish, Thorny Suntan, a color guaranteed to match anything. Against her poxed skin, it looked more like Thorny Sunburn.

"Wear your favorite color," Drew had suggested, so Maryl had chosen a red satin jumpsuit. Cinched about her tiny waist was a silver belt, linked with a lion's-head buckle. Gazing at the ceiling-mounted monitor, she saw Jonah Wiggins part the curtains, walk center stage, and salute his audience.

Jonah had once been a minor cog in the wheel of Valerie's production agency, and Maryl had studied the clippings pasted inside her mother's scrapbook. Jonah posing with Buzzy Beeson, after a guest appearance on the comedian's show. Jonah during his short stint as a game show host. He had begun his career as a Country-Western singer, and in the early photos he resembled Our Gang's Alfalfa, complete with cowlick. Today, all that remained of the Oklahoma country boy was his bachelor status and a slight drawl. If the show's conversation lagged, and it rarely did, Jonah would sing Ledbelly or Guthrie.

Now, Maryl wanted to place her forked fingers between her teeth and whistle. She'd known Jonah was handsome, but—*oh, Drew, I never told you that my real hero in G.W.T.W. wasn't Rhett Butler. I was hopelessly in lust with Ashley Wilkes. Margaret Mitchell's Ashley, not, with all due respect, the movie's Leslie Howard.*

If she remembered correctly, and she did, Margaret Mitchell's Ashley had drowsy gray eyes and his voice was . . . drawling? Yeah, drawling. And resonant. *Didn't resonant mean pulsating?* Maryl stroked the soft silk of her jumpsuit. Under a sheer bra, her nipples hardened. She pictured Jonah in a Confederate uniform, tight breeches hugging his lean hips, emphasizing the pulsating throb between his legs. Damn! She had edited one too many salacious manuscripts.

She studied the TV monitor again. Forget the Confederate uniform. Sheep had been sheared for Jonah's charcoal slacks. A sacrificial lizard had donated its skin for Jonah's boots. Jonah headed his own clothing line. His dress shirts and sports blazers were all stitched with the tiny logo of a spouting whale.

Thick beach-sand hair was styled short, and his eyes were the same color as a koala's fur. Maryl watched him tease his audience and band leader with a topical monologue. The audience responded by applauding or groaning enthusiastically.

Michelle, introduced after a commercial break, didn't look

nervous. She crooned her new ballad, traded quips with Jonah, and promoted her album. Then, reluctantly, she exited stage left. Maryl hoped her own interview would go as well.

The band leader played a fanfare and the audience went wild.

"Lord, lord," Maryl whispered, borrowing Michelle's lament. "It's Pat Huxley."

Pat Huxley, affectionately called "Pat Python," was a small chunky comedienne who burst through the stage curtains as if she could hardly wait to open her glossed mouth and release the venom from her fangs. A Scandinavian actress had once said, "She hux her victims to death." Thus, the python appellation. Pat's clothes usually dripped with glitzy spangles or feathers and ruffles, unflattering to her busty, overweight body.

She began her comedy routines with the question: "Do you want to hear a secret?" The audience would scream *yes,* and Pat would launch her act—sexual insinuations and digs at celebrities, delivered in a breathy, little-girl voice.

Maryl thought Pat's nickname was a slur to all honest pythons.

This evening La Python wore raspberry pants and overblouse, decorated with a sequined galaxy. Maryl recognized Capricorn, Aries, and the Gemini twins, before she grew dizzy and the sequins blurred. Pat's hair was a brassy, henna-hued blonde, her eyes a brassy, henna-hued hazel, and her plucked eyebrows resembled the erratic line on a lie detector's graph.

Her monologue and conversation with Jonah took up most of the remaining show. *Maybe there really is a God and I've been spared,* thought Maryl, just before a stagehand ushered her to the wings, where she caught the end of Jonah's introduction.

"And now it is my pleasure to present the Rosebud girl, Mary Bradley."

Maryl walked downstage toward Jonah's antique desk, shook

his warm hand, then sat on a cushioned chair between the host and Huxley.

"That's not my name," she mumbled, placing her wrists in her lap, upside-down, hiding the rash.

"What did you say, darlin'?"

"My name is Maryl. It rhymes with Carol. The 'y' is silent."

Ordinarily, Jonah would have apologized and corrected his pronunciation. But he was still annoyed at the wild ride to the studio, and his favorite writer had presented a multiple list of complaints directly before air time—an ultimatum. Jonah could almost feel the tiny red devil who perched on his shoulder.

"The why is silent?" he asked, winking at the audience.

"Yes, sir."

"What about the what?""

"What?"

The audience tittered, catching the pseudo Abbot and Costello exchange.

Jonah said, "Why is the why silent, Maryl-who-rhymes-with-Carol?"

"I don't know. It just is."

"Tell us, Maryl Bradley, why did you decide to become a model?"

"I don't know," she repeated, afraid to say something wrong. "I guess I was seduced by—"

"Seduced?" Pat Huxley smirked.

"Yes. Seduced by the promise of fame and fortune. But it's not like that at all. I mean, I make money, of course I do, but it's really very hard and—"

"Seduced. Hard. Umm . . . that's good." Pat smirked again.

"It just happened, I guess," Maryl said.

Jonah swallowed a yawn, wondering why they had booked this too-tall mouse with the flaming mop of hair. Then he happened to catch her image in the television monitor. He blinked, looked at his guest, the monitor, his guest again.

As always, the camera emphasized each individual ingredient of Maryl's face, creating a gourmet feast of charismatic appeal. The audience had caught the same image in banks of huge TV screens, set high above the stage. They gazed upwards, enjoying the beautiful vision, waiting expectantly.

"Models have to be so skinny," said Pat, standing and stretching her short, heavy body. The camera shifted, catching her motion, and the audience laughed. "Models can't eat very much, can they, dear?"

"Yes. No. I mean yes, they can't eat very much," Maryl said. "I have friends who exist solely on honey, for energy. I don't think it's healthy, but I've never had to worry. I've always been too thin."

Shit, thought Jonah. The red-haired model was looking directly into the camera and had missed a certain gleam in Huxley's eyes. Hadn't the Python recently spent a week at an exclusive weight-reduction spa? Hadn't she failed miserably and turned the experience into a comedy routine?

"I tried to be a model once," said Pat, seated again but leaning into camera range. "Then I had this *intimate* talk with a model friend. She said she had met this *gorgeous* man, a famous singer. Then they, you know, did it. When they finished, the man turned to my model friend and said, 'That was like a fast-food meal. A good roll, but where's the meat?' "

After the laughter had died down, Pat continued, "My friend turned to her lover and said, 'Speaking of meat, you lied about the size of your . . .' " She glanced toward Jonah. "Weenie."

"Pat!"

Jonah's admonishment was lost in the crescendo of applause.

"I know something that's interesting," Maryl said, somewhat desperately.

"What's that, darlin'?" Jonah wondered if he should insert a commercial and tell Python to shut up. What the hell. The show was nearly over and if Pat became too raucous they could bleep her dialogue.

"Well, it's my name again," said Maryl. "I was born on the same day as Marilyn Monroe, and named for her. Maryl is my nickname. For the record, I don't think Marilyn committed suicide. I believe she was mur—"

"You look remarkably well preserved to have been born on the same day as Marilyn Monroe." Pat quirked an erratic eyebrow.

"I meant the same date, June first, only I was born on June first, 1954."

Jesus, thought Jonah. He had never met a woman who would confess her true age before millions of TV viewers. Interesting.

"That reminds me of another story," said Pat. "I had this *intimate* friend named Marilyn, and she met this *gorgeous* man, a famous politician." Pat winked. "About a week after they had, you know, done it, my friend got a phone call. 'When can I see you again?' asked her politician. And she said—do you want to hear a secret?"

"Yes!" screamed the audience.

"Marilyn said, 'I can't see you, lover. I've got the seven year itch.' " Pat swiveled her chair toward Maryl. "Do you ever get it, dear?"

"Get what?"

"The seven year itch. Herpes. Stop scowling at me, Jonah. Can't I say herpes on TV? It's not weenie. Oh my God, look at the model!"

A miserable Maryl, her queasy stomach cramping more every moment, had reached from long habit to push her glasses up the bridge of her nose. Not finding the familiar frames, she began to scratch the rash on the back of her hands. The camera caught her confused face, her shoulders and upper arms moving. It looked as if she was scratching something in her lap.

The camera swiftly moved to Pat, who was shouting, "She does have an itch! Was it Bryan Edwards? He's big now, and divorced. I've heard he's dating Hugh Hefner's ex-plaything. Tell us everything, Mary, or Marilyn, or whatever the fuck *(bleep)* your name is." Humming the theme from the old *Howdy Doody Show,* Pat sang, "It's true confessions time, it's true confessions time."

"I . . . I wasn't . . . you . . . you horrible bitch," cried Maryl, and fled.

She ran from the stage, found herself in a hallway, and opened the nearest door, lettered PRIVATE, stenciled with a huge star. Apparently, it was Jonah's personal bathroom because blue-penciled monologue scripts lay scattered across a shelf above the sink.

Gasping for breath, she slumped on the floor, then realized that she wasn't exactly gasping for breath. She was making horrid little sounds, not unlike the terrified bleats of a goat. She tried to stop the bleats, but couldn't. She wanted to faint, but—for the first time in her life—she couldn't.

After what seemed like hours, Maryl felt a hand clasp her shoulder. Looking up, she met Jonah's worried gaze.

"I've been searching all over for you," he said. "The studio guards insisted you were still in the building."

"The show—"

"Forget the show. Are you sick, darlin'?"

"No. I've been bleating."

"Bleeding?"

"No, bleating, like a goat. Oh, God. I lost my cool and sounded so stupid."

"You didn't sound stupid. The audience booed Huxley and started chanting 'Maryl, Maryl.' In any case, it was all my fault. Putting you on the same stage with Pat Python was like throwing an unarmed Christian to the lions. I should have stopped her. I'm not usually so insensitive, just ask my mother. Aw, don't cry. The program's taped. We'll edit out . . . Maryl darlin' . . . please don't cry." Jonah knelt, gathered her into his arms, and licked her tears away. Then he covered her quivering mouth with his.

Maryl kissed him back.

Jonah took her uptown for a late dinner, laughing while she ate everything on her plate. "Models have to be so skinny," he teased.

They taxied to Jonah's sumptuous apartment, and barely had time to enter the vestibule and kick the door shut before she was tearing at his shirt buttons. In turn, he ripped her favorite jumpsuit down the front, then her sheer bra, then her panties.

She caught her breath as Jonah's lips traveled from the base of her throat to her taut nipples. "I've been waiting for this my whole life," she said. His tongue was a conductor, sending electric currents throughout her entire body. "Oh my God, Jonah, I can't stand up. I'm going to fall—"

"Sweet," he murmured.

"—in love with you."

Three weeks later they were married.

One month later the network moved Jonah's show to California.

Chapter Ten

Hollywood, California

Outside the Polka-Dot Unicorn, foggy mist impregnated sidewalk cracks, giving birth to shadows. Although most of the Cinderellas and Prince Charmings had established their astrological connections and flown the coop, a few celebrants lingered, their eyes glassy, their magic wands fragmented by roach clips. A cowboy named Francis, known as The Duke, was hunched over a curb-side trash can. A prostitute named Jane, known as Doe, watched dispassionately.

"What a way to make a living," Doe muttered. "I shoulda stayed in Fort Wayne. C'mon, man, I ain't got all night. Straighten up and let's get the hell outta here."

The Duke shut his eyes and sank to the pavement. The trash can followed, spewing its contents.

Doe knelt and retrieved The Duke's wallet. "Empty, you bastard!" Holding her breath, she searched his puke-soiled clothes. Nada. Not one red cent. The cross 'round his neck looked gold-plated, so she stood, yawned, and walked away.

Shadow-snakes slithered across The Duke's prone body. A dog lifted his leg, peed on The Duke's left boot, then barked at a Volkswagen whose bright round headlights pierced the fog.

Inside the Polka-Dot Unicorn, a cocktail waitress, recently transplanted from Denver, unhooked her padded bra, scratched the furrows beneath her breasts, and donned an orange and blue Denver Broncos T-shirt. Reaching into the pocket of her khaki shorts, she removed a wad of bills and handed the bartender his share.

"Thanks, Trish." Adding the money to his tip-snifter, the bartender shot a worried glance toward the blonde woman whose head slumped a few inches above a booth's table. Should he call Randy McNeal again? With relief, he watched the door open. Pointing to his watch, he mimed a pained expression.

"What happened, mate?"

"I don't know, McNeal. She's been like that all night. I told Trish to cut her off but Trish says she ain't drinking booze, just club soda. Of course, Trish swears she once screwed Jack Nicholson so who can believe anything *she* says."

"Thanks for ringing me up." Randy slid a twenty across the bar's polished surface, walked over to the booth, sat next to Anissa, and gently nudged her slack body. "Are you feeling a skerrick under the weather, darlin'?"

"Alfy question," she said. "Of course I'm under the weather. If there was no weather there'd be a big void and we'd all die. I want to die."

"What's wrong, love?"

Unfocused gray eyes stared at him. "Kathleen . . . landlady. Told her I was leaving . . . big fight . . . pictures . . . said sell pictures to the Senator. What's your word? Flog?"

"Kathleen plans to flog photos of you to your father?"

"Yes. With men. Or flog to me. Lots of money." Long lashes fluttered across her pale cheeks. "Go 'way."

"You're not drunk." He had a horrible thought and searched her purse, then all four denim pockets. Nothing. Frantic, he finally found an empty container of sleeping pills buried deep within the booth's vinyl cushion crease. "Anissa, get up!" He shook her roughly. "Wake up, damn it!"

"Too late. Go 'way."

Randy carried her to his Volkswagen and sped toward his

apartment. Pinching her nose shut, he poured his cream-vinegar-eggs mixture down her throat. Then, despite her protestations, he walked her around his living room for eight hours straight.

Afterwards, he called an ex-lover, a part-time nightclub bouncer and stunt man. Soon Randy held the photos and negatives in his hands. While Anissa watched, he shredded them.

"I once tore up a ten-thousand-dollar check and flushed it down the toilet," she said.

Three days later she signed the lease on an empty apartment next door to Randy's. Their duplex, in the middle of a steep hill, was converted from what had once been a flourishing Monastery. Other dwellings surrounded a life-sized statue of Jesus. Small animals wandered through the shrubbery. Squirrels, rabbits and chipmunks seemed to prey and pray at the base of Christ's sculpted feet while only a few blocks away the famous HOLLYWOOD letters pierced the sky and Sunset Boulevard shone with irreverent glitz.

Randy introduced Anissa to his producer, Maxine Graham, who promised to keep her in mind for the next *Children of the Night* casting call. Even though, Maxine said, she was being wooed by *Morning Star.*

Anissa furnished her apartment with a used convertible couch, an old stuffed armchair, her black and white portable TV, and Tramp. Jacob had shipped the cat to L.A.

"What the bloody hell are you doing now?" asked Randy, one week after Anissa's Maxine-Graham introduction."

"Nothing."

"Why do you lock your doors and draw the shades?"

"I'm scared."

"Of what?"

"Men. They still look at me."

"Most blokes admire a beautiful woman, Anissa. Kathleen's

washed her hands of you. She wouldn't dare try anything naughty. What's this?" Randy fingered a shapeless brown smock.

"A new dress. I sewed it myself."

"You have a closet full of flash gear."

"If I wear this, no one will notice me."

"That's true," Randy said sarcastically. "Your dress is the same color as the bloody smog."

The next day Anissa stood in front of the bathroom mirror, picked up a sharp scissors, and cut her hair close to the scalp.

"Holy shit," Randy bellowed when he saw the result. "You look like Ingrid Bergman playing Saint Joan of Vista Del Mar Avenue."

Yet he had to admit that the haircut made Anissa's haunted gray eyes even larger and her face ethereal. Rather than the saintly Joan, she could have been cast as one of the Monks who, long ago, had silently shuffled toward the top of their hill.

I'm buggered, Randy thought. Anissa's body looked transparent, the skin stretched tight, and she would only eat if he shared meals. She left the complex to buy groceries she never cooked, or to sit on a park bench and watch the children who swarmed over the playground.

Why am I bothering with that nit? Angry, stymied, Randy decided to try one last gambit. During a humid, storm-slurpy night, he knocked on her door.

Anissa wore her brown, ankle-length smock. Two new items adorned her stark white living room walls—a silk-screened angel and a framed newspaper review of a University of Wisconsin student production, including a grainy cast photo. An old western flickered on the TV screen, but she had turned the volume all the way down. Tramp slept, draped across the window sill.

"I thought I wasn't supposed to drink," she said, gesturing toward Randy's Cuervo Gold bottle.

"You're not, but tonight we're celebrating. A mate of mine is directing Tennessee Williams' *The Glass Menagerie,* and I'm playing Tom. Look, love, I brought a bag of chook and chips."

"Chicken and fries," Anissa translated, giving her friend a wan smile. "You know what? The only play I've ever acted in was by Tennessee Williams."

"I'll bet you were a beaut. Which one?"

"*Streetcar.*" She nodded toward the framed newspaper review.

Randy poured tequila into a plastic water tumbler. "Here, Anissa, down the hatch."

It took only one drink.

"I don't like this stuff anymore," she said, her voice catching on a sob. "I want to die."

"Why?"

"Because I don't want to live."

"That's no answer. It's like 'because I said so.' You're not living. You're barely existing. What's wrong, Anissa?"

"My heart's broken," she replied in a small, tired voice.

"That's bloody bullshit!"

Randy wanted to cuddle the thin, shaking girl whose face, all eyes, reflected such pain. But he stifled that impulse. Sympathy wouldn't cure her, not until he ascertained the reason for her recent regression.

"Talking about a broken heart is like emoting a line from my soap," he continued. "It's a speech from one of your old memory movies. Hearts don't break, Anissa, not if they're healthy, and your precious Joseph Weiss didn't die."

"He did for me!"

"Then you've fulfilled your period of mourning. You've punished yourself for whatever it is you think you've done. Shit! It's not your brother, is it?"

"*Half* brother!"

"Why do you visit the playground every afternoon? Why do

you watch the little tykes?"

"I don't like you anymore, Randy. Go home."

Frustrated, he threw the tequila bottle at a wall. Glass shattered, sending the cat for cover. At the same time, thunder drummed the sky and rain snapped against the window panes.

Anissa scooped up Tramp. Holding him against her breasts, she smoothed the fur that had bristled like a white porcupine.

"Why do you watch the tykes?" Randy persisted.

"I don't know."

"I think you do know."

Still holding the cat, she turned the television's volume all the way up. Unidentifiable music blended with the sounds of loud hoof beats.

Randy punched the off button.

Anissa curled her fingers into fists. Tramp responded by unsheathing his claws, but she didn't even wince. "Go home, you Aussie bastard!" she screamed.

"Why, love? Why do you watch the little nippers?" Randy sank onto the couch and crossed his arms. "Why?"

"I watch the kids because . . . because . . . our . . . my baby would be there if he had been born. I wish . . ." She wept, unable to continue.

"Okay." Randy pulled Anissa into his lap while Tramp wriggled free. "Hush. No. Don't hush. Cry it all out. It's not your fault. The abortion was not your fault. It happened, it's over, there will always be an ache, a scar, but it's over. That's my good girl, my good sweet girl."

When the gasping sobs had become small breath catches, Anissa looked into Randy's blue eyes. "I don't know how you can have such patience with me," she said, "but I feel ever so much better. I give you my word, Randy darling. No more sleeping pills. No stupid tears, either. I just hope I have the opportunity to help you as much as you've helped me."

The next day Anissa auditioned and was awarded the role of Laura in *The Glass Menagerie.*

Following the first performance, Maxine Graham pushed her way backstage. "I have a new part coming up on *Children,*" she said. "What the hell happened to your long hair?"

"My haircut was the result of a religious vow," said Anissa, winking at Randy. "I live in an old Monastery."

"*Merde.* Grow it back. I want it long again by next week."

"Yes, ma'am."

"What's the part, Max?" Randy asked.

"Cyndi's sister."

"That's a small role. The grapevine says you've considered a ghost for Pablo." He tilted Anissa's chin. "Look at this face, Max. Celestial. Chimerical. Ingrid as Joan of Arc."

Three weeks later Anissa floated across the TV screen, a celestial, chimerical, Ingrid Bergman-ish ghost. Five days later the first fan letters arrived. All were addressed to Anissa Cartier.

Which meant, said Maxine, that viewers had read the credits. Which meant, thought Anissa, that viewers were into ghosts.

So what? She was getting paid for having fun. Nova or galaxy star, she had achieved an unanticipated, serendipitous success. And success, be it sugar-coated or saccharine, smelled like perfume.

Los Angeles, California

"No, no, no!" The director took off his glasses and pinched the bridge of his beaky nose. "Maryl baby, this is a TV commercial, not some goddamn spread in one of your fashion mags. Perfume is seductive. Nobody wants to screw a skunk."

"Jesus, Tony."

"Okay, lousy metaphor. Here's a better one. Drowning in money. Do you have any idea how many women watch soap operas?"

"For the record, my big brother says soaps are called soaps

because they were sponsored by soap manufac—"

"Bullshit! Soap is squeaky clean while perfume is pornographic."

"Don't you mean prurient?" Absently, Maryl patted the head of the tame tiger standing by her side. Then she pulled up the bodice of her red mini-dress. "Why bother covering my nipples? Why not let it all hang out?"

Tony gazed at her critically. "Not much there to hang, baby."

She stared directly at his crotch and threw his words back at him. "Not much there to hang, baby."

"Bitch!" screamed Tony, who, rumor had it, put thick rolled-up socks inside his underwear. "Freaking bitch!"

Maryl held her breath and counted to ten. "If you think that by calling me names you'll make me feel seductive, you're sadly mistaken."

"You might not believe this, dollbaby, but most models would give their left tit to work with me." He sank onto his director's chair. "All I have to do is snap my fingers."

"Then snap."

"I wish I could, but *Morning Star* wants you. Rosebud wants you. You're their goddamn spokeswoman."

"Spokesperson."

"No, woman. That's what you don't understand. The women who watch *Morning Star* want to get laid by Drew Flory, and we have to guarantee they smell good."

"Give me a break!"

"That's a terrific idea. Take ten, fifteen minutes. Find a deserted corner and masturbate."

"You're disgusting."

"Yeah, but very successful."

Jonah Wiggins strolled onto the set, hugged his wife, and whispered, "He's right, Maryl."

"About masturbating?" she asked, flabbergasted.

"No. About being successful. Do you have a dressing room?"

"If you can call it that. Chair, table, mirror."

"Does it have a door?"

"Well, yes."

Shading his eyes from the glare of lights, Jonah looked at Tony. "Leave us alone for half an hour, okay?"

When Maryl returned to the set, she glowed from within. Her face was radiant. Her eyes still glittered lustfully. Her skin above and below the red mini-dress seemed phosphorescent, as if the tiger had rubbed his tawny body against her body, igniting sparks.

"Oh God, oh shit," breathed Tony. "Someone turn on the wind machine. Hurry! Never mind new makeup. Leave her face the way it is. Her lips look bruised, that's incredible. Okay, doll-baby, bend over and pet the tiger. Tickle his chin. Now run his tail across your breasts. Shit, I'm getting a hard-on. Uh, sorry Jonah."

"No problem. Maryl, stop laughing."

"I can't help it, Jonah. I keep thinking about Pat Python. After they had, you know, done it, the model turned to the tiger and said . . ." Maryl giggled helplessly.

"Terrific, baby," Tony crooned. "Beautiful, dollbaby. Wet your lips. Toss your head. Stare at the camera. Glance toward Jonah. Look at the tiger. The camera again. Yes, yes, yes!"

New York City

The curtains opened.

Delly paced up and down the wings as *Duck Pond Sonata* cast members joined their hands together and bowed.

"Let's skip the curtain call," she said.

"Don't be silly," Jon said. "That's what turns you on."

"You turn me on, Griffin."

"I wish," he said under his breath.

The curtains closed then opened again.

Delly stood center stage. Dipping into a deep curtsy, she said, "Quack, quack." Then she lowered her body to the boards and stretched out on her side, knees slightly bent, face toward the audience, eyes shut.

Well, almost shut. Through her spiky, mascara-caked lashes, she could see people rising from their seats. Her freckled nose inhaled perfume and fur. The applause was deafening.

Mom and Uncle Sam had flown in from Chicago for *Duck Pond*'s premiere. Jules and Samantha Perry had bought tickets, too. Then, at the very last minute, their baby-sitter canceled. And yet, during every single performance, Delly anticipated Sami's arrival. Every performance she waited for Princess Pretty to prance on stage and shout, "Sing my doodahs, Delly-Dog!"

It never happened, of course. But the prospect gave Delly the motivation to explore her character's vulnerability and create an almost obsessive torment.

The critics compared her to Julie Harris. Jon, they said, was spicy Tennessee Williams and peppery Arthur Miller, seasoned with a sprinkle of salty Neil Simon.

Following the reviews, the lines at the box office were very long. Six weeks later, Paramount called and—

Still in her semi-fetal position, Delly completed the ritual she had begun opening night.

"This is for you, Daddy," she whispered.

Rising, she blew fingertip kisses toward the balcony.

It was like blowing on a dandelion puff.

No. It was like tossing a handful of diamond stars toward heaven.

Delly Diamond stars.

Wishing stars.

Act Two
Chapter Eleven

Los Angeles, California

From hidden speakers, Kim Carnes sang about Bette's eyes.

Randy turned the stereo's volume down. "Are you sure you want to go with me, Anissa?"

"Absolutely. I've never been to a gay lounge."

"How many people have? It's not on everybody's agenda. People usually prefer Disneyland and Universal Studio."

Anissa shuddered, remembering eight years ago. June, 1973. Universal Studio. Buzzy Beeson.

Recently, she'd encountered Buzzy at a movie preview. He was into drugs again. Saggy-chinned, unfocused, the famous comedian kept mumbling something about how Anissa starred on TV with his only son, Drew.

Bringing her attention back to Randy, she said, "I should explore different sensations, lay the groundwork."

"A visit to The Playground won't help you lay anything or anybody. Lesbians don't exist in Soapland."

Seated on the sofa, Randy stared down at Anissa. Dark blue denim contoured the rump that seemed glued to his living room floor. Her toenails gleamed amid cotton puffs. At age twenty-nine, she looked innocent, wholesome, a blonde dairymaid from Wisconsin. Currently, she played Charlotte on *Morning Star,* TV's most popular daytime drama. The writers had conceived Charl as a goody-goody, but Anissa had dubbed her "the slut next door."

"I don't know what to wear," she said, removing the toe-puffs. "How does one dress for a gay lounge?"

"A bra is not required, my lady, but a top and shoes might be appropriate. On the other hand—"

"No shirt, no shoes, no service," she finished, directing one pink-polished fingernail toward the sign above Randy's front door. During a rumble at the Unicorn, instigated by some Marlon Brando motorcycle clones, she had stolen the Unicorn's sign, and it now joined the memorabilia that adorned her best friend's room.

Several pots were hidden in woven macramé cradles, suspended from ceiling rafters. The pots held English ivy, Boston fern, and Pothos plants, whose fronds looked like the veins on an old woman's hands.

Across one wall hung framed posters—the Marx Brothers in *Animal Crackers,* Walt Disney's 1938 *Snow White,* and the 1947 classic, *Gentlemen's Agreement.* The most prominent poster displayed Rock Hudson, James Dean, and Elizabeth Taylor in *Giant.*

Montgomery Clift publicity stills dominated another wall, depicting the handsome star in cinematic scenes from *Red River* to *The Misfits.* Between the Clift stills were photos of Randy's early stage successes.

Wooden-shuttered windows filled a third wall.

The last partition included a fireplace, surrounded by various-shaped mirrors. Flanking the hearth, bookcases overflowed with bound scripts, novels, and rocks of all sizes. HE WHO CASTS THE FIRST STONE read a framed needlepoint.

Plump, chintz-covered cushions were nestled in white wicker furniture. A wispy Yorkshire Terrier named Oscar Wilde had made one of the wicker chairs his personal property, and black tufts of fur had become part of the patterned chintz.

From his own cushion, Randy leaned sideways to scratch

Oscar's ears. "Damn dog. This furniture is . . . was new and very expensive. Shoo, you alfy mutt. Get down!"

Oscar bared small fangs and snapped at Randy's fingers.

"Shame on you, Wilde Oscar, biting the hand that feeds you." Anissa grinned. "Such a ferocious, macho bugger, just like your devoted master."

Propelling himself from the sofa, Randy landed on top of Anissa. They wrestled briefly until he pinned her arms above her head.

"Stop!" she yelled. "You'll smear my polish."

"Screw you."

"Is that an Australian expression?"

"G'day, love, screw you."

"I wish you would. I haven't been laid in years."

"Celibacy was your idea." Randy nodded toward the Thorny Pink nail polish tattoo that garnished her bare breast. "What's that supposed to be?"

"A roo with a joey in its pocket."

"It looks more like a boomer fannywhacker."

"Is fannywhacker another word for kangaroo?" Playfully, she arched her back and rubbed her breasts against Randy's naked chest. "Or is it a humongous penis?"

"A boomer fannywhacker is a large marble," he said, releasing her arms and sitting back on his heels.

"A marble? Aussie galah fink! My tattoo is an herbivorous leaping marsupial mammal. Anyone with an *American* brain can see that. Did I ever tell you I flunked Zoology, along with English lit and botany?"

"Yes."

"You smeared my roo's tail, so now I must visit the loo and wash it all off." Anissa simulated tears from the corners of her eyes. Not quite Bette Davis eyes, but close.

Carnes finished her last song, and a new record clicked into place—Judy singing about the boy next door. Leaning back against the white wicker legs of the sofa, Randy shut his eyes and thought about Anissa, the girl next door. She kept insisting he had saved her life when it was really the other way around. He had fought her booze and pills, but she had fought his demons.

He had always been haunted by demons, even before he discovered that he was a queer. According to Webster's, a queer differed from what was usual or normal while a queen (same page) was an effeminate homosexual. He knew he wasn't effeminate, but the scary demons vanished when Anissa was present. They were scared of *her*. Because, from the very beginning, she had never allowed his queerness to override her feelings for him. Anissa called it common sense. He called it sensitivity. Despite her lonely childhood, despite the ill-fated affair with her half-brother, Anissa was the most compassionate person he had ever met.

Garland's last note rebounded off heaven and wafted toward Carnegie Hall. The sudden silence was jolting, until it was interrupted by Anissa's sweet voice. "Are you asleep, Randy?"

He opened his eyes and gazed up at the lovely woman who stood above him. "When you reach my advanced age," he murmured, "you daydream a lot."

"Advanced age?" Anissa tossed her hair, cascading once again toward her waist. "You're only thirty-five, Aussie."

"That's this life. In my previous existence I was a princess and one of Cleopatra's handmaidens."

"Are we discussing ghosts and things that go bump on the set? Remember my first role? Pablo's deceased lover?"

"The viewers ate it up."

"I can't imagine why. It was indigestible. I'll never forget whispering my seductive dialogue to a bored camera crew. Then, when they finally edited my scenes onto the tape, I looked like a

Kewpie doll wrapped in toilet paper. God, I couldn't wait until I was reborn on *Morning Star,* a flesh and blood character. I'll bet you had something to do with my reincarnation, Randy, considering that you were once a magic princess."

"I didn't say magic, and don't make fun of me. I believe in reincarnation. Did you know that throughout history famous people have died and been born on the same date? For instance, Robert Benchley, U.S. humorist, died on November twenty-first, 1945, the same day Goldie Hawn was born. When the doctor slapped her tiny rump, Goldie probably emitted her first giggle."

"And on the day Hitler perished, Maxine Graham was born. I still say you had something to do with *Morning Star,* darling."

"Impossible. Maxine doesn't let a mere actor contribute plot treatments."

"Not true." Anissa bent forward and scratched Oscar's furry rump. The ecstatic Yorkie licked her fingers. "Ever since Max left *Children* and became *Star*'s producer, the grapevine's been on overtime. They say Drew Flory can 'contribute' to Maxine any time he feels like it. They say he has her wound 'round his little finger, but I have a feeling she's wound 'round a different part of his anatomy."

"Have you met Caleb yet?"

"Just an introduction."

"He's a beaut."

"Why, you randy bugger! Stay away from Drew Flory. Don't you know that according to all the columns you and I are supposed to announce our pending nuptials any moment?"

Anissa disappeared into the kitchen, then walked back through the living room. Anchoring Coke bottles beneath her armpits, she buttoned a checkered red and white shirt with colorful flowers embroidered on each breast pocket.

"Is that a new deodorant?" Randy asked, staring at the bottles.

"Don't change the subject," she said, handing him a Coke.

"What's the subject? Our engagement?" Downing the soda in five swallows, he placed the bottle on his bookshelf. "The reporters pair us because you refuse to date. If you're attracted to Flory, go for it."

"Who said I was attracted to Drew Flory? I'm not even sure I like him. Besides, I have you."

"If David was here, I'd kick your beautiful butt next door."

"David's the one with the beautiful butt. We have the same taste in men, and they always prefer you."

"Too right. But visiting The Playground won't improve that situation." He stood, stretched, donned a white shirt, and stepped into snakeskin penny loafers.

"Anyway, I don't need sex," Anissa said.

"Bullshit! Everyone needs to be naughty once in a while. If I really were a magic princess, I'd wave my wand and have the perfect mate appear. The quintessential Prince Charming."

"He'd probably fall in love with you, not me. Darling, why don't we get married?"

Randy removed Oscar from the wicker chair and watched the little dog leap back up again. Finally he said, "It would be a great way to get even with your father. If you married me, you couldn't give Jacob his prized grandson."

"That's not true. Lots of gay men have children."

"Not me, Anissa. I can't *make* children."

"That doesn't matter. I love you, Randy. You could sleep with David, I wouldn't care. I love you so much, and even though you deny it, my heart would still be broken if you hadn't been around to fix it with your verbal bandages."

"I've told you before. Hearts can't break."

"The Oz wizard says that hearts will never be functional until they can be made unbreakable."

"The Oz wizard said that hearts will never be *practical* until they can be made unbreakable, and anyway, the wizard was a charlatan."

"I love you, Randy. I love—"

"Belt up, Anissa. Are you ready?"

"Yes. Do I look okay?"

"You're a beaut," he said sincerely, meaning more than her physical appearance. "Let's hit the road, jackeroo."

Leaning back against the Volkwagen's headrest, Anissa lifted her face toward the starry sky and felt breezy curlicues caress her hot cheeks. Had she really asked Randy to marry her? How many times had she promised herself she'd never bring the subject up? Because rejection was painful, and anyway she'd already been pregnant, aborted, married, annulled.

Was there a grain of truth in Randy's revenge remark? Was she trying to get back at Jacob? No. She loved Randy, plain and simple. Well, maybe not so simple.

"Randy," she said, lowering her face, "aren't you afraid of being recognized?"

"Do you mean people will ask for my autograph? Or discover that I'm gay?"

"Yes. Both." She felt her cheeks flush. "Gay."

"My darling jackeroo, everyone knows."

"I didn't at first," she said, smiling at the nickname. Randy had several pet names for her. Before leaving their duplex she had donned a denim vest and boots, and a jackeroo was an apprentice cowboy.

"I don't broadcast my sexual preferences," Randy said. "On the other hand, I'm not a leading man like Rock Hudson."

"Are you serious? Rock Hudson's gay?"

"Anissa, please forget I said that."

"Said what?"

"Thanks." He tweaked her nose. "I just do my own thing and

try to get along. Hold on, stop sign."

She admired the play of his thigh muscles as his feet hit the clutch and brake pedals. Calvin Klein double pleated, cream linen slacks hugged Randy's lean hips. A carefully cultivated tan enhanced his face, emphasizing the blue of his eyes, and his hair was sun-bleached, as if the golden-beige undercoat and brown stripes of a tiger had merged. His voice was masculine, his body athletic, his style heroic. What a waste, she thought, although it wasn't a waste to Randy, and anyway, who was she to judge?

"Once upon a time, I attended this celeb-studded Hollywood bash," said Randy, maneuvering his Volks around a sleek white Cadillac. "Among the guests was Pat Huxley, that viperous bitch who considers herself an entertainer. Do you know who I mean?"

"Of course. Pat Python. But I'm not famous enough—"

"Just wait, roo. When you win your Emmy she'll add you to her roster."

"If I win, when I win, I'll quote Helen Reddy's wonderful Grammy speech. 'I'd like to thank God because She makes everything possible.' "

Randy laughed. "That particular night, the night of the party, I walked through the room and heard Huxley talking to another guest, a woman with so many wrinkles in her neck she looked like she wore chains of flesh. They were nattering about character actor Christopher Coombs."

"I had such a crush on 'Topher' when I was a kid."

"So did I. The wrinkled woman asked Huxley if Topher's companion was a fruit, her word, because he wore an earring, spoke in a high voice, and fluttered his wrists."

"I didn't know Christopher Coombs was . . . is gay."

"He's not. He's bi. Topher has eclectic tastes. A prostitute friend of mine says she has to dress like a little girl before he can make it with her."

Anissa shuddered. "Okay. Sorry. The woman asked Pat Huxley if Topher's mate was gay. Then what?"

"Huxley smiled and smirked." Randy raised his voice a couple of octaves. " 'That just proves how appearances are deceiving,' she said. 'I know a young actress who swore she was *intimate* with Coombs and he performed quite well. Topher's friend played college football and he's married with two kids. You can't tell a book by its cover, my dear.' Shit, Anissa. Topher's mate was a raging queen. Huxley's such a bloody nit."

"One more question. Don't they mind at the studio? Earlier you said gays didn't exist in Soapland."

"I exist discreetly off camera, so they don't mind. As a matter of fact, they're moving me over to *Morning Star.* I'm being written out of *Children of the Night.* Maxine is aware of my past, present and future, yet she requested me for a new character."

"Randy McNeal, why didn't you tell me?"

"I was saving it as a surprise. There's a bottle of special wine stashed at The Playground."

"What's the part?"

"Adam, the manager of a health club. My love interest is Charl."

"Me? The script has been leading toward Charl boffing Cal. What a slut!"

"I believe they plan to exploit our off-screen relationship. Naturally, there's a slight hitch. Maxine says that Adam will also be naughty with Hannah."

"And Charl doesn't like that, huh?"

"We'll have to wait and see. No advance scripts, remember? Maxine wants more bloody Australian accent, after years of trying to lose it and sound American."

Anissa burst out laughing. "Since I met you . . . dear lord, Randy, since I met you . . ." She caught her breath. "I don't go to the bathroom, I go to the loo. I flog instead of sell, hire instead of rent. I wave to nippers rather than small children. I wear gear, not clothes, flash gear if I'm dressed up. I have mates rather than friends. I get buggered, which does *not* mean covered with bugs, and I sing 'Waltzing Matilda' in the shower. Lose your accent? Hah!"

"Be fair, Anissa. I'm bloody well Americanized."

"Oh, yeah? Prove it."

"I eat fast food. Does that mean the food is firmly loyal, as in *fast* friends? How about *fast* asleep? Maybe the burgers and chips are wild, for example they run around with a *fast* crowd. Or maybe they're merely promiscuous. Never mind, we've arrived."

They left Randy's car in an overflowing parking lot and walked toward the portal of a large complex. A sign above the door read THE PLAYGROUND and the entrance was guarded by a pair of winged gargoyles. One of the grotesque stone images sported a June Allyson pageboy. The man who collected cover charges stamped the back of Anissa's hand with a red star. On the wall near the turnstile, a painted arrow indicated the way downstairs to The Merry-Go-Round and The Swings.

"The Merry-Go-Round is primarily for women patrons," Randy explained. "The Swings is a room that can only be opened with special keys purchased by Playground members. Inside, X-rated movies are played continually on a large screen."

"Are you a member?"

"Yes, but I don't care for X-rated movies." Randy shrugged. "On the other hand, my mate David has this thing for Stallone."

"Oh, my God! Don't tell me—"

"No, Anissa. Stallone made a porn flick once, that's all. We're keeping to the main floor. It's called The Seesaw."

"Merry-Go-Round? Swings? Seesaw? They're not awfully subtle, are they?"

"Why be subtle? Look at this toney crowd. I had Chris reserve my usual table."

"Who's Chris?" Anissa asked. But her question was lost in the crush of bodies as Randy guided her toward a small round table in front of a raised stage.

He signaled a waiter, who soon arrived carrying a bottle of Tyrrell Red and two goblets.

The waiter wore cut-offs and a black sleeveless T-shirt. His biceps bulged. "You picked a good night for your celebration, McNeal," he said. "The Countess is due to appear."

"Thanks, Chris." Randy shoved a ten dollar bill inside the handsome waiter's tight denim pocket.

"Countess?" Anissa stared at Randy.

"Soon there will be a show on that stage. The Countess is its star tonight, and he's world famous."

"*World* famous? We never heard of him in Milwaukee and Madison. Did I ever tell you that I'm the niece of a Countess?" Raising her glass, she gulped wine.

"Slow down, roo. Are you jumpy about being here?"

"No. Yes. Maybe a little."

"Relax. Half the mob is straight. They come to dance, act toney, or gawk."

Anissa glanced around the room, her eyes adjusting to the dim lighting, emphasized by black walls with red trim. Randy was right. Several tables included mixed couples. Near them sat a man and woman, sharing hugs and kisses. The girl was cute rather than beautiful, but she had incredible eyes, a color somewhere in between her dark green corduroy slacks and lime blouse. *Damn, I've been staring and she's caught me.*

"Are you gay or straight?" asked the girl.

"Delly, shut up," her partner said.

"I just wondered, Jonny. She's so pretty."

"My friend here has had a few too many," said her companion.

"My name's Delly Diamond. Can . . . may we join you?" Without waiting for an answer, the petite girl maneuvered her chair next to Anissa. "This sourpuss is Jon Griffin. I know it's a cliché, but you look familiar. Are you *moo*-vee stars?"

"I'm Anissa Cartier and this is Randy McNeal. We both have roles on daytime dramas."

"You talkin' soap operas? I don't watch soaps. Junk."

"Christ, Delly." Jon groaned. "Sorry, folks."

"Don't apologize for me, Griffin, and don't tell me what to do. This is my celebration, not yours."

"Celebration?" asked Anissa.

"Yup. Just lost a part in a *moo*-vee." Delly made a pair of horns with her thumb and pinkie. "Moo, moo, *moo*-vee."

"She's drunk as a skunk," said Jon with an embarrassed grin.

"Why are skunks drunk? Why do we pay through the nose? Why do we say cold as hell?"

"Okay, Delly, that's enough. We're leaving."

"We can't leave yet. I haven't found the click."

"The click?" Randy raised his eyebrows.

"That line from *Cat on a Hot Tin Roof.* Paul Newman says it to Burl Ives or Elizabeth Taylor or somebody. I forget."

" 'The click that I get in my head that makes me peaceful,' " said Anissa, then quoted the entire passage.

"That's it!" Delly shouted.

"Isn't she a beaut?" Randy smiled. "You're a bloody wonder, roo."

Anissa felt her cheeks bake. "I seem to have this thing for Tennessee Williams."

Delly raised her hand to her head and curled her fingers into a the shape of a gun. "Let's play Russian roulette. Click, click, bang. Peace."

"C'mon, honey," Jon pleaded, "let's go home."

"No. I wanna chat with my new friends here and we haven't even danced."

"You're too tipsy to dance."

"Am not." She stood up, swaying, and turned toward Randy. "Will you dance with me, Mac? Is that your name? I forget."

Randy started to rise, but Jon had already jumped from his seat, sending his chair to the floor with a crowd-muted crash.

"We're leaving right now," he said, "even if I have to carry you out."

"Don't you dare!" Delly sat down and grabbed the edge of her chair tightly with her hands. "You go home, Griff. I'll celebrate all by myself."

"She's really a nice girl, but she tends to act nuts when she's had too much scotch, which doesn't happen very often." He turned to Delly. "Let's go, before you make a total ass out of yourself."

"No! You wanted to come here. You thought it would cheer me up. I wanted to slash my wrists."

"With what? The sharp edge of your teddy bear? You're acting like a baby."

"Baby is something you have between your legs. That's from Jonny's play," she told Anissa. "Only the line goes, 'Baby is something born between your legs, quack, quack.' "

"I'm leaving, Delly." Jon turned toward the exit.

"Adieu, mon cher monsieur."

As Jon walked away, a tall, bearded man asked Randy to dance. Then there was silence.

Delly stirred the ice in her drink with her middle finger. "I'm sorry," she finally said. "I should have left with Jon. I'm screwing up the evening for you and Mac."

Poor thing, thought Anissa. She looks so vulnerable. In a town where a woman could freeze yogurt with one frigid glance,

Delly's vulnerability stood out like a sore thumb, and the phrase *wet behind the ears* came to mind. "Don't fret, kiddo. I've had one too many myself. Want to talk about it?"

"Not really," Delly said, then suddenly found herself telling a sympathetic Anissa the story of her life, starting with her move to Manhattan.

"After I turned twenty-one, a trust fund from my father came due and I didn't have to worry about money. I continued my acting lessons while attending auditions. Then I got a call-back and a second call-back and was cast in an original drama, produced by the legendary Joseph Papp, directed by Mike Nichols. A 'small but pivotal role.' "

"Good for you." Anissa patted Delly's shoulder.

"Jon and I celebrated. I got drunk that night, too. You know what? I can count on one hand the number of times I've been drunk, actually half a hand. There's this warning thing inside my head, the click I guess, that tells me I should quit or I'll become sick or whatever. My whatever that celebration night was a patch of ice. I slipped and broke my leg. Badly. Plaster cast and crutches. Naturally, I lost the pivotal role—the part was very physical and couldn't be rewritten to include crutches. I grit my teeth whenever I hear the expression 'break a leg.' "

"You poor baby."

She reminds me of me, thought Anissa, *except I didn't break my leg. I broke my heart, even if Randy says hearts don't break.*

"Jon found some investors and had his play *Duck Pond Sonata* produced," Delly said. Then she told Anissa how Jon had insisted that a brand-new actress, an unknown named Delly Diamond, perform the lead. She was familiar with Jon's script so her audition had been unstressed, even though the director said she'd have to act stressed in her role as a marginally retarded girl named Virginia. After try-outs and multiple revisions, they'd finally opened on Broadway and the reviews had been outstanding. One critic even compared her to Julie Harris.

Anissa whistled. "That's a real compliment. What's the plot line?"

"Virginia shares her fantasies with the ducks who populate a pond bordering her sanitarium. She's raped by a neighboring farmer, but nobody believes her story because the old codger's one hell of a rich, powerful bastard. But she's pregnant, so they blame it on one of the funny farm employees. Her mother is notified, takes her back to the city, and locks her up inside a small room. When she has the baby, Mommy dearest takes it away from her. Virginia escapes from the apartment and returns to the duck pond. She wades into the water, telling the ducks she wants to join them, become one of them. She has a long monologue and she quacks. That sounds funny, but it wasn't. It was sad. At first we used live ducks, but they were a bitch to direct, so we played a tape instead. The theme music was the ugly duckling song from the movie *Hans Christian Andersen.* That was my idea."

"Now I understand the baby is born between your legs bit."

"Jon couldn't decide if he should kill off Virginia, so he let the audience imagine the ending either way."

"Wait a sec. I read about your play in the *Times.* Didn't Paramount purchase the rights?"

"Yup. They hired Jon to script the film. That's why we moved here. But this time Jonny couldn't get me screen-tested for Virginia and they cast Amy Irving. Rats! I think I'm going to cry."

"Go ahead. Be my guest, Delly. I don't blame you."

"No, I'm okay. I guess that long confession was my click. I'm soberer. More sober? Jon's right, Anissa. I'm not usually like this, inviting myself to your table and acting so rude. I'm sorry. Which soap do you star in?"

"You don't have to be polite, Delly."

"I really want to know. Please?"

"*Morning Star.* I play Charl, a goody-two-shoes. Except I have a feeling the writers are planning to turn her into a first-class bitch soon. We have a producer named Maxine Graham and a new head writer, Judith Pendergraft. Rumor has it that our esteemed producer doesn't care for one of the women on the show, a character named Hannah. They're adding a man named Adam, whom Charl becomes involved with, and Charl might try to kill Hannah. That's all conjecture, the Adam plot. Damn, you can't possibly understand what I'm talking about."

"It's fascinating. I thought *Duck Pond* was filled with evil, but it's sort of introspective and there *are* some funny lines. Your soap sounds nasty."

"I'm a second-generation soap addict, Delly. The way Maxine and Judith Pendergraft work, we don't get scripts ahead of time. So I'm in the dark about what's supposed to happen, and I can't wait to hit the studio and find out."

"You get scripts the same day?"

"Usually a day or two before, sometimes a whole week. Fortunately, I have a memory like a sponge and—"

"Show time, kids." Returning to their table, Randy sat next to Anissa, across from Delly.

The dance floor's laser beams were eliminated. Spotlights directed at the platform illuminated a chubby announcer who introduced the first performer, Miss Olivia. Clothed in a long blue gown with a high cowl collar, the entertainer pranced on stage. Soundtrack music from *Xanadu* flowed statically from overhead speakers. Swaying in time to the music, Miss Olivia tried to lip-synch lyrics.

"He looks like a woman until he turns around," whispered Anissa, watching Miss Olivia's blonde wig flip with every hip thrust. "His back is definitely male."

"You can't disguise a man's shoulders and back," Randy said.

"It's a different shape than a woman's."

Each of the following entertainers had trouble lip-synching, but the audience didn't seem to mind. Several men approached the stage and waved money as the songs played on without pause.

There was a fanfare. The Countess appeared from a corner entrance. He wore skin-tight black leather pants, a red sequined top and an orange Orphan Annie wig. The spotlight's rays bounced off the ruby choke-necklace that adorned his ebony throat. Donna Sommer's *Last Dance* blasted from the speakers as moist red lips mouthed the lyrics.

"It's unreal," Anissa said. "If I passed your Countess on the street, I'd think woman, unless I walked behind him. You're right, Randy. You can't disguise a man's back."

The Countess encored twice. His tight pants bulged with contributions. Finally, he dabbed at his streaming brow with a handkerchief, threw the handkerchief at the waiter, Chris, then exited stage left.

Laser beams darted across the empty, darkened stage. "I'm going to explore downstairs," Delly said.

"When you're finished, we'll drive you home," Randy said.

"Why don't you spend the night at my place?" Anissa winked. "We can have an old-fashioned pajama party and confess our sins. They say confession is good for the soul."

"Jonny says confession can be turned into a bestseller, especially in L.A. and Washington. Thanks, you guys, but I'll taxi home."

Delly wrote down Anissa's phone number. Then she descended steps and entered another dimly lit room. A few couples glided across the small dance floor. One overworked waitress serviced tables. At least a dozen women lined up in front of a mahogany bar.

"Can I buy you a drink?"

May I, thought Delly, staring at the woman whose cap-toothed smile gleamed. "Thanks. I appreciate the offer, but—"

"No obligation, sweetie pie. I'm not a man who has to get laid after putting out for a couple of cocktails. What are you drinking?" She signaled the bartender, who scurried toward them.

"Scotch," said Delly, "with a splash of soda."

"I'm Judith Pendergraft." The woman swept bleached hair away from her forehead. Her perfectly round blue eyes were fringed by stubby, mascara-caked lashes. A black silk dress, bloused on top, was gathered at her waist by a multi-hued belt.

Delly introduced herself. "Your name sounds familiar, Ms. Pendergraft. I know. You're the head writer for *Wishing Star,* the soap opera."

"*Morning Star,* and we prefer daytime drama. But I seldom talk business when I'm having fun. Come with me to my table and join my friends, Delly Diamond."

"People, uh, my friends are waiting upstairs."

"I understand. It's been a pleasure meeting you." Judith signaled the bartender. "Have one more drink, sweetie pie."

Delly felt the first drink hit like a bolt of lightning. "I'm not a pie, sweetie," she said. "Pies are easy. They always say easy as pie. What does that mean?"

"I guess it means that pies are easy to eat."

"Hey, smarty-pants, why do they say drunk as a skunk?"

"I'm not sure," Judith said, giving Delly's question serious consideration. "Skunk means an obnoxious person. Drunk as an obnoxious person makes sense, doesn't it? Won't you please join my party? No skunks allowed."

Delly's mind raced. Judith Pendergraft was a professional contact. No obligation. No skunks. She looked down at the liquid swirling in her glass, the same color as the golden glints in her sister Samantha's eyes. Sami would never let an opportunity like this pass.

Defiantly, Delly finished her drinks and staggered toward Judith's table, even though she felt drunk as a skunk, easy as pie, cold as hell, and was afraid she'd have to pay through her freckled nose.

Chapter Twelve

Blinking open her eyes, Delly found herself on top of a strange bed. *I will not say where am I,* she thought. "Where am I?" she said.

"You fell asleep," replied the blonde, cap-toothed woman who reclined next to her.

Delly glanced around the room and saw herself reflected in the mirrored walls and ceiling. On top of an end-table was a crystal lamp with a pleated shade that diffused pink light. The blonde woman's bed, if it was her bed, had a padded crimson heart-shaped headboard and purple satin sheets.

"How did I get here, Ms. Pen . . . Pender . . ."

"Judith. You don't remember?"

She smiled and Delly thought she looked like the Gold's family cat, Southern Comfort.

Squeezing her eyes shut, Delly let images whirl. She had met Judith's friends and downed glass after glass of Chivas. They had all left The Playground together. Judith's friends had helped her into a white Cadillac, then supported her up the walk toward Judith's Brentwood home.

She recalled drunkenly reciting her monologue from *Duck Pond Sonata.* She had sung the *South Pacific* and *Bye, Bye Birdie* scores. She'd been a goddamn Gold star! Everybody had praised her, hugged her, petted her, especially one tall woman with red hair, who looked like Woody Woodpecker.

Then what?

She couldn't remember because the click had finally arrived, along with a dark void. "Did someone carry me upstairs, Judith?"

"Yes."

"You?"

"Yes."

"I'm sorry."

"It was my fault, Delly. I felt responsible. I shouldn't have plied you with Chivas. But even drunk you were so friggin' cute. And very talented."

"Why didn't you call a cab? I mean, before I passed out?"

"You couldn't remember your address."

"Oh, God. I'll never drink again. What time is it?"

"Late, early, it doesn't matter. You have a beautiful body. Wouldn't you feel more comfortable without your clothes?"

She shook her head. "I know we met at The Playground, Judith, but I'm not, I've never—"

"Made it with a woman. I understand."

"I'd better go home now," she said, sitting up. Her motion caused the sheets to slide down and she saw that Judith was nude, her body large, well proportioned. Delly felt the room spin. "Oh, God, I think I'm still sort of drunk."

"Do you feel sick, sweetie pie? The bathroom's right there, behind one of the mirrored doors."

I'll die before I throw up in front of a famous screenwriter. Delly gritted her teeth. "I'm so embarrassed, Judith. Maybe if you help me to a guest bedroom where I can lie down for a while until everything stops whirl—"

"Turn over on your stomach."

"Why?"

"Turn over, pet. I won't hurt you."

She complied, and felt Judith's strong hands massage her neck and shoulders. The dizziness settled into a distant blur.

Instinctively, she drew closer to the comforting strokes. "That feels good," she said, "but anything else is wrong."

"Tell me why it's wrong."

"I don't know. It just is. I couldn't—"

"Of course you couldn't. Leave everything to me."

"I think—"

"Don't think. Perhaps this is unfair, Delly, but I want you very much, and I can help you. I'm respected at my network. It's true. Don't look at me like that. In my business it's drive and talent, not sexual preference. Earlier tonight, before you drowned yourself in Chivas, you said something about letting a movie role slip through your fingers. Have you considered daytime drama?"

Reaching into an end-table drawer, Judith pulled out a cold-capsule-shaped pill. Snapping it open, she held it under Delly's nose.

"Oh, please, don't." Delly felt a new wave of dizziness and everything went spinning again. "Hey, I'm a swan," she cried, clambering to her feet and standing on the mattress. "Wheee, I'm flying, just like Peterfuckinpan." She saw colored lights reflected in the mirrored walls and heard firecrackers sizzling.

Had she really said Peterfuckinpan? She hardly ever swore. Samantha was the one who swore. Delly Diamond was drunk as a skunk, stoned as a skunk, dizzy good, not dizzy bad. *Wheeeee.*

Judith laughed and clapped her hands.

Delly sank down onto the mattress and lay on her back. Judith's face swam into focus. Delly zeroed in on Judith's eyelashes, caked with mascara. The lashes crept forward until all Delly could see were—

Spiders! Hairy spiders!

Pushing Judith away, turning over on her stomach and wriggling toward the edge of the bed, Delly had a clear image of Samantha. Once upon a long time ago, Sami had tripped over a cobblestone and allowed Jim-with-the-pimples to fondle beneath her sweater.

Sami had traded breast for Dick—Dick Clark.

Delly's head stumbled over cobblestones. "I want," she managed.

"Anything," Judith said. "Just name it."

"I want a part on *Morning Star.*"

Chapter Thirteen

"*Pre*senting Miss Wiggy. She's a virgin . . ." The emcee paused for titters. "This is her first time, so let's put our hands together and make her feel welcome."

The hazy beam from a spotlight hop-scotched across an empty stage.

"Okey-dokey, here she comes. Misssss Wiggy!"

As if playing hide-and-seek, the spotlight darted left and right, up and down, and the emcee's toupee began to sweat. "Miss Wiggy, where the fuck are you?"

His last five words rebounded off a ceiling that leaked when it rained.

"Miss Wiggy's kinda' shy, folks." Distant thunder sounded like a stomach growl as the emcee turned his face toward the wings. "We won't bite ya, kid."

A man from the audience shouted, "Speak for yourself!"

Maryl just stood there, her heart slamming against her chest.

Speak for yourself was the reason why she stood there, half hidden behind the side curtain. Because her modeling career and marriage to Jonah Wiggins had become too perfect, irksomely idyllic. Because she wanted to use her brains rather than her body. Because a second career as a stand-up comic was ludicrous. Because she'd rejected the insane notion then become obsessed by it.

Flipping through various newspapers, she'd read about the comedy club that had supposedly launched Pat Python.

Tonight was Amateur Night. The audience wouldn't expect perfection, so why did the stage seem a million miles away? Why did the spotlight look as if it might burn her skin, or at the very least give her skin cancer?

She had disguised her slender body with a padded pink dress that probably added seventy-five pounds to her bust, waist and hips. She'd covered her flaming mane with black Cher-hair that fell below her butt. It was Monday, August twenty-fifth, and Marilyn Monroe Bradley Florentino Wiggins, model model, model wife, was gone with the wind. Pre-senting Miss Wiggy.

"Speak for yourself," she said under her breath.

Stomping center stage, she met the emcee's angry glare with a timid smile. Then turning toward the audience, she immediately forgot every single joke she'd memorized.

Get a grip, Miss Wiggy, she admonished, silently. *Use your brains. Improvise.*

"Last night I saw a movie with a happy ending," she said, gripping the microphone stand. "Everyone was glad when it was over."

She heard a few embarrassed coughs and her stomach-knot tightened into a hangman's noose.

"My lover and I weren't compatible," she said. "I'm a Capricorn and he's a jerk."

Silence. Maryl wanted to run away but her low-heeled pumps felt as though they were nailed to the floor.

"I read in the paper where Xerox merged with Wurlitzer," she said, "so I guess they'll soon be selling reproductive organs."

Did she hear a few snickers? Yes. Briefly, she thought about telling her old slut-bitch joke, but she had a hunch dirty jokes wouldn't fly. How about dirty politics?

"There are two sure things in life," she said. "Death and taxes. Except death doesn't get worse with each session of congress."

Laughter? Yes! A few people even applauded.

Encouraged, she said, "Last February President Reagan called for deep cuts in domestic spending, but proposed an increase in the defense budget. I guess it's the fathead not the overhead that makes government so costly. A few weeks ago . . ." She paused and waited until the laughter died down. "A few weeks ago Reagan authorized production of the neutron bomb. Have you ever stopped to consider that government regulations are like catsup? You either get none or a lot more than you want. Patrick Henry ought to come back and see what taxation *with* representation is like." Then, just for grins, she said, "My lover and I weren't compatible. I'm a Democrat and he's a jerk."

Democrat worked while Capricorn didn't. Maryl filed that information in the back of her mind, even though she knew she'd never use it. Even though, by the time she'd finished her routine, she had experienced baptism. She'd been initiated, sanctified, purified. She'd confirmed that she had brains.

No. Not really. *Miss Wiggy* could speak for herself.

The club owner waited in the wings. "That was great, Miss Wiggy." He gazed at her critically. "This is just a suggestion, but you might consider fat jokes. Can you come back next week?"

"I'll think about it," Maryl said, thanking her lucky stars that she'd given him a fictitious phone number.

"I loved your reproductive organ joke," he said with a smirk.

"Thanks."

Her padded bosom moved toward the backstage exit. Her padded waist, hips and butt followed. She probably looked like the mongrelization between a ship and a tugboat—the *Titanic* and Little Toot.

Maybe she should forget this second career bullshit and have a baby.

★ ★ ★ ★ ★

Perched atop the cab's roof, a rectangular placard advertised *Raging Bull.* Robert DeNiro flaunted bird doo-doo. No wonder he clenched his fists.

With that thought, Delly dug her nails into the seat as the cab careened around a corner. Her body adjusted to the jouncing motion, but her head felt as if it had been severed by huge teeth. Dinosaurian whiplash. What a great idea for a horror movie. "The Raging Tyrannosaur Taxi Who Ate Hollywood." Jon could write the screenplay.

She squinted at her watch. 10:30 A.M. America had already received its weather report from Today-Good-Morning. She didn't need a weather report. It was Tuesday, Aug-twenty-sixth, and it was smog hot. It was the morning after the night she'd grabbed the merry-go-round's gold ring and discovered it was brass.

"Third house on the left," she said, wincing when the dinosaur's tires lunged through a puddle as big as Poland.

With a screech of brakes that reverberated inside her head, the cab finally stopped. She handed the driver the fare Judith had handed her. "Keep the change," she said, oh so hung over.

Hangover city. Hang-ups hung out to dry like soiled laundry pinned to a dirty clothesline. Never again. Delly stumbled up the rain-slick path, unlocked her front door, took a couple of deep breaths, and walked into her living room.

Jon was busy at the typewriter. Bare-chested, barefoot, he wore faded jeans with air-conditioned knees. His typewriter sounded like the click-clack of a runaway train. Delly pressed her hands against her temples. Three aspirins and a Bloody Mary hadn't helped. Never again!

"That girl we met at the Playground invited me to sleep over," she said, her voice oozing sincerity. Because Anissa *had* invited her. Without waiting for a reply, she showered. Then she pulled on a pair of jogging shorts and her favorite Superstar T-shirt.

"I should have called," she said, re-entering the living room, "but I couldn't remember our new number." Another semi-truth. She'd forgotten her new address.

Jon turned his back on the typewriter. "I'm sorry about last night, Delly. We should have stayed home."

"Home?"

"Don't you consider this home, honey? We haven't been here very long, but I think it beats our New York apartment. I suppose you could have stayed back East. After *Duck Pond*'s reviews, you'd have been cast in another play." The corners of his mouth twitched. "But I need you to cook my meals."

"Right." Delly returned his grin. She hated cooking with a passion. Jon had once accused her of being the only domestic chef he knew who could fuck up Jell-O.

She glanced around the living room of their small rented house on Martel Avenue, not far from Paramount Studios and downtown Los Angeles. Last week they had unpacked the last carton and tried to make their new nest cozy. Two lovebirds caged in a strange city where gung-ho Disney disciples worshipped squeaky rodents and nasal ducks, not to mention Cinderella and Snow White—the ultimate con ladies. Especially Snow White, who had escaped reality by invading a cottage inhabited by a number of grumpy, bashful, happy, dopey, sleepy, sneezy, medicinal dwarfs. Employed dwarfs, no less.

Samantha loved Snow White. In retrospect, Delly realized that her sister had been titillated by the thought of sharing her bed with seven lovers. *Ménage a sept.*

With a sigh, Delly wriggled her tush onto a royal blue canvas director's chair with DIAMOND stitched in white. The chair next to her read GRIFFIN. In front of her, Daddy's books rested on a coffee table. To her left, a teak wall unit held a TV, a stereo, record albums, and photos of her family. Mom and Samuel smiled from their wedding picture. A perpetually youthful William Gold looked like a perpetually youthful John Garfield. Next to Daddy's picture was Samantha, surrounded by Jules and her gaggle of kids. Will and Juliet and the twins, Carrie and Nellie, named for Mom and *South Pacific*'s Nellie.

The other half of the living room had been turned into an office. Beneath a picture window, bordering one wall, rounding a corner, were a file cabinet and two steel desks: Jon's area, organized with research books, pens, pencils, phone, typewriter, paper, colorful binders and paper clips.

"Do I consider this home, Jonny? Of course I do. It's just that things are so different from what I expected." Without warning, she began to cry.

Jon walked over to her chair. "Aw, Dell, don't."

"No, please, I can't tolerate your pity."

"Then how about dishing out some pity for me?"

"What do you mean?"

He sat, leaning against his embroidered name. "I didn't tell you last night because it was 'feel sorry for Delly' time, but the studio is messing around with my play. Someone at the top has decided the last scene is too 'down.' Forget that Ali died in Ryan's arms. Paramount wants a happy ending."

"How can Virginia live happily ever after?"

"Easy. Remember the guy who never appears on stage? The one who was blamed for impregnating Virginia?"

"Our invisible male nurse. We used to make jokes about the size of his invisible penis."

"He's my hero now, played by John Travolta or Michael Douglas or Jeff Bridges. Travolta or Douglas or Bridges falls in love with Virginia."

"What? Falls in love?"

"Yup. You see, Ginny's not really retarded. Just an unhappy childhood, her bitchy mother, all revealed in therapeutic flashbacks during her escape from the city. In my new version, she's rescued from the duck pond by Travolta. Or Bridges."

"Or Douglas. Are they serious?"

"Very. There's more. Virginia gets rescued in the middle of a storm, Amy Irving with wet curls plastered across her face, background music by Bob Seger and the Silver Bullet Band. Meanwhile, the farmer who screwed Ginny gets trapped at the back of his barn while flood waters rush toward him. He's the one who drowns. 'It's time we developed a sweet love story,' said one producer. I mentioned the word paradox. They had an answer for that, too. The paradox is now whether or not Virginia should keep her baby. Can she really love it? Can Travolta love it? Perhaps, they suggested, we should show the rape and delete the pregnancy. But then we'd have to ax Mom, and Shirley MacLane has already expressed an interest in play—"

"Are you going to change it?"

"What choice do I have? The studio even dangled a literary carrot. Paramount'll make a deal with some publisher and I'll write the 'sweet love story.' We're talking mega-bucks."

"But it's not your concept."

"Come on, honey, that's the same tone of voice you used last night when you put down soap operas."

"Sorry." She remembered the carrot Judith had dangled inside her mirrored bedroom. "Hollywood's a town without pity, Jonny. Let's play the dialogue game."

"Now?"

"Yes, now."

Delly had once described their dialogue game to Carolyn Ann during a long-distance telephone conversation. "You see, Mom," she'd explained, "when Jonny has a terminal case of writer's block and he's threatening to get a 'real job,' we act out the scene that's bothering him, improvise together."

Jon leaned forward in his chair. "Who do you want to play?"

"I'll be Virginia's mother and you can play the farmer."

"Talk about changing concepts."

"All right. I'll be Virginia and you can be John Travolta."

"Let's do this scene without dialogue." Kicking off his jeans, Jon knelt by the side of her chair, kissed her eyes shut, licked at the tears that still stained her cheeks, and ran his hand underneath her shirt.

She responded. Her body. Her mind. Her heart. Her soul. An orgasm began to build, like waves crashing against a moat's wall. Thank—

"God, Griff, I wish . . . I want . . ."

"Tell me."

She fell from her chair, into his arms, then straddled his waist, staring at his toes. Without dialogue, she let her fingers do the talking.

In turn, Jon carried her toward the castle's uppermost parapet while she urged him on to even greater heights. Until they spiraled downward, landing together on the crest of a wave.

"I almost forgot," he said. "You had a phone call from a Vance Booker. He made me write down his number and repeat it twice. You're supposed to call him back ASAP."

"Do we know a Vance Booker?"

"He says he's the casting agent for *Morning Star.* What's a morning star?"

"When did he call?"

"Just before you got home."

Maybe, thought Delly, the merry-go-round's ring wasn't tarnished after all.

"What's a morning star?" Jon asked again.

"*Morning Star* is the name of a soap opera. Last night I met the producer, Judith something."

"Judith something was at The Playground?"

Delly nodded. "She was with a bunch of people, but I guess I made a good impression. I'll use the bedroom extension to call Booker, so you can get back to your writing."

Entering the bedroom, she hesitated, staring at the phone. Did she really want to do this?

Don't be stupid, she thought. *Judith's merely keeping her promise. Besides, I'm not guaranteed a part. Judith said I'd have to audition, just like everyone else. Even if I'm lucky enough to pass the audition, that doesn't mean I have to visit her house again.*

Sinking onto the bed, Delly stared across the room, toward the shelves filled with her doll collection. Raggedy Ann stared back, an enigmatic smile on her painted lips. Barbie still retained her last elaborate hairstyle. Mortimer Snerd had once belonged to Carolyn Ann. So had Shirley Temple, clothed in a red and white dotted pinafore. The rest of the shelves held an assortment of stuffed bears, including one dry-cleaned, mink teddy-bear named Feiffer. The oldest bear, Mumpsy, was missing its button eyes.

"What should I do, Mumpsy?"

Vance Booker answered on the first ring.

"Fantastic," he yelped, after Delly had introduced herself. "We're looking for a young actress to play the role of a mental patient, rooming with one of the characters on the show who has checked into the hospital to escape what she thought would be a murder charge when she gave a poisoned drink to the woman engaged to the man who took her virginity."

"Whoa. What did you say?"

"I'm supposed to set up an audition for you to read for the part of a character in a hospital's mental ward. Her roommate is Charl, played by Anissa Cartier, our rising star. Charl checks herself into the hospital to avoid a murder charge and she needs someone to talk to so the viewers will know about her diabolical schemes—her escape, another murder attempt, the usual. Are you interested?"

"Can . . . may I call you back? Give me ten minutes." Delly dropped the receiver on the cradle before Booker could reply.

She borrowed one of Jon's scratch pads and a sharp pencil. Then she pawed through her purse until she pulled out the piece of paper with Anissa's phone number.

"Please be home, please be home. Damn it! Why don't you answer your—"

"Hello, this is Anissa Cartier. I can't come to the phone right now. Leave a message at the sound of the beep. Beep."

"Hi, Anissa. This is Delly Diamond. We met last night at The Playground. I was hoping—"

"Hello? Delly? I'm here. That was me, pretending to be a recorded message. You wouldn't believe the kooky calls I get for Charl, even though my number's unlisted. I used to have an answering machine but the damn thing broke. I was in the shower. That's why it took me so long to answer."

Delly told Anissa about Vance Booker. "What should I know when I call him back?"

"Aside from time of interview, you might want to find out if the job's an under-five."

"What's that?"

"Exactly what it sounds like. It's a separate pay category where the actor can only say five lines with as many words as necessary. A long time ago Vance was an under-five, and he's never forgotten. He still talks in run-on sentences."

"Boy, does he ever."

"An under-five is the next step up from being an extra. You might also ask if the character's a day player. You work for only one day but your character is identifiable, so you'll never work on the show again unless the same character is needed. Am I going too fast?"

"No. What else?"

"Ask Vance if the part will recur."

"Recur? Come back?"

"Right. There's no contract that says you'll come back, but chances are you will. No guarantees, but you could connect with the viewers and a contract would come later. You want a recurring character."

"Thanks, Anissa. Now I can sound as if I sort of know what I'm talking about. Anything else?"

"I don't think so. By the way, how did you get your interview with Vance?"

Delly's mind raced. "After I left you and Mac, I bumped into your producer, Judith something."

"Pendergraft."

"Right. I told her about *Duck Pond.* She mentioned this new part, a crazy kid, then suggested that I might be right for it. Type-casting, huh?" Anxious to change the subject, Delly said, "I once had a pen-pal named Anissa. Her last name was Stern and she lived in Milwaukee."

"Are you *my* Delly? Delly Gold? My God! I sort of wondered about the name last night, but—"

"So did I. Well, I would have, but I was a bit, well, you know. And, obviously, you're *my* Anissa. Can you say small world?"

"You should have no problem auditioning, Delly. You've starred in everything from *South Pacific* to *Our Town.*"

"That was high school. Besides, I sort of exaggerated in my letters. My sister—"

"How I used to envy you."

"Me? Why on earth would you envy me?"

"Your school activities. Cheerleader. Glee club. The boys you dated. What ever happened to that 'older guy'? The one you met at the basketball game. The one who lived in . . . Broken Neck?"

"Great Neck. I guess we sort of lost touch."

"I'd love to work with you, Delly Gold. Remember last night

when I said rumor has it that Charl might try and kill off Hannah?"

"I remember everything you said, even though I can't remember all of last night." Delly felt her cheeks flush. "This morning was hangover city. Never again."

"I think I told you we don't see our scripts ahead of time."

"I guess Vance Booker does. He said Charl would be checking into a mental hospital and I would be her roommate."

"Great, Delly. Your part might be very important."

"It's not my part yet. Should I know anything special about Booker?"

"Special?"

"Sometimes Broadway directors have these idiosyncrasies."

"Oh, I see. Vance looks like one of Santa's elves. He's short, with wispy white hair and pink cheeks. He's sweet but nervous, and he has a tic in his right eye. I'm sure the tic is the result of our esteemed producer, Maxine Graham. If anything goes wrong with casting, the wrath of Maxine comes down on him. There's a special red phone, a hot line from Maxine's office, and if it rings, Vance knows he's in trouble. If it doesn't, he waits for it to ring. The Chinese water torture in reverse. Thus, his nervous blink. Don't let it throw you."

"Does he get in trouble often?"

"Only once since I've been on the show. He cast Scottie Fitzgerald. We call her Zelda for obvious reasons. She plays Hannah, and bitchy is an understatement. The grapevine says Zelda was Pendergraft's recommendation. Am I going too fast for you again?"

"No. But suddenly I'm scared."

"Don't be. Piece of cake. Just recreate your Virginia role. You'll be fine."

"Assuming I pass the audition, how long does it take to appear on the show?"

"Hard to say. Tomorrow they're pre-taping, introducing Adam, a new character. So that should set the chain of events in motion."

"Say a prayer for me, Anissa. Oh, lord, you just stepped from the tub and I've kept you on the phone."

"No problem. By the way, Mac's name is Randy and he plays Adam."

"Randy. Sorry."

"Good luck, pen-pal."

"Thanks, pen-pal. 'Bye for now."

Delly immediately called Vance Booker. The part wasn't an under-five, was not a day player, and would recur. Vance set their interview for Friday.

That gave her three days to study the soap's story line.

She moved the portable TV into her bedroom so she wouldn't disturb Jon, and explained the plot to him three nights later. From the bed, they watched Jonah Wiggins, whose guest star was the famous Rosebud model, Maryl Bradley.

Delly thumbed the remote, turning the volume lower. Then she leaned back against her pillows and said, "*Morning Star*'s characters live in a small town called Wayne County."

"The town square has a statue of John Wayne?"

"Nope. Statues are covered with pigeon poop and everything on *my* soap is squeaky clean, at least externally. Anyway, I'm not sure there is a town square. The characters all mingle together at the local nightclub, hospital, or health spa. Wayne County also has a local drugstore with a doddering pharmacist, not to mention a local mansion where the town matriarch, who has been on the show forever, lives alone."

"No local whorehouse?"

"The entire town is a whorehouse. For instance, the first scheme involves my friend Anissa. Charl's a virgin. Anissa says they're about to introduce Adam, and bang, Charl will be deflowered. There's this girl named Hannah, the niece of the town matriarch. Hannah's rich. Snooty. According to Vance Booker, Charl poisons Hannah. I'll bet she steals the poison from the pharmacist, Mr. Norman."

"Who? Hannah?"

"No. Charl."

"I'm lost."

"Sorry. Charl gets screwed by Adam and tries to poison Hannah."

"Okay. Got it. Go on."

"There's this guy named Caleb—" Delly stared at the TV screen. "Wow, she's beautiful. I've always wanted to look like Maryl Bradley, tall and slender. I'll bet she was a swan from day one. Where were we? Caleb, right? They call him Cal. He runs the local newspaper."

"Hold it. I thought you said there's a local lounge, hospital, drugstore and—"

"The *Wayne Gazette* isn't housed in any building. Cal mentions his newspaper stories at other locations, and talks to his secretary, Betty, over the phone. I don't think Betty exists, either. Cal is messing around with Nurse Marybeth and a rock singer, Tabitha Catherine, also known as Tabby Cat. Cal wends his way into the affections of Lady Nancine, the town matriarch."

"Why is she called Lady?"

"She was once married to a British Lord. Cal suspects Lady Nan is involved with a drug smuggling operation, headed by a sleazy stud named Marlon."

"Brando?"

"No. Just Marlon. A one-name sleaze."

"You learned all this in three days?"

"There's more. A bunch of subplots. For example, take married doctors, Marshall and Lizzie."

"You take 'em," Jon mumbled.

"Marsh and Lizzie are married in real life. I remember reading about them in my movie magazines. They were both young film stars, like Robert Wagner and Natalie Wood, but they fizzled out. Marsh and Lizzie once dominated *Morning Star*'s plot. Now they're relegated to smaller slots and—"

"Wait! You're losing me again. What did you say about Robert Wagner and Natalie Wood?"

Delly heaved an exasperated sigh. "Nothing. I used them as an example of young, married film stars. You're not listening."

"I am listening. How else would I know about Robert Wagner? By the way, a wagner is a happy dog."

"Please listen. I'm almost finished. Tabby Cat—"

"The rock singer?"

"Yes. Tabby's pregnant and might have an abortion. The black police chief, Malcolm, wants to marry her. That's it."

"That's it? So far you've brought up issues of abortion, miscegenation, drugs and murder. What happened to sodomy and child pornography?"

"Give the show a chance. I only watched three days' worth. And stop nibbling my belly-button."

"I'm helping you rehearse for your audition, superstar. Take off that damn T-shirt. I plan to drive you crazy."

"You won't have to drive very far," she whispered.

The next day Delly entered the *Morning Star* studios.

Vance Booker's office was cluttered with scripts, résumés and casting breakdowns. She had to shift several agent submissions from her chair to the carpet before she could sit.

Anissa had been spot-on. Booker looked like a stereotypical North Pole elf. He wore Ben Franklin glasses atop a bulbous nose. The half-lenses magnified his tic. As he studied Delly, he said, "Fantastic. I was hoping you'd be small because the character we're casting isn't a child but she acts like one and due to tragic circumstances she's reverted to childhood."

"Mr. Booker?"

"Vance."

"Well, you see, uh, Vance, I'm not all that familiar with TV auditions. I mean, until recently, I've never, well, hardly ever watched soap operas."

"Daytime drama. Look, cookie, you'll read for me today. Next week you'll audition for Maxine Graham." Blinking non-stop, Booker glanced toward a red phone.

"What's the name of my character, Mr. Book . . . uh, Vance?"

"Doris or Dora." Shifting through the chaos on his desk, he located a script and flipped through its pages. "Here it is. Pandora. She has this guilt thing because she believes she killed her best friend. Can you play guilt?"

"You bet." *Piece of cake!*

"Fantastic. Take these sides and learn your lines. You have fifteen minutes."

"Wasn't Pandora forbidden to open a box sent by the gods?" Delly reached for the pages. "Didn't she open it anyway and let loose a swarm of evils upon mankind?"

"It's just a name, cookie."

Chapter Fourteen

Framed by a flaming window, Maxine Graham writhed while Manderlay burned. "A fire is good for ratings," she said.

Drew Flory stood on the ground below the mansion's window. "Rebecca," he shouted, "let down your hair!"

"That's Rapunzel, you fuckwit." Maxine's eyeballs oozed from their sockets and her skin peeled in strips, until all that remained was a skull.

"Cut and print," said Alfred Hitchcock. "Judith, you can put your face on now."

"Merde, Hitch baby. My name is Maxine Graham and I'm melting, mellllting . . ."

The phone rang, interrupting Anissa's nightmare. Fumbling for the receiver, she stared groggily at the clock on top of her new color TV. Digital numbers solidified into focus: 12:07. Midnight-oh-seven.

She tried to think. It was six nights after her visit to The Playground and she was inside her apartment, watching Hitchcock's classic movie, *Rebecca.* At least she had started out watching *Rebecca.* Now, the *African Queen* chugged through a murky quagmire.

Tramp's head rested on one of her breasts and his tail coiled around another. When she moved, the cat's sharp claws tried to secure a foothold.

"Ouch!" She placed Tramp on a couch cushion and brought the receiver to her mouth. "Hello, this is Anissa Cartier," she said. "I can't come to the phone right now. Leave a message at the sound of the beep." She yawned. "Beep."

"Roo, I need your help. Are you there? You're playing bloody machine, aren't you? Please help me."

"Randy? What's wrong?"

"Can't talk now. Pay phone. Gas station. Can't. Be. Seen."

The disjointed words and sentences were punctuated by sobs. Suddenly, the phone went dead.

"Randy? Shit!" Anissa thumbed the cradle, slammed down the receiver, and aimed her remote. Hepburn and Bogie faded into oblivion, leaving behind the mugginess of an African swamp. Anissa's window air conditioner fought a losing battle. She dabbed at her sweaty forehead with the hem of her nightie. The sun must have passed its torch to the moon like some damn relay racer, she thought, just before the phone rang again.

Grabbing the receiver, she said, "Randy, tell me what happened."

"Disconnected. Mistake. Stupid."

"I meant . . . never mind. Where are you?"

"Pay phone at gas station. It shuts down at midnight, the station not the phone, and I'm out of bloody coins."

"Give me the number. I'll call you back."

"No. Please. Just come. Hurry."

"Where *are* you?"

"Malibu."

"Malibu? I thought you and David drove to San Francisco for the weekend." She took a deep breath. "Tell me exactly where you are and how to get there."

She listened carefully, said goodbye, hung up, and quickly dressed in denim shorts and a white T-shirt. Running a brush through her hair, she twisted the long strands into one thick braid. Then she splashed cold water on her face.

Her green Mustang had been falling apart and repair bills

clogged her glove box. She inserted the ignition key. Feeling like a rat in a claustrophobic maze, she heard the engine cough, wheeze and die. Did her car have incurable lung cancer? Christ, it smoked enough. Turning the key again, she gingerly pressed the accelerator with her right sneaker, and heard a horror-movie-screech. Finally, the engine cleared its throat and settled into a steady, hostile buzz.

"Just get me to Randy, you rubber-hoofed monster," she half-threatened, half-pleaded, shifting into second gear.

His directions were easy to follow. Challenging cops, Anissa drove expeditiously, parked, then raced up a staircase toward a third-floor beach condo.

Inside, an overturned sofa and chair provided an effective detour through the living room. Pillows lay like soft cemetery headstones amongst snowy drifts of spilled stuffing. Smashed stereo equipment and a shattered mirror made a bristly, splintered trail toward a balcony. The balcony's sliding glass doors were open and in the distance Anissa could see an ocean view.

"Watch out for the glass, roo." Randy's anguished voice came from the other side of the room.

He wore khaki shorts and a brown golf shirt, stained with streaks that looked like dried seaweed. Cross-legged on the floor, underneath a framed scenic print of Switzerland, he flipped through the pages of a paperback dictionary.

"Come see, roo," he said, his voice a childish whine. "This book doesn't have shithead so I looked up idiot, which means 'a mentally deficient person with intelligence in the lowest measurable range.' That's me. An idiot."

Sniffing at ocean breezes and a strange metallic odor, Delly edged around the sofa, dropped to the floor, and cradled Randy's head on her shoulder. The sound of a radio wafted from the rear of the house. Van Halen.

"Who owns this beach condo?" she asked.

"David."

Gently releasing Randy, she stood up. "Where is he?"

"In the bedroom. No! Don't go in there!"

She sat on her heels, facing Randy. "Is David hurt? Sick?"

"Dead. David's dead."

"Oh my God! What happened?" Briefly, she glanced toward the balcony. "Did David fall? Jump?"

"My mate's dead. I don't know what to do."

"How did David die?"

"He had a bloody heart attack." Randy laughed, a high shrill wail.

"Stop it!" Without taking time to think, Anissa slapped him across the face. "Calm down and tell me what's going on."

The hysterical laughter ceased abruptly and his eyes clouded with tears. "I told you hearts don't break, but I was wrong. They do if they're attacked."

Standing again, she pulled his unresisting body up with her. "Show me David. Now!"

Obediently, Randy led her toward the back of the house. He halted at the bedroom entrance and pointed his finger.

Anissa saw a blood-soaked body draped across the bed. The metallic odor was very strong. A small radio perched on top of an antique bureau.

Randy made an about-face, returned to the living room, and slumped down, assuming his former position against the wall.

Anissa sat next to him. "Tell me what happened."

"We got into San Francisco last Thursday. David said we were being followed. He refused to leave our hotel room. But we finally did, Friday night, down a service elevator. This beach house belongs to David's auntie, only she's in New York. David promised to water plants and collect mail, so he had a key . . ."

"He had a key," she prompted.

"Yesterday, Saturday, David began to relax. This morning he went to church, and tonight we ate at a local pub. Steamed crabs. White wine. Boiled shrimp. It was overcooked, the shrimp. They shouldn't charge those prices if they make something wrong. The crab was smashing, but the shrimp tasted rubbery. Chewy, Anissa, like raw chook."

"Raw chook," she repeated, dazed by his recitation, full of detail but lacking any real emotion. "Go on, Randy. What happened after you ate supper?"

He gave her a belligerent glare. "That's your bloody problem. You're too nice. You won't complain. I grizzled and they took it off the bill. I said shrimp shouldn't taste like raw chook and they agreed. You have to grizzle if you want satisfaction. Or you can't get no sat-is-faction."

As if stuck in some horrible Hitchcock nightmare sequence, worse than her Maxine Graham dream, Anissa heard the bedroom radio—Jagger singing about going to a go-go.

"Don't move," she said, a rather stupid request under the circumstances. She climbed a kitchen counter and jumped down, landing on tile. Searching through cabinets, she found a bottle of sherry and poured the remains into a coffee mug. Then she returned to Randy, grasped his chin, and opened his mouth.

He swallowed automatically.

She glanced around the littered living room. "Is the phone working? Should I call the police? You can tell them—"

"No, Anissa, please. I'll tell *you.* After we ate, we walked along the beach. David thought he saw someone lurking and insisted we come back here. I grizzled, said he was a spoilsport. I called him paranoid, said we could be in 'Frisco if he hadn't been such a bloody nark. My poor mate. Oh, God, my poor mate." Clambering to his feet, Randy leaned against the wall.

"What happened?" she cried desperately.

"There was a knock on the door. David said, 'Don't answer.' I laughed and said, 'Have some more grog, mate. Maybe you'll see the ghost of Monty Clift.' David looks like Clift, the reason why I have all those stills on my living room—"

"Randy!"

"I opened the door. David's ex-lover stood there. He's a big bloke, called Popeye because he likes to boat and has muscles. Isn't that an alfy name?"

"Yes, totally alfy. Tell Anissa what happened next."

"Popeye was drunk. He shoved me back and walked inside. He was holding an ice pick. Wait a minute." Randy bent forward, retrieved the dictionary, and thumbed through its pages. "Here it is. Ice pick. 'A pointed tool for chipping or breaking ice.' It doesn't say anything about breaking hearts. See?"

Rising, she untangled his fingers from the paperback. "I see. What happened after Popeye walked inside?"

"A freaking ice pick. Why not a chain saw? I just stood there, frozen stiff. *Frozen,* roo, get it? I didn't even try to stop Popeye when my mate struggled and the stereo shattered and David shattered and my life shattered. I'm such a beaut at pouring puke remedies down throats, but I couldn't move against a big prick holding a little pick."

"Randy darling, don't blame—"

"Popeye didn't touch me, not at first. I just stood there and watched him attack David's heart. Popeye wore a dirty sweatshirt and cut-off daks, and beneath his daks I could see that he was big, Anissa, and ready. Sometimes a bloke can't get an erection when he's drunk. Not Popeye. He was big. He walked toward me. I threw pillows. He slashed at them with the ice pick. Then he heard a noise and left flat out. David . . ."

"Go on, Randy. Please."

"David's eyes were open, staring. He had no pulse. I carried his body into the bedroom and called you. My father was right.

I'm a loser. A drongo."

"Are you absolutely certain David's dead?"

"Yes."

"Why didn't you call the police?"

"My coins were all used up."

"Doesn't Auntie's phone work?"

"She had it temporarily disconnected."

"What about the neighbors?"

"They couldn't hear Popeye. David always played the radio and the stereo at the same time."

"I meant *phone*, Randy." Anissa tried to keep her frustration under control by carefully placing the dictionary on a bookshelf between Mailer and Michener. "Surely one neighbor will let us inside when we—"

"No. Please. Publicity. Maxine. I once told you they accepted me for what I am. They would never . . . my father . . . what am I going to do?"

"We have to call the police, Randy. Wait. Let me think. What's your relationship with David?"

"My relationship? Anissa, for Christ's sake!"

"Sorry, I didn't mean personal. Isn't he your stockbroker? Was that a nod, Randy? Okay. So if you were seen with him in San Francisco, it was a business meeting. Did anyone recognize you here in Malibu?"

"No. Just Popeye."

"Damn! The pub. They would remember, especially after you complained."

"No, they wouldn't."

"Why not?"

"I was disguised. David didn't like it when fans asked for autographs. I have special gear. A long black wig and a beard."

"What about your car?"

"It's at home, on the street. We used David's Mercedes. He

was so proud of that macho, status motorcar."

"Fingerprints. Did Popeye wear gloves?"

"I don't know."

"Think, Randy, think!"

"Why would he wear gloves, Anissa? It's summer. You don't wear mitts in the summer."

"Never mind, you're right, the cops will find him through his fingerprints. They'll find our prints too, but if we both stick to one story—"

"Stop it!" Randy swiveled and pounded on the wall. "I don't know what the bloody hell you're talking about."

She turned him around and wiped his perspiring brow with the edge of her T-shirt. He smelled hot and sick.

"Listen, Randy. It doesn't matter if you were seen in San Francisco, or even Malibu. You kept your appointment with David, stock business, then spent the night with me. I'll swear to it. I was all alone in my apartment. I watched an old movie on the telly. *Rebecca,* starring Lawrence Olivier. Delly called and thought the voice in the background was you."

"Olivier's British."

"Of course he is, darling, but sometimes it's hard to tell the difference. I mean, Brit and Aussie sound the same."

"No, they don't."

"Hush. I'm still thinking. Remember your story about Topher Coombs and his gay mate? Pat Huxley said that appearances were deceiving. She said Topher's mate was married. So we'll drive to Vegas and get married. Maxine will be livid when I don't show up at the studio, but she'll be thrilled when she hears—publicity! Think of the publicity, Randy. We were together all night and decided to get married. That will stop any rumors."

"I grizzled with an accent."

"What?"

"At the pub. I grizzled with an accent."

"Randy, you spent the night with me."

"The cops will put it together. People know David's my mate."

"If the cops question us, I'll insist that David was alive when we left him."

"I can't marry you. I can't let you lie for me."

"You can't stop me. Change your clothes. Hurry."

He staggered down the hallway, and stopped midstep. "This is mad, Anissa. We won't get away with it. I wish Popeye had killed me, too. Oh, God. I can't think."

"I'll think for both of us. Please listen, Randy. You didn't kill David, and you couldn't fight Popeye. He was armed with an ice pick. That's the same as a knife. Do you understand?"

"No."

She heaved a deep sigh. "We'll discuss it later. Are your clothes in the bedroom closet?"

"No. Auntie's closet was filled with flash gear, and we planned to leave early tomorrow. I packed a suitcase. It's in the bedroom."

"Okay. Stay here."

Entering the room, Anissa averted her gaze away from David's broken body. She would pretend this was a scene from her soap. David was a day player. He wasn't dead, just acting.

Vaguely, she recalled performing from her own script, outside a college library. She had been successful, hadn't she?

It wasn't your child, Joe.

David isn't really dead.

Grabbing Randy's suitcase, she bolted from the room.

Anissa drove through downtown Las Vegas, parked, paid for a marriage license, then drove again until she found a white chapel with colorful neon lights. From outside speakers, Sinatra sang about love and marriage going together like a horse and carriage.

She drove a Mustang. It was an omen, right?

Randy repeated his vows as if a script prompter fed him lines. "I, Stuart McNeal, take Anissa Helene Stern Cartier to be my lawfully wedded wife, to love, honor and cherish . . . please, Anissa, I can't do this."

"Yes, you can."

"So help me God."

Barely past noon, the temperature topped one hundred. Vegas shimmered and Randy sweated. He looked so sick, Anissa registered at the Sahara.

They had to walk past a pool where people ate or drank breakfast, and one obese woman shouted, "Ain't that Charl and Adam? Adam looks like he lost a bundle. Did ya lose all your money, Adam?"

When they reached their room, Randy cried himself to sleep in Anissa's arms. Exhausted, she couldn't fall asleep, so she watched TV while her arms grew numb from Randy's weight. Soon the *Morning Star* theme music sounded.

Randy stirred but didn't open his eyes.

Anissa watched her show, taped less than a week ago. Randy, strong and virile, strutted in the midst of exercise equipment. The camera scanned Wayne County's health spa, then pulled in for a close-up; Adam kissing Charl. Everybody agreed that Randy was the best kisser in Soapland. Charl's mouth opened under the onslaught of Adam's lips, and even Anissa could see that Charl lost her breath. Adam tossed his head and laughed.

You'll laugh again, my darling, I promise.

In his sleep, Randy moaned and muttered, "David . . . Popeye . . . ice pick . . . help."

"I'll help," she whispered. "Trust me. I love you."

She eased his head from her shoulder, onto the pillow. Then, reaching for the bedside phone, she had a sudden image of Maxine Graham. Eyes oozing. Skin melting. Skeletal jawbone unhinged as she said, "*Merde,* what a nice surprise. When did Randy switch gears, my dear? I always thought your relationship was more like sister and *brother.*"

Anissa bolted for the bathroom, where, for the second time in twelve hours, she splashed her face with ice-cold water.

Oh, God, she thought. *I can still smell David's blood. No. That's my blood. I've got my damn period.*

Wadding up her shorts, she stuffed them inside the bathroom trash can. Another omen? Hadn't she once stuffed a bloody wedding dress into a gas station's trash can?

Before leaving Vegas, Randy would buy her a new pair of shorts, souvenir shorts, with an I-heart-Vegas logo.

I heart Vegas.

I heart Randy.

She turned on the shower, shed her T-shirt and bra, and stood under the pelting spray. Lathering her body, she sang about love and marriage going together like a horse and carriage. Because she was a soap opera star.

Soap. Opera. Get it?

After her shower, she dug through her purse until she found an emergency tampon.

"Sorry, Senator," she said, "but that's the way the wind blows and the estrogen flows."

Wrapped in a white terrycloth hotel robe, her hair turbaned by a bath towel, she perched on the edge of the bed. As she waited for the operator to place her Maxine, person-to-person call, she suddenly remembered an old Charlie Chan line: *Bad alibi like dead fish. Cannot stand test of time.*

Chapter Fifteen

The restroom had fluorescent lighting.

Standing in front of the mirror, Delly critically inspected her blue jeans and Jon's white shirt, the scalloped edges falling below her knees. Were her long shaggy bangs too childish? How about her curly ponytail?

She had wanted to look like a disturbed teen. Instead, she looked like a 1940's bobby-soxer; a pubescent Shirley Temple. All she needed was cuffed jeans, saddle shoes, and Cary Grant. Then she could be Delilah-Shirley-Temple-Diamond.

Didn't Delilah give Samson his haircut outside some Shirley Temple? For the first time in years, Delly wanted to share her name-joke with her sister. *Old habits never die,* she thought. *They don't fade away, either.*

The audition script called for Pandora to carry a doll, so Delly had picked Raggedy Ann from her collection. Her reading was to take place inside Maxine Graham's office. The office door gaped open. Vance Booker greeted Delly, his right eye blinking unintelligible Morse code.

Judith Pendergraft leaned against a wall, next to a window.

Maxine was short, thin, fidgety, an electric wire searching for a socket. Black hair, frosted with silver, reached the tips of her sharp shoulder blades. She wore a transparent blouse that showed brief cleavage beneath a frilly slip's bodice. The blouse had escaped the waistband of a straight black skirt. Several bracelets encircled her bony wrists. The bracelets jangled as she crushed out her cigarette and immediately lit another.

"This is Echo Foster, Miss Diamond," she said. "Miss Foster will cue you."

Delly recognized Tabby Cat.

"Let's get started," Maxine said.

Echo gave Delly a thumbs-up, then recited the first line. Delly, as Pandora, responded.

"Do you have an agent?" Maxine asked, after the reading.

"No." *Did I blow it?*

"Can we reach you at the number on your résumé?"

"Yes." *Damn, I blew it.*

Maxine shook a new cigarette free from her crumpled pack. Vance fumbled for a lighter. Maxine huffed smoke rings toward Pendergraft.

Judith coughed, and Delly suddenly realized that the writer hadn't acknowledged her presence. In fact, Judith seemed downright bored.

They'd probably offer the part to Amy Irving. Or someone named Irving. Or someone who looked like Amy. Or someone whose name started with the letter A.

For three days Delly wouldn't leave the house. Why hadn't she asked if they'd call, win or lose? Next time she'd pretend Jon was her agent, so he could nudge and end the suspense. "Sorry but your client didn't get the part. She sounded sane and we need crazy."

The Platters were harmonizing "My Prayer" on the radio when Delly heard the front door close—Jon returning from a visit to his health club. In a desperate moment of domesticity, she was kneading a lump of raw hamburger meat. A box of bread crumbs and three eggs decorated her kitchen counter.

She dropped an egg when the phone rang.

"Hello? Hello?" Delly watched goopy yolk drip from the

counter. She listened, said "Okay, thanks," then replaced the wall phone's receiver and stared down at the spattered squares of pebbled tile.

"Aw, Dell," said Jon, "there'll be other parts."

She raised her head. "I got it. I got Pandora. They want me."

"That's great."

"They offered a year's contract. Five hundred and fifty dollars a show. Anissa said fourhundredtwentyfive's minimum."

"Slow down, honey."

"They must have really liked me, Jonny. Vance promised I'd have one show a week for a full year. I start September fifteenth. Math has never been my strong suit. What's five hundred and fifty times fifty-two?"

Jon laughed. "Do you want to celebrate? Call Anissa and her new husband and visit that bar where all the *soap stars* hang out?"

"The Polka-Dot Unicorn?"

"Right."

"Are you serious? I'd probably get drunk, slip on a patch of ice, and break my leg."

Jon glanced through the kitchen window, at the sunny back yard. "Yup. I see what you mean."

"I want to celebrate," she said. "Oh boy, do I ever. Let's make mad, passionate love."

"I should shower first."

"I can't wait that long."

"I didn't shower at the club."

"I don't care." She unbuttoned his shirt and pressed her face against his damp chest. "Yum. You smell like Man."

"I smell like sweat socks. Speaking of enticing aromas, is that a new perfume? Eau de Toilette Ground Beef. I like it, Delly. Very basic. Very me Tarzan, you Jane."

"Anissa says they never used that line in the movie."

"When did you discuss our favorite jungle stud with Anissa?"

"When I delivered a wedding present. It was from both of us."

"And what did *we* give the happy couple?"

"Mark Twain, Nathaniel Hawthorn and Herman Melville."

"I thought they were dead."

"I found a quality edition of works by U.S. authors. The book cost a fortune, but what the heck, it's only money. Anyway, Anissa has this amazing recall for movie lines."

"Yeah. The click thing. I remember."

"Weismuller thumps his chest and says, 'Tarzan.' Then he taps Maureen O'Sullivan on her chest and says, 'Jane.' Tarz had a rather limited vocabulary, but he didn't need words."

"Neither do I." Jon scooped her up in his arms, carried her into the bedroom, placed her on the bed, stripped her jeans, and shrugged off his shirt.

"Hurry," she urged.

"Even Tarz can't make love through denim." Jon unzipped his fly. "What are you doing?"

"Helping. Did your jeans shrink? I want to lick stamps and envelopes. I'm so hot. What's the name for a woman's hard-on?"

"A wet-on?" His mouth covered her breast while one hand crept between her thighs.

"See? I've got such a wet-on. Hurry, Tarz. No. Don't hurry. Yes. Hurry."

Later, with the hamburger meat and broken egg shells still decorating the kitchen counter, they shared a pizza.

"I want to create the best soap character ever," Delly said. "Do you remember my New York acting teacher, Don? The one who came after Madame Sourdellia?"

"Sure. Tall and skeletal. White hair. Yellow teeth from chain smoking. Fingers stained with nicotine."

"People always thought he was Andy Warhol and stopped him on the street for autographs. Don's a fabulous teacher. He takes characters and helps you find a way to make them like real life. The audience can identify and love you or hate you because they recognize themselves in the situation. Do you understand?"

"Not really."

"There are no emotional memories. People don't have them in real life, at least not on the surface. Interesting people don't go around feeling sorry for themselves all the time."

"Sure they do."

"No, Jonny, not interesting people."

"Sorry, but I disagree. I like up-front emotions. I think that's healthy."

She chewed a piece of pizza crust. "Okay, take Pandora."

"I just did. Or did Jane take Tarz?"

"I'm serious. I don't want to create a character dripping with self-pity. Viewers like their TV friends full of hope, no matter how hopeless the situation."

"I thought the soaps presented epic problems so that viewers can believe their own lives aren't so awful."

"No way. Viewers want happy endings, with hugs and kisses."

"So do I. But not always on the screen."

"Sorry. I forgot about *Duck Pond*'s altered concept. Look, there's a fine line. In the soaps the viewers want sex and drama, not pitiful characters. They can't empathize with someone totally pathetic. You wouldn't love me if I whined and wailed all the time."

"I'd cuddle and comfort you."

"That could become tiresome."

"I'd want you to comfort me." He lifted her chin with his index finger. "Isn't it time we got married? Or will your sister stop you?"

"What do you mean?"

"Samantha got married so you won't."

"Sami has nothing to do with it. Anissa once said, 'Most marriages don't add two people together. They subtract one from the other.' "

"Who was she quoting? Elizabeth Taylor? Zsa Zsa Gabor?"

"No. Liz and Zsa Zsa love being married. Anissa quoted James Bond in *Diamonds Are Forever.*"

"Well, marriage or no marriage, I plan to love *my* Diamond forever."

They shared the last slice of pizza, mouth to mouth, teeth to teeth, tongue to tongue. Then, ignoring the goopy egg on the tiles, they sank to the floor and consummated Delly's role as Pandora. Again.

On September thirteenth, an Emmy was presented to Daniel J. Travanti for his leading role in *Hill Street Blues.* Delly, Jon, Anissa and Randy watched the televised special together.

"Travanti attended the University of Wisconsin," Anissa said. "I met him years later, during my college production of *A Streetcar Named Desire.* If anyone deserves his success, Dan does. He's paid his dues."

"Who did you play in *Streetcar*?" Delly asked.

"Blanche, the Vivian Leigh role. My half-brother, Joseph Weiss, played the Brando role."

"Is Joseph still an actor?"

"Joe prefers emoting before a judge and jury. He's a lawyer. I love him to death, but not as much as I love my new husband." Anissa hugged Randy, then stuffed his mouth with popcorn.

The popcorn traveled down his chin, un-chewed, landing in his lap, where his hands rested. Actually, they didn't rest, thought Delly, since Randy constantly clenched and unclenched his fists, pumping them up and down as if he held a couple of weapons. Knives, maybe. Randy sounded normal when he spoke, but his blue eyes looked glazed over. Maybe he was on some kind of drug.

Two days later, Delly stood outside the *Morning Star* studio.

New York would already have the bite of fall in the air, she thought, while California was still summertime, summertime, sum-sum-summertime. Instead of a seasonal nip, there was the nippy anticipation of a new TV season. Which shows would conquer Nielson's nightly ratings? During the day it was *Morning Star* versus *General Hospital.*

The building looked like a film noir creation—dark complexioned, mournful, wicked. Even the sky above had been bleached gray, while in the distance black birds soared like crooked parentheses.

At the studio entrance, a security guard sat inside his booth. Delly scribbled her initials next to her name on the roster. With a Scatman Caruthers smile, the guard waved her through.

My first day as a soap star, she thought. *Twinkle, twinkle, little star.*

She walked down a flight of stairs, turned left, entered through double doors, and was greeted by a cast mural.

Doctors Lizzy and Marshall smiled sincerely. They'd never be sued for malpractice.

Next to Wayne Memorial's staff leaders were Nurse Marybeth and Dr. Ron.

Another group included Caleb, Charlotte—long blonde hair blown by invisible breezes—and Adam. Leaning suggestively against Adam was Hannah.

To the right of Hannah stood Lady Nancine. Then Marlon the Drug Smuggler, scowling attractively.

Mr. Norman, the town's doddering pharmacist, and Malcolm, the black police chief, could have stepped straight from a Norman Rockwell painting. In fact, everyone looked like that.

Even the rock singer, Tabitha Catherine.

Tabby Cat had been painted with short, porcupine-quill hair. A pink streak zigzagged down the middle of her dark spiky strands. Earrings dangled to the top of her jumpsuit. Delly remembered reading opposite Tabby at the audition. Without the wig, Echo Foster's shoulder-length hair was ash-brown.

Delly squinted. There was lots of room for her character. She could see herself standing directly behind Charl and Cal. Charl, Cal, and that crazy kid, Pandora. No, not crazy. The trick was to take the dialogue and make it sound natural, sane, so that viewers would emphasize with that *sick* kid, Pandora.

Saluting the mural, she strolled toward a reception desk. The young woman talking on the phone had Tabby Cat spiked hair, dangling earrings, and she chewed gum like a grazing cow. Delly had met Rosemary twice: Vance Booker's interview and Maxine Graham's audition.

Spying Delly, Rosemary pulled the receiver away from her ear and covered its mouthpiece. "Good luck, kid," she whispered.

A short flight of stairs led to the first floor, which included Vance's office, several writers' alcoves, and a waiting room furnished with comfortable chairs, sofas, and three color televisions, all tuned to various daytime dramas. Delly walked past the waiting room and entered the nearest restroom.

Her stall contained fresh graffiti. MAXINE SUCKS read one notation, to which someone had added COCK. Underneath cock, someone else had scribbled:

I'M CHRISTIAN AND I DON'T WANT TO READ DIRTY WORDS

Under dirty words it said: HOW DO CHRISTIAN COCKS TASTE?

LIKE DREW FLORY

YOU TASTED DREW, CHRISTIAN? LUCKY YOU!

Delly grinned at the graffiti, tucked her Superstar T-shirt inside her green cords, and re-tied her sneakers.

Exiting the restroom, she climbed another flight of stairs, found herself in a hallway, and remembered Anissa saying that part of the old building had once been a sound stage for silent movies. Delly sped past a door lettered PROJECTION ROOM, then Maxine Graham's office.

Next came the dressing rooms and a wardrobe room, jam-packed with clothing racks. Delly saw Tabby Cat's sequined jumpsuits and Lady Nan's fur-trimmed dressing gowns. One rack held nurses' uniforms. White shoes and stockings were scattered underneath.

Right next to Wardrobe was the makeup room. Small cubicles for individual makeup artists lined the walls. At one end, beauty salon sinks looked like gape-mouthed monsters waiting eagerly for hair-wash victims. The area was filled with the hum of conversation. It smelled like talcum powder, shampoo, underarm deodorant and hair spray, especially hair spray.

Delly took a few steps forward. Then she just stood there, frozen, until a familiar eye winked and familiar lips smiled.

"Anissa!" Delly sagged against the door frame. "Thank God."

"Hi, pen-pal. Confusing, isn't it?"

The beautiful actress rose from her chair. Feeling like an eager, tongue-lolling puppy, Delly scampered toward her.

Anissa's blouse had paper toweling for a collar, and her long hair, skewered onto oversized rollers, looked like fat, flaxen caterpillars. Dark liner and sooty lashes enhanced the friendly pussy-willow eyes.

"I'm wondering why I agreed to do this." Delly implored the ceiling, then focused on Anissa again. "I've never been so scared in my life. Maybe they should paint my portrait on the mural downstairs and send me home. I can't remember my lines."

"Relax. We have time before our scenes are shot. I'll show

you around. Randy's here and so is Echo, who told me your audition was spot-on."

"What a great name, Echo. How did she think of it?"

"She didn't. Her parents did."

"It's her real name?"

"Yup. Her mother was pregnant and on vacation, visiting the Grand Canyon. Dad went exploring while Mom rested. Then Mom went into labor and yelled for help. Her voice—"

"Echoed down the canyon. I love it."

The object of their conversation strolled into the makeup room and gave Delly a hug. "You made quite an impression at your reading, Delly. The other auditions were mere formalities."

"Thanks, Echo. I need all the positive feedback I can scrape together for the taping this afternoon."

"I'm not making it up to give you confidence. You should have heard Pendergraft. 'Well, that's that,' she told Maxine. 'We've found our Pandora.' Max puffed on her ciggie. 'Loved the doll, nice touch,' she said, smoke billowing. Judith said, 'I want her, Max.' Vance stopped blinking. Anissa says I talk too much."

"I didn't say you talk too much. I quoted Johnny Carson's comment about Pat Huxley. 'She doesn't need a sharp knife at the dinner table. Pat cuts her food with her tongue.' "

"I take that as a compliment. It's called wit."

"It's called nasty rumor-mongering."

"Whatever. Do I have time to give Delly a survival course?"

"Be my guest, but let her sit in the makeup chair. Marla should arrive any moment to create Pandora's hairstyle."

Delly said, "Who's Marla?"

"Head honcho hairdresser," Echo stage-whispered. "She's having an affair with Marlon. Marla and Marlon. Sounds like two fish fucking."

"Wait a sec," Anissa said. "Last week you told me Marla was

sleeping with Dr. Marsh."

"Nope. I heard Marsh is sleeping with Marybeth, and his wife is lusting after Drew. Everybody lusts after Drew."

"Not me."

"Shit, Anissa, you have Randy. I guess Maxine has Drew, even though she continues to audition male extras in the projection room next to her office. Ah, the scent of old cellulose film. An actor's aphrodisiac."

Anissa frowned. "I wish they'd pack up those ancient reels and send them over to UCLA. Damn fire hazards!"

"I believe the affair between Judith and Zelda has run its course," Echo continued. "Scottie's on the skids. Hey, Delly, watch out for Mr. Norman. He's always peeking at naked boobs. Drew Flory, busy bastard, also has an ongoing affair with that Rosebud model, Maryl Bradley. She sends him suggestive telegrams that sound like steamy romance novels."

"And Tabby Cat is screwing our director, Peter Peterson. We call him Peter-Peter-Pussy-Eater."

"Shut up, Anissa." Echo grinned. "Speaking of pussy, Tabby must get ready now. I'm on before you."

Marla fussed over Delly's hair, finally settling for a duplicate of the audition style: curly ponytail and shaggy bangs.

The wardrobe mistress presented Delly with a blue and yellow, vertically striped housedress. It was too large and very long.

I'll have to develop my character from the inside out, Delly thought. *Clothes won't help.*

Anissa's blue smock was shapeless, as well, but she was tall enough to look chic, despite the unflattering garment. Following her friend, Delly ascended twelve steps until she reached the top floor's cavernous studio.

"Wow," she breathed, awed. "This place is the size of a full New York City block." Glancing up, she instinctively ducked at the sight of dozens of grid lights stretched across the ceiling. "Those spots look like black vultures."

"Our only vulture is Maxine," Anissa said. "See that piece of glass set into the wall at the end of the grids? Behind the glass is a tiny room with miniature TV screens, speakers, and telephone lines. Max supervises the show from there. If she's angry, her voice booms from above and sounds like God. Sometimes you can hear her walking across the set, her heels tapping. It's scary. I'll escort you through Wayne County, Delly, but be very quiet. They're shooting Tabby's scenes."

Anissa nodded toward a set filled with small, round tables, chairs, a bar area and a raised stage. Echo stood on the stage, a microphone held close to her lips. Drew Flory and Nurse Marybeth sat at a ringside table.

"Our club is called The Echo Chamber in a tribute to you know who," Anissa whispered. "Peter named it. Over there is Lady Nan's living room and bedroom set. I wish I could steal some of the authentic antiques."

"God, I love antiques. I plan to spend my salary on collectibles. Jon says I'm nuts but—"

"Shhhh."

"Sorry."

Delly looked left and right, as she and Anissa traveled across the concrete floor. Drugstore, health spa and police station were all portable sets; only the nightclub and mansion permanent. At the very end of the studio was a sparse bedroom with bars at the window, followed by an area filled with colorful plastic furniture and what looked like a nurses' station.

"Those are for our scenes," Anissa whispered. "Bedroom and recreation room in Wayne Memorial's mental ward. By the way, the sets change overnight for the next day's shoot. Take a deep breath, Delly. Echo's scene just wrapped."

"Wrapped," Delly echoed, her mouth dry, her heart beating

against the pulse in her throat.

Anissa's glossy lips turned up in a wicked grin. "Don't be scared. Soon fourteen million people will be introduced to Pandora, roommate to Charl, the all-American slut next door. What's fourteen million people compared to the Super Bowl and the Academy Awards?"

Peter Peterson strolled into view. The director had dark hair, mink-brown eyes, and a drooping Wyatt Earp mustache. He gave Delly a hug.

"Easy scene," he said. "Pandora's introduced to Cal. Cal's investigating the attempted murder of Hannah. He suspects Charl. Cal already knows, from Marybeth, that Pandora's here because of a mental breakdown, after her best friend Robin was killed in a car crash. Then we'll go straight to the next scene, where Charl is happy because Pandora didn't give away her big secret, that she's pretending to be insane. Dialogue, blah, blah, blah, the doll bit. Ready, Delly?"

"You bet."

They walked through the first short sequence.

Drew Flory's even better looking in person, Delly thought. Drew Flory. The name sounded familiar. Good grief. Drew Florentino. Could this hunk be Samantha's teenage crush? Delly would ask him later—if she survived.

She didn't. Her dialogue with Charl was a disaster.

Nervous, forgetting every acting lesson, Delly talked too loud, giggled through every line, and just about rolled her eyes.

I'm acting cliché crazy, she thought, unable to stop.

Delly, Anissa and Peter all turned at the sound of high heels tapping.

"Come with me." Maxine grasped Delly's arm by the elbow.

Delly stumbled alongside the producer, down two flights of stairs, until they entered a small room. The furniture was tacky—an old stuffed couch, card table and chairs, a scarred, scroll-framed wall mirror. Beneath the mirror was a thumb-tacked sign that read: ~~CRITIQUE SESSION~~ BITCH PITCH.

"I don't know what that was, but you just gave the worst impression of insanity I've ever seen," Maxine said. "You were perfect at the audition. Did we make a mistake?"

"I'm sorry."

"Don't apologize, and please don't tell me you'll be better. That's obvious. You couldn't get any worse." Maxine tucked her blouse into the waistband of her skirt. "I've phoned down to the writers. They'll alter the script and delete Pandora's dialogue. She'll just nod her head. While the writers are revising, we'll shoot your scene again. If you repeat the previous performance, we'll tape it a third time. With the new, silent version."

Delly let out the breath she didn't know she'd been holding. "Thank you. Oh, thank you."

The cameraman focused on Delly's green eyes, bright with unshed tears.

Anissa held a floppy rag doll with black button eyes and loops of wooly, red-orange hair.

To ensure her roommate's silence, Charl suggested that she and Pandora become best friends. Charl would take Robin's place in Pandora's heart.

"Best friends don't tell secrets about each other, do they?" Charl held out the rag doll. "If you keep my secret and help me escape from this dreadful hospital, you can play with my baby."

"Do you mean it, Charl? Can . . . may I really play with your baby?"

Eyes wide, a grin splitting her face, Pandora crushed the doll to her chest, held it away for a heartbeat, then kissed its red cloth cheeks.

"My baby," she whispered as the camera zoomed in for a close-up.

Background music reached a crescendo.

Ten days later, fourteen million viewers met and fell in love with Pandora, nicknamed Panda, and Delly learned that Maxine had never phoned down for script revisions. Delly's performance had been achieved through fear and intimidation.

Delly was grateful, but she hated Maxine all the same. With relief, she discovered that everyone else loathed the producer.

Cast members swore that Max would kill for higher ratings. Echo conjured up a backstage phantom named Mr. Ratings, who, she said, would someday kill Maxine Graham.

Chapter Sixteen

The kitchen radio played Billy Joel.

Anissa looked at her *Chien* calendar. Above numerical boxes, an evil cat named Ronnie hung meaty bones on an outdoor Christmas tree. Behind an electrified White House fence stood starving dogs, their tongues lolling.

The caption read: LET THEM EAT BISCUITS.

In a few short weeks, Anissa would celebrate her thirtieth birthday and her five-month wedding anniversary. Replenishing her *Chien* coffee mug, she sat at the kitchen table and let flashbacks flicker.

Upon their return from Vegas, Randy had stood by her side for publicity photos, his arm draped casually across her shoulders. Later she discovered a slight discoloration on her right shoulder—pressure from his fingers.

They received congratulatory letters from Aunt Theresa and both sets of parents. The McNeals, who were back home in Australia, sent their new daughter-in-law a white lambswool sweater.

Helene scribbled her note on flowery stationary. Bobby Hoffman, she wrote, had married a girl named Monica, nicknamed Moose. Young Karl Dietrich was still a bachelor. Joseph Weiss practiced law in Chicago. "I watch MORNING STAR every day," she wrote, "and I don't believe you really meant to poison Hannah."

Jacob was especially effuse with his praise, and Anissa felt a stab of wicked pleasure when Randy read the letter and said, "I can't give you children, roo, can't even try."

"That's okay. I don't want a baby."

"Anissa, remember when you said if we got married you'd never interfere with my lifestyle? I'm giving you the same option. You can be naughty with anyone you choose."

"No, Randy. I'll concentrate on being a good wife and a good mother to Oscar Wilde and Tramp."

"That's us, roo. Cats and dogs may get along but they don't breed. I should have been neutered like your bloody cat. If I had, David—"

"Nothing's changed, Randy. We'll be fine."

They weren't fine. Every night Randy woke screaming. He replayed the murder scene over and over. "What happened to David was not your fault," Anissa kept repeating, over and over.

Every day Randy waited for the newspaper. There was no mention of David. Or Popeye.

Somebody managed to keep the murder under wraps, Anissa thought. Could Popeye have lurked until she and Randy left the beach house? Could he have buried David's body? Even if he had, what about the blood? The shattered mirror? The splintered stereo? The pillow stuffing? Was Popeye an incredibly efficient interior decorator?

Every hour Randy expected to see the flashing lights of a police cruiser pull up to their curb. He listened for the loud knock on their door. "Mr. McNeal, you have the right to remain silent . . ."

Silence prevailed. Nothing happened, and nothing was worse than something.

Randy said, "Why don't the coppers question me? A bloke can't just disappear. Why didn't David's auntie raise an alarm?"

Anissa decided to pay a visit to the beach house. Driving closer, she saw the FOR SALE sign. She parked, climbed the stairs, and pounded on the door. No answer. No neighbors. She jotted down the phone number on the sign, called, and was told that the property was under contract. No, the company wouldn't give out any information about the previous occupants, sorry, goodbye.

We've been incredibly lucky, thought Anissa. *Why can't Randy see that?*

Randy saw nothing, except the TV. His nightmares didn't go away so he sat until dawn, staring hollow-eyed at the screen, clenching and unclenching his fists, as if he held Popeye's lethal ice pick. His muscled body grew slack and his tan faded. By necessity, his role as the health spa instructor diminished. Randy didn't care. Often, he forgot his lines while everyone else adlibbed. He could still kiss. He was still the best kisser in Soapland. The ultimate irony, Anissa thought.

Maxine sat behind her cluttered office desk. "*Merde,* Anissa," she said. "Since your marriage, Randy has thrown his career down the toilet. Is a straight relationship too stressful?"

Here we go again. Anissa coughed to hide her hesitation. *Please, God, help me think of a believable it's-not-your-child-Joey lie.*

"We're fine," she replied. "I was practically living with Randy before we got married."

"Then what's with this depression bit? After your Vegas surprise, following all that delicious publicity, Judith and I talked about beefing up Adam's part." Maxine lit a cigarette and blew smoke rings toward the projection room window. "Of course, that's impossible now."

"Randy doesn't gab about his personal life, Max, but I guess I can tell you. We want a baby. Randy had his sperm checked. It's low. Don't worry, this will pass. Give him time."

"Time is the one thing we can't afford to give. We've had letters. Soap fans are so fickle, my dear." Her ashes missed the ashtray and dotted the untidy pile of papers scattered across her desk. "Say la vee. Adam has to go. Randy's fired. Would you tell him, Anissa? I don't want to hurt his feelings, especially when he's so depressed."

Drew Flory discovered Anissa, huddled on her knees inside the deserted Wardrobe room. She cried so hard, her whole body shook. Kneeling, he grasped her by the shoulders. "What is it? Are you sick? Hurt?"

"Go 'way."

"Slow down and breathe." Drew shook her gently, wondering if he should slap her face. Before he could raise his hand, she crumpled, falling forward, her hot tears soaking his pant leg. He leaned over, covering her body with his, holding her tightly.

Finally, inevitably, the painful sobs became small shudders, the shudders occasional quivers. Drew shifted, sitting with his back propped against the wall. He settled Anissa in his lap, her head resting beneath his chin.

"Sorry," she gasped. "I haven't cried like that in years."

"Do you want to talk about it? My sister Maryl says I'm a good listener."

"Not now, Drew, please. Maybe later." A ghost of a smile curved her lips. "Maryl Bradley? She's your sister?"

"Yes."

"Romantic telegrams," she whispered.

"What did you say? I couldn't hear you."

"I've got to go home, Drew, but I'm so tired I can't move." Her long lashes fluttered. "God, I'm cold. Maxine made me cold." She snuggled closer. "I wish Echo's phantom, Mr. Ratings, really did exist."

Drew hummed softly. After a while he looked down at Anissa's flushed face. Even asleep, her beautiful mouth trembled with every breath, and he wanted to destroy whomever had caused those tears. Was it Randy? Aussie bastard! No, wait. She said Maxine made her cold. What had Max done to her?

I could kill that bitch in cold blood!

Since murder was against the law, Drew used every ounce of his star status to convince Maxine that Judith should write Adam off on vacation, leaving the door open for reinstatement. Then he responded to Anissa's impulsive thank-you kiss with a barely audible, "No big deal." Because he would gladly slay fire-breathing dragons for her, and Maxine was merely a tiny dragon, puffing cigarette smoke through her nostrils.

Unfortunately, the indefinite hiatus had an unpredictable result. Randy now stayed inside the apartment day and night.

Anissa had never relinquished her half of the duplex, so she suggested that Randy cut through the connecting walls and create one large complex. "You can produce, direct, even star in any production you choose," she said. "Use my apartment as a rehearsal hall. Jon Griffin has a file full of original plays. He wrote lots of stuff before he hit with *Duck Pond Sonata.*"

"That's a ripper plan," Randy said.

During the next few days he sketched blueprints for the building's conversion, penned lists of actors who might be interested in the project, and read through Jon's scripts.

Anissa congratulated herself, then awoke one morning to find the blueprints and list of actors crumpled, tossed into the kitchen trash can. Clenching and unclenching his hands, Randy sat in front of the TV.

After her taping at the studio, she hurried home. When her schedule called for a day off, she puttered around the apartment—cleaning, dusting, preparing tempting meals. One night she discovered that Randy furtively fed the gourmet tidbits to Oscar. The little dog grew fat.

"Anissa, shove off!"

For once the TV was silent. Randy sat on the sofa, a crossword puzzle in his lap, his fingers clutching a pencil like a bloody ice pick. Anissa had been dusting his rock collection. Now, as if for the first time, she noticed his sunken eyes and the dark pockets underneath.

"Why don't you take a nap, darling?" she said. "You've got pouches under your eyes, big as a roo's."

"Belt up, Anissa. Please."

"You have to snap out of this, Randy, see a psychiatrist."

"What's the point?"

"You can talk to him about what happened."

"I know what happened. I killed David."

"You didn't kill David!"

"I wouldn't believe we were being followed. I opened the beach house door. I'm responsible."

"No, Randy. That's why you have to see a doctor."

"This isn't working." He raked his fingers through his hair. "Please, darlin', shove off."

"I could go grocery shopping. Would you like something special for dinner tonight?"

"Forget groceries, Anissa. Ring up Drew Flory."

"What does Drew have to do with anything?"

"I'm not a dill. I watch *Morning Star* every day. You two are mad for each other."

"Randy, I've never—"

"I know. That's what I mean. You've got to leave me alone. I can't stand all this bloody kindness. Drew loves you, Anissa. Why let me screw up your life?"

"You're not screw—"

"If you leave me alone, I'll see your quack."

"Quack?"

His lips twisted into the semblance of a smile. "Doctor. I'll visit your bloody shrink."

"Promise?"

"I'll end this nightmare, and that's a promise. Do me a favor and move into the apartment next door? I need to sort things out."

"Okay, Randy, we'll try it your way."

Anissa's life settled into a new pattern. She would meet with Drew and Delly to study lines and rehearse scenes. She slept in her old apartment. The Christmas holidays approached so she invaded Randy's living room, stringing Christmas cards across the fireplace mantel, decorating a tiny tree with silver tinsel and red velvet bows. Randy even agreed to attend the Jonah Wiggins New Year's Eve celebration party, a coveted invite.

Christmas Eve was lucky, thought Anissa. By December twenty-fourth, Randy would have exorcised his demons.

Meanwhile, her husband seemed happier, healthier. The TV no longer played. Instead, Randy spent his time writing inside a loose-leaf notebook. Discarded pages were shredded so completely, Anissa couldn't decipher his notations. He hadn't seen a "quack" yet, but his writing was just as therapeutic.

Wasn't it?

Feeling stupidly superstitious, she unwrapped a new *Chien* calendar; one of Drew's Christmas presents. January depicted the puppy, Bootsie, looking up at a shelf filled with boxes of dog biscuits. The biscuits were just out of reach and the caption stated: DON'T BE TOO OPTIMISTIC. IT'S IMPOSSIBLE TO SMILE AND WHISTLE AT THE SAME TIME.

Twelve days before Christmas, on a nasty overcast afternoon, Anissa squinted toward the sky from her seat in Drew's black Porsche convertible.

"After Wisconsin," she said, "I can't get used to California weather at Christmas time. I want the sting of snowflakes landing on my face, catching in my lashes. I crave the smell of wet woolen mittens and knitted mufflers. I long for the ambiance of a sharp chill in the air. And I feel like barfing every time I see Santa Claus in a pair of jogging shorts."

Drew grinned. "Are you pensive or grumpy?"

"Randy would say I was grizzling. I guess it's my bloody car needing repairs again. I should buy a new car like you did, Drew. I have the money. But Randy says my Mustang is a classic, and, well, it's aged well. Physically, I mean. It's more beautiful now than the day I first drove it." Anissa scratched at a small hole in her jeans, breaking a fingernail. "Why is the sky so murky?"

Drew grinned again. "This may sound profound, and I could be wrong, but I think it's because it's going to rain."

"I don't mind snow but I hate rain." She pictured a young girl seated on a University of Wisconsin courtyard bench, her red sweatshirt drenched, her regal braids dripping rainwater. "Grizzle, grizzle, grizzle. Bitch, bitch, bitch."

"Speaking of bitches, are you aware that Maxine and Judith have slanted the scripts toward a Cal-Charl love affair?"

"But Charl's stuck inside Wayne Memorial's mental ward."

"When has locale ever stopped a love affair? Max says the ratings will soar."

"Bloody ratings."

"Ratings make the world go round."

"I thought love made the world go round."

"Not for Maxine." Drew pulled his Porsche against the curb. "We've arrived, Charl. See you tomorrow."

"Thanks for the lift, Cal. I'll check on Randy. If you linger a few minutes, I'll retrieve Jon's scripts. I keep forgetting to give them back to Delly. You're driving past her house, aren't you?"

"Yup. I'll wait right here, honey."

I'll wait forever.

Those three words came to mind as he watched the leggy actress scamper down the path.

It started to rain a split second before he heard Anissa's desperate screams. Racing toward the duplex, he could distinguish a few disjointed sentences.

"Untie the rope. I can't reach. Oh, God. His poor, tortured neck. Joey! Drew! Somebody, anybody, help!"

Randy's notebook included a will, leaving everything to Anissa. One page listed specific instructions for his funeral. Other pages contained muddled notes to David. Randy wrote the scene at the beach house as a short story, changing the ending so that he and David overpowered Popeye, then used the pick to chip away at a block of sculpted ice.

After filling their glasses with Drambuie, Stuart said, "Let's make a toast."

"Alfy word, toast," David replied. "It sounds like burnt bread."

Those were the last words on the last page. Then Randy hanged himself in the same bathroom where he had once wrapped Anissa inside a fluffy pink towel.

Dry-eyed, she attended the memorial service. Dry-eyed, she torched fireplace logs, burned the Christmas cards and tree, and systematically pulled prints and posters from the wall, adding them to the blaze. The Marx Brothers lost their silly grins. Snow White, Prince Charming, and seven dwarfs sacrificed themselves on the flaming pyre. Gregory Peck and Rock Hudson soon joined the mélange.

Drew watched passively, but gathered her into his arms when she began to discard the Montgomery Clift movie stills.

"Let me go," she said.

"Burning Clift won't bring Randy back."

"I don't want to bring him back. He's reconciled, peaceful."

"Jesus, Anissa, do you believe death conciliatory?"

"Yes. No. Maybe. Don't fret, Drew. I'd never commit suicide, mainly because I'm not sure I accept the concept of heaven and hell."

Releasing her, he glanced at the fireplace. "Let's stop burning stuff and head out for something to eat."

"I'm not hungry."

"I know, honey, but food is one of the first steps toward overcoming suffering."

"You s-sound like m-my m-mother."

Convinced that Anissa was finally going to cry, Drew extended his arms.

"I'm not going to cry," she said. "I'm too angry. Randy had no right to leave me alone."

"You're not alone," Drew said, his voice very soft.

For five days Anissa played Charl with habitual ease. Her expression altered for the cameras. Afterwards, her eyes resumed their haunted stare and her face looked like rigid white marble. Drew couldn't break through her shell. He prayed for a repeat of the wild-weeping episode inside the Wardrobe room, a therapeutic cry, but it never happened.

Maxine sent Anissa to Wisconsin, a promotional tour. "I'm not insensitive," she told Judith. "We'll shoot around Charl while Anissa recuperates in the friggin' bosom of her family."

Chapter Seventeen

Madison definitely had the ambiance of sharp chills in the air. Temperatures dipped below zero. Salvation Army Santas wore thermal underwear underneath shabby red velveteen. Inside black boots, their toes froze. Duetsch Department Store sold out of every pair of mittens, every earmuff, every jacket, every woolly sock in stock.

University of Wisconsin students skated on Lake Madison, then drank coffee and 3.2 beer inside the well-heated Rathskeller.

Newspapers headlined people freezing to death because they couldn't pay their electric bills.

At Hillhouse, radiators hissed. Fireplace wood sizzled when snow fell down the chimney. The entire bottom floor reeked of singed hot chocolate. Steamy, lavender-scented water permeated the upstairs. Helene's bedroom had so many electric heaters plugged into wall sockets, Anissa thought her mother's TV might short-circuit. But luckily—or unluckily—it didn't.

On *Morning Star,* Cal wrapped up the Marlon/Lady Nancine smuggling caper. Marlon died in a shoot-out, then—surprise!—came back on Christmas day as his twin brother. The whole cast sang jingle bells (*oh, what fun*) except Charl and Pandora, who "celebrated" the holidays inside Wayne Memorial's mental ward. During the party, Hannah tried to seduce Cal, who obsessed over Charl's absence.

Helene watched the show obsessively. Corpulent, her hair

still styled like Mamie Eisenhower, she expressed sorrow for Adam's death.

"My husband's name was Randy, Mama. Stuart Randy McNeal."

"Do you think Adam exercised too much, dear? I read somewhere that too much exercise can cause heart attacks."

Jacob's body was wizened, his face a map of wrinkles. He asked Anissa if Randy had impregnated her before he "kicked the bucket." When she said no, Jacob didn't even bother to hide his disappointment.

Invitations were issued for a January birthday party.

Anissa dreaded the event, but remained silent because Helene wanted to "show Charl off."

I'm not Charl, Mama. I'm your daughter, Mama. I'm a juju, Mama.

"Holy shit, I'll bet that's real gold." Bobby Hoffman ran his thumb across the embossed letters that embellished Anissa's birthday-party invitation.

He tried to wipe away a greasy fingerprint, smudging the invitation even more, then carefully leaned it against two ceramic figures saved from the top of a wedding cake. The miniature groom wore a black tuxedo and stovepipe hat. The bride's foot had been broken in a fall from the bureau to the wood-planked floor. Monica had glued the bride's foot back on—backwards.

Rather than a wedding picture, the bureau sported a black and white photo of Roy Rogers. "I love Roy," Monica had once said, "because he stuffed Trigger. Ain't that a hoot?"

Owls hooted, thought Bobby, turning away from Roy's photo. Focusing on his wife, he said, "You can't wear that outfit to a fancy party."

"The hell I can't." Monica looped a Garrison belt through

her brown chinos. A yellow plaid shirt struggled to contain her breasts. Her stomach bulged above the tight belt as she bent forward and tucked her pegged cuffs inside her pointy-toed boots. "I ironed my pants and shirt good, Bobby Bear, and polished my boots. Ain't you proud as punch?"

I'd like to punch your freaking stomach!

He stared at Monica's belt buckle. "You gotta' have a nice dress somewhere. I wore my suit," he said, flaunting blue pants and jacket, a white shirt, and a black bow tie.

"I saved my wedding gown inside a garment bag." She nodded toward the bedroom closet.

Wish I could zip you up inside your garment bag. It's plastic, ain't it? How long would it take you to suffocate?

"Do ya want I should wear my wedding gown, Bobby?"

It wouldn't fit, you stupid bitch.

"Of course not, Moose," he said. "Maybe a prettier blouse and skirt. Please? For me?"

"No way, José. I don't have to get all fancied up to meet one of your old hoo-ors."

Hoo. Hoot. Monica looked like an owl with her short brown hair, round eyes and beaky nose. When they had wed, fifteen or twenty pounds ago, Bobby's friends had made sly remarks about his new bride's oversized titties, and he had practically burst through his Fruit of the Looms.

"Nissa ain't no whore," he said.

"Funny how she never mentions you in all them magazine articles, Bobby. *TV Guide* never said one itty-bitty word."

"They didn't say one word 'bout Karl Dietrich neither, and she married him."

"That husband of hers who just died was some looker. I woulda had him stuffed." Monica laughed.

Bobby glanced around. Covering their walls were animal heads, mounted on wooden plaques. At first the unusual decor had fed his lust. Now it made him want to puke.

"Nissa don't talk about us to reporters 'cause we were kids," he said, staring into the marbled eyes of a full-grown buck. Bambi's father?

"Oh, pardon silly me," Monica huffed. "I forgot how you was brought up in that hoity-toity house."

"Aw, Moosie, don't. I married you. I . . . I love you."

I'd love to see you hanging from the light fixture, your throat cinched by that stupid belt. I'd love to see your head mounted on the wall.

"Why don't we stay home tonight, Bobby Bear? I bought me some new lon-jur-ray."

"Are you crazy? I . . . we . . . you've got to meet Nissa."

"Why? 'Cause you once had the hots for her?"

"She had the hots for me!"

"Bullshit! I seen her on TV, buster. She's got class, like a princess. You ain't her type."

Bobby's chipped tooth flashed. "We were in love. But Jacob laughed when I told him I wanted to marry Nissa. So she got stuck with that drunken asshole, Karl. Then she married some faggot actor."

"Fag? You gotta be kidding. Her actor was more man than you. I seen him on TV, pumping iron. You won't exercise. You won't even go hunting."

"I hunt up dead cars and fix 'em." He glanced toward the stuffed trophies and felt his guts knot. "I think hunting with a high-powered rifle sucks."

"If we stay home tonight, I'll let you suck." Unsnapping her top buttons, she thrust forth her breasts.

Bobby ignored his wife. "Jacob didn't think I was good enough for Nissa. Well, I done great. Got myself the biggest car repair shop in Madison."

"Should we skip the party, Bobby?" Monica's eyes blinked

owlishly. "You want I should put on my new lon-jur-ray?"

"Snap your shirt, Moose. Your tits are hangin' out."

Karl Dietrich Jr. had ordered a subscription to *Playboy,* but he used his father's name because they gave doctors a rate-break.

Doctors always got rate-breaks, even though Karl couldn't understand why any pragmatic practitioner would want Miss January hanging 'round his office. Unless he was a baby doctor and he needed a man to donate sperm.

Placing the magazine on the kitchen counter, Karl poured another three fingers of Wild Turkey, gulped it down, belched twice, then dropped the plastic tumbler and clutched his belly. *Forgot to insulate my stomach. Shame on me.*

He staggered to the refrigerator, tugged at the handle until it opened, and drank straight from a milk carton. "Anissa once said that Wisconsin's a goddamn dairy state," he muttered, white liquid dripping from his mouth, staining his green and gold Packers sweatshirt. *Shit, sour! The milk's sour! Oh, God!*

Dropping the carton, he watched white globs puddle on the linoleum. A rancid smell invaded the kitchenette. Retching, he turned toward the sink. Tears streamed down his face while mucus ran from his nose.

He filled the sink with water and lemon-scented Joy, hoping the detergent would dispel the milk odor. Then he filled a new tumbler with whiskey. *Shame on me!* His hands shook and the Turkey sloshed and he had a feeling he'd soiled his underpants.

"What the hell, have to change my clothes anyways." Turning slightly, he focused on a Mickey Mouse wall clock. "I've been drinking since three this afternoon, Mickey. Hey, it's nearly seven. Time flies when you're having fun. I swore I wouldn't drink till Anissa's party. Hey, Father and Mother will be knocking on my door soon. Do I have time to shower? I'd better. Hey, maybe I should squirt Joy under my armpits."

Karl staggered toward his bathroom. "Joy to the world," he sang, "my armpits stink."

After washing and toweling his pudgy body, he put on a Jonah Wiggins shirt and a gray wool suit. Then he lassoed his neck with a pre-knotted, poinsettia-patterned tie. His hair had thinned so much the scalp showed through. His eyes looked bloodshot so he poured half a bottle of Visine over the pupils, blinking at the sting. Swiveling left and right, he stared into the mirror. Shit on a shingle! Anissa would soon see a fat failure who had flunked out of medical school and who now lived above his parents' garage. Ostensibly, he was his father's Office Assistant, a glorified nurse who wore soft-soled shoes.

"When I'm completely shit-faced," he told his reflection, "I'll dream that my ex-bride is dead, on top of a slab, with a tag tied 'round her big toe. To Anissa, from Karl. I'll dream I'm performing an autopsy. First, I'll cut up her beautiful January breasts."

Fondling his erection, Karl recited the months of the year. In his head, he pictured body parts and Playmates. April looked like Anissa.

He filled a toothpaste-encrusted glass with tap water and swallowed a Quaalude.

Shame on me!

A diamond birthday bracelet sparkled from Anissa's wrist as she wended her way down the long staircase. She wore a dark gray velvet gown with crimson puff sleeves because she knew that Randy wouldn't want her to wear black. "Jerry Lewis was right when he said that funny had better be sad somewhere," she murmured, gazing toward the funny-sad people clothed in formal attire.

"Nissa *does* look like a princess!" Bobby entered the house, Monica by his side, just in time to watch Anissa's slow descent. "She's even wearing a crown."

"That ain't no crown," Monica said. "It's a tee-aira."

"At least she didn't dress in pants and boots." Bobby hurried away from his wife. "Nissa," he said, meeting her at the landing, reaching out to give her a worshipful touch.

Anissa blinked, and for a brief moment her fragile exterior shell cracked. Childhood memories flickered. She recoiled, stepping backwards, nearly falling. Then, abruptly, she turned toward her mother, who sat in an oversized wheelchair.

By Helene's side stood Karl, Jr. Returning his soft hug, Anissa was unable to comprehend the expensive suit. Instead, she pictured him in white pajamas with red hearts and Cupids.

"Merr' Chris'mas," Karl slurred. He pictured her wearing a tag tied 'round her dead toe—To Anissa, From Karl—and without another word, he lumbered toward the downstairs bathroom.

Ignoring Karl's strange behavior, Helene said, "How do you like your party, Charl? Are you having a good time?"

"The party's fine, Mama. Thank you."

"Lady Nancine's party didn't have as much food as our party, and Hannah shouldn't flirt with Cal. He's *your* boyfriend."

"Yes, Mama. Please excuse me, Mama. I'm thirsty."

Bobby intercepted her at the mahogany sideboard, directly in front of the cut-glass punch bowl. Once again, she abruptly turned toward another group of guests.

Bobby's face flushed at the sound of Monica's derisive laughter. Angry, frustrated, he grabbed her fur-lined parka, propelled her out the front door, dragged her down the path, and shoved her inside their red Corvette.

"Where's your jacket, Bobby Bear? You'll freeze your balls off."

"Shut up, Moose."

"She didn't say one itty-bitty word to you. Nissa, you said, your mouth full of sugar, and your big TV star didn't even know you."

"Shut up!" Ignoring the stick shift, Bobby yanked at Monica's belt buckle. Then he peeled her chinos and panties down to her boots.

"Atta' boy," she urged. "Didn't you have no fun at your fancy party?"

"You're asking for it."

"You're lucky somebody asks for it. Guess Nissa don't have the hots for you no more, huh? Can you get it up, Bobby Bear?" She snorted. "That's what I thought. Let's go home and I'll put on my new lon-jur-ray."

Inside Hillhouse, Anissa wandered through the room.

"No, the writers haven't told me how Charl will escape from the hospital," she kept repeating.

Later she could recall nothing about the party, except the image of Karl in pajamas, until the front door opened and a tall man entered. Joe's face was older while an unfamiliar mustache shaded his Voight-Redford lips.

By his side stood a tiny Asian woman, her black hair styled in a pixie cut. Grasping Anissa's hand, she said, "We were so sorry to hear about your loss, Mrs. McNeal. Joe wanted to send you a letter, but we decided to tell you in person when Jacob insisted we attend your party."

"Thank you. Please call me Anissa."

"And I'm Kathy. Kathy Wong-Weiss."

Joe put his arms around both women, guiding them away from the doorway. "You never heard about my marriage," he said. "I assumed Helene would tell you. I'm so sorry, angel. I sent an announcement to your studio since I don't have your home address."

"I rarely get my studio mail." Turning toward Kathy, Anissa said "Congratulations" and hugged the smaller woman. Then she faced Joe again. "Have you become a famous lawyer yet?"

"No. I'm an ordinary attorney, working for Chicago's Civil Liberties Union. That's where I met Kathy. But we plan to move to your neck of the woods soon."

"Joe just passed the California bar exam," Kathy said.

"So did she," Joe said, his voice oozing pride. "We're going into private practice, Weiss and Wong-Weiss. I don't see my father much, Anissa. I've paid back my tuition and—"

"You can't be serious, Joey. Jacob owed you much more than an education. I hate him. Don't you?"

"Since I don't work for him, Jacob owes me nothing, and I can't hate him. He's become so old and powerless."

"I must greet our hostess," Kathy said over her shoulder, as she walked toward Helene's wheelchair.

"Your wife's sweet, Joey. I'm happy for you."

"Thanks, angel. Are you all right?"

"Remember when I told you about The Kaiser and Dolf?" At his nod, she whispered, "I'm a juju."

"That's ridiculous. You didn't kill the cats."

"I killed our baby and my husband."

"No, Anissa. Jacob was responsible for the abortion and—"

"Don't you understand? I failed Randy."

"How did you fail him?"

"I don't know. But I must have, 'else why'd he die?"

"Anissa, there's a reason for everything. I realize that's hard to accept, but it will become easier, I promise. After Jacob told me about my mother, I loved and hated her at the same time. Now, I just love her."

Reaching into his pocket, he pulled out a small box. "Happy birthday. Kathy picked this out, but the inscription's mine." From another pocket, he retrieved a pad and pen. "Give me your phone number. I'll call when we arrive in California." He wrote down the number. "What's that Jack Paar thing you used to quote all the time?"

"Paar said, 'To restore a sense of reality, I think Walt Disney should have a Hardluckland.' "

"Right. Please remember that I love you."

"I love you too, Joey."

As he headed toward Kathy, Anissa retreated up the stairs to her bedroom. Opening her birthday package, she removed a flat gold charm, shaped like an angel. It was inscribed: TOGETHER WHEREVER WE GO.

She scribbled a note to Helene, signed it Anissa/Charl, and placed it on her pillow. Her coat hung inside the downstairs closet so she mashed her puffed sleeves under a blue cardigan, called a cab from her bedroom phone, walked down the back staircase, and slipped out a side entrance.

Goodbye, Senator. Joey may be able to forgive you, but I can't. Goodbye, Mama. See you from the telly.

The cab ride was a blur. The flight to Chicago then LAX was a blur. Her watch looked blurry, but it had to be around three A.M. when she knocked on Drew's door.

He answered her frantic pounding with a muffled oath. His body was draped in a blanket, his hair mussed, and his sleepy black eyes registered anger, then confusion.

"May I come in?" she asked, her voice hoarse.

"Of course. What happened?" Ushering her inside, Drew studied Anissa's flushed face. Her eyes were too bright. Her hair escaped a tiara, falling down her back in long rat-tails.

"Jacob. Party. Joey." She wanted to say more, but her teeth kept chattering.

Belting her bathrobe, a tall, slender woman entered the living room.

"You have company," Anissa managed. "I'm sorry, Drew. I couldn't go back to the duplex. Delly's taking care of my cat.

Echo adopted Oscar. The apartment's em-empty, and I didn't know where else to g-go."

"I'm not company. I'm Drew's sister, Maryl. You must be Anissa. Oh my God!" Maryl ran forward and supported the swaying figure while Anissa, at long last, burst into tears. "Drew, she's burning up with fever. Here, take her while I find some extra blankets. Yours will do for a start. Never mind the blushes. I've seen you naked."

Scooping Anissa up in his arms, hearing her sobs, feeling her tears scorch his bare chest, Drew followed his sister's red hair toward the bedroom.

For three days Drew and Maryl took turns sponging Anissa's body with cold cloths, force-feeding her hot tea, chicken broth and antibiotics.

On the fourth day she opened her eyes, finally fever free, and saw Drew sitting in a chair by the side of the bed.

"You need a shave," she rasped. "Maxine'll be pissed."

"Don't ever do that again. You scared the hell out of me. Why on earth would you leave Wisconsin in the dead of winter . . ." He took a deep breath, but it didn't help. "Why were you wearing a stupid sweater?"

"The sweater isn't stupid, Drew. I was stupid."

"What were you thinking?"

"You. I was thinking you."

Rising, he turned and walked across the room. Anissa saw his broad shoulders shake. "Are you crying?" When he didn't answer, she struggled to the edge of the bed, lowered her feet, and tentatively found the carpet with her toes. As she took a few steps forward, Maryl's nightgown brushed her ankles.

Drew made an about-face. Tears streamed down his cheeks. "Anissa, get back in bed!"

"I was thinking you," she repeated. "I was cold on the outside, burning hot on the inside, and it wasn't my fever. I heard you call my name. I felt you reaching out, hugging me, even when my plane flew through a storm. I hate rain. I'm afraid of rain. But then I heard your voice."

Swiftly crossing the room, Drew pulled her into the circle of his arms. She felt fragile, a crystal vase, yet there was an inner core of strength. He remembered how, as a boy, he had watched a willow during a violent storm. The wind had whipped branches, leaves had swirled, and the tree had arched, bent nearly to the ground. Holding his breath, he'd waited for the wood to snap. But it hadn't. After the storm blew away, the willow stood erect again—nude, strong, proud.

Anissa sighed. "Maybe I imagined your voice."

"No. You didn't. I've loved you silently for such a long time, but that night I called out your name, in my sleep. Maryl woke me and we talked. Then I went back to bed and dreamed you stood outside my door. Only it wasn't a dream. When you began to cry, reality set in, and I realized that you were my whole world."

She felt his unshaven chin caress her forehead. "Randy wanted us to be together. He said you loved me."

"I don't think I've ever *not* loved you. Do you love me?"

"Yes. Oh, yes."

"Welcome to my world." He pressed her face against his heart. "Welcome home, Anissa."

"Drew?"

"Yes?"

"Make love to me."

He stroked her hair. "That's not a good idea, honey. You're still very weak."

"Then I'll take a rain check. You see, I'm not afraid of the rain anymore."

Chapter Eighteen

Wearing beige shorts and a white sleeveless blouse, Delly sat at Jon's desk.

Her brain played hopscotch.

Hop. In an old movie they would show how the months passed by ripping pages from a calendar. Usually, there'd be background music.

Skip. September, October, November, December, January, February, March, April, May. Now it was June. Delly had played Pandora for nine months, and she felt as if she'd given birth to a monster, or at least a monstrous problem.

Jump. Maxine had the option of renewing contracts every thirteen weeks. Judith Pendergraft dictated to Maxine, so Delly had spent three more evenings at Judith's Brentwood home.

Hop, skip, jump!

Like an overweight train, *Morning Star* chugged along. As Pandora's dependency on Charl grew stronger, Charl became more manipulative. Hannah had survived the poison attempt, so Charl made elaborate plans to escape from the hospital. She would kill Hannah again, then sneak back inside. Pandora would provide an air-tight alibi.

"No problem," Delly told Jon one morning, over a home-cooked breakfast of rare bacon and fossilized eggs. "All Charl has to do is steal a key to the supply closet, pilfer a nurse's uniform, break out of the hospital in the dead of night, and abduct a staff member's car from the parking lot. Meanwhile,

Pandora hides the gun, knife, poison, whatever, inside her baby."

"Baby?"

"Her doll."

Like a paint-by-numbers picture, various elements of the plot emerged slowly. Nine months. Delly felt like a stale piece of bread in a moldy loaf.

No, not bread. Twinkies. Drew had once said that roaches, Styrofoam and Twinkies would survive after the world was nuked.

Twinkie, twinkie, little star.

Dropping her ball-point pen, Delly crumpled another piece of paper. How come Jonny could create brilliant monologues while she couldn't even write her own name? Except for calendar pages, stale bread, and twinkie stars, her mind was blank.

She glanced through the window, staring at the familiar scenery, focusing on her elderly neighbor, Mrs. Grady, who was walking, or being walked, by her Shepherd-Collie. The large dog halted to water the palm tree at the edge of Delly's front yard. Mrs. Grady wore a long blue dress and a hat festooned with artificial flowers. Even though the sky was sunny, cloudless, a black umbrella crooked Mrs. Grady's arm. Suddenly, a jogger jogged by. The dog barked and propelled himself forward. Mrs. Grady's feet nearly left the ground. She looked like a surreal Mary Poppins. Then the street became empty, silent, a Hollywood set waiting for the director to yell, "Three, two, one, action!"

"What are you doing?" Entering the living room, Jon shook his thick hair, still glistening from a health club shower.

"I'm so glad you're home, Jonny. This is impossible."

"What's impossible?" Scooping up several discarded scraps from the floor, he tossed them toward a wicker trash basket.

"I'm sorry about the mess, honey. I started fooling around,

trying to devise Hannah's murder weapon. Gun, knife, sharp chopsticks. Then I tried to think of a background for Pandora, but it's not working." She sighed. "I can't write my way out of a paper bag."

"What's with the background? You've been playing the part for months."

"I know. But Pandora's merely a tape recorder that Charl talks into. All the other characters have backgrounds, even Marlon's twin brother. I should give Pandora a history so I can know her better, act her better."

"Okay, I get the gist. Would you like to brainstorm with me? A variation of the dialogue game?"

"That would be great, Jonny. Thanks."

"Come away from my desk. Plunk your curvy rump on top of your director's chair. Good girl." Jon hunkered down, directly in front of her knees. "Does Pandora have a last name?"

"No. Just a nickname. Panda."

"Let's make her last name Chinese."

"Why not Greek?"

"It could be Greek, I suppose—the Muse and all—but the panda comes from the mountainous regions of China and Tibet. How do you feel about Panda Wang?"

"That's a good soap name, but I prefer Panda Chan. I love Chan movies and Anissa quotes Charlie all the time."

"I've changed my mind, Delly. We don't want a Chinese name. You'd have to look ethnic."

"Anissa calls Charl the all-American slut next door. Maybe Panda should be the all-American mental case. Pandora Lizzie Borden. Panda Borden took an ax, gave her mother forty whacks. When she saw what she had done—"

"She gave dear Hannah forty-one."

"No. Charl's supposed to knock off Hannah. I'll suggest an ax. What a great weapon, all that blood. Gosh, where can they hide an ax? Maybe Mr. Ratings will find Charl's ax and knock off Maxine."

Jon walked into the kitchen and returned with a couple of ice-cold beers. "Didn't we once look up our zodiac signs on the back of a menu?"

"Yup. You were born under the sign of the tiger. You are sensitive, emotional, and capable of great love. I'm the snake. Rich in wisdom and charm. Whoa. Are you saying I should call myself Pandora Snake? I hate snakes." She shuddered.

"Weren't there examples, on the menu I mean, of famous people born under various signs?"

"Yes. I remember because some were so relevant. Caruso was born under the sign of the rooster, Davy Crockett the horse. Your tiger included Mary, Queen of Scots. She lost her head."

"I won't lose mine. I want to be rich, not royal. Let's see. Your sign included Lincoln, Darwin, Edgar Allan—"

"Poe! Pandora Poe. I like it, Jonny."

"Okay, honey, Pandora Poe it is. Now, let's create your background."

Delly gazed up at Jon. "I want Pandora normal. That's very important."

"Define normal."

"Well adjusted. Reasonably sane. That way her craziness is more traumatic."

"Okay, normal childhood. Your parents produced two and a half children. Mom's a school teacher. Dad's civil service. Mortgaged home. An Irish setter named Big Red."

"How about a Cocker Spaniel named—"

"Joe Cocker?"

"Very funny. The normal family would call its dog Lassie or Spot. Come to think of it, what average family would name their daughter Pandora?"

"Mom's an English teacher. Are you sure you want normal,

Delly? Closet skeletons are much more fun."

"Pandora got sick when her best friend was killed. I'll settle for an uncomplicated, typical childhood. Brownies, Girl Scouts, the most popular girl in school. Cheerleader?"

"But of course. Pandora went steady with the high school basketball jock."

"No, not basketball. Football."

"Whatever. Good student. Scholarship to college."

"Majored in home economics?"

Jon laughed. "How about art history? Joined the best sorority. Became engaged to an anthropology major. Lost her cherry in the back seat of a Chevy."

"Almost lost it. Didn't go all the way."

"Why?"

Delly placed her beer bottle on top of the coffee table. "Not every sweet thing gets screwed on the back seat of a Chevy."

"It doesn't have to be a Chevy."

"Pandora's a virgin, okay?"

"Okay. Pure Pandora Poe. We know about the car accident, right?"

"Yes. Three couples leave a frat party. They're all drunk. Pandora changes seats with Robin and they hit a telephone pole."

"Is Pandora the only one who escapes unhurt?"

"Yes. Robin dies. Another girl goes through the windshield and is disfigured for life. The fiancé turns into a veg—"

"That was in the script?"

"No. Just Robin. She was crushed to death."

"Christ, Delly, what a sadistic mouth you have."

"The better to eat you with, my dear. I think we've done enough background probing for one evening. Let's lick stamps and envelopes."

"Do I get Pure Pandora Poe or Deadly Delly Diamond?"

"Flip a coin."

"Jungle studs don't carry loose change." Lifting her from the chair, Jon slung her over his shoulder. "Tarzan will take his chances. Frankly, I wouldn't mind Crocodelly."

"That's croco*dile.*"

"A crocodile is a phone used for bullshit conversations."

"Smarty-pants. I meant the thick-skinned, amphibious dile."

"You're not thick-skinned, my love. I wish you were."

"Why?"

"It would make your acting career so much easier." *And our lives.*

Maxine Graham's office desk was covered with blue-penciled scripts, anchored by boxes that held the remnants of Chinese take-out. An empty Planters Peanuts jar held pens, pencils, paper clips and chopsticks. Two ashtrays overflowed with lipstick-tinted cigarette filters. A portable TV, next to the phone, televised a rerun of *Cagney and Lacey.*

Perched on the edge of a love seat, Drew thought about how it must be every man's fantasy to sleep with Cagney and Lacey—a *ménage a trois.*

Maxine paced between the love seat and her desk, then halted mid-stride. "Have you eaten enough bean curds, Flory?"

"More than enough. Thanks, Max."

"You're welcome. I invited you here to discuss Cal." She turned the TV's volume lower and retrieved a lined pad, filled with spidery handwriting.

"Anything wrong?"

"Au contraire." Her gaze touched upon his *Chien* T-shirt—Chien sandwiched between Mary-Wanna and Streisand—and his black chinos and sock-less sneakers. "Your fan mail has increased daily, especially since Randy's timely demise."

"Timely? Jesus, Max."

"All right, unfortunate demise. In any case, we must increase the sexual tension between Cal and Charl. Mental rape, Flory, mental rape." Shifting a container of siew mai, finding the edge of her desk with her backside, she scrutinized his face. "Why that brooding Heathcliff scowl?"

"Is this late-hour discussion leading up to a new plot?"

"Of course." She glanced down at her pad. "Judith thinks we should put Cal in danger. A location shoot, Mexico or Nassau. Buried treasure or buried bodies."

"Shit, Max, I want to do prime time and feature films. Jon Griffin is scripting a new movie for Paramount and I'm up for the lead."

"What about your contract?"

"Screw my contract."

"I'd rather screw you."

Drew stood, walked over to the projection window, and stared into the dark room next door. He knew better than to give Max such a perfect cue line. She was trying to make rumor reality. Years ago he would have indulged her for the hell of it. Now, even if he wanted to, the famous sex symbol couldn't get it up.

Turning away from the projectionist's window, he sat on the love seat again. "I'm sorry, swee' pea," he said, intentionally using the pet name he'd coined for her. "But you're not just a piece of ass. I respect you too much."

Maxine lit a cigarette and coughed. "Okay," she said, "where were we?"

"Nassau. Mexico. Look, swee' pea, I have to go home. If you want my admittedly biased opinion, I think the foreign shoot idea stinks."

She shrugged. "Aside from the ultimate consummation with Charl, what do you suggest we do to increase our ratings?"

"Since when do actors dictate plot treatments?"

"Since I say so."

"How the hell do I know what you and Pendergraft have in store for Wayne County? We don't even see advance scripts."

"*Merde!* Do you think we don't know about Wardrobe?"

Drew grinned. General script outlines were delivered to the wardrobe room because costumes had to be stitched in advance. "Gosh darn, Miss Graham," he drawled. "We poor, dumb, insecure actors only hang out in Wardrobe 'round contract renewal time, just to see if our character's gonna have an illness or accident comin' up."

"You were never poor, dumb or insecure in your life, Flory. Talk to me!"

"About *our* script? Well, we all know Scottie will die soon. Frankly, I can't believe she's lasted this long. She eats sushi every day for lunch, with tons of garlic. No mints. No mouth-wash. And Cal has to kiss her." Drew winked, but Maxine didn't respond. "Okay, okay, my suggestion is to speed up the bits between Charl and Pandora."

"We've been considering that. Maybe we could even have Pandora rebel, act gutsy, fight back."

"Max, I'll make a deal with you. Cut Cal's part, at least temporarily, and I'll drop negotiations for Jon Griffin's new film. My Movie of the Week just wrapped. Dick Clark has scheduled me for a *Pyramid* guest spot. I promised to shoot a perfume commercial with my sister, Maryl Bradley. In a few short weeks, Cal can solve Hannah's murder. Am I being fair?"

"What about Judith's idea? Buried treasure?"

"Every soap is dealing with exotic locations. I think it's a waste of money. Romance equals ratings. Lots of sex and 'mental rape.' We can dig for buried treasure in Lady Nan's basement. Our ratings soared during Tabby's pregnancy. By the way, I thought the miscarriage was a cop-out."

"Say la vee. Rosebud Cosmetics insisted. No, demanded." She shrugged again. "They weren't ready for a relationship between Tabby and Malcolm, even though we swore up and down it would be platonic, a peck on the cheek. But some biggie didn't want white pecking black."

"Are you considering another story line for Delly?"

"Not really. Pandora has served her purpose. What can we do with Pandora after Charl is cured?"

"But the viewers love her."

"Viewers are so fickle, my dear."

"I think you underestimate our fans." He glanced at his watch. "Are we finished? Anissa's waiting for me at home."

"What? Are you two living together?"

"Not in the sense you mean. We're sharing my apartment while she recovers from Randy's suicide."

"But that was six months ago."

Furious, Maxine tried to hide her reaction. Did Mr. Respect leave the beautiful Anissa untouched?

A shame Pandora couldn't be released from the mental ward while Charl stayed locked up forever.

After all, Delly was no threat.

Summer had slipped away faster than a Venice Beach roller skater navigating a slippery boardwalk.

With that thought, Delly braked her Audi for a stoplight, heard the clutch squeal, and wondered if one oiled a clutch. She knew nothing about the mechanics of a car engine, and could care less. She'd rarely driven in Manhattan. Subways had transported her east side, west side, all around the town.

It's September. I hate September. It reminds me of Mr. Hailey's candy.

Why did she suddenly remember that? It had happened a million years ago, the day she'd name-joked Hans Jewish Andersen and Delilah Old. Sweeping her bangs away from her forehead, she peered into the rearview mirror.

Delilah *Old.* Christ, she had wrinkles. No, not wrinkles. Eye-smudges. She looked like a damn raccoon.

Pandora has to be young, not old.

For a person who'd once denounced soaps as junk, Delly had, pervasively, changed her mind. She now thought about soaps day and night, and was almost as passionate as Maxine about ratings. Today she wore a *Morning Star* T-shirt. Her new script perched on the passenger seat, surrounded by outdated trade newspapers, a sweater missing three buttons, and a Chien coffee mug. On top of the Audi's dash was a magazine devoted to soap stars, headlining Drew Flory. This Saturday he'd appear in a made-for-TV-movie.

Geese honked. No, cars honked. The light had turned green. Her clutch squealed. The Beatles sang about a yellow submarine.

"Panda has lots of studying to do, Ringo," Delly told her car radio. "Lots of lines to learn. No time to fix supper. Maybe Jonny will order a pizza. No. Better not ask Jonny. He's mad 'cause Panda's been a naughty girl."

The radio announcer introduced Jim Croce, and the musical strains of *Bad Bad Leroy Brown* drifted from the one dashboard speaker that still worked. "Bad bad Pandora Poe," Delly sang. "Bad-est kid on the whole damn show."

Jonny had no right to be mad. It wasn't as if Delly was having an affair with another man. Jonny couldn't understand that Delly didn't visit Judith's house. It was Panda who played with Judith on the bad bad satin sheets. In fact, bad bad Pandora Poe had accepted another Brentwood invitation for Saturday night.

"Boy oh boy," Delly told the radio. "Jonny's gonna be mad at Delly."

But Panda had to see Judith. The new script, right there on the seat, had Charl starting a fire. During the confusion, Charl would steal a nurse's uniform. The last page of the script had

Panda trapped in the fire.

"You are one silly Panda," Delly said. "The writers can't kill you off. They need you for Charl's alibi. Her knife's hidden inside your baby. On the other hand, Charl's meaner than a junkyard dog. Charl could take my baby away. Then they wouldn't need Pandora."

Pulling into her driveway, parking behind a silver Rabbit convertible, Delly scowled. Why did Jonny always drive the new Rabbit? Then she remembered that it had been her own suggestion since Jon had a business luncheon at Paramount.

She rescued her script from the debris, entered the house, and admired her cozy love nest, now an antique showplace. The two royal blue director's chairs, glass coffee table, and Jon's desks and file cabinet were the only pieces of furniture that remained from their early weeks in Hollywood.

Surveying the living room, she felt her mouth turn up at the corners. Their couch was an Empire gilt-bronzed meridienne. The TV, VCR, and stereo components rested on a seventeenth century English Coffer. A refinished mahogany Chippendale table held the framed photos of her family. An American highboy of curly maple stood nearby, flanked by an Arrow Banks rocking chair. Velvet throw pillows, embroidered with silver and gold birds, covered the couch.

Jon sat in front of his new computer. He raised one eyebrow, but didn't stop tapping away at his keyboard. God, she loved his hands.

Walking into the bedroom, she ran her own hands across the polished wood of an antique four-poster, bought at auction, guaranteed to have been at least one night's respite for George and Martha Washington. Then she pulled a knee-length red kimono from her painted Burgess wardrobe. Next to the wardrobe was an English chest with one of her most prized possessions on top—a late-nineteenth-century puss-in-boots inkwell, whose cat peeped out from the inside of a shoe.

Her doll collection now included an early baby doll that said Ma-Ma when its arms were pulled. She had cashed one entire paycheck for a French Jumeau fashion doll of unglazed porcelain, whose enormous eyes and pout reminded her of Samantha.

Most of her salary was lavished on antique furniture and dolls. Sometimes she dragged Jon to auctions or flea markets, and he had bought an authentic Humpty Dumpty mechanical bank of heavy cast metal with bright enamel paint. Circa 1890, it was in perfect condition, but the evil grin on the clown-like face bothered her. Maybe it brought to mind a long-ago birthday cake and Samantha's snide comment: *Your 'nitials spell dog.*

"No, they don't," Delly told Humpty. "Not anymore."

Was that the real reason she'd changed her name to Diamond?

Belting her robe, clutching her script, she strolled into the living room and curled up amidst the plump couch pillows. For a while she watched the swinging pendulum on a Seth Thomas Post Office clock. Eight-oh-five. Eight-ten. Her stomach growled. Was Jonny hungry? He hadn't said one word and his keyboard sounded angry. Well, she wasn't going to speak first.

"George and Martha wouldn't approve," she said. Jon's bare shoulders glistened with creative perspiration. Staring at the white space between his bronzed back and the waistband of his jeans, she felt an almost overwhelming desire. "We're not keeping up with tradition, Jonny. Didn't President and Mrs. Washington screw themselves silly inside every Colonial home and tavern?"

"Do you honestly believe George and Martha screwed in *our* bed, Delly?"

"Yes. Why wouldn't they?"

Jon stopped typing. "Georgie's wooden teeth would have

hurt Marty's ponderous bosom."

"Little Joe Cartwright craved a ponderosa bosom," she said. *Not great, but good enough for a grin,* she thought.

Jon didn't crack a smile. Abruptly, he threw a mug filled with pencils against the wall. The pencils landed in pick-up-stick positions as Jon said, "Why are you doing this to us, Delly?"

"What are you talking about?"

"Pendergraft called to confirm."

"Oh, that. Panda has to see Judith."

"Don't give me that Panda shit."

"Jonny's mad at Panda. Bad, bad Pandora Poe."

"Quit *Morning Star,* Delly. It's not worth your romps on the casting couch." Rising from his chair, he ran across the room, grabbed her script, and hurled it toward the pencils.

She screamed when he clutched the lapels of her kimono, wrestled her to the floor, and straddled her body. Then she stopped struggling. "Don't be mad, Tarz."

He groaned. "What am I going to do with you?"

"For starters, you can take off your jeans."

"Please quit the show."

"Please make love to me."

Delly felt his weight crush her breasts. Her legs circled his butt. He slid inside, withdrew, slid inside again. "Ah, Jonny, don't tease." There was a loud series of knocks on the front door. Jon raised his head, listening. "Don't stop," she gasped, arching her back. "I wish . . . I want . . ."

He lowered his head and nosed her robe apart. She felt him leave a trail of feathery kisses down her belly until he reached the dark, moist triangle between her thighs. His tongue snaked out and caressed, while his fingers typed erotic messages across her swollen nipples.

The door knocks were punctuated by the doorbell. Once again, Jon raised his head. "What the hell?"

"Ignore it," she managed, on the verge of an orgasm. "Girl Scouts selling cookies. Religious nuts."

"Are you expecting someone? Anissa?"

"No."

"Did you order a pizza?"

"No."

"Maybe Paramount sent revisions."

"At night? Jonny, please . . . rats!" She watched him step into his jeans and walk toward the door. Every sound was exaggerated. His footsteps. His hoarse cough. The zipper on his jeans. Her heart slammed against her chest. Her spit tasted salty and bitter, as if she'd swallowed semi-sweet, chocolate-covered peanuts. Sitting up, she tried to re-wrap herself in the folds of her robe and tidy her tangled hair. Then she heard a familiar voice.

"Well, it's about time. My cab drove away. I saw two cars in the driveway and lights in the window, so naturally I assumed you were home. Did I interrupt anything important?"

CHAPTER NINETEEN

"This isn't how I pictured your decor," Samantha said as she explored the living room.

"How did you picture it?" Delly remembered her sister's habit of caressing surfaces, and her stupefaction turned to prickly petulance when Sami's fingers traced the English coffer.

"I don't know, Dell. Beaver-Cleaver-ish, maybe."

"Come on, Sami, that's not me."

"That's my *perception* of you." She glanced around. "This stuff's pretty, I guess, but it's so old."

"Older stuff's worth a fortune," said Jon, grinning at what he probably thought was meaningless familial banter.

Delly knew better. She wanted to erase Jon's grin with her knuckles. Instead, she said, "What are you doing here, Sami?"

"Aren't you glad to see me?"

"Sure," she replied, thinking how most sisters would have hugged, kissed. But Samantha wasn't demonstrative with women, not unless she wanted something very badly. "Why didn't you call, Sami? We had no idea you planned a visit."

"This isn't a visit. I've left Jules." She shrugged off her London Fog. Beneath the trench coat, she wore designer jeans and a short-sleeved sweater in her favorite burnt-orange color. Flinging her coat toward the rocker, she fumbled inside her purse until she'd extracted a crumpled cigarette pack and a gold-plated lighter. "Do you mind if I smoke?"

Yes!

"No," Jon said.

Studying Sami's tight jeans and sweater, Delly decided that her sister looked more voluptuous than fat. Palomino hair tumbled down Sami's back in a carefully-contemplated shag. Her makeup was applied flawlessly, with more flair than flash, and her skin resembled the porcelain Jumeau doll.

"You must be Delly's boyfriend," she purred, extending five dark red fingernails toward Jon.

"Guilty." Shaking Samantha's hand, he grinned again.

"Can . . . may I have a drink? I hate flying, always count the nuns and babies on board. I figure God won't strike down nuns and babies."

Jon laughed. "I'll prepare one of my specialty drinks. Better yet, I'll fix drinks for all of us."

Delly watched him head toward the kitchen. Then, squaring her shoulders, she faced Samantha. "How are the kids?"

"Fine. The twins are almost potty trained. Isn't that a dopey word? Potty? Sounds like a plant. Uncle Sam gave me this marvy British nanny for Chanukah. Remember the guest room where we used to stay when we were sick? I swear it still smells like crushed grapes. Remember how we hated tea and Daddy would sweeten it with grape jelly? Jules took out the grape arbor and built a jungle gym for the kids. Nanny sleeps there."

"Where? The jungle gym?"

"No, silly, the guest room. Was that a joke?"

"Yes. Does Jules know you're here?"

"He does now. I sent him a telegram."

"Of course. A telegram. Why am I not surprised? What did you tell the kids?"

"That I'll bring them to Hollywood when I'm settled." She crushed out her cigarette in a cut-glass candy dish. "Will wants Sting's autograph. How come you look so shocked? I couldn't arrive on your doorstep with four screaming brats."

"Brats?"

"Actually, they're all sweet, especially Juliet, but I couldn't intrude on you with an entourage. You don't have room for Nanny, so you'd have to baby-sit."

"Me? Sami, I've got a full-time job."

"You do?"

"Yes. I play Pandora on—"

"That's not full time."

"I beg to differ. I rehearse, study lines, and—"

"Well, that's why I didn't bring the kids."

Jon returned, balancing three steaming mugs. "Coffee, Kahlua, and raspberry liqueur," he said, setting the mugs on the coffee table. "My specialty."

Samantha gave him a deliquescent smile. "That looks marvy," she said, "but I really must count calories. I've lost thirty pounds. Is it okay if I bunk in your house for a while?"

Watching her sister turn her luminous gaze on Jon, Delly gulped her drink too quickly and burned the roof of her mouth. She slipped into the kitchen, filled her mug with straight liqueur, then walked back in time to hear Jon say, "So naturally we want you to stay with us."

"How long?" Delly said.

"Until I get acclimated," Samantha said. "Why? Is there a problem?"

"Not really. We have a second bedroom. But Jon and I both need peace and quiet, especially Jon."

"Then I'd better find myself a hotel."

"That's stupid," Jon said. "You'd have to pay for meals, rent a car—"

"Well, okay, if you insist. Trust me, I'll be mouse-quiet. Jon darling, would you fetch the largest suitcase?"

"I'll fetch them all."

Delly felt the potent liqueur hit her stomach like a fireball.

June Cleaver wouldn't consume raspberry thunderbolts of forked lightning, but then June wouldn't buy expensive antique furniture. Ward would piss his pants over the Arrow Banks rocker, great for making love in, especially when one wanted rocking. Did Ward and June make love? Sure they did. At least twice. Wally and the Beaver. *I'm heading for the click too fast. Better slow down.*

What the heck. How often did a beloved twin sister drop in out of the blue for a permanent visit? Only Samantha could have planned her arrival so perfectly. Only Samantha could have timed her entrance during the climax.

Making an effort to walk straight, Delly entered the kitchen and refilled her mug. When she returned, Jon had carried all but one piece of luggage through the hallway, into the guest room. Samantha opened the remaining suitcase and pulled out two denim jackets lined with mink. She tossed a small jacket toward Delly, then handed the other, larger jacket to Jon.

"Thanks," he said. "I'll wear this to my next Paramount meeting. They always make more concessions if they think you're solvent."

"Too expensive," Delly said. "We can't accept—"

"Don't be silly. You should see the markup on furs. Where's your piano?."

"Piano?"

"You know, that funny-looking piece of furniture with eighty-eight black and white keys. Mom plays one."

"Sami, we have no room for a piano."

"Yes, you do. If we move this dopey couch closer to the TV, we can squeeze the piano over there, in the corner."

"It's not a dopey couch and we don't need a piano."

"I do, Dell. I've been taking voice lessons from this darling gentleman who used to star in operas. I had to audition to become his student, but he liked me and put me ahead of the others on his waiting list. I need the piano to practice on. La, la, la, and all that shit. I'll buy a small one, I promise." She fondled the family pictures. "You can put these on top, Dell, just like Joan Crawford did in her movie Daisy-something. Or was that Lana Turner? God, I love Lana Turner movies. Some people even think I look like her. What do you think, Jon?"

"There's a resemblance."

"No, I meant the piano."

Delly said, "You plan to become a singer?"

"I *am* a singer. I just need a gig."

"Sami, it's not that easy. Jon, tell her."

"It's not that easy," he said, sitting on the couch.

Samantha sat next to him, crossed her legs, and leaned back against an embroidered cushion. "Sure it is. While Dell was wasting her money on acting lessons, I turned my trust fund over to my stepfather, Samuel Curtis, and he made me a big fat profit. I can afford backup musicians and you can find me an arranger, Jon. I know you have contacts within the film community. I've thought about this for a long time. I want to pay my share of the rent, too."

Delly's head whirled. Pay her share? How long was Sami planning to stay? A piano? Practice? La-la-la? Peace and quiet? Desperate, she focused on Jon. *Say something!*

"Don't worry about the rent," he said.

"I won't free-load and . . . oh my God, Monty!" Leaping up from the couch, Samantha ran toward the guest room. When she returned, she carried a tiny animal. "Folks, this is Ricardo Montalban. He'd bark hello but he's sedated."

"A rat!" Delly screeched.

"Don't be silly. Monty's a Chihuahua. He's pure-bred, with papers a mile long."

"Ricardo Montalban?" Jon stared at the small creature.

"I wanted a name that sounded Hispanic, and I've always

loved *Fantasy Island.* Fantasies are fun, don't you agree?"

Montalban wriggled from Samantha's grasp, staggered over to the American Shaker rug, lifted his leg, and arced a stream of urine toward the rug's braided edge.

"I'll pay to have it cleaned," Samantha said.

She brought her rat but left her kids behind, thought Delly, carefully placing her empty mug on the coffee table.

This time Samantha offered her sugary smile to both Jon and Delly. "Monty's trained, really he is. He's just nervous from the long trip, aren't you baby boy? Itsy, bitsy, pretty baby. I'll keep him inside my room at night. Obviously, he doesn't eat much. I almost named him Anorexia, but it sounds like a girl's name. Have you had supper yet? I hate airline food so I gave mine to a nun. Why don't I whip up omelets? You two can go back to whatever I interrupted when I knocked on your door."

Samantha's words blurred. Delly lost the coherency at Anorexia. She swayed and felt Jonny's hands steady her.

"Are you okay?" he whispered.

"No." She watched her sister stroll toward the kitchen, trailing fingerprints across every surface. "Jane drank too fast on empty stomach."

He gave her a rueful grin. "Tarzan's jungle juice like boxer's punch."

She felt an overwhelming desire to claim Jon as her own by playing their wacky definition game. "Boxer, underwear," she managed. "Punch, Hawaiian."

"Hawaiian is what comedian Phil Silvers used to say. Jesus, honey, are you planning to throw up or pass out?"

"Throw up."

"I'll hold your head," he offered, propelling her toward the bathroom.

"Never mind." She stopped abruptly. "June Cleaver."

"What about June Cleaver?"

"She'd never toss her cookies. I'm so dizzy, Jonny."

He scooped her up, carried her to their four-poster, and placed her on top of the quilt.

"That dog's awful," she wailed. "I don't want a piano. I want to make love and now we can't."

"Sure we can, after your sister goes to bed."

"Oh, God. Now the bedroom's spinning." She squeezed her eyes shut. "Make love to crocodelly. Please?"

"We can't right now." He stroked the tangled hair away from her forehead. "I wish we could."

"Why did she come here?"

"We can handle it. Tomorrow I'll call musical arrangers and start looking for a rental house. Pass out, my love. I'll tell Samantha you're studying lines for tomorrow's show."

"Monday."

"What?"

"My next show's Monday. The taping, I mean."

"Samantha doesn't know that."

"Tell her my job's full time."

"Okay. And later we'll lick stamps and envelopes."

Jon watched long lashes shade Delly's pale cheeks. She lay sideways. The kimono revealed the sexy curve of her small breasts, and he realized they hadn't made love in ages. She should find a good shrink. She was on the verge of a mental breakdown. Unfortunately, Jon knew all the signs. *Duck Pond*'s Virginia had been inspired by his little sister.

Maybe he should take the bull by the horns, so to speak, and get rid of Pendergraft himself. He had clout, contacts, and he could request, as a personal favor, that Delly be cast in Spielberg's next film.

Staring down at her small, firm body, Jon felt an erection build. To hell with Samantha. Spitting on his fingers, he inserted his hand beneath Delly's robe. He would lubricate her quickly, penetrate quickly, and—

"Jon? Dell? Where are you? The food's ready."

Eyes still shut, Delly felt Jon remove his fingers.

"I'm coming, Samantha," he yelled.

But he didn't have time to come. Neither did I.

Delly heard the bedroom door close. Opening her eyes, she focused on Mumpsy, the old stuffed bear that Daddy had given her when her fever had soared and her glands had swollen and she'd stayed in the guest bedroom and sipped cup after cup of Daddy's medicinal grape jelly tea. "If I catch your mumps," Samantha had said, "I want Elvis records, not some dumb baby toy."

Before Randy's suicide, Delly had watched Anissa feed Oscar Wilde a can of Alpo, goopy and pungent, straight from the can.

Even with the door shut, Sami's omelets smelled like Alpo. Well, why not? Hadn't she cooked one for Delly-Dog?

"The stars at night are big and bright," Delly sang. "Deep in the heart of Hollywood."

Twinkie, twinkie, little star, she thought. *Like a Diamond.*

The convertible top was down, so she maneuvered her arms into a hooded gray sweatshirt. The hood would keep her ponytail from blowing apart.

Jon had asked her to cancel the Judith appointment and she had said yes. So why was she sliding her white middy-blouse, short blue shirt, argyle knee-socks, and white sneakers behind the Rabbit's steering wheel?

For a trip to the drugstore, of course. They needed toothpaste and shampoo and toilet paper, especially toilet paper. An extra person used lots of Charmin, not to mention charm.

Sami could be so charmin'.

Delly had lathered her body with lemon-scented soap, but the aroma of Sami's heavy Ninja perfume filled the Rabbit's interior. She had borrowed the convertible to "acclimate." Acclimate meant a shopping spree on Rodeo Drive, where she had accumulated a dozen boxes, a gilded, jewel-encrusted bird cage, a portable TV, and a parking ticket.

Trust me, I'll be mouse-quiet, she had promised. But her rat barked at shadows or at the newly purchased parrot, Sinbad, who swore a blue streak. Sami couldn't exist without background noise. Her new color TV perched on the guest room bureau. Sami was addicted to Johnny Carson, Jonah Wiggins, and the not-ready-for-bed-yet movie channel. Meanwhile, in the living room, a reel-to-reel never ceased its repetitive music.

Then there was the piano, the damn upright piano. Delivered this morning, its light wood veneer clashed with Delly's antique furniture. Sami had tested chords all day, playing scales, chopsticks, la-la-la.

Jon had escaped to his health club.

Compulsive in her personal habits, bathing at least twice a day, Samantha was sloppy about leaving soiled clothes draped over Delly's "dopey couch." A brush filled with strands of palomino hair lay next to the family photos. Pantyhose curled, like sleeping snakes, on top of the rocker.

Montalban used the braided rug as his personal toilet until Jon scrubbed the spot and covered it with newspaper pages—the entertainment section, which included TV listings.

Tonight Drew's movie of the week would be telecast. Anissa had invited Delly to watch, but she had a previous engagement, a shopping spree at the ole drugstore.

Making a sharp right turn, she dovetailed the Rabbit into a driveway and parked behind a white Cadillac.

Judith wore an ankle-length paisley caftan that slimmed her wide hips. "Hello, Pandora," she said. "How are you?"

"Fine. Do you have any Charmin?"

★ ★ ★ ★ ★

Jon had traveled the length of an Olympic-sized pool, swimming lap after lap, automatic, mindless activity. Finally, exhausted, he headed for home.

He had asked Delly to cancel her Saturday Pendergraft appointment, using her sister's unexpected visit as an excuse. Delly had agreed, but when Jon turned into his driveway he saw that the silver Rabbit was missing.

Mouth-watering odors permeated the house. Samantha stood on the glass coffee table, barefoot, harmonizing with Paul Williams. Paul sang about finding the rainbow connection, and Samantha was a glossy-lipped Muppet.

Her piano guarded the room like a grinning sentinel.

"Hi, Samantha. Where's Delly?"

"Hi, Jon. She said something about a rehearsal for her show."

"Shit!"

"I know what you mean. Work, work, work. All work and no play makes Delly a dull girl, right?" Samantha turned off the stereo. "I cooked us some dinner. I'll serve it in here."

Ignoring the dull-girl remark, Jon let his body sink into his director's chair. Then he kicked off his sneakers. Maybe he should phone Delly and beg her to come home. No. He was tired, couldn't deal with Pendergraft right now.

He couldn't deal with Pandora, either.

Samantha entered the room, her hands mittened by pot holders. Two plates rode atop her stuffed palms. The food looked delicious—steaming volauvents, surrounded by baby potatoes boiled in their skins.

"That looks great," he said. "Delly can't cook."

"Since my marriage all I've done is experiment with food." Samantha flung her pot holders toward the rocker. "You never met Jules, did you? Christ, I forgot. You never met me."

"I feel like I know you. Delly—"

"Jules was gorgeous in high school. Tall, captain of our basketball team. A shame he's not athletic beneath the sheets. He wants to shoot baskets, but all he can hit is the backboard." She grinned impishly. "Am I embarrassing you?"

"Yes."

"Jules is still tall, but very heavy. It's probably my fault since he gobbled my food down. Now that I'm gone, maybe he'll lose a few pounds. I think Delly's too thin, don't you?"

"No, not really."

"How do you like my new piano?"

"It's nice."

"Nice? It's marvy. Listen."

Jon watched her dance toward the piano. She wore an I-heart-NY, oversized T-shirt, stenciled with a huge red apple. Her breasts bounced beneath the white cotton material. No bra. Delly rarely wore a bra, but her breasts didn't balloon like her sister's did. Not that Samantha's were rubbery. On the contrary, they were statuesque. And why was he comparing breasts?

After playing a few simple background chords, Samantha's voice soared into a haunting melody that Jon had never heard before. A girl crooned to her infant about his father, a civil rights activist, soon to be released from prison. Samantha's vocal range changed several times, and she slid from octave to octave with ease. First, a husky contralto, then a high soprano.

Despite the cliché lyrics, Jon's throat felt lumpy as the lovers reunited, only to be torn apart again. The young father, handcuffed, was transported back to jail, where he would serve additional time for visiting his new son.

"You're terrific." Rising, Jon applauded. "Where did you find that song?"

"Inside an old attic trunk. My mom wrote it. That's why I need an arranger so badly, for all the other instruments. Do you really like my song?"

"It's great. Have you got more?"

Samantha sang a second ballad. This time the lyrics told about a photographer who fell in love with an imaginary subject, a composite of several different models. Upon his death, a negative was found clutched in his fingers. The developed picture showed the photographer and his dream girl, walking hand-in-hand through the misty fog.

Once again, Jon felt moved by the sentimental lyrics.

"Mom wrote that song, too. It's called 'Portrait of my Love.' A bit *Wuthering Heights,* but what the hell."

"Samantha, I'm curious. No, baffled. Why didn't your husband recognize your incredible talent?"

"He was jealous. One night I sang at a party. When we got home he slapped me." Her bottom lip quivered and her amber-tinted eyes brimmed over with tears. "Jules said everyone made fun of me because I sounded like our old family puss, Southern Comfort. Jules said I was so fat I looked like a cartoon opera singer. I was hurt, but mad, so I spit in his face."

"Don't cry. Hush, honey, it's all right. You're safe now."

"After I spit, he hit me again, bloodied my nose."

"Poor baby, don't cry."

"So I kicked him in the balls."

Instinctively, Jon's hands traveled to his crotch. A woman could never feel the pain, he thought, feeling the pain.

"I was wearing heels with pointy toes," Samantha continued. "Jules left me alone after that night. I had an affair with my voice teacher. He taught me how to control my vocal range. He couldn't get me to stop smoking . . ." She paused, her tears shining like crystal. "You're not being polite, are you, Jon? You think I'm good, don't you?"

"Better than good. Professional. Terrific."

"Thanks." She wound her arms about his neck.

Jon felt her heat and stepped backwards, encountering the

coffee table. Off balance, he leaned forward to compensate, and they both tumbled to the floor. Samantha didn't release her hold, straddling his hips, nibbling at his earlobe.

"Enough," he yelped. "Uncle!"

"I want you, Jonny."

"No, you don't."

"Yes, I do. I can't get pregnant. My tubes are tied."

"Delly—"

"Will never know, I swear to God." Samantha unzipped his jeans and pulled them free from his legs. Next, she removed his shirt and tugged her own shirt over her head. "Take my undies off," she urged.

"I hate to hurt your feelings, Samantha, but we can't do this."

"Yes, we can. Consider it a therapeutic fuck. Please?"

Jon had heard women use the F-word before, numerous times, but Samantha made it sound like a caress. He felt her tongue lick, the warm saliva leaving an erotic trail across his nipples.

I spit at him. Jules hit me, bloodied my nose. Poor, brave Samantha. Slowly, Jon's arms moved on their own accord, pulling her body up along the length of his, stroking her plump curves. He buried his face in her large breasts, tasting new, exciting flesh. *I've been faithful,* he thought, tugging her panties down, feeling her wriggle free from the silky material, feeling her silky hair tickle his throbbing groin. *I've been King Arthur while Delly lusts after Sir Judith Lancelot.*

"What a marvy bod you have," Samantha purred.

She needed him, made him feel like Jon Lancelot, a knight in shining armor. Carefully, he maneuvered their bodies until she was on her back, a defenseless turtle.

"Do you want me to suck you?" she asked, fondling his erection. "I've never done it before, but—"

"No, honey, this is my gift."

She was larger than Delly there, too, and Jon felt as if he'd entered a wet, heated cave. He couldn't get enough of Samantha's swollen nipples, the musky scent of her perfume, and her voice urging him on, singing his name.

God, he was a bastard, screwing Delly's twin sister, but he couldn't stop. He felt Samantha's imperative contractions and timed his own response perfectly.

"You're so marvy," she panted. Directing his first finger toward her anus, she quivered like an orgasmic cheerleader.

Jon withdrew, flipped her over, and penetrated. She rocked back and forth, delirious with passion.

"HolyMaryMotherOfGod!" she screamed, and he had just enough time to wonder where a nice Jewish girl had learned that particular phraseology before she flipped him.

Even though she'd never sucked a penis before, she managed to practically swallow him whole.

Like a boa constrictor ingesting a live rat.

Chapter Twenty

Delly stared at her reflection in the octagonal mirror above Judith's wet-bar.

Except for her knee-socks, she looked like a high school Mariner.

As a Mariner cheerleader, Samantha's petite feet had sported white ankle-boots. She'd worn a sexy sailor outfit with a skirt that flipped, showing her butt. To make the squad you had to be able to turn a cartwheel.

Orange and blue pom-poms.

Jules and Neeley running down court, dribbling, scoring.

Dribble, dribble, six foot star.

Listen, Delly, your sister thought I was real good.

Delly Good-as-Gold had never opted to become a Mariner. She had wanted to play Nellie Nurse. Instead, she'd played a sailor, clothed in white bell-bottoms that etched her panty line. She prayed she wouldn't get her period, and God had answered that small prayer. Thank God for small favors.

However, God had a weird sense of humor, allowing Delly's classmates to witness her loss of virginity. But that had led to her physical transformation. Had God wanted Delly to take control of her life?

So why was she losing control now? Why—

"Are you staring into the mirror?"

"Huh?"

"Why are you staring into the mirror?" Judith repeated.

"What do you see?"

"I see Pandora's box."

Judith laughed. Then she held out a thick crystal glass. As Delly sipped her second scotch-splash, they discussed the new script. Charl's fire was a ruse, Judith promised. Panda would remain unscathed. The writers were considering a romance between Panda and Cal.

"But they can't," Delly said. "Cal and Charl belong together. C my name is Charlotte and my husband's name is Cal. We come from California and in our baskets—"

"We've simply kicked the idea around, sweetie pie."

"Panda can't love Cal. Panda's pure."

Judith's butt plowed a rocking chair's cushion. She patted her lap. "Sit, Pandora."

"No. Panda has to go home." Watching Judith's eyes narrow, Delly felt her control slip a notch. "Why are you looking at me like that?"

"Panda has to go home," Judith mimicked. "I wonder which role is honest."

"What do you mean?"

"Don't look so friggin' innocent. Save it for the cameras. Do you prefer to play the dull Delilah, who lost an Oscar-winning role in her boyfriend's movie, or the Delly who hides inside Pandora's skin so that she can become Pendergraft's pampered pet?"

"I'm acting, Judith."

"Of course you are."

"I'm Pandora Poe at your house or on the *Morning Star* set."

"Pandora Poe?"

"We . . . I gave Panda a last name."

Judith laughed. "Poe. That's priceless. From Edgar Allan, I presume. Did you ever read his short story, 'The Magic Paw'?"

" 'The Monkey's Paw.' Yes. But it was written by W. W. Jacobs, featured in an Edgar Allan Poe anthol—"

"Whatever. Remember the third wish, canceling the other two wishes? Do you want to wish away *Morning Star?*"

"No."

"Then sit on my lap, Miss Pandora Poe."

Delly sat. She placed her thumb inside her mouth as Judith's hand crept under her skirt. The Chivas had dulled her senses and, after all, control had definite sexual connotations. Lay down the law. Be on top of. Delly giggled and her thumb popped out. "That tickles, Judith. Panda wants her pill."

"Later."

Control! "No, Judith, now!"

"Patience, pet. Patience is the art of concealing your impatience. I have a nice evening planned, a surprise."

"Goodie, goodie, good as gold. Panda loves surprises."

The doorbell rang.

"I do believe my surprise has arrived." Judith shifted Delly and rose from the rocker. "Wait here, pet."

A few moments later, Judith returned, followed by two women. "Pandora, I'd like you to meet Mayella and Beverlee. Beverlee spells her name with two friggin' eees at the end."

Delly stood and curtsied.

"Judith, she's precious," said Mayella.

Shoulder-length cinnamon hair had been pulled away from Mayella's forehead, exposing a prominent widow's peak. Tiny blue eyes, like buttons, crinkled at the corners.

Beverlee had short reddish hair, the color of paprika, and a long sharp nose.

She looks like Woody Woodpecker, thought Delly. *I think we've met before. Where?*

"I watch your show all the time," Beverlee said, "even tape it when I'm working. I'm a model."

"Do you know Maryl Bradley? She's a model and the sister

of a very close friend of mine."

"I model shoes, dear. Maryl Bradley and I don't run in the same circles."

Delly accepted a new drink from Judith. "Where's the surprise?"

"This is the surprise. A party. Later we'll play games."

"Panda doesn't want to play games," Delly whispered, her tummy cramping. "She wants to go home."

"What did you say?"

"Nothing." *It's not your home anymore. Samantha. Montalban the rat-dog. Sinbad the Parrot.*

Judith glanced at her watch. "Make yourself comfortable. Flory's show is about to start."

"Goody, goody." Delly clapped her hands.

Opening the door to a French Provincial cabinet, Judith tapped the buttons on a television, then walked across the room and settled into her rocker. Delly sat on the couch, next to Beverlee. Mayella folded her body, powwow style, on Judith's new, lush, cream-colored carpet.

Large printed credits flashed across the TV screen. Drew's name was above the title, along with Shirley Jones and Melissa Sue Anderson.

The plot was simple—a man in love with both mother and daughter. Delly maneuvered back and forth between the wet-bar and the couch. *Sorry, Cal, I wanted to watch your movie sober, but Panda hasta get drunk as a skunk.*

For two hours, minus commercial breaks, Drew wooed both Shirley and Melissa Sue. As the film ended, he drove away to die of a fatal, undefined illness, leaving Mom and kid united in mutual sorrow.

Judith watched critically, then smiled during the last scene, and Delly thought her eyes looked very yellow in the room's recessed lighting.

"I know the genius who wrote that piece of shit," Judith said. "Oh, well. The movie's been hyped for weeks and Flory was his usual charismatic self. Maxine'll be pleased."

"I thought it was sad. And beautiful." Beverlee sighed. "He sacrificed his happiness to die all alone, just like—what's that animal that dies all alone?"

"An elephant," Delly said, remembering when and where she'd met the shoe model before. Once. At The Playground. Beverlee had been part of Judith's entourage.

"Game time," Judith said. Opening another cabinet door, she retrieved a camera.

Delly felt woozy. "Pander hasta go home now," she slurred. "Her sistah's waitin'."

"Yes, pet, I understand." Judith held both hands behind her back. "Choose, Pandora. Left or right?"

Delly pictured script pages—Panda trapped in a fire. She pointed, opened her mouth like a baby bird, and washed down the Quaalude with Chivas.

"Wheee, I'm a swan," she cried.

"Drink some more, Pandora, that's a good girl."

"Scotch tastes like Sami's eyes. Panda's flyin'. Ladybug, ladybug, fly away home, your house is on fire and Judith'll burn."

"What does she mean by that?" Mayella's brow beetled.

"Pandora wants to set me on fire," Judith said, "and she knows just how to do it. Don't you, pet?"

"No. I meant Max. Set Maxine on fire. Mr. Ratings."

"What? Who?" Mayella looked as if she needed a dictionary.

"Cast joke," Judith explained. "Maxine thinks it's a hoot."

The living room spun. Through wisps of cotton candy, Delly saw a brand new movie-of-the-week. Starring Judith, Mayella, and Beverlee. Delly Diamond's name filled the screen, above the title. Surprise! The movie had been shot in Judith's living room. Opening scene: famous scriptwriter hands actress a full glass of amber-eyed scotch. Actress drinks.

Beverlee: "Careful, Judith. Pandora's already had too much. She'll puke or pass out, like she did last time."

Delly: "I threw up last time?"

Beverlee: "No. You passed out."

Judith: "She's developed a high tolerance, and she won't lose her inhibitions unless she's zonked."

Beverlee: "There's a big difference between zonked and passed out."

As if on cue, Delly's legs buckled and she fell. The puddle of spilled Chivas looked like Chihuahua piss. Judith would be pissed.

Oh, no. Delly Diamond had to throw up. Was that in the script? Once upon a long time ago she'd sworn she'd never throw up in front of a famous—

She heaved twice and waited for more, but that was it. So why did the room kept spinning?

Beverlee: "What did I tell you?"

Judith: "Help her upstairs. Shit! My new carpet's ruined."

You can't say shit on network TV.

Giant scissors cut, censoring, and Delly's movie-of-the-week faded into oblivion.

"Help her upstairs," Judith repeated.

Mayella and Beverlee clasped hands, forming a swing. They carried Pandora to the mirrored bedroom. Judith followed with her camera.

"Would you like to swing with a star?" Delly sang, her head turning cartwheels.

Just like a Mariner cheerleader.

Drew turned off the TV.

"Well, that's that," he said. "Rotten, huh?"

"You looked sexy." Anissa's brow furrowed. "What happened

to Melissa Sue Anderson's blonde hair? Didn't she have blonde hair in *Little House on the Prairie?* When did she become a brunette?"

"Anissa . . . why the hell are we discussing Missy's hair?"

Clothed in a pair of jeans and nothing else, Drew sat on the edge of a red-bordered Turkish Prayer rug. Anissa reclined on their beige corduroy couch. She wore bikini panties and one of his old pin-striped shirts. Lazily, his fingers Braille'd her feet. She was the only woman he'd ever met who wasn't ticklish.

The floor lamp cast its muted glow. White walls were filled with posters from his Community Playhouse days, joined by Maryl's magazine covers. Warhol's Marilyn Monroe surveyed the room from above the glass screen and brass andirons of a tiny fireplace.

"You weren't performing Shakespeare," Anissa said. "Honest, Drew, you were fine. Everybody did a wonderful job."

"Quote it."

"Don't be silly."

"Go on, quote some memorable lines from my wonderful disease-of-the-week flick."

" 'Oh, darling, how strong you look.' "

"What the hell was that? No one says—"

" 'Strong enough to bring us both back to life, if you don't want to die.' Quote, unquote."

"Oh, I get it. *Love Story,* right?"

"Numskull. Lawrence Olivier to Merle Oberon in *Wuthering Heights.*"

"Sorry."

"Love is never having to say you're sorry." Anissa giggled.

"At least you compared me to Olivier."

"Belt up, Drew. The acting was fine, your emotions sincere, and I lost myself in your character. You looked so sad."

"I was thinking about *Morning Star*'s iron-clad contract," he grumbled. "Speaking of our beloved soap, I have no monopoly in the emotions department. You're incredible and Delly's an expert."

"You know what Delly told me? She said she keeps tweezers inside her smock pocket. When Pandora's due to cry, she turns away from the camera and plucks a hair from her nose. Makes her eyes water. I've been worried about Delly. She shifts into character at odd moments."

"What do you mean?"

"She's Pandora even after we wrap."

"We all do that, keep in character until we can shake it off."

"But I've seen Delly transform at home. All of a sudden she'll evolve into Pandora. It's weird."

"Maybe she's teasing."

"No way. She changes in the blink of an eye."

"How do you respond?"

"I adlib Charl to her Pandora. Then I say I have to pee, or fetch a glass of water. When I return from the bathroom or kitchen, she's Delly again."

"I'll have a talk with Jon, find out what's going on."

"Thanks." Momentarily, Anissa remained silent, lost in thought. Then she smiled, stood up, and unbuttoned her shirt so that her breasts were partially revealed. "Hello, Cal," she said, her voice Charl-husky. "Let's find an abandoned supply closet and screw our brains out."

"Are you showing me how Delly transforms?"

"No."

"You're serious?"

"Yes."

"Sorry, honey, but I'm exhausted. So far today I've made love to Tabby Cat, three nurses, and Lady Nan."

"I can bring you back to life again."

"Forget the supply closet. Let's celebrate my movie debut

with a night on the town. What do you say?"

"I say no."

Drew stood, stretched, then wandered aimlessly, adjusting a window drape, straightening pictures. "There's champagne."

"You can drink champagne, if you think it'll help."

"Help what?"

"Stop pacing and listen. I love you. I want you."

"Anissa, I can't."

"Yes, you can."

"You don't understand."

"Yes, I do. Maryl told me what you told her the night I showed up on your doorstep, the night I was so sick."

"Then you know I can't."

"I don't expect Superman, Drew. I don't want a super hero. I love *you,* not some macho fictitious character."

"I love you, too. Give me time."

"Drew, listen, please. I adored Randy, worshipped him, but I can't handle another celibate relationship." She knelt, crying.

Drew looked down and saw the uncomplicated depths of pure love in her wet eyes. He felt her slender arms clasp him about his legs as she buried her face against his thigh. Hot tears seared all the way through his jeans to his skin.

"Don't cry." Kneeling, he gathered her into his arms.

He saw himself in front of a stage curtain. Every woman in the audience looked like his beautiful Anissa. He sniffed her flowery scent and felt her heartbeat, but he had already burned his candle at both ends.

Sobbing, she raised her face and her breath blew out imaginary flames.

Anissa, his only love, the only woman he had ever really wanted or needed.

He finished unbuttoning her shirt and pushed it free from her shoulders.

Rising, Anissa stepped from her panties.

Rising, Drew stepped from his jeans.

Naked, their eager bodies blending, he tasted her sweet breath in a long kiss. Then he tensed, unsure, afraid.

"I lied," she said. "I lied about a celibate relationship. I don't care if you kiss me until dawn. I don't care if we cuddle or fondle or feast on each other. I don't care if you never penetrate, because you're already inside me. I carry you inside me every waking moment. I carry you inside my heart. You don't have to prove anything, Drew, because you're already a part of me. When I sleep, I sleep you. When I breathe, I breathe you. When I laugh, I laugh you."

"When I love, I love you," he said, lowering her to the Turkish Prayer rug.

Prayer, however, was the last thing on his mind. Later he might offer up a prayer of deliverance, but right now he felt delightfully, deliciously pagan.

So did she.

"Oopsie-daisy, don't fall down," said Mayella, guiding Delly inside. "Shit, Beverlee, I don't like this. Pandora's gonna faint. Or scream."

"So what? It's her house. If she screams, somebody'll find her. I hear a dog. Let's go."

The two women shut the front door behind them.

"Oopsie-daisy, don't fall down," Delly said, her voice raspy. "London Bridges falling down. Lloyd Bridges falling down. Jeff and Beau Bridges, falling down."

Feeling Pandora-crazy, sounding Pandora-crazy, she crept along the dark hallway until she reached her bedroom. Damp clothes stuck to her body and her hair still dripped water from the compulsory shower she'd taken after Judith, Mayella and Bev—no! She didn't want to think about that or she'd scream again. And this time she wouldn't be able to stop.

Thank God Mayella had driven her home in the Rabbit, Beverlee following, because crazy Pandora would have driven her car into a tree, maybe on purpose.

Samantha's perfume permeated the house, even the master bedroom. Shivering, Delly undressed and slipped under the quilt.

"Delly, is that you?" Jon's voice sounded sleepy. "Why are you wet? Is it raining?"

She burst into tears, straining her already raw throat. Then she buried her face against his chest.

"What's the matter, honey?"

"I hate her. I'm never going there again, Jonny. I'm quitting the show. I'll give my notice on Monday, help Sami get settled, find another job, learn how to cook."

"Okay, baby, okay."

"Do you know the cradle song? Cat's in the cradle, little boy blue? Mayella's little boy blue. Beverlee's man in the moon."

"God, Delly, what happened?"

"Tired. Sleep."

"No. We've got to talk."

"Can't. They gave me tranquilizers."

"How many?"

"Two, three, I forget. They had to hush me. But I wouldn't hush so they gave me a shower."

"Jesus, Delly!"

"I love you," she said, and promptly fell asleep.

"Wake up," he pleaded, but she didn't stir. She slept deeply, her lips slightly parted, her breathing relaxed, rhythmic.

Still, it wouldn't hurt to keep a vigilant watch. Naked, Jon stood by the window. Darkness turned to dawn. Mrs. Grady's dog watered the palm tree and barked. From Samantha's room, Montalban sounded a reply.

Samantha. She had offered herself to him on a silver platter. No. A silver spoon. Cat's in the cradle, silver spoon—what was that all about? He loved Delly, but he was a playwright, an author, not a shrink, and he honestly didn't know what to do, what to say.

Standing guard against nebulous shadows, watching the world outside his window awaken, Jon found himself humming snatches of Harry Chapin's popular song. Then, kneeling by the bed, he brushed the tangled bangs away from Delly's forehead and kissed her pale lips.

"No, please, leave me alone."

"Okay, baby, sleep it off. Christ, I need some caffeine."

He tiptoed down the hallway. He paused outside Samantha's room, walked forwards, backwards, then entered and locked the door.

Samantha was nude, awake, waiting. "Fantasies are fun," she said. "Don't you agree?"

"Delly's asleep. We have to be very quiet."

"I sing when I fuck, darling."

She spread her legs and stroked with her fingers until her body quivered, on the verge of an orgasm. Aware that Samantha was addictive, wanton, uninhibited, Jon remembered a Paramount luncheon toast: "May all your pleasures become habits." He should leave the guest bedroom now, before this "habit" continued, before he was beyond redemption.

Wasn't he already beyond redemption?

"Come here, Delly's boyfriend." Samantha's voice sounded urgent. "Hurry!"

Jon swiftly crossed the room, covered her mouth with his, and swallowed her orgasmic anthem. At the same time he thrust deep, plunging into a maelstrom of imperative contractions. He was grateful for the dog and parrot since their barking squawks disguised his own involuntary moans. His coming was abdominally painful, a guilty, perverse pleasure, but a pleasure nonetheless. He issued forth a steady stream of desire, even while he held Samantha's hands at bay, avoiding her sharp, scarlet fingernails.

Samantha sang.

Monty barked.

Sinbad squawked.

And Delly slept, curled up on the bed where George had supposedly screwed Martha.

Chapter Twenty-One

Delly didn't quit the show.

"I'm glad you confided in me first," Anissa said, following Monday's taping. "Play the story line to its conclusion and audition for other parts while you're still employed."

Delly slanted a glance toward her friend. Anissa looked radiant, glowing from the inside out. Her scene this morning with Drew—wow! Even Maxine, seated inside her booth at the end of the vulture grids . . . even Maxine had boomed, "That's friggin' fantastic, Charl!" Something had happened over the weekend, thought Delly, something friggin' fantastic.

"You don't understand," she said, desperate to explain, afraid she might lose Anissa's friendship if she did.

"Yes I do, Delly. Everybody's restless."

Like poison ivy, Drew's movie of the week had infected cast members with dreams of prime-time maybes. They were congratulatory, yet behind Drew's back they itched and bitched. Except Anissa, who seemed to thrive on the daily grind, who claimed her ascension to soap stardom was "hereditary."

Ordinarily, Delly would have itched along with the others. But today she was too consumed with indecision.

Should Pandora tell Charl about Beverlee and Mayella?

What if she did, and what if Charl mentioned Little Boy Blue and Man In The Moon to Echo? Delly could imagine Echo's knife-tongue slashing.

Maybe it was better to keep her lips sealed, keep on playing

Pandora, quell all rumors. At any rate, she wanted to forget Saturday night—a horrible dream.

Reality was Samantha.

Audition musicians arrived in endless rotation. Delly's small house throbbed with sound. Beer bottles and overflowing ashtrays littered every surface. Delly wished she could transport her valuable antiques to Lady Nan's mansion.

Samantha wanted to call her group Little Toot and the Engineers.

"Remember our favorite kid story, Dell?" she said, spooning yogurt between her glossy lips. "Daddy always read it out loud before we went to sleep, the story about the engine who kept saying, 'I think I can, I think I can.' "

"Little Toot was a tugboat," Delly said.

"Toot has certain connotations." Jon sipped his breakfast coffee. "You'd lose mass appeal."

"To hell with mass appeal. Drew's father started with a cult following." Samantha's eyes glittered. "Drew Flory. That's another score I have to settle." She shook her mane of palomino hair. "Never mind. Only kidding. Water under the bridge."

"Drop the name Toot," said Jon, "and I'll ask Drew to call his father. Maybe Andrew Florentino can devise a comic strip featuring your group. Drew said Chien once sang with the Temptations. Or was it the Beatles?"

"Little Toot was a tugboat," Delly said. "The little engine who could didn't have a name."

"Okay, Jon." Samantha pouted prettily. "I'll call myself Samantha and the Engineers. It's a bit innocuous, but I'll know what it really means. For the record, toot's not so bad. Don't look at me like that. I'm not into drugs. Singing's my turn-on. Haven't you heard me sing when I—"

"Take a shower. Me, too. Your *sister* says I sound like Tarzan." Thumping his chest, he gave a Weismuller whoop.

Delly waited for Jon to voice objections over the audition invasion, but he remained amused and agreeable as he tracked down possible arrangers and played host to the influx of applicants.

Samantha made her selection on a Thursday night. She sat next to Jon, an embroidered pillow wedged between her lower back and the back of the couch. "Piano, FDR," she said.

"Absolutely." Jon turned toward Delly, who slumped in her director's chair. "His real name is Franklin Delano Roosevelt Orowitz. Swears his parents named him that, hoping he'd become President. He can barely reach the piano pedals and he wears Elton John sunglasses. Would you fetch us some popcorn, honey?"

"I'm not Montalban. Fetch it yourself."

"Poor Dell," said Samantha. "She feels left out."

"I do not."

On his way to the kitchen, Jon patted her head.

Damn, he does think I'm Sami's rat-dog!

"I can't make up my mind about the drummer," said Samantha, upon Jon's return.

"That woman drummer was—what's your word? Marvy."

"No, she's not." Samantha flicked her gold lighter, pursed her lips, and blew a cloud of cigarette smoke toward the light fixture. "I want an American drummer, and she's Canadian."

"That's a stupid reason," said Delly. "After all, Paul Anka's Canadian."

"Hey, it's *my* band and I don't want any friggin' foreigners, okay?"

Jon nodded, but Delly knew the real reason behind Sami's decision. She didn't want another female in the group.

Seated again, Jon said, "How about the guy with the black-rimmed glasses?"

"Buddy Holly's ghost?" Samantha pressed her hand against

her heart. "Do you think those marvy curls are natural?"

"Are you selecting musicians based on their gender, curls, or talent?"

"Give me a break, Dell. Jay Salerno's a fine drummer. They call him 'The Salamander.' By the way, Jon, I told Barnum he was hired before he left the house."

Delly remembered Barnum because she'd been home for his audition. Tall and dark, chocolate icing atop a devil's food cake, Barnum was a master on the bass guitar. The gifted musician could play strings and horns, too.

Samantha tapped her chin with her index finger. "Do I need back-up vocalists?"

"No," Jon said. "You're good enough to carry it solo."

"Well, if you insist. That leaves the lead guitarist. How about Rattlesnake?"

"Who?"

"Don't you remember him, Jon? His real name is Steve something. He's skinny. Wore a tight jumpsuit, warm-up socks and ballet slippers. Mick Jagger without the lips."

"Rattlesnakes are poisonous," Jon said with a grin.

And diamonds are hard, thought Delly. So why did she feel like bursting into tears? Because Delly Diamond was flawed while Samantha Gold shined? Because Pandora was on the skids while Little Toot chugged her way up the harbor's watery mountain, reaching for her twin sister's star?

Twin. Twin-kle. Twinkle, twinkle, brand new star.

"Rattlesnake would attract groupies," Samantha said. "I'll capture the men in the audience. Barnum will attract jigaboos and jackamammies—"

"Samantha Vivian Gold!"

"Do those words offend you, Dell darling?"

"Daddy would turn over in his grave, and I won't tolerate racial slurs in *my* house."

Samantha's eyes sparked but she merely said, "Sorry," then turned to Jon. "Rattlesnake's young, cute, sexy. I'm singing Mom's two ballads, of course, but I've developed a repertoire of 1950s standards. Women love to orgasm while they dance. I know I did."

Delly blinked. "What do you mean, a repertoire? Good grief, Sami, have you landed a job already?"

"Didn't Jon tell you? I'm the opening act for a jig . . . for a *black* comedian who scored high marks on the *Jonah Wiggins Show.*"

"Where?"

"Vegas."

"How?"

"My New York singing teacher has clout."

"When?"

"Soon."

"Congratulations." Delly forced what she hoped was sincere cheer into her voice.

"It's probably a long shot. I mean, no one's coming to see *me.*"

"Don't put yourself down," Jon said. "You have more talent . . ."

He paused, and Delly could almost swear his cheeks reddened. Had she missed something?

"Jon darling," Samantha purred, "would you do me a big favor? I've found an old furnished house within my price range, big enough for me and the kids. I know it's late but the agent gave me a key, and if you could drive me there, well, to be perfectly honest, I need a man's opinion. Suppose I sign a rental agreement and the roof caves in or something? Want to come along for the ride, Dell?"

"No, thanks. I've got lines to study."

"Would you fetch us a six-pack and a blanket, Jonny?"

"Why do you need a blanket?" asked Delly, watching Jon head for the hallway linen closet.

"In case we want to sit. The house is filthy."

Jon returned. "I couldn't find an extra blanket. Will a sleeping bag do? There's one in the trunk of the car. Are you sure you don't want to join us, Delly?"

"What the heck. I'll tag along."

"If the house is old and furnished," he said, "there might be junk stored in the attic."

"Junk?"

"Antiques."

"Since when are my antiques junk?"

"Don't fight," Samantha said. "I almost forgot, Jonny. Bring along a can of bug spray, please. Is there such a thing as snake spray? The agent said snakes might be lurking."

"Snakes?" Delly shuddered. "I've changed my mind. I'll stay here."

"Well, if you insist."

Delly caught her breath at the familiar refrain, and almost changed her mind again. Samantha looked like an illustration for Little Toot. Her eyes gleamed and cigarette smoke *whooshed* upwards, like the smoke from Little Toot's smokestack.

"Goodbye, Dell," she said. "Don't wait up."

Toot, toot, tootsie, good-bye.

Toot, toot, tootsie, don't cry

Jon found an arranger, Garrison Smith, a Harry Belafonte lookalike. He took Carolyn Anne's ballads and enhanced the haunting melodic themes.

Samantha turned thumbs down on the old house, which, she said, had bats as well as bugs.

FDR, Salamander, Barnum and Rattlesnake appeared at all

hours for impromptu meals, not to mention impromptu practice sessions.

Montalban barked non-stop.

"Shut the fuck up," squawked Sinbad.

Delly tried to ignore the damage to her beloved antiques. Even the new piano had cigarette burns.

"I'll pay for repairs when this is over," Samantha promised.

Say something, Jonny, Delly pleaded silently. But Jon took an office near Paramount to pen a new script while waiting for *Duck Pond*'s final edit. Publication of his novel was due soon, too.

The *Morning Star* story line peaked with the approach of Hannah's demise. Scottie Fitzgerald swore that after her last scene, as corpse, she would leave for Italy to star in a film. Delly wondered if Italian restaurants served sushi. Fortunately, Italian spaghetti, western or otherwise, was flavored with Scottie's two favorite spices: sex and garlic.

Drew's TV movie had topped the ratings. Now his agent negotiated with CBS, submitting one of Jon's old screenplays for the network's consideration. Called *The Groundhog Murders,* Jon's script involved a Jack-the-Ripper-ish killer. Drew would play the clue-hunting brother of a slain victim. Rumor had it that, if successful, Drew's character might spin off into a series.

At long last, Samantha left for Vegas.

Chapter Twenty-Two

The hotel room was small. Guests probably didn't spend much time sleeping, thought Delly, as she brushed her hair away from her forehead and anchored the thick strands with rhinestone-crusted barrettes.

No Pandora bangs. No ponytail. Tonight she'd watch her sister's debut with adult panache.

Her dress was an ebony sheath, gathered in an abbreviated bustle. One strap kept the bodice from falling.

"Better not slump," Jon teased, sitting on the edge of their bed. He wore a dark gray suit and his shirt matched the smoky blue of his eyes. "You look good enough to eat," he added, patting the bedspread.

"Daddy used to tell Mom that," Delly said somewhat wistfully as she paced back and forth between a mirrored dresser and a window.

"Nervous, honey?"

"You bet. I don't know if Sami has butterflies, but I have a few competing for an Olympic medal in Lepidopteran Gymnastics."

"Do you wish Delly Diamond was backstage warming up?"

"No way, Jonny. I couldn't sing in front of an audience. I tried once, in the fifth grade. Disaster! Sami had to come to my rescue, and I've never forgotten the humiliation. If I was on stage tonight, I'd faint."

"That's bullshit! You'd be great. It's like falling off a horse and climbing back on top again."

"Maybe. But I didn't climb then and it's too late now." Delly spun into a pirouette. "I can't wait. Music by Carolyn Ann Gold. Mom should be here. I wish I hadn't promised Sami I wouldn't tell Mom."

"Samantha thought about inviting your mother and step-father, but she's afraid she might fail."

"She's not afraid of failure, Jonny. Even if she mixed up the Little Engine and Little Toot, her basic philosophy is 'I know I can.' "

"Samantha's more vulnerable than you realize, Delly. She tries to hide it but she's scared. That tough act is a facade."

"Poor Samantha."

"Aw, be fair. She's worked very hard to make her Vegas debut a success."

"I know."

"Rehearsals day and night. She takes one break a day, to watch you on your soap. She thinks you're terrific."

"Yeah, sure. She watches Drew Flory and plots revenge."

"Revenge? Why?"

"She used to date Drew a long time ago. Until he dumped her. I suppose I should warn him. Anissa, too."

"You're overreacting."

"Am I?"

"Yes." Jon leaned back against his pillow. "Come here, you gorgeous thing."

"No. Come here."

"What are you doing?"

"Admiring the view."

"So am I."

"Thanks. But I meant the view from our window." Delly sensed Jon's approach.

"What view? It's a parking lot."

"Forget the cars and look at the sign. I once squinted up a movie marquee and pictured my name there. I never pictured 'Samantha and the Engineers,' but it's almost the same. One day Sami's name will appear above the comedian."

"And my Diamond will shine from a movie marquee." Circling her body with his arms, he dipped his hands beneath her bodice. "Why is it such a turn-on to make love in a hotel?"

"Because it's new, different, and we don't have to wash the sheets. Whoa, leave my breasts alone. They're not slot machines. Do you expect coins to fall out from under my skirt?"

"Absolutely. Can you feel the handle on *my* slot machine? It's tickling the cleft in your curvaceous butt."

"We don't have time."

"Sure we do. We'll skip dinner."

"I'm all dressed up."

"This is Vegas. We can play strip poker." He pulled Delly over to the dresser and mimed dealing cards. "What do you have?"

She scooped up her imaginary cards and glanced down. "A full house," she said, her voice smug.

"I dealt myself four aces, and four aces beats a full house. Take off your dress." He mimed reshuffling. "What do you have?"

"Wait a sec. Let me hang up my new dress so it doesn't wrinkle. Okay, I have four aces."

"Too bad. I have a royal flush."

"What? I thought four aces were best."

"Nope. You lose. Take off your panties." He shuffled and dealt. "What do you have?"

She brought her splayed hands closer to her face. "I've got a royal flush. Too bad. You lose."

Jon removed his clothing, every stitch. "No," he said. "I win."

The hotel's entertainment hall, adjacent to the main casino, filled rapidly. The new comedian had been touted all week, and the celebrities who ringed the stage included Buzzy Beeson, Rex Smith, Mort Sahl, Jerry Lewis, Jonah Wiggins, Maryl Bradley, and Pat Huxley.

Thanks to Samantha, Jon and Delly sat up front, their small table close to Huxley's party.

Delly watched a pregnant woman approach. Tall and fine-boned, her brown eyes tilted slightly at the corners and her red hair was bunned in back, circled by a string of pearls. She wore a simple white maternity dress, partially covered by a mauve silk scarf, and her expression was impish rather than beautiful.

"Hi, folks, we've never met," she said. "I'm Maryl Bradley Wiggins. You're Delly Diamond, Pandora on Drew's soap. And you must be Jon Griffin. Drew thinks you're a genius."

"Drew's the genius." Jon stood and offered Maryl his chair.

"No, thanks. The show's about to start. Jonah had a few days off so we decided to catch his comedian and sign up Samantha Gold, if she's as good as the advance publicity says she is."

"She is," Delly said.

"That's right. Anissa did mention that Samantha's your sister. I believe I'll sit after all." Maryl slid onto Jon's chair and folded her arms above her belly. "I'll bet you're excited, Delly."

"She's more nervous than excited," Jon said.

"I know what you mean." Maryl smiled. "Drew and I are thirteen months apart. Still, I can always tell when he's up to something. We have this invisible bond."

"Samantha and I are twins," Delly said, "but we don't seem to have that bond you're talking about. I wish Anissa and Drew were here."

"Me, too. A shame they had to shoot Dick Clark's quiz show. Cal and Charl and a bunch of *General Hospital* soap stars, all for charity. Oops, Jonah's beckoning. I'm not sure I'll see you later. The baby usually sends me to bed early." With a grace that belied her pregnancy, Maryl rose from the chair.

"She's lovely," Delly whispered, as Jon sat and the curtains opened.

FDR, Salamander, Barnum and Rattlesnake posed at their instruments. Salamander issued forth a drum roll. The stage darkened. One muted spotlight covered Samantha's entrance.

She wore her favorite burnt orange, a skin-tight dress that sparkled with hundreds of marmalade sequins. Both side seams of the long skirt had been slit to the waist, revealing abbreviated panties that molded her hips and buttocks. Strapless, the gown strained to conceal Samantha's breasts, and the audience gasped when she raised her arms to embrace the spotlight.

Delly admired her sister's face, framed by carefully tousled palomino hair. Lipstick glistened and black kohl emphasized the amber glints in Sami's eyes.

Signaling her musicians, she sang her mother's haunting ballad about the photographer and his dream vision. A moment of silence followed her last note. Then the audience erupted, rising and applauding. Pat Python sobbed audibly.

Samantha took several bows, and Delly saw that her sister had lost fifteen, maybe twenty more pounds. How could she have done that so quickly? Diet pills? Diet soda? Cocaine? What had she said? *Just for the record, toot's not so bad.*

At the end of her performance, Samantha received another standing ovation, sang three encores, and the comedian who had yet to appear was already history.

" 'I awoke one morning and found myself famous,' " Delly said to Jon. "Byron. Anissa quoted that line after Drew's movie-of-the-week."

Samantha had reserved a hotel suite for her victory celebration.

She knew she'd be a hit, thought Delly. Scared? Vulnerable? Not even close.

Capturing Rex Smith, silencing the guests, Samantha joined the handsome singer in a duet from *The Pirates of Penzance*. The room didn't have a piano or drums, but Barnum and Rattlesnake provided background music.

"More!" the guests screamed.

Someone shouted, "Play it again, Sam!"

She did, a solo this time.

Mort Sahl and Jerry Lewis traded quips. Buzzy Beeson, on the wagon, performed an old Vaudeville routine. A poker-faced Samantha played straight lady, feeding him lines.

Barnum and Rattlesnake took a break, first flicking the room's radio switch to an all-music station. Guests pushed furniture up against the wall.

Caterers arrived with champagne and hors d'oeuvres.

A soap fan asked Delly for her autograph. Jon winked and slipped away. After scribbling her name, Delly searched the hallway and saw him embracing Samantha, next to the elevators.

Delly gulped down her champagne, turned back into the suite, and bumped into Rattlesnake, who asked her to dance. He gyrated his sweaty body against hers, and his smell made her sick to her stomach. She tried to settle the queasy feeling with more champagne. Then she watched Jon dance with Sami, afraid to take her eyes off them, afraid the orange dress would disappear, afraid the marquee outside the hotel would suddenly read: ELOPED WITH JON.

Unlike a telegram, she couldn't paste a marquee inside a scrapbook.

This is Vegas, she thought. She could marry Jon tonight.

She saw him clasp his hands about Samantha's waist, shifting her from one of his hips to the other in a classic jitterbug move. Sami's spiked heels flew off and her breasts finally escaped the gown's bodice. Laughing, she tucked them back inside, then gave Jon a kiss while flashbulbs exploded and cameras clicked.

Outside the restroom, Delly heard voices behind the closed door.

"Isn't Samantha Gold beautiful? I'm getting my hair colored and cut like hers."

"It wouldn't help. You have no breasts."

"I can fix that, too. Isn't her boyfriend cute?"

"The tall guy who looks like that old movie star, Tyrone what's his face?"

"Yeah. Some girls have all the luck."

Tears salted Delly's champagne. As the gossipy women exited the restroom, a hand grasped her arm and propelled her inside.

Maryl shut the door and locked it. Then she said, "You look like you've lost your best friend."

"What are you doing here?" Delly placed her empty champagne glass on the sink's marbled surface. "I thought you planned to go to bed early."

"Jonah wants to sign Samantha, so I decided to tag along. Why the tears? Come on, Delly, 'fess up. My brother Drew says I'm a good listener."

"You wouldn't understand."

"Why not?"

"Because you're perfection."

"Ouch. What an awful compliment. Forgive me, Delly, but are you jealous over your sister's successful debut?"

"No. Yes. I don't know. Not her success."

"What then?"

"I guess it can be summed up in two sentences. My father called me Smarty-Pants. He called my sister Princess Pretty."

"Oh, I see. You'd rather be pretty than smart."

"I want to be both."

"Who doesn't? Look, Delly, you can purchase beauty at any hair salon or cosmetics counter, but you can't buy smart."

"Have you ever heard that song about the ugly duckling, Maryl?"

"Sure. The other birds told him to get out of town."

"I'll bet you were a swan from day one."

"Nope. I was an ugly duckling. Too tall."

"I was too short."

"I was too skinny."

"I was too fat."

"I wore braces."

"So did I."

"And glasses." Maryl smiled. "Aren't you going to say you wore glasses?"

"No. You win. Who turned you into Cinderella?"

"A photographer named Bryan Edwards, but he wasn't my Prince Charming. I really hate that fairytale. Want to know why? I'll tell you why. Cinderella never took control of her life. You might say she won the lottery but never bothered to invest in a ticket. You see, Delly, that damn fairy godmother gave Cinderella a Bob Mackie gown, Rosebud cosmetics, René Lalique slippers, and a Rolls Royce coach, but Cindy had nothing to do with it. She didn't rise from the ashes and say, 'I'm gonna change my life. Wash my face and clothes, tidy my hair, hitch a ride to the ball, and charm the bejesus out of Prince Charming. Afterwards, I'll start a cleaning service, hire some chimney sweeps, rake in the bucks, buy back my father's chateau, and send my wicked stepmother packing.' "

"Are you saying it's okay to be an ugly duckling if you have character?"

"Very good. For the record, Cinderella and I have a lot in common. My magic wand was a camera and Prince Charming turned out to be a talk show host. I never took control. Things just happened."

"Shit happens."

"No, Delly, dreams happen. That's why the story of Cinderella has survived over the years."

"Maryl, I don't get your point and I know you have one."

"I caught you on Broadway in *Duck Pond Sonata* and I've watched you on *Morning Star.* You're terrific, Delly. You make me laugh and cry. Still, I sense a certain uncertainty. As if you're saying take me as I am or not at all."

"What's wrong with that?"

"Nothing. You play crazies very well. But you should try to grow, stretch, expand that marvelous talent. Find a new part. Experiment."

"Boy oh boy, it's easy to give advice when you're rich and famous."

"I'm sorry."

"No. I'm sorry. I appreciate your concern, Maryl, really. Nobody ever talks to me like you just did. Jon says to quit *Morning Star.* Anissa tells me to stay. I'm scared to rise from the ashes and start my own cleaning service. What if I fail?"

"What if you don't?"

There was a loud pounding on the bathroom door and somebody shouted, "Hey, did you fall in?"

Someone else said, "I'm gonna pee my pants."

Maryl unlocked the door. "Sorry, ladies, we were swapping swan stories."

As Delly exited, she heard one of the women say, "I'll bet swan's another word for cocaine."

Delly hugged Maryl good night. Then she returned to the perimeter of the improvised dance floor.

"There you are," said Jon. "Samantha wants you."

Samantha wants you. Delly feels left out. Fetch. Roll over. Sit up and beg—

Forget it! She wouldn't beg Jon to marry her.

He led her to the front of the room. "Remember," he said.

"It's like climbing back up again."

"What do you mean?"

"The horse."

"What horse?"

Samantha's arms twisted around Delly's shoulders like a snake. "Presenting the Gold sisters," she said into the microphone. "For your entertainment we'll sing a medley from *South Pacific.*"

"No!" Delly shook her head, the motion causing dizziness. But Sami's long fingernails dug into her bare shoulder and the brief fainting spell went away. She couldn't remember all the words to "Some Enchanted Evening," but Sami covered her memory loss.

"Play it again, Sam!" Pat Python screamed.

"Pray it again, Bootsie," slurred Buzzy Beeson, whose wagon had apparently tipped over.

Red hot anger replaced Delly's awkward embarrassment.

Bad, bad Pandora Poe, she thought, *meaner than a swan-cocaine-junkie, bad-est kid on the whole damn strip.*

Strip poker!

Grinning wickedly, she lowered her strap, raised her skirt, and began to bump and grind.

Salamander beat out a drum roll on the coffee table.

"Take it off, take it all off," Buzzy Beeson chanted.

Samantha captured Delly's arm. "What the hell do you think you're doing?"

She tugged her arm free. "Sing my doodahs, bitch."

"Stop it, Delly. Jonny, stop her."

"Why?" he said, drunk as a skunk. "She's on top of the damn horse."

The guests clapped in a mesmerizing rhythm. Lord, thought Delly, she had to take something off. What? Her bra? No. She wasn't wearing a bra.

Securing her hem beneath her chin, tugging at her pantyhose, she heard a few coins pelt the floor. Suddenly, she remembered Maryl's words about how you could buy pretty but not smart.

Smarty-Pants was not for sale!

Dropping her skirt, Delly held up her hands and waited for silence. "The Gold sisters are played out," she said loud and clear. Then she turned her face toward Samantha. "Pack up and leave my house or I'll kick your butt all the way back to Bayside. And if you think I'm kidding, I'll start by sending your Mexican rat to the pound."

"Tonight I opened mouth, inserted foot," Maryl said, snuggling closer to Jonah and kicking their bed covers free.

"So what else is new?" Jonah's voice conveyed his smile.

"I told Delly Diamond she needed to stretch, expand, but I think I was talking about myself."

"You're expanding." Jonah patted her belly.

"I'm serious, honey. I felt drawn to Delly. In a way she reminds me of me. The ugly duckling syndrome."

"Knock it off, Maryl. You're beautiful."

"Not really. The camera makes me beautiful. You make me *feel* beautiful. Darling, if I was an ugly stepsister, rather than Cinderella, would you love me?"

"No." He raised himself up on one elbow. "But not because of ugly or pretty. I wouldn't love Cinderella, either. Do you understand?"

"I guess."

"Look, sweetheart, if you were an ugly stepsister, you wouldn't be Maryl. If you were Cinderella, you wouldn't be Maryl. In both cases, you'd have different personas. I fell in love with Marilyn Monroe Bradley Florentino, not some fairytale image." He placed her hand on top of the bulge between his thighs. "Do you know how much I love you?"

"Yes. Me too, you. One more question. You've seen Delly when I play the tapes from Drew's show. Are you saying she wouldn't be adored if she weren't so vulnerable?"

"That's an awful example. Delly's playing a role."

"No, Jonah. She's exactly the same off-screen."

"Maybe vulnerability is one of her assets."

"Maybe. But I had this stupid urge to grab her shoulders, shake her hard, and tell her to grow up. At the same time, I wanted to cuddle her. Does that make any sense?"

"Absolutely. Maryl, you said you were talking about yourself when you told Delly she needed to stretch. What do you mean?"

"I don't know. Yes, I do. I wish . . ."

"Wish what?"

"I wish I could create something memorable. I never told you this, Jonah, but I once played a stand-up comic—before we got pregnant. It was amateur night at one of those comedy clubs and I was so scared I almost fainted."

"Poor baby."

"Poor nothing. I made the audience laugh."

"Then why'd you quit?"

"Because I was pretending to be a woman named Miss Wiggy, just like I pretend to be this model named—"

"Maryl, what do you want?"

"I want to negotiate world peace or write a best-seller or solve a murder."

"Solve a murder?"

"Use my *wits* to achieve success . . . my brain power. I told Delly you couldn't buy smart."

"Sure you can. Would you like to be affiliated with the talk show? Secure guest stars? You could become more involved with my clothing line, maybe even schedule fashion shows."

"Thanks, Prince Charming, but that was Cinderella's

disadvantage—or her dilemma. Your generous offer is simply another magic wand."

"Are you unhappy, darling?"

"No. That's the problem. I've found my Prince Charming and passively accepted happily ever after."

"Why do you consider happy passive?"

"Never mind. Pregnant babble. Speaking of magic wands, I can feel yours growing."

Straddling Jonah's body, she began to spasm, proving that happy wasn't passive after all.

"To hell with Cinderella," she gasped, "and fuck Prince Charming!"

Back in their room, Jon fumbled with the tiny buttons on Delly's dress.

"Forget strip poker," he said. "It takes too long. Let's play Farmer in the Dell."

"Leave me alone. You're drunk and I'm mad."

"Why are you mad?"

"The horse bit."

"I was trying to prove a point."

"Really! I suppose you believe that if you throw someone into deep water, they'll swim."

"Well, that's true. Isn't it?"

"No. They doggie paddle and look ridiculous."

"You didn't look ridiculous."

"I did at first."

"But you overcame the odds, honey. This is Vegas and you beat the odds. You had that crowd in the palm of your hand."

"I had them in the crotch of my panties. In any case, that's not the only reason I'm mad."

"C'mon, honey, let's play Farmer."

Farmer in the Dell, improvised when Jon had created the

farmer-Virginia scene for *Duck Pond*, was a variation of their dialogue game and the signal for a sexual romp. Delly scowled. "Play your dumb games with Samantha."

"I can't play Farmer in the Sami. That makes no sense." He took off his clothes and stretched out on top of the bed. "Okay, we'll lick stamps and envelopes."

"Stop it! No more games!"

"What's the matter?"

"I saw you and Sami."

"What did you say?"

"I saw you together, in the hallway."

"From the hallway? But I locked the guest room door." He tried to sit up. "You're right, I'm drunk. Can't think straight. At first I didn't want to, I swear. But Samantha called it therapeutic and you were at Pendergraft's house and I was so frustrated. I know that's not a good excuse, and I hated myself, and I'm sorry you found out because it's over and done with. Christ, you saw. Why didn't you say something before now?"

"You slept with my sister? You made love to Sami?"

Jon sat up and shook his head. "What are we talking about? You said you saw Sami and me. What did you see?"

"Tonight I watched you hug and kiss in the hallway, next to an elevator. Then you danced and kissed again."

Jon's head buzzed while sour champagne traveled up his throat. "Jesus, I'm so stupid."

"The old house. Sleeping bags and snakes. Bugs and bats."

Jon swallowed. "There was a house. Sami really did want me to check it out."

"You made love, right?"

"No, Delly, we fucked. There's a big difference. I make love with you, only you."

"I feel sick."

"I'm sorry, baby. I can't tell you how sorry I am."

"Anyone but Samantha!"

Jon watched with horrified fascination as Delly shivered. Her body altered its shape, shrinking, and her dress seemed too large for her childish frame.

"Panda feels sick. Panda can't breathe."

Alarmed, sobering rapidly, Jon staggered to his feet. "Easy, baby," he said. "Take one breath at a time." Lifting her, he sat on the edge of the bed. She straddled his lap, sucking her thumb. "Don't," he pleaded. He slapped her hand away, caught part of her face, and her thumb popped out.

"You bastard," she yelped, flailing out at him. Losing her balance, she slid from his lap to the floor.

"I'm sorry." Jon knelt beside her. "I didn't mean to hit so hard. Damn it, you were sucking your thumb!"

Delly crept up onto the bed, curled into a tight ball and said, "You don't hit Panda when she sucks your—"

"It's me, Sami, hi." The door opened. "I couldn't help eavesdropping. Is my sister drunk, Jonny? Or is that a scene from her stupid soap?"

"Go away!" Jon shouted.

"Sure. If you come with me."

"Are you insane? Get out of here!"

"I'm high, Jonny. Beeson shared his toot and I need to get laid. Delly doesn't deserve a lover like you. Do you know what she did after I married Jules? She stole my prom dress."

"That's what I wore when I met you, Tarz. I guess Jane swings like a pendulum do. I guess Panda's not so pure after all. She's a slut. No. A slug. Slug is what you put in a slot machine if you want to cheat the house. Everybody cheats."

"Christ, what's wrong with her?" Samantha began walking toward the bed.

"We've only just begun," Delly said. "Jules gave me a mink teddy, drenched in semen. I had it dry-cleaned."

Samantha's mouth twisted into an ugly scowl. "Jules said he loved Delly best. I kicked him in the balls. He never slapped me, that was a lie, but you swallowed it, Jonny, hook, line, and sinker. So I swallowed you. Don't you want me, Delly's boyfriend? Why pretend?"

"Samantha, if you don't get out of here—"

"Oh, shit. I broke my sworn vow, promised I wouldn't confess to Delly-Dog, promised I wouldn't mention the marathon sex on her dopey couch."

"You're right, Jonny," Delly said. "My antiques are junk."

"I've already been offered contracts," Samantha said. "You can see the slobber on the pages. They're all drooling, crawling on their hands and knees, trying to lick my butt. You can have my butt, Jonny, anytime. He loves my butt, Dell."

"You bovine bitch!" Enraged beyond reason, Jon clenched his fists. In another moment he'd sent her reeling.

Samantha's eyes glittered. "When you come crawling, I'll kick *your* balls," she said. Then she left the room, slamming the door behind her.

Jon lay on the bed and pulled Delly's body close to his. "It'll be all right, baby. I'll make everything right again."

She sat up and stared at her thumb. "Danny Kaye sang about an ugly duckling, but he also sang about Thumbelina. She was a tiny little thing. I feel so tiny, Jonny. I want to fly away, find some place soft, and disappear."

"I love you, Delly. I've always loved you, from the first moment we met." He swallowed a sob. "Mercy, Delly."

"It's *merci, mon—*"

"Je lai pardonne de m'avoir offense."

"I forgive him for having offended me," she translated. "You speak French. That bit at the restaurant . . . you're such a fraud . . . just like my sister."

"Forgive me."

Momentarily, she was silent. Then she said, "I've been captured and locked inside a box . . . Pandora's box. Do you know what I think? I'll tell you what I think. Those stupid gods sent Pandora the very first television set and told her not to plug it in. If she did, they said, she'd let loose a swarm of evils upon mankind."

"Forgive me, Delly. Please. I love you."

"You can't love me, Jonny. I'm stuck inside a TV—Pandora's box. Don't you see? If you divide an image into a collection of small colored dots, your brain will reassemble the dots into a meaningful image. I'm just a pixel, Jonny. You can't love me because I don't exist."

Intermission

He was surprised by California's grit and grime. In the movies it looked so clean—bleached beaches and bleached blondes.

The first woman he met was dark-haired and her legs looked like a burnt field of weeds. She said her name was Jane but people called her Doe, and she was a Notre Dame football fan. He said his name was J.S. and he was a Packers fan. They had a lot in common, he said.

"Yeah," she said. "We got a lot in common. Like, legs. You got hairy legs and I don't shave mine. I'll get them waxed after you've paid."

"Pay? Jesus!"

"He'd pay, too. This is Hollywood. Unless you're a big-shot producer or director, you pay."

"How much?"

"A hundred."

"For a C-note, I get to shave your pussy."

She laughed. "There's a razor in the bathroom."

An hour later she wasn't laughing. Notre Dame had lost a fan and the morgue would soon have a new Jane Doe.

Christ, the porn, he thought, strolling down Sunset Boulevard. Los Angeles was an X-rated movie, projected on an outdoor screen.

Splitting the smoggy sky, a billboard advertised Sean Connery's new film, Never Say Never Again.

Men and women sported pierced ears.

Sounds from a ghetto blaster pierced his own ears: Joe Cocker and

Jennifer Warnes were up where they belonged.

He felt as if he was where he belonged, and nobody would never say he was a failure again.

A fancy apartment didn't suit his needs, so he found himself a nondescript motel that rented by the month. All he needed was a bed and a color TV with good reception. "My wife is hooked on soap operas," he told the motel manager.

He didn't have a wife.

A wife, however, justified the magazine pictures taped to his wall. Let others get their jollies jacking off from posters of Farrah-the-faucet. His imaginary wife preferred Anissa Cartier. So did he.

He loved Charl. But if she didn't love him back, she'd die.

Act Three
Chapter Twenty-Three

Hollywood, California

Vanessa Williams briefly won the Miss America title.

"I know why she was disqualified," Maryl said, her voice smug.

"Her provocative photos?" Clearing dirty dishes from the TV tables, Anissa grinned when Maryl captured the last microscopic crumb of chocolate mousse pie with her index finger.

"No, not her photos." Drew turned off the TV. "It's because Ms. Williams doesn't have three names. Right, Maryl?"

"Right. You're so smart. And they say a man's brains are in his quick."

"My quick is feeling very patriotic these days. It keeps wanting to salute."

"What the bloody hell are you nattering about?" Anissa implored the ceiling.

"Explain it to her, Drew." Maryl grabbed her purse. "I have to go home now, check out Jonah's patriotism."

On October 16, 1983, the Baltimore Orioles defeated Philadelphia four games to one, proving that birds were more powerful than Phillies, and Delly collected her World Series bet from Anissa—fifty cents.

Samantha Gold appeared on *The Jonah Wiggins Show,* following guest star Pat Huxley. "Poor Python, she's no match for your sister," said Maryl, watching the show with Delly. "Jonah will have to bleep half their conversation."

New story lines developed on *Morning Star.* Cal investigated Hannah's murder with a vengeance. Charl recovered from her "mental illness" and moved back into the hub of Wayne County's social sphere. Her romance with Cal was consummated.

Despite her numerous deceptions, viewers still regarded Charl as a pure goddess. Aware of that attitude, the writers scripted changes. On a visit to Pandora, Charl said that Hannah had been killed *before* her escape from the mental ward. "I'm not sure I could have gone through with it, Panda," Charl admitted. "But it doesn't matter. Hannah was already dead."

"She was?"

"Yes."

"Like Robin?"

"Yes, dear. God wanted Robin for His own nest," Anissa improvised, because Delly's dialogue hadn't been in the script. "Play with your baby now, Panda, and I'll visit you again real soon."

Afterwards, Anissa confronted Delly inside the makeup room. "Are you feeling all right, love?"

"Sure. Why?"

"That Robin bit was an adlib."

"It was?"

"We're lucky Maxine didn't catch on. I guess she's preoccupied with Marybeth."

Ratings had soared when Nurse Marybeth became infatuated with an elderly, distinguished drifter who had mysteriously appeared in Wayne County. The viewers were just beginning to realize that the stranger, played by Christopher Coombs, was really Marybeth's long lost father.

"Topher" Coombs was Maxine's latest coup. The gracefully aging actor had been a movie staple for three decades. In his early films he sported a pencil-thin mustache, and he always played the hero's best friend. During the 1970s he'd starred as a detective in one short-lived TV series. Until recently, he'd toured the regional dinner theater circuit.

His hair had silvered attractively. His mustache and beard framed a sensual mouth with very white teeth, and he appeared much younger than sixty-something.

One afternoon he invited Delly to his dressing room. "I hear you've been given your walking papers," he said.

She winced. "My contact hasn't been renewed."

"Damn shame." His white teeth flashed. "We've hardly had a chance to know each other."

"Damn shame," she repeated while her mind raced. *I wonder how much influence he has with Maxine. I wonder if he can get Panda reinstated?*

Topher rummaged through his wardrobe, pulled a bottle from the pocket of his topcoat, and poured straight bourbon into a couple of water glasses. "Here, baby."

"I don't drink anymore, Mr. Coombs. I had a sort of nervous breakdown."

"Dear child, I understand."

No, you don't. Samantha Gold's a shooting star while Delly Diamond's a falling star.

"Maybe I will have one drink." As Delly shook her bangs away from her eyes, she caught her reflection in the dressing room mirror. She had just finished her last scene with Anissa. The shapeless gowns had long ago given way to a variety of sleepwear, and today Pandora wore ruffled shortie pajamas.

Seated on a wooden chair, Topher leaned back against the dressing table and patted his legs. "Sit on Daddy's lap, baby."

Anissa said that Randy said that Topher has a thing for whores dressed up as little girls. "I must change my clothes now, Mr. Coombs. Good luck on the show." Delly drained her glass and headed for the door.

"Maybe I can talk to Miss Graham, convince her to let you stay."

"Would you, Mr. Coombs?"

"Call me Daddy, baby."

"Panda would be ever so grateful, Daddy."

"Pour yourself another nip and sit on Daddy's lap."

"I shouldn't drink, Daddy."

Because Panda was sick this morning. Delly's pregnant. Las Vegas. Strip poker. Delly forgot to pack her pills, so Panda has to suffer. Will Topher really talk to Maxine if Panda lets him touch her jammies?

It was worth a try. What did she have to lose? Anyway, Topher's casting couch was preferable to Judith's, and booze would help dull her senses.

Delly filled her glass with the last of the bourbon. She took deep gulps.

Panda's tummy flip-flopped then settled.

Delly aimed the empty bottle toward a wastepaper basket.

"No, no, baby, not there," Topher said. "Hide the bottle in my coat pocket. That's a good little girl. Come here and finish Daddy's drink."

She did, again gulping quickly. Then she straddled his lap and felt his hands fondle her breasts. He panted and his breath smelled like a Peppermint Patty wrapper. He unzipped his slacks. Above his shorts, he wore an elastic band to flatten his belly.

"Panda drank too fast," Delly whimpered. "Panda's dizzy."

"Daddy will make you feel better."

Leaning back in his chair, Topher tugged her ruffled panties down her hips and thrust his fingers between her thighs, just like Mr. Hailey, the man in the drugstore, the man who'd given her all that free candy. The come-out-come-out-wherever-you-are, ollie-ollie-income-tax man. Topher even had a Santa-belly and whiskers. Delly then did something she'd wanted to do for more than twenty years. She slapped Mr. Hailey's face.

Topher's very white false teeth plopped out and fell into his lap.

Wriggling backwards, Delly screamed, afraid she might get bitten.

Then she screamed again. And again.

On the *Jonah Wiggins Show,* the one with Samantha, Pat Huxley had told of an actress who auditioned for a famous horror film director on the proverbial casting couch. The ingénue's orgasmic screams had led to a starring role in one of his movies.

"Stop it," Topher said. "Shut up! Somebody will hear . . . what do you want, missy? Money?"

Delly swallowed her next scream. "I want to stay on the show. You said you'd talk to Maxine."

"Yeah. Okay. Sure. You got it."

Delly stood and hitched up her panties. "For every part, scream, scream, scream," she sang.

"Get out of here, I'm not kidding. You're a nut case."

The bourbon was playing silly buggers in her tummy. Who used to say silly buggers? Randy. She was afraid to move, afraid if she did she'd throw up.

Topher's face dripped perspiration, revealing age-wrinkles beneath his carefully applied makeup, and all of a sudden Delly knew he'd never talk to Maxine. Not in a million years.

So she threw up all over his false teeth.

"What's the matter, baby?"

"Don't call me baby." Delly lifted her face from the pillow and stared at Jon through swollen eyes.

"Do you want to tell me what's going on?"

"No."

"Delly, you run inside the house without a word, gulp down

three aspirins, bathe for an hour, hit the bed, and—"

"I've been fired."

"Fired?"

"My contract wasn't renewed."

"So you'll find another role, one that's different, better."

"True." Sitting up, she retied the sash on her red kimono. "Drew's agent has agreed to represent me."

Jon watched her light a cigarette, a new oral addiction. But cigarettes were preferable to thumb, even though you couldn't get cancer from thumb.

"Has Samantha returned from Vegas?" Delly blew smoke toward the Humpty Dumpty bank.

"Yes. She flew in for Jonah's show, flew back, then returned for good today. She cleared out her things while we were both away from home and left a note on the piano, which by the way is now ours, a thank-you gift. Do you want to see it?"

"The piano?"

"No, the note. Are you okay, honey?"

"Sure. Tell me what it says."

"She's moving in with Rattlesnake."

"Did she take Montalban or is he another thank-you gift?"

"He's gone."

"Sinbad?"

"He's still here, inside the guest room."

"Maybe I should pluck his feathers and roast him for Thanksgiving dinner."

Jon walked toward the doll shelf. Then he turned and said, "Marry me."

She shook her head. "*Duck Pond*'s a success. They say you and Amy will be nominated for Oscars. Sami's songs have hit the charts. And I've been fired."

"So?"

"I have to get my career on track first, Jonny."

"Why?"

"Arthur Treacher once said—"

"Anissa once said."

"Anissa once said, 'In Hollywood success is relative. The closer the relative, the greater the success.' By the way, she's pregnant. Drew looks cocky. So does Cal." Rising from the bed, Delly grabbed an ashtray and snuffed out her cigarette.

"Do they plan to get married?"

"Yes. Listen to this, Jonny. *Morning Star* will use an authentic minister when Cal and Charl tie the knot. Then Anissa and Drew will repeat their vows for real. Before I forget, keep a week from Friday night open. The cast plans to give me a good-bye party at the Sawmill. Maxine and Judith have *not* been invited. Anissa and Drew will be there, of course, along with Echo and Peter, Lizzie and Marshal—remember them?"

"I think so. Doctors, right? Didn't they once operate on Robert Wagner?"

"You have a phenomenal memory."

"Fee nominal? Doesn't that mean insignificant? Trifling?"

"A trifle is candy made from chocolate, butter and sugar."

"Have some sugar, sugar." Tilting her chin, Jon kissed her. "The new movie I'm working on has a perfect part for you, and I have enough clout to insist you be cast."

"I thought Barbra Streisand wanted to read your script."

"She does, but there's a great supporting role."

I always play the supporting role.

An organ sounded a wedding march, but the tune that ran through Anissa's head was "Frankie and Johnnie."

She glanced up at Drew. He looked resplendent in a black tuxedo whose color matched his eyes. Even here, even now, thick, dark brown hair fell across his forehead and she ached to push it back.

Would he ever do her wrong? He'd have many opportunities. Why had she agreed to this marriage? Because of the baby? Because she was so head over heels in love with Drew Flory, she couldn't release her breath without sighing his name?

Oh, lordy, how they could love!

Anissa wore an empire-style gown, designed to hide her slight tummy bulge. Multiple layers of tatted antique lace fell to the tips of her heeled sandals. Creamy ribbons had been woven through the lace. A square-necked bodice enhanced her breasts and her gauzy veil was attached to a circlet of fresh flowers.

She and Drew stood before the minister.

"To love, honor and cherish, until death us do part," she repeated, thinking how Randy would approve. He believed in reincarnation. Maybe a compassionate divinity had slipped Randy's soul into the fetus that now rested beneath her heart.

Drew placed a gold band on her third finger.

"I pronounce you man and wife," intoned the minister.

"Beautiful," said Peter. "Maxine?"

"That's a wrap," she said, her voice booming from the overhead speakers.

Drew kissed his new bride. "Okay, darling," he said, "let's get married."

"Yes, let's," Anissa replied without hesitation.

An aroma of singed beef and hot au jus filled the room. The house specialty, prime rib platters, had just been delivered to *Morning Star* cast members. Seated at sawmill tables under redwood beams, other diners gaped at the familiar performers. Several people approached, brazenly asking for autographs.

After the platters had been removed, Drew tapped his water glass with a fork. "I'm not going to make a speech," he said, and grinned at the spontaneous applause. "Charl?"

Anissa stood and presented Delly with an enlarged photo of

the studio mural, signed by the cast. Then she held out Pandora's striped smock from the first day's taping. "When you look at this," she said, "always remember—"

"That I can be an actress in spite of my costume?"

"Actually I was going to quote Zsa Zsa. 'Ze only place men vant depth in a woman is in her décolletage.' "

Sporting a Tabby Cat pink and black spiked wig, Echo returned from a trip to the restroom. "What did I miss?"

"Charl's quote," Delly said.

"Not Charl, Anissa," Drew amended. "One day Anissa, as Charl, will step up to the camera and deliver her own lines. I thought she'd do it during our wedding. She had that look in her eyes."

"How could you see a look beneath my veil, Cal?"

"What would you have quoted, Anissa?" asked Heidi Hesselman, who played Nurse Marybeth. "Something about wedded bliss?"

"Okay, gang, you asked for it. 'I hate television. I hate it as much as peanuts. But I can't stop eating peanuts.' Quote, unquote."

"Jimmy Carter," Drew guessed.

"Orson Welles," said Anissa. "Enough quotations, people. Tabby has a gift for Delly."

Reaching beneath their table, the wigged actress held up a neon-lettered sign that read: THE ECHO CHAMBER.

"Echo Foster!" Peter placed his arm around her shoulders and squeezed. "You thief! If I don't kill you, Maxine will."

"Oh, pooh. Make another sign." Echo downed her glass of champagne. "I'll kill our Max off first, before she can do me in. I'll sabotage her sky booth, booby-trap her speakers so that the sound pierces her eardrums and penetrates her tiny brain."

Delly joined in the applause, giggling as each cast member suggested elaborate, goofy ways to murder Maxine Graham.

"Mr. Ratings lurked yesterday," Echo said, "disguised as a delivery boy from the Deli. Maybe he'll stab our Max with a sharp Kosher dill."

Anissa said, "They fired Topher Coombs."

"You're kidding," Heidi squealed. "I wondered why he was missing from our wedding scene, but I figured he was nursing one of his famous hangovers."

"He was, but that's not why he got axed . . ." Echo paused for effect. "Statutory rape," she stage-whispered. "Maxine tried to hush it up."

Heidi said, "How did *you* find out?"

"I happened to be strolling past Maxine's office when I heard the ruckus. Topher, the sly sleaze, took a motel room and invited some dumb mother to bring her little girl there for an audition. Mom waited outside. You can guess what happened. Luckily, the kid screamed bloody murder and Mom fetched the motel manager before too much damage had been done."

"Shit," Heidi swore. "Topher was my plot treatment."

"Anyhoo," Echo continued, "Topher threatened Max with dire consequences if she broke his contract, even mentioned something about cutting off her balls. We might have a new little girl on the show since that was Mom's condition not to press charges. I, for one, wish they'd arrest Topher. But you know how Maxine feels about adverse publicity."

"Maybe Topher will murder our Max," Drew said. "If he cuts off her balls, she could bleed to death."

Jon held Delly's hand under the table. Midway through the celebration, she felt his fingers clutch hers tightly, and she followed his glance toward the Sawmill's entrance.

Samantha walked through the room, flanked by her arranger and a young actor. The towheaded boy, who looked barely older than his shoe size, had his arm draped around Sami's shoulders. His fingers brushed her low-cut, sleeveless, beige suede vest. A matching skirt and boots completed her outfit.

Delly watched Sami slide her butt across a redwood bench at the front of the room. Oblivious of other diners, she kissed the boy, then placed her hand on his jean-clad groin. He squirmed, aroused or embarrassed. Sami laughed.

Goodbye, Rattlesnake, hiss-off, thought Delly.

Sami's arranger, Garrison Smith, said something. Sami sat up straight, her hands clasped together, as if she were a naughty girl who had been chastised by her teacher.

Jon said, "Do you want to leave?"

"How can I leave my own party? I'm okay."

"Champagne?"

"No, thanks. I'm on the wagon." She reached for a cigarette and flicked a tiny gold lighter several times. "Sami left this behind. Damn thing doesn't work. Out of fluid, I guess."

Jon tossed her a box of restaurant matches.

There was the sound of a drum roll.

The Sawmill's band leader introduced Samantha and induced her to join him. She winked at the audience, then raised her arms for silence. "I want to dedicate this song to my dearest sister, actress Delly Gold . . . I mean, Delly Diamond. She's just been fired from her soap opera, *Morning Star,* but she's here tonight, folks, celebrating. Or maybe she's plotting her revenge against the show's producer and director."

Only Jon heard Delly's gasp amid the cheers from Anissa, Echo, and the rest of the cast members.

"This is a brand new song," Samantha continued. "To sing it, I need my dearest composer and arranger, Garrison Smith."

Garrison took over the piano. Samantha turned to the other band members. "See if you can follow me, boys," she said.

The ballad had a country-western flavor. Its lyrics told about twin sisters in love with the same man.

That's not one of Mom's songs, thought Delly. *Sami and Gar-*

rison must have composed it together.

Anissa wended her way around the long table and knelt by Delly's chair. "Drew tracked your sister down through her agent. She told him to go straight to hell, do not pass go, but when he mentioned your goodbye party—"

"Why did Drew invite her? Why?"

"Another surprise. What's wrong?"

Delly flung her legs over the bench, stood, whirled about, and fled.

Staggering upright, Anissa turned to follow.

Jon gently grasped her arm. "I'll take care of this."

Losing sight of the small figure in red slacks and white blouse, he headed for the restrooms.

Delly stumbled outside and zigzagged across the parking lot. *Where's the car? There it is.* Leaning against the Rabbit, she dug through her purse for her key ring. *Where's the key?* Turning her handbag over, she watched its contents spill to the ground. Receipts, makeup items, pen, wallet—where were the damn car keys?

"Keep your tongue in your pocketbook," she cried, pounding her fists against the Rabbit's window.

"Can I help you, Miss?"

May I, thought Delly. She squinted toward the bearded man who wore a sweaty cowboy hat. He held a six-pack of Bud.

"What's the matter, baby?" he asked.

"Panda can't get in her car."

"Did you lock the keys inside?"

"I guess."

"Maybe the restaurant has a coat hanger."

"Panda wants to go home."

"Don't cry, Panda. I'll take you home." Placing his free arm around Delly's waist, leading her away from the Rabbit, he maneuvered between two cars, and pressed his body against hers. "You're cute, baby doll. I was gonna sit out here in the parking lot, drink my brewski, and listen to the music. Then you come along like the answer to a prayer."

"Music. Awful."

"You don't like country, Panda?"

"No. Dizzy. Kiss me, Jonny."

"I'm not Johnny. They call me The Duke."

"If Panda lets you touch her tatas, will you talk to Maxine?"

"Sure." Placing his six-pack on the hood of a Plymouth, The Duke unbuttoned Delly's blouse and reached around her back to unhook her bra.

"Did you hear Samantha?"

"Samantha who?" He cupped her breasts with his hands.

"Goody, goody, Panda will sing for you." She pushed his fingers away and climbed up onto the Plymouth's hood. Blouse unbuttoned, bra dangling by one strap, she sang, "Some enchanted . . . when you meet a strange . . . when you see a strange . . . damn it, I can't remember the words!"

"That's okay, Panda. We'll go to my place and listen to Toto's new album."

"Toto's a dog, silly."

"No. I meant—"

"There's Jonny." She shaded her eyes, even though there was no sun, and surveyed the parking lot from her high perch. "He's looking for me. 'Bye."

Climbing down from the Plymouth, she hooked her bra and ran toward the Rabbit. "Jonny, here I am. The car's locked and I dropped my purse."

"Why is your blouse open?" he asked, helping her gather the spilled items.

"I want to lick stamps and envelopes."

"Soon." He pushed the buttons back through their loops. "Here's an idea. How about visiting your mother over the

Thanksgiving holidays?"

"A vacation, Jonny?" At his nod, she said, "That's a wonderful idea."

"I'm almost finished with my script revisions. You fly to Chicago and I'll join you there."

"Okay. Tomorrow I'll call Mom. Then I'll collect my stuff from the studio. They don't tape on Saturdays."

Delly reached inside her pants pocket for her crumpled pack of cigarettes. She withdrew her hand and looked with surprise at her set of keys.

"My tongue was in my pocket all the time," she said and burst into tears.

"Wake up, sleepyhead," Jon said. "It's almost noon."

Delly stretched. "Why did you let me sleep so late?"

"Because you needed it. We had quite a workout last night. It was good, wasn't it?"

"When she was good, she was very, very good, and when she was bad—"

"Is that your quote for the day?"

"I'm running dry. I'll have to call Anissa."

"She phoned earlier. Said not to wake you, that she'd try again later."

Delly reached for a cigarette.

"Don't smoke, honey. Tarz dove into river and fought crocodiles to bring Jane fish." He retrieved a tray from the dresser. Next to a thick sandwich, fresh flowers nodded from Delly's puss-in-boots inkwell.

"Tuna fish, Jonny? First thing in the morning?"

"It was either tuna, leftover pizza, or parrot. Our cupboard is bare."

"I'll learn how to shop before I learn how to cook."

"I'll hire a shopper and a cooker. I love you just the way you are." He glanced at his watch. "I'm off to the health club. Tarzan requires rejuvenation. Do you need the Rabbit?"

"Yes, please. Jane has to swing through Hollywood and Vine. Errands. Groceries and lighter fluid. Thanks for breakfast, Tarz, and the flowers."

"You're welcome. Let's eat out tonight and pick up groceries on our way home. Tarzan can carry heavy sacks."

"I thought sacks was a department store."

"Very good, Smarty-Pants. I love you. 'Bye."

Through her open window, Delly heard the loud chug of the Audi. Then she wolfed down half a sandwich and called Carolyn Ann.

"My part on *Morning Star* ended, Mom, so I thought I might fly to Chicago, visit you and Uncle Sam."

"How marvelous, darling. I'm sorry about your show, but you'll find another part. You're such a gifted actress."

"Aw, you're just saying that because you're my mom."

"When does your plane land? I'll start plucking the turkey."

"Whoa, Mom. It's still a week away. What's all that noise?"

"Juliet, Will, Carrie and Nellie. Jules flew them out, poor man. He couldn't cope very well after Nanny quit. Samantha canceled part of her concert tour to search for a house. She's going to stay in California, says she has lots of irons in the fire. I didn't approve of her leaving Jules, but I guess it will all work out in the end. When are you going to marry Jon?"

"Maybe I should wait."

"You've waited a long time, Delly."

"I meant my visit, Mom. You and Uncle Sam are full-up."

"Don't be silly. Thanksgiving is for family. What's one more in this crowd? Juliet, no!"

Delly heard a loud crash.

"I've always hated that old vase." Carolyn Ann laughed.

"Gee, Mom, I don't know if—"

"Samantha will arrive in a few days. We'll have a family Thanksgiving. Is Jon coming, Delly? I consider him family."

"Sami's flying to Chicago?"

"Didn't she tell you?"

"No. I . . . we haven't talked much lately. We've both been so busy."

Delly stared at the Humpty Dumpty mechanical bank, her heart slamming against her chest. *It wants to kill me. It wants me to kill me.*

"I'll have my piano tuned," said Carolyn Ann. "You and Samantha can sing together. What was it you used to say all the time? Oh, yes, I remember. The Gold sisters, da-dum."

"Wait a minute, Mom," Delly said, striving to keep her voice calm. "The visit isn't definite."

"Why not?"

"Panda . . . Pandora might be reinstated. Panda . . . I have to stick around until I know for sure, be available if they need her . . . me. Jon has to finish his script. Panda . . . I only called because there's a slight possibility she . . . we can make it."

"Are you feeling all right, darling?"

"Party last night. Samantha sang. Late. Tired."

"Get some sleep, darling. Juliet, no!"

Another crash.

Delly Diamond sat on the wall.

Dumpty Delly had a great fall.

"Delly, are you still there?"

"Yes. I'll let you know, Mom. About Thanksgiving. Love you."

Delly started to hang up the receiver. Instead, she tugged the cord from the wall and flung the phone toward her doll shelf. Barbie, Shirley, Mumpsy, and other dolls tumbled to the floor. Frantically, Delly searched through the mess until she found the French Jumeau doll.

She walked through the kitchen, stepped barefoot into the

backyard, walked toward a wooden shed, entered, tripped over a rake, and felt a nail scratch her heel. Ignoring the pain, she grabbed a hammer from its pegboard.

That won't work!

Dropping the hammer, she reached for a hatchet.

Back inside the house again, she methodically demolished the piano's exterior. Discordant music filled the room as she banged the piano keys with her Samantha look-alike Jumeau doll, laughing when its porcelain features splintered.

Music by Toto.

Ding dong, the wicked bitch is dead.

She opened the door to the guest room and stared at Sinbad. Parrot poop littered his cage.

Pandora Borden took an ax, gave the parrot forty whacks. When she saw what she had done—

She showered, scrubbing her body with lemon-scented soap. She dressed in green corduroy slacks, a pink blouse, and white sneakers. Then she brushed her hair into a Pandora ponytail.

I'm off to see the Wizard.

Lions and tigers and bears, oh my.

She glanced at the ruined piano, smiled, strolled outside, locked the front door, and slipped behind the wheel of her Rabbit convertible. Pulling out from the driveway, she narrowly missed Mrs. Grady, who was walking her giant mutt.

Follow the yellow piss road. Road show. Road hog. Road kill. Parrots and rabbits and dogs, oh—

"My aching head," she cried.

Interlude

Propped against two foam-rubber pillows, he watched a commercial for Rosebud perfume.

The red-haired model lit his fire, but she wasn't Charl.

Only Charl could make him burn.

The red-haired model rode a white stallion. A man sat behind her, hugging her waist. They galloped along a beach, waves splish-splashing against the shore. The perfume was called FANTASY.

"Escape into Fantasy," said the man on top of the horse, "and make all your dreams come true."

He recognized the voice. Caleb. Cal. Drew Flory.

Flory, hah! Probably a fake name, shortened from Florstein or Florowitz. A Jew. He could always tell.

Hollywood was full of Jews. They changed their names, even Michael Landon—Little Joe, for Christ's sake—and they had plastic surgery. He knew this for a fact because the biggest Jew of them all, Phil Donahue, had once interviewed some plastic surgeons.

He'd have to rescue Charl from the Jews.

He watched the white stallion gallop into a sunset. Then he saw the Morning Star *logo, heard music, and Charl appeared.*

So did Cal! Again! Shit!

Mentally erasing Cal from the scene, he focused on Charl. Dreamy eyes and creamy skin, but she wore too much makeup. He'd rub that stuff off when they were finally together.

He felt himself coming and gave in to the sensation, arching his back, writhing with exquisite agony. Then he wiped himself clean with a tissue, sat up, and opened a bottle of Wild Turkey.

Turkey! Thanksgiving!

He'd been in California three months, and it was time to set his plan in motion.

Time. Did he have time to rewind the tape and watch Charl's scene again? He had to go to work soon. A real waste since it was Saturday and they didn't shoot the shit on Saturday. Should he call in sick?

He'd taken the job because it got him through the gates, into Charl's studio. He'd seen Charl but she never saw him.

Bitch!

After rewinding the tape, he flopped down on the bed. "C'mon, Charl," he said. "Light my fire."

Too much lipstick. Too much gunk on her eyes. At least they couldn't screw up her hair. Long. Blonde. Soft as corn silk.

"Come on, Charl, light my fire. Light my fire, light my—"

Chapter Twenty-Four

Fired, thought Delly.

Would Henry let her enter the studio without Maxine's permission? Why not? After all, Wayne County was one huge mental ward and she was the star mental case.

"I stopped by to pick up my stuff," she told him.

"Will you be long, child?"

Leaning against the security booth, which looked like a tollbooth, she said, "Fifteen minutes, half an hour. Anybody else here today?"

"Vance Booker, but he left."

"Judith Pendergraft?"

"Haven't seen her. Miss Graham is upstairs in her office, and Miss Anissa—"

"Anissa's here, at the studio?"

"Yep. She had a meeting with Miss Graham."

Delly smiled. Even though he was perpetually posted at the entrance, Henry knew everything that went on inside the building.

"I was sorry to hear about you leaving the show," he said.

Her smile faded. "Say la vee."

"Hush, child, don't you be sounding like her!"

The hate in his voice was unmistakable. "How come you don't get along with Maxine, Henry?"

"Miss Graham tried to get me discharged, only she called it early retirement. She wanted to hire another guard, that man who delivers food from the deli. Miss Graham took him inside the projection room for his audition, but it didn't work out. He's still toting sandwiches. How was your goodbye party, Miss Delly?"

She stared at him, confused by the change of subject.

"Last night at the Sawmill," Henry said. "I saw Miss Echo sneak a prop from the show. Did you have fun?"

"Yes. Sort of." Delly tossed Henry a fingertip kiss and entered the building. As always, the wall mural greeted her. Hannah and Topher had been eliminated. However, Echo's phantom, Mr. Ratings, hadn't killed off Pandora yet.

Pandora stood behind Cal and Charl, with only her face, neck and shoulders visible. Her left cheek rested against the rag doll's carroty hair. Soon Panda and her baby would be gone, as if a ghostly eraser *whooshed* through the building, rub-a-dub-dubbing. Hey, what else could you do with a crazy person? In the real world, mental hospitals had names like Peace-haven-rest, and they were filled with insurance patients. Which was funny when you thought about it—and who wanted to think about it?—because most of the crazies roamed the streets, un-caged.

Too bad Panda didn't have insurance—wait a sec! Change Panda's ponytail to shaggy gold hair, change the color of her eyes, and Samantha Gold could be the Panda on the mural.

After all, we're twins.

Uncomfortable with that revelation, Delly climbed stairs to the third floor.

Maxine's door gaped open. Seated behind her cluttered desk, the producer nibbled a pencil. She looked like a beaver. No. A termite. The kind of termite they always showed in nature movies, eating wood, magnified a bazillion times. An Emmy stood on Maxine's desk, next to a yellow legal pad covered with scribbles.

Scribbles and doodles and dots, oh my.

E my name is Emmy.

Oh, Auntie Emmy, there's no place like home.

Too bad the bad, bad Pandora Poe was kicked out of Wayne County. Now she's homeless. Un-caged.

Delly knocked and entered.

Maxine looked up. "What can I do for you, dear?"

"I came to collect my things and . . ."

"Yes?"

"Maxine . . . about Pandora . . ."

"You did a fine job, Delly. We were very pleased."

"If you were so pleased, why'd you kick me off the show?"

Maxine lit a cigarette. "Honorable dismissal is not a kick in the pants, dear."

"Why couldn't you and Judith cure Pandora?"

"Without her illness, there is no Pandora."

"That's not true. She could be released from the hospital and settle in Wayne County."

"As what? She couldn't be a nurse or a doctor. She couldn't go back to school or suddenly start a business. She has no background."

"Yes, she does. I gave her a background, a whole history, even a last name."

"That's nice."

"Don't you believe me?"

"Of course I do."

"Judith once said something about a relationship with Cal. Pandora and Cal."

"I don't have time for asinine *bon mots,* Delly." Maxine puffed smoke toward the projection room window. "Cal and Charl were married *a la belle etoile.*"

"Under the stars?"

"Right. Don't you remember our lovely outdoor wedding?"

"Panda wasn't in that scene."

Max sounds sarcastic, thought Delly. With sudden insight, she realized that Max was jealous of Charl and Cal. No, not Charl and Cal. *Anissa and Drew.*

"Why couldn't Pandora come between Cal and Charl?" Delly said, playing on Maxine's jealousy. "Pandora could work at the newspaper. That way she'd be close to Cal."

"There is no newspaper."

"Sure there is. *The Wayne County Gazette.*"

Maxine sighed, stood, led Delly toward a small love seat. "Sit down, dear, you're shaking like a leaf. That's better. Would you have us build a new set, just so Pandora can write classified ads and hustle Cal?"

"No. But she could be a reporter, help Cal solve Hannah's murder."

"A former mental patient as an investigative reporter? Get real, Delly."

"This is daytime drama, Max. You can do anything you want."

"Even if it were possible, we're way over budget. You have no idea what Toper Coombs cost us. That bastard threatened to sue if we didn't buy him out of his contract."

"You can cut my salary."

"We're planning to introduce a new character," Maxine continued, ignoring Delly's desperate offer.

"I know. The little girl who Topher—"

"A new singer for the Echo Chamber."

"What? But Tabby Cat—"

"I probably shouldn't be telling you this, Delly, and I'll trust you to keep it a secret." Maxine's finger grooved her lips. "Tabby's going to be arrested for Hannah's murder. Meanwhile, we've been auditioning singers."

"Max, I'm a singer. My whole family is musically inclined. My mom writes songs and my sister—" Delly swallowed. "My sister is Samantha Gold. We *both* sing, Max. It's in our genes. Maybe you haven't heard of Samantha yet, but—"

"*The* Samantha Gold? We've been talking to her agent about the new part."

"My sister? You've been talking to my sister's agent?"

"It will probably be a short stint, but we need a vocalist and Samantha wants national exposure. I had no idea she's your sister. Ummm, maybe we can use that."

"Right. She could be Pandora's sister and—"

"No, not the show. I meant publicity. You'd do that for your little sister, wouldn't you?"

"My *little* sister?"

"I meant age, Delly, not size. You and Samantha could hit the talk shows, pose for pictures together, and—are you all right, dear? You're white as a ghost."

Delly reached for her mouth with her thumb. Instead, she withdrew a cigarette from her purse.

Maxine's lighter flamed. "Tell you what. Samantha has to audition, just like everyone else. If she doesn't work out, I'll have Vance give you a call. I suppose we could turn Pandora into a singer, but please don't get your hopes up."

Up, up and away, in a beautiful balloon.

"You're a fine actress, Delly, and I'll be happy to recommend you for another daytime drama."

The Wizard's balloon flew off without me.

"I have work to do, dear."

Click your heels three times.

"Judith wants me to jot down some ideas, the new singer's plot treatment. Maybe she can come between Charl and Cal. Yes, that might fly. Thanks for the idea, Delly."

Click. Click. Click.

"You can visit the set any time, dear."

Was it all a dream?

"And don't forget, Delly. Pandora can always recur."

Rising from the love seat, Delly walked into the hallway and closed the office door behind her.

She plowed through Wardrobe, tossing clothes left and right, hoping to find a future script outline and verify that Tabby Cat would be arrested for Hannah's murder. But no script magically appeared, so she wandered into the makeup room.

A smile split Anissa's lovely face as she lowered a can of ginger ale to the dressing table's surface. "Delly, what luck. I called this morning, only you were asleep. I'm so sorry about last night."

"That's okay. It doesn't matter."

"I know Samantha's been a pest, but until I spoke to Jon—"

"Pest? Oh, Anissa, that's funny, an 'asinine bon mot' to quote Maxine. Sami seduced Jon. She's poisonous, like a snake, and she's been hired for *Morning Star.* Max just told me. Max said Sami would have to audition, but she's great at auditions. Remember our pen pal days? I lied. Sami played all the roles, every single one. Sami was the cheerleader, not me, and she belonged to the glee club and—"

"Calm down, love. Take a deep breath. It will be all right, honest it will. There were times in my life when I felt everything had turned sour and I wanted to die. I'll tell you a secret, Delly. Even Drew doesn't know. I once tried to commit suicide. Randy saved me. Too bad I couldn't save him."

Secrets! Delly was tempted to blurt out her secrets. Mr. Hailey. Jules. Judith. Topher. But the little voice inside her head warned, *Keep your tongue in your pocketbook.* Biting her bottom lip, she retrieved two capsules from her purse.

"May I have a sip of your soda, Anissa?"

"Sure. What kind of pills are you taking?"

"Tranquilizers. Judith gave them to me."

"Easy, Delly, don't get hooked on downers."

"I won't."

"For what it's worth, my Aunt Theresa used to quote from the Bible. Her favorite line was about the morning stars singing together and the sons of God shouting for joy. I'm paraphrasing, of course. It's from *Job,* the answer to a 'when' question, but Aunt Theresa believed it meant things would get better."

"Point taken. Jonny feels awful about my sister. Anyway, it's his turn to grab the spotlight. Everybody adores his movie, and his book is climbing toward the top of the bestseller list."

"You must be so proud."

"I am." She smiled tremulously. "We need the money, now that I'm unemployed. I owe astronomical amounts on my furniture, and Jon supports a retarded sister."

"He does?"

"Yes. We had a long talk after Sami's Vegas debut. *Duck Pond*'s Virginia was inspired by Jon's little sister. She's institutionalized. Recently he shifted her to a private sanitarium with the best of facilities." Delly sighed. "Speaking of secrets, I'm sort of pregnant."

"How can you be sort of pregnant?"

"I haven't seen a doctor yet, but I've skipped a couple of periods and I forgot to bring my birth control pills to Vegas."

"Have you told Jon?"

"No."

"Why not? He'll be deliriously happy."

"Do you think? After he told me about Virginia, I wondered. Genes and all that. How did Drew take it when you announced the big event?"

"He laughed and cried." Anissa fiddled with her ginger ale can. "Delly, I wish you wouldn't gulp down tranquilizers. It's not good for the baby."

"How are *you* feeling?"

"Great. Bugs is fine, too."

"Bugs?"

"During my last checkup, the doctor put that gizmo that measures the heartbeat on top of my belly. Drew was with me and he threw his voice. It sounded as if my stomach said, 'What's up, Doc?' We've been calling the little nipper Bugs ever since. Why don't you come home with me, Delly? We'll concoct a celebration dinner. On second thought, I'll cook. You can keep me company."

"Maybe later. Right now I want to collect my stuff."

"What stuff?"

"A sweatshirt, a baseball cap, and my doll."

"The doll belongs to the show."

Delly retrieved a cigarette from her purse and flicked her lighter several times. "Damn, nothing works right." Rummaging through her purse again, she mumbled, "I bought some lighter fluid—never mind. Here's a box of Sawmill matches."

"Leave the doll at the studio, Delly. Don't take Pandora home with you."

"How can I take her home when she doesn't exist? Maybe I'll introduce Pandora Ghost to Mr. Ratings and they can both kill our Max. Anissa, what the heck are you doing?"

"I know it sounds alfy, but I'm being followed." She secured a brown wig with bobby pins. "I guess you could call this wig a disguise."

"Followed? You're kidding."

"I wish. It's been happening for two, maybe three months. An overzealous fan, I suppose. Once I tried to confront my bothersome 'groupie,' but when I turned around all I saw was that delivery guy from the deli. I couldn't see his face, he was too far away. He waved. Then he turned into Maxine's office while I walked toward Wardrobe."

"Does Drew know about your 'groupie'?"

"Sort of."

Delly grinned. "What kind of answer is sort of?"

"I made a dumb joke out of it, quoted Brando. 'If you want something from an audience, you give blood to their fantasies. It's the ultimate hustle.' "

"Forget Brando. Have you told the police?"

"Told them what? That I suspect an overzealous fan is following me? There haven't been any letters, phone calls, or threats. The police would think I'm bonkers, if not downright paranoid."

"Be careful, okay?" Delly bent forward and gave her friend a hug.

"Please come over tonight. I can call Maryl. Drew bought that new version of Trivial Pursuit, Silver Screen. He swears I've memorized all the answers, but I haven't, so we can play fair and square and—"

"Anissa, you're babbling."

"I know. But I have a feeling—" She took a deep breath. "You're cracking up, Delly."

"An egg cracks." *Humpty Dumpty had a great fall.*

"So do people. I'll wait and we can leave together."

"I'm fine, Anissa. Double or nothing."

"What?"

"Trivial Pursuit. I'll give you a chance to win back our World Series bet."

"Deal. Call me later?"

"Yes."

"Promise?"

"Yes."

"And you'll tell Jon about the baby?"

"Anissa, please."

"Okay, okay, I'm history."

Delly watched her friend leave, then glanced around the makeup room. She could see Samantha, instant center of attention. Sami wouldn't have to appear in a shapeless shift on her first day. Max would want to emphasize Sami's cleavage, dazzle the viewers. Marla, head honcho hair stylist, would ooh and ahhh over Sami's palomino mane.

Delly reached for a blonde wig and put it on. There! Now Panda looked like Sami. No. Panda looked like Charl.

Standing in front of the dressing room mirror, she combed the long wig-strands. Then she paused, her arm suspended.

Someone's spying on me.

She saw nothing.

Anissa gave me the jitters.

Placing her comb on the table, Delly left the makeup room, entered the prop alcove, searched until she found Pandora's doll, walked downstairs, and slipped into the room where Maxine and Peter gave critique/bitch sessions.

Grabbing an ashtray, she sat against the wall, directly beneath the window. She saw discarded clothing sloppily draped over card table chairs. On the old couch, near the door, lay her hooded sweatshirt and Dodger's baseball cap. Nurse Marybeth had abandoned a Stephen King novel, *The Stand,* and it lay face down across the corner of the card table.

Focusing on the wood-framed mirror, Delly could imagine Maxine's reflection, her mouth moving. Sami would receive her share of criticism. Nobody was immune, not even the great Samantha Gold. Or was she? If Sami could out-bitch Pat Python, couldn't she manipulate Maxine Graham?

Delly fumbled through her purse, found her box of restaurant matches, and lit a cigarette. The tranquilizers were working. She yawned.

Marlon Brando claimed that fame was the ultimate hustle. Delly had proposed that Pandora hustle Cal. Maxine said no, maybe Samantha. What about Judith? Could Judith alter the concept? But Judith had ignored Delly, ever since Little Boy

Blue and Man in the Moon. Actors didn't live happily ever after, after all. They didn't live forever, either.

Even swans died.

Anissa had once said, "People have great respect for the dead in Hollywood but none for the living," paraphrasing Errol Flynn.

If Maxine died, would she be respected? Delly had a feeling Max wanted love and respect even more than she craved high ratings.

What about Delly Diamond?

You can't buy smart.

Could you buy respect? How? With money? Not in Hollywood. With talent? Absolutely. Judith was a prime example. She'd once said that drive and talent earned respect. But that would make Maxine an object of respect, and she wasn't. The Mr. Ratings bit proved it. The bathroom graffiti proved it.

Delly yawned again. Then, very softly, she chanted, "Delly Diamond took an ax, gave her producer forty whacks. When she saw what she had done, she gave Pandora forty-one."

Chapter Twenty-Five

A portable TV played the tape from a future episode of *Morning Star.* Lost in her own fantasies, Maxine slumped on the office love seat, one hand in her lap, her fingers curled around an Emmy.

Emmy, an alteration of Immy, the nickname for image orthicon.

Maxine coughed. The room smelled like fumy antiperspirant. Elizabeth Taylor had been quoted as saying "There's no deodorant like success." Maybe Maxine could convince Elizabeth Taylor to cameo, just for fun. Ratings would soar.

Lighting another cigarette, Maxine sniffed. Christ, it stank to high heaven in here. Carefully placing Emmy-Immy on the floor, she stood, walked behind the love seat, and tried to open a window. The frame inched up then stuck. *Merde!* Returning to the love seat, retrieving her statuette, she pictured Drew Flory.

She had earned Drew, damn it, and she had the perfect plan for making him obey.

The fire started on the first floor, one floor above the cast mural. It began as an infant, teething on Vance Booker's résumés and photographs. Then it crawled toward the critique room.

Directly above the fire was Maxine's office. It had once been a sound stage for silent films and the uneven walls looked as if they'd been erected by the same animator who created Roadrunner cartoons. Covering Maxine's desktop were scripts, anchored by remnants of pastrami on rye, a polystyrene cup of potato salad, and a garlic pickle. Abandoning Emmy-Immy, retrieving the pickle, Maxine pictured Drew again. Then she closed her eyes and sucked on the pickle.

Below, the fire skipped early childhood and grew a punk-rock hairdo. It possessed a teen's eclectic appetite, consuming several items before it regurgitated Stephen King. Then, slithering backwards through the exit, the fire paused in the hallway and rummaged around for more food. Anorexic, it dieted and almost died. Gasping for breath, it discovered a pile of newspapers stacked in an open doorway. Saturday's comics beckoned. The fire nibbled *Peanuts.*

Above, Maxine glanced toward the window used by long-ago projectionists. Darkness cloaked shelves filled with cellulose film.

As she focused on the wall opposite the projection room, she pictured Drew's taut butt.

With a smug smile, she returned her gaze to the projectionist's window.

After devouring the comics, the fire swiftly chewed up sports pages, an editorial deploring the U.S. invasion of Grenada, and President Reagan atop a horse. Still hungry, the fire traveled inside the doorway and discovered a closet. A pyramid of cheap toilet tissue enhanced the back wall.

Drew had better obey me or I'll blacklist Anissa, Maxine mused. She had file folders in cans of film, hidden inside the projection room, where no one would ever find them. The files contained photographs of Big Stars in compromising positions. If Drew wouldn't compromise, if he continued to defy her, she'd sell the photos.

Kathleen Kaye, bless her heart, had saved one set of Anissa

Cartier photos, which she'd happily sold to Maxine. Wouldn't an exposé rag love to get their grubby paws on those pictures?

Then there was Buzzy Beeson, sly sleaze. Buzzy wasn't a bad director, considering that his camera had been hidden behind the hotel's drapes. And Buzzy, needing cash badly, had sold his Anissa weekend to Maxine. If Drew disobeyed her, Anissa would be washed up. Because viewers were fickle and the industry was cruel and self-serving—just like Maxine Graham.

Below, the fire grew into adulthood, danced up the supply closet wall, lapped at the ceiling's paint, and snaked through microscopic floor-cracks. Discovering dessert, its hissing voice became a roar of approval.

Once again, Maxine gazed dreamily at the white wall opposite the projection room. A pattern of light flickered. Startled, she jumped to her feet, turned, and stared at the projectionist's window. This time, instead of darkness, she saw flames reaching high for cans of cellulose film.

Shit! The file folders! Maxine took one step forward.

The projection room exploded. Glass fragments flew across the office with the impetus of a missile. One shard severed an artery in Maxine's neck. She fell, holding Emmy-Immy against her silent heart.

The fire licked its long fingers and searched for another victim.

Connie Francis crooned, "Who's sorry now-wow-wow?" Behind her, Buddy Holly played the drums. "Panda Poe," he sang. "Pretty, pretty, pretty, pretty Panda Poe."

The food delivery man waved a huge Kosher dill. "One ana two ana three," he chanted, each word encased inside a champagne bubble, just like a Chien *cartoon. Who's sorry now segued into where-*

the-boys-are, and Connie Francis segued into Samantha Gold. Sami sang, "Some enchanted evening, when you fuck a stranger."

Her marmalade bodice fell to her waist. "Oops," she said, yanking her breasts up. "Oopsie-daisy, don't fall down."

"Don't slump, Samantha," Maxine Graham said.

Sami said, "Go to hell, do not pass go."

"Merde! *I meant it as a compliment," Max said. "You can play the scene bare-assed naked if you want."*

"Okay." Sami made an about-face. Her gown was backless and her butt shone in the spotlight. "Where the boys eat," she sang, "someone waits for meow."

Three paws rum-tum-tummed Buddy Holly's drums. Even though Southern Comfort had needle-sharp claws, rather than high heels, he sounded like Maxine Graham on a bad-weather day. "Poor crippled cat," Max said. "But if he's cured, I'll have to fire him. Ladybug, ladybug, fly away home, your house is on fire, your pussy will burn."

Samantha said, "Don't talk dirty."

Delilah Gold sat on a chair in the middle of the stage. She looked like a harlequin—black makeup and white, diamond-shaped tears. "Doodah," she said.

Delly lay in a heap, her face resting against the stuffed body of her doll. Her wig had slipped off and it lay on the floor. The messy strands looked like a Muppet who'd been caught in the crossfire from a drive-by shooting. "What a stupid dream," she said.

Buddy Holly. Maxine. Sami. Southern Comfort. She tried to fit the jumbled images together but her brain felt too muzzy.

She needed a nicotine fix, but her box of matches and pack of cigarettes were missing. Had she smoked them all? She couldn't remember. Rising, she yawned, coughed, stretched, coughed. The room was foggy, the air stinky with the odor of singed material and burnt paper.

She rubbed her eyes free from drugged sleep and coughed

for the third time.

Oh, no! Scooping up her rag doll, she ran. Outside the critique room, a charred trail marred the hallway carpeting and smoke billowed from a supply closet.

She climbed the stairs two at a time, but halted when she heard the sound of a thunderous explosion. The walls shook. So did the floor.

Everybody in New York had warned her about earthquakes.

"Panda's scared," she whimpered. "Humpty Dumpty told Delly something bad would happen."

Anchoring the doll beneath her arm, she covered her ears with her hands. Somehow, she reached the second floor, stumbled down the hallway, and came to another halt.

"Look, dolly, flames. The hospital's on fire. Thank God it's not an earthquake. Oh, no! Panda's trapped. But Judith promised Panda wouldn't get killed in the fire. Did Judith change her mind? Silly Panda. This fire's make-believe. They don't use real fire on TV. Delly should complain to Peter because the smoke is making Panda cough. Where are the cameras?"

Panda's on the wrong floor! That's why Peter's cameras are missing.

Ignoring the flames that lapped at her sneakers, Delly sidled up to an emergency exit. With an almost superhuman effort, she managed to open the heavy steel door. Then she paused on the stairwell, pressing dolly against her stomach.

"Panda has a tummy ache, Dr. Marsh. Peter, please cut this scene."

Despite painful spasms, Delly grasped the railing and climbed higher. She tried the door to the main studio but it was jammed. Maybe the vultures were trying to escape. Maybe they blocked the entrance. Did Maxine sit inside her sky-booth, surrounded by soaring, grinning grid-vultures?

"Oh, no. Max'll be mad. Panda's supposed to be in the fire while Charl steals a nurse's uniform." Delly wiped at her tears with the doll's pinafore. "Oh, wait, I know. Judith changed the script and Panda's getting married to Cal. Didn't Judith once say that Panda and Cal would fall in love?"

Charl's trapped in the fire.

Panda's gonna get married.

Maxine said the wedding was outside.

Delly reached the top step. She pushed at another steel door. It opened, and she found herself on the roof. Looking up, she chanted, "Star light, star bright, first star I see tonight—"

What else had Maxine said? Oh, yeah. Something about Cal and Charl getting married under the stars. Carefully placing her rag doll on the roof's asphalt surface, Delly sank to her knees and clasped her hands together. "I, Pandora, take thee, Cal, to be my husband, for richer or poorer, until death . . . until death . . ."

Wait a sec. Maxine said Cal and Charl, not Cal and Panda. Too late. Cal and Panda were married, which meant Cal couldn't marry Charl until death do us part, or death threw a party, or something like that.

Where's my script?

Where's the prompter?

Where's the camera?

Where is everybody?

Chapter Twenty-Six

The Audi had developed a bronchial wheeze. Chugging up the driveway, it sputtered and stalled. Jon turned the ignition key, pressed down on the accelerator, and released the clutch petal, but he knew the car wouldn't start again. Things were going well, financially. Maybe he should buy a new car, a matching Rabbit convertible. Twin bunnies. No, definitely not *twins.* He'd find a small pickup to cart Delly's auction antiques. That would save them money in the long run.

"We'll turn you into a planter," Jon told the Audi. Then, whistling a discordant tune, he unlocked the front door, entered, and saw the piano. *What the hell!*

A burglar? Christ, was he nuts? Why would a burglar smash the piano but ignore the TV, VCR and computer? Someone high on drugs? Someone who had been interrupted while robbing the house? Someone still inside the house?

Furtively making his way down the hallway, Jon spied a hatchet.

"I'm armed, you bastard!" he shouted, grasping the tool's handle and inching open the guest room door.

Sinbad the parrot, freed from his cage, perched on top of the curtain rod. Feathers decorated the floor and bedspread. Had someone tried to kill Samantha's bird? Why?

The phone rang.

Jon slammed the guest room door shut, quickly scanned the bathroom and master bedroom, then ran back into the living room and grabbed the receiver.

Anissa's voice gushed a jumble of words.

"Slow down, honey," Jon pleaded.

Drew's voice, calm and steady, took over. "We were watching TV," he said, "while waiting for Delly to call. Anissa invited her—and you, of course—for supper tonight. There was a news bulletin, a fire at the *Morning Star* studio."

"Is it bad?"

"The worst damage is on one floor. They have it contained, practically out. Smoke—"

Jon heard a *thunk*—had Drew dropped the phone?—then Anissa's voice again.

"The old projection room exploded," she said. "Delly—"

"What about Delly?" Traveling the length of the cord, Jon reached for the TV knob.

"She was at the studio when I left this afternoon. I . . . Drew, tell him."

"Jon, Delly's on the roof of the building."

"The roof?" He focused on the TV screen. Smoke poured from studio windows. A small figure posed on the roof's edge. "Why doesn't she come down? Is she hurt? Scared?"

"They say she's threatening to jump. Anissa and I were about to leave when we decided to call you one more—"

"I'm on my way. Drew, wait! My car won't start."

"We'll swing around and pick you up. Stand outside. Every minute counts."

With a shaky hand, Jon hung up the receiver. Staring at the hatchet, he wanted to smash the TV screen. If he did, maybe the image of Delly would fade and she'd be safe at home.

Safe? He glanced toward the ruined piano, saw the shattered doll. Its eyes were missing, its nose was broken, its mouth oozed porcelain, and it looked like a corpse.

★ ★ ★ ★ ★

Drew double-parked. With Anissa and Jon, he quickly wove through the gawking spectators, the fire engines, the police cars, and an old man who looked up at the building and cupped his mouth with liver-spotted hands. "Jesus loves you!" the old man shouted.

A cop restrained the two actors and Jon at the security booth.

"I know the girl on the roof," Jon said.

"Sure, buddy. Step behind the ropes."

"Miss Anissa, Mr. Drew," Henry cried. "They say Miss Delly wants to jump."

"Tell the police we came to help," Anissa said.

"It's all right, these people are her friends," Henry said, but Jon had already pushed his way through and sprinted for the studio entrance.

Drew and Anissa followed.

More police congregated on the roof. Drew stopped to explain while Jon continued running.

Delly's pink blouse and green cords were black with soot. Only her glazed eyes and the doll seemed free from carbon grime.

"Go 'way!" she screamed. "Go 'way or I'll jump!"

"Honey, it's me, Jon," he said, making a desperate effort to restrain himself. Because he wanted nothing more than to finish his journey across the roof and gather Delly into his arms. "I came to take you home."

"Panda can't go home. Maxine said so."

Jon stepped forward as Delly moved closer to the roof's edge. "Honey, let's talk. I love you."

"Panda's tired of talking. Blah, blah, blah. It doesn't do any good. No one listens."

"I'm listening. Tell me why you want to jump."

On the ground, firemen set up tall ladders. The crowd buzzed like a swarm of mosquitoes—insects collected by a special effects crew for the climatic horror movie scene. A spotlight pierced the sooty sunset, and its bean illuminated Delly's body.

The crowd cheered.

Delly gave a jerky bow, then shaded her eyes. "Make them turn it off!" she screamed. "Turn it off, turn it all off. Or Panda will fall. I swear she will."

A cop spoke into an aerial transmitter and the light beam dipped away.

"Why do you want to jump?" Jon repeated.

"Panda will get her name in the news. Hollywood has respect for the dead. And Sami can't do it better."

"But we made plans to fly to Chicago for Thanksgiving, remember? Don't you want to see your mother?"

"I was going to tell her about the baby."

"Delly, if you jump you'll lose your baby," Anissa said.

Jon said, "What baby?"

"She's pregnant."

"Oh my God! She didn't tell me! Why didn't she tell me?"

"She promised she'd tell you tonight. Delly, did you hear me? You'll lose your baby."

"Too late, Charl." Raising her arms, stretching them out like wings, Delly moved closer to the roof's edge. The doll dangled from her fingertips.

"No!" Jon shouted.

Dropping her arms, Delly maneuvered one leg over a raised cornice. Then she stood there, poised like a ballerina about to arabesque.

"Let me try," Drew said. Thrusting his shaking hands inside his jeans pocket, he smiled. "Hello, Pandora."

"Hi, Cal. What are you doing here?"

"I came to visit you."

"Charl's over there, Cal."

"I know, but I came to see you. I love you very much."

"I love you too, Cal." Delly pressed the doll against her stomach. "Panda's sick, Cal. Maxine said if she's not sick there is no Panda. But you can tell Max that Panda's *really* sick. It's not pretend. Her tummy hurts."

"Maybe you'd feel better if you gave me a hello-hug?"

"Panda can't hug you, Cal."

"Why not?"

"Panda has to fall off the roof."

"No!" Jon shouted, moving forward.

"Hush," Anissa said, holding him back.

Drew said, "Why do you have to fall, Panda?"

"Because it's in the script."

"It's not in my script."

"Yours is different. Judith wrote a new script for Panda. Panda let Judith tickle her so she wrote a special part. Topher tickled Panda, too, but she slapped his face. He was so mad he lost his teeth so he couldn't talk to Maxine. Delly talked to Maxine, but she said Sami's gonna' sing on *Morning Star.* Did you hear me, Cal? Sami's gonna' be on Delly's show. The Gold sisters, da-dum."

"Panda, listen. If you jump, you'll hurt the doll."

"My baby, Cal?"

"Yes. Your baby. Her insides will come out."

"I'll land first. My baby can be on top."

"People who fall turn somersaults. You might land on top of your baby. You might even crush your baby."

"That's true, Cal. What should Panda do?"

"She should let Cal take care of her baby."

Delly lowered her leg to the asphalt. She extended her arm, then pulled it back, cradling the rag doll against her breasts. "You won't grab Panda, will you? She has to jump. Hollywood respects the dead."

"I won't grab. I promise. You can trust me, Panda."

"Charl says I shouldn't trust anybody."

"She didn't mean me. Charl trusts me."

"No. She only trusts Panda. She said so. Charl tells Panda all her secrets, not Cal. She didn't tell Cal about—"

"Hannah? About escaping from the hospital in a nurse's uniform? About the knife?"

"Charl did tell you. Charl must trust you, Cal."

"That's right, Panda. Let me have your baby."

"Okay." Delly took a few steps toward Drew.

Slowly, he removed one hand from his pocket and stroked the doll's carroty wool strands. "What a pretty baby," he said.

"Take good care of her, Cal."

"Yes. I will." Grabbing Delly's wrist, he pulled her close. She struggled wildly.

Jon ran forward, placed his hands underneath her knees, and swung her up into his arms. Then he carried her away from the roof's edge. "Her sneakers are burned," he moaned, "and her pants are covered with blood."

"She's having a miscarriage," Anissa said. "Oh, God!"

Delly stopped struggling when a cop covered her body with a blanket. From Jon's arms, she twisted her head and stared at Drew. "I trusted you, Cal," she said, then closed her eyes and slumped against Jon's chest.

Watching Jon race toward the stairs, Drew put his hands on Anissa's shaking shoulders. He massaged gently, hoping to release her tension, hoping the repetitive motion might somehow release his own tension.

"I should have stayed with her today," Anissa cried, pulling away. "I knew she was upset. And I was the one who mentioned suicide. She reminded me of Randy."

"Bullshit! Randy was on a guilt trip. You can't make me believe Delly felt guilty about leaving the show."

"But she did, Drew. Delly honestly thought she'd let Pandora down."

"Listen to yourself. You're talking as if they're two different people."

"She was so damn vulnerable. I should have stayed with her, said something, *done* something."

"Thank God you told me about playing Charl to her Pandora. That saved her life."

"Let's go. Hurry. The ambulance has already left for the hospital."

"I'll drive you home, then find Jon and bring him to the apartment." Drew patted her belly. "You and Bugs need to get some rest."

"Are you bonkers? I couldn't rest."

"Vacuum the carpet, put up a pot of coffee, clean Tramp's litter box, cook some veggie soup."

"Okay."

"Promise?" he asked, startled by her capitulation.

"Samuel Goldwyn once said, 'If you can't give me your word of honor, will you give me your promise?' "

"I don't give a shit what Goldwyn said! Anissa, I'm sorry. I didn't mean to yell. Delayed reaction. Please don't cry."

"I can't help it, Drew. I'm partly to blame and nothing you say can change that."

"Let's all share the blame—there's plenty to go around. Delly's right, you know. We weren't listening."

Entr' Acte

In the confusion he'd managed to steal a fireman's uniform, just as Charl had once stole a nurse's uniform. Then he'd sneaked up onto the studio roof.

But the actors had gone home and the moon's spotlight shone down upon an empty stage.

Why hadn't Charl run from the burning studio into his arms?

He was ready to offer comfort, then love. He had tried to save her, but the police pigs kept him away, behind the ropes. He heard one pig say there was a dead body—deader than a door nail.

Charl?

His stomach churned and his brain sizzled. Charl's friend, Pandora, had tried to jump. Should he jump?

His gaze encompassed the roof until he focused on a forgotten rag doll whose button eyes stared up at the sky.

Swearing a blue streak, he grabbed the doll, thrust his arm back in a classic major league pitcher's pose, and hurled the doll, hard as he could, over the side of the roof.

Later, he sat on the edge of his lumpy motel mattress and pressed a cold gun against his hot forehead.

Suicide leaps were for girls.

TV images flickered—a taped Rosebud commercial. Why couldn't a VCR edit out commercials?

He had written a short note. In it he said he didn't want to live without Charl.

They could have been so happy together. Now it was finished, over, door-nail dead.

He watched the whole show until the music sounded and the credits flashed, until he saw her name. Then he lowered his gun, walked to the VCR, and pressed rewind.

Raising the gun to his forehead again, he glanced at the screen. Shit! While the tape rewound, Charley Brown and Snoopy were celebrating Thanksgiving.

Charl was dead and they were giving fucking thanks!

His first finger applied trigger pressure.

Wait!

Should he play the tape one last time?

Coward! Do it now. Count to three. One. Two. Two and a half—

Chapter Twenty-Seven

Staggering into Drew's apartment, Jon sat heavily on the beige corduroy couch. "She didn't tell me about the baby," he said. "The real baby, not her damn rag doll."

"Your clothes are covered with soot and blood," Anissa gasped.

"Couldn't change clothes, had to wait for Delly's emergency D and C. The doctor swears she's fine, but she's sedated and will probably sleep—oh, God, blood. I'm sorry. Your couch."

"Forget the couch." Drew sat next to his friend.

"I should be at the hospital."

"No way." Anissa's hands spanned her hips. "I'll run a hot bath and you can borrow a shirt and jeans from my husband. You're almost the same size."

"Drew's taller."

"Don't argue with my wife." Watching Anissa walk toward the kitchen, Drew placed his arm around Jon's shoulders. "She's incorrigible, stubborn as a mule. When all else fails, she'll quote you into submission. I had to marry her to shut her up."

"I wanted to marry Delly."

Anissa returned and set a bowl of steaming vegetable soup on the coffee table. "Get down, Tramp, you naughty puss. That's for Jon."

"Thanks, Anissa, but I'm not hungry."

" 'Food is one of the first steps toward overcoming suffering.' Quote, unquote."

"Jesus! Now she's quoting me," Drew said.

Jon tried to mirror Drew's grin, but his mouth quivered and his face fell forward.

"Okay, okay." Drew held his friend tightly. "That's good. Tears are good. Cry, Jon. Cry for Delly. Cry for all of us."

Anissa knelt on the prayer rug. When Jon's outburst had subsided, she handed him a wad of tissues. "Does Delly still think she's Pandora?"

"No. She was groggy, doped up. She didn't remember the fire or the roof. She kept mumbling, something about how Humpty Dumpty wanted her dead and she couldn't be put back together again. She said she fell asleep and dreamed about Maxine and Buddy Holly. Buddy Holly, for Christ's sake! If only I had stayed home this afternoon, driven her to the studio—"

"Stop it, Jon! I just went through that same bit, and I know better than anyone else in this room what guilt can do to a person."

"I'm sorry. You're right." He blew his nose.

"How did Delly take the miscarriage?"

"Nothing. Blank. I'm not sure she understood."

"Poor Delly." Anissa clasped her hands over her stomach.

"All right, that's enough," Drew said. "We don't have time for this. We've got to be practical."

"Delly just lost her baby." Anissa stared at Drew as if he'd sprouted wings. "What if it had been Bugs? What do you mean, practical?"

"Before we left the studio, I heard the cops talking. They're saying the fire was the result of arson. Who do you think will be blamed for Maxine's death?"

"Delly? You can't be serious."

"Who else was there?"

"I don't know."

"Delly had opportunity and motive."

"What motive?"

"Anissa, forget she's your friend. Delly was released from *Morning Star.* When she talked to Maxine, she discovered that Max planned to cast her sister Samantha in a brand-new part. Delly's mind could have snapped."

"Obviously, it did. But when I saw her she was unhappy, not vindictive."

"You don't know what was going on inside her head."

"Neither do you!"

"Anissa, please." Jon's hands formed a time-out T, his palm pressed against his fingertips. "Arguing won't get us anywhere, and Drew's probably right."

"Are you telling me that you believe Delly could have set the fire?"

He shrugged. "This morning she seemed resigned, almost relieved, but she gets so weird over Samantha. I think Delly destroyed Samantha's piano, hacked it to pieces. That takes angry strength. She might have tried to kill Samantha's parrot. If Delly, as Pandora, did start the fire, I'm sure she never meant to harm Maxine, but I'll have to call an attorney, just in case."

"Eat your soup, take a bath, and get some sleep." Anissa's voice was now calm, steady. "You can't help Delly unless you do."

"First I have to call—"

"I know a great law firm, Jon. Trust me." Anissa's fingers moved toward her breasts, where a small angel charm swung from the end of a gold chain.

The framed sign above a floppy-cushioned sofa read:

The law doth punish man or woman
That steals the goose from off the common,

But lets the greater felon loose,
That steals the common from the goose.

Anissa glanced around the cozy Weiss and Wong-Weiss conference room. Behind an oak table were bookcases, filled with law volumes and mystery novels. Fragmented sunshine sliced through two windows and formed puddles on a plum-colored carpet. Another wall held several framed posters, including Humphrey Bogart as Sam Spade, Raymond Burr as Perry Mason, and Charlie Chan.

"Good old Charlie," Anissa said. " 'Bad alibi like dead fish.' Did your wife choose that poster?"

"No. Kathy thinks Chan's too stereotypical. Bogie is hers, and she's been shopping for the quintessential Spencer Tracy, *Inherit the Wind* poster."

"Who wrote that bit about the goose?" Anissa pointed to the sign.

"That famous philosopher, Anonymous. It's from the eighteenth century. Sit down, angel."

"Have you seen Delly yet?"

"Kathy is chatting with her right now."

"Are you going to take the case?"

"Of course. But at the moment there is no case. The police are investigating, searching through the rubble. Your friend Delly seems to be a victim, not a perpetrator."

"Our security guard, Henry, insists that nobody was inside the studio except Maxine and Delly. Drew thinks Delly's mind could have snapped. Jon says she gets weird over her sister, Samantha. Delly tried to kill a parrot that belonged to Samantha and she bought lighter fluid on her way to the studio. She told me so, even though she lit her cigarette with matches. She even mentioned something about Pandora working with Mr. Ratings."

"Who the hell is Mr. Ratings?"

"A backstage ph-phantom. Echo . . . one of the actresses . . . it's a long st-story."

Joe handed her a tissue box, cleverly disguised as Oliver Wendel Holmes. Joe waited until her tears had become sniffles. Then he said, "Anissa, do you believe Delly set the fire?"

"Drew said she had opportunity and motive."

"Forget opportunity and motive. Do *you* believe she set the fire?"

"No, Joey. But maybe, just maybe Pandora did. Which brings me to my next question. If Pandora torched the studio, does that mean Delly's guilty?"

CHAPTER TWENTY-EIGHT

District Attorney Russell Benton snapped his red suspenders.

With a wince and a flinch, Susannah Benton curled into a naked body ball on their king-size bed. Then she pulled the blanket up around her chin. Rusty's suspenders sounded like a bullwhip. Glancing toward her husband, she surreptitiously slipped a peppermint Lifesaver between her pouty lips.

"Don't bother," he said.

"Don't bother what?" She sat up and tossed her brown hair, styled in the blunt cut popularized by figure skater Dorothy Hamil.

"The candy, Suze. You've already doused yourself with Bombay perfume."

"I drank one double martoonie, that's all." Her bare toes touched an empty Bombay gin bottle, hidden beneath the sheets. "Leave me alone, Rusty. I've got a splitting headache."

Susannah squeezed her eyes shut and wondered for the umpteenth time how she had ended up as the wife of a district attorney.

Directly beneath her high school yearbook picture they'd printed: THE NEXT DORIS DAY. But Doris, singing "It's Magic," had risen to major stardom with her first movie. Until 1953, life for Susannah had been magical. Then everything turned shitty.

After winning a local beauty contest, she'd fled Alabama to find fame and fortune in Hollywood. To hell with Doris Day.

Susannah had breasts. She'd be the next Jayne Mansfield.

Instead, she became a beauty operator, then part owner of an exclusive beauty salon, and her one claim to fame was a bit part in *East of Eden.* Well, not a bit part exactly, more like an extra. But she had met James Dean, which left all other men out in the cold. Dead or alive, Dean was the quintessential stud.

Russell Benton's wife, Grace, had been that California rarity, a native who didn't drive a car. Susannah drove to the Benton's Beverly Hills estate to wash, cut, and set the woman's iron-gray hair. Grace Benton was flat-chested. When Susannah—age forty and aging rather well—met Rusty, she displayed her enormous assets like two inflated rubber buoys tossed to a drowning man.

"Lawyer Benton, sir," she'd purr, batting her eyelashes. "I bought this bra because the ad promised cross-your-heart support. Put your hand here. Now here. Does that feel like support to you? Isn't there a law against false advertising? Can I sue the brassiere company?"

Grace Benton died of heart failure while Susannah was tweezing her bushy gray eyebrows. Rusty came running, felt his wife's neck pulse, and turned to comfort an hysterical Susannah. Comfort led to sex.

Twenty years older than her husband and disgustingly wealthy, Grace had no children. Rusty inherited. He gave a few bucks to charity and started thinking: *politics.*

After the funeral, with the scent of flowers clogging her sinuses, Susannah comforted Rusty. He wasn't James Dean, not by a long shot, but he did have one enormous asset, and it wasn't the size of his penis.

"Can you buy me a movie part?" she'd ask, placing his hands on her buoys. "Then I could sign autographs at political rallies."

Benton needed a new wife. Susannah was available, built like a brick you-know-what, and last but not least, the district attorney believed his public would respond favorably to a woman who was neither too old nor too young. So they wed, a big mistake, kind of like signing up for the *Titanic*'s maiden voyage because the ship's façade wasn't marred by all those ugly lifeboats.

Now, five years later, Susannah opened her eyes and watched her husband button his yellow pajama top.

Rusty looks like a lemon, she thought, wishing she could peel him into twists to garnish her martoonies.

Her gaze followed as, weaving a ring-studded hand through his profusion of silver hair, he paced back and forth, pounding the carpet with his bare feet.

Rusty was a war hero.

True.

He had established a reputation as a stern taskmaster who gloried in putting criminals behind bars "where they belonged."

True.

A dynamic public speaker, he threw his opponents off balance with an aw-shucks demeanor, and he hinted that he'd been born and raised on a farm in West Virginia, where he milked cows, churned butter, and toppled outhouses on Halloween.

False.

Susannah knew that he had been raised in Trenton, New Jersey, and had graduated from Princeton University.

Presently, he was being backed by big business interests who needed their own personal politician. The other party's incumbent was due for reelection and Rusty wanted to be California's next State Senator.

"What an opportunity," he hollered, halting in front of their wall-to-wall closet. "Only in Hollywood, America."

"Only in Hollywood, what?"

"Haven't you been listening? Or is your brain too saturated with gin?"

"You, um, said something about Delly Diamond, the actress who set fire—"

"Not just any actress, Suze. A soap opera star. Think of all that delicious publicity."

"Publicity?" *Once I shook James Dean's hand and he kissed me on the forehead.*

"You're not usually so dense this early in the evening."

"Leave me alone, Rusty."

"Not tonight. Tonight we're celebrating. Soap operas, Suze, you watch them often enough. Look, I'm prominent in Southern California, but I have to become as well known in Fresno, San Francisco, Sacramento—never mind. All I need is one big court case with newspaper headlines."

"Headlines," she echoed.

"If you ever read anything except movie magazines, you'd know that your husband made the front page of the *Times* today. 'In Hollywood, America, fame is no excuse for the perpetration of a heinous felony,' announced Russell Benton during an impromptu press conference."

Picking up the newspaper, Rusty threw it against the wall.

Susannah winced, flinched, and chewed her bottom lip until a drop of bright red blood appeared. "Congrats, darling," she said. "I'm so proud of you."

Grinning, he sauntered toward the bed. Susannah wanted another martoonie. Badly. Rusty looked like the shark in *Jaws.*

He retrieved his suspenders and tied Susannah's wrists to the headboard. Then he snapped the elastic while she pictured sharks. Sharks lived in water, right? Wrong. They lived on Hollywood sound stages, had toothy *Jaws,* and were nicknamed Bruce. Who thought up the name Bruce? Steven Spielberg? Richard Dreyfus?

Water, water everywhere, but not a drop to douche.

God, her throat and vagina were so dreyfus, so dry.

Didn't Richard Dreyfus kill Bruce the Shark in *Jaws?* Where was Richard when you really needed him? Or Steven Spielberg? Or James Dean?

"Help," Susannah whispered.

Oh Susannah, oh don't you cry for me, for I've come from Alabama.

Poor Delly Diamond. Wait until Rusty displayed his toothy *Jaws* inside the courtroom. Poor Pandora.

Poor Susannah, oh don't you cry for me.

After all, she had fortune if not fame.

Picturing James Dean and Richard Dreyfus, she dug in her heels and arched her hips. "Congrats, Bruce," she moaned.

But Rusty, busy inserting his erection between Susannah's pouty lips, didn't hear her slip of the tongue.

Marilyn Monroe Bradley Florentino Wiggins waddled across Anissa's kitchen. Setting a frying pan on top of the stove, she beat three eggs into an earthenware bowl. Then, thumbing the toaster's knob down, she turned toward Anissa. "What are you scowling at? The newspaper?"

"Yes. There's a story about the district attorney who's handling Delly's case. Russell Benton. What an asshole. Honestly, Maryl, if you weren't staying here I'd go bonkers."

"Then it's lucky our new house needs renovations and the old one has already been signed, sealed and delivered."

Anissa chewed a saltine cracker. "Stupid biscuits are supposed to settle my stomach. I passed the morning sickness phase weeks ago but stress is causing tidal waves. How are *you* feeling?"

"Great, except I'm due to hatch the first professional woman field goal kicker."

"Tell me again how soon you're due to hatch."

"I think I've started my tenth month."

"What?"

"You heard me. The doctor must have miscalculated." Maryl tossed her eggs into the pan and smiled at the satisfying sizzle. She buttered four pieces of toast, and absently brushed crumbs from her maternity jeans and oversized Chien T-shirt. "Jonah and I have agreed on one name. We both like Joan."

"Me, too. For Jonah?"

"No. Of Arc. Put your sneaks on, Anissa. It's time we played Angie Dickenson."

"Angie Dickenson?"

"Okay, you're right. We both can't be Pepper." Maryl studied Anissa's white slacks and white silk Hana Sung top with its goldtone buttons and black sweatshirt trim. "Cagney and Lacey," she said.

"What the hell are you talking about?"

"You look like Chris Cagney, except your belly has pooched and your hair—"

"Maryl!"

"We're going to play detectives, find the person who set the fire."

"Impossible. The police haven't discovered one clue."

"Nothing's impossible. Don't forget that Maryl Bradley, professional model with shit for brains, once edited an historical romance writer into literary sainthood. I even suggested Ed use the pseudonym Edwina Cartwright. We'll start with the food delivery boy."

"The food delivery boy left the studio before the fire began. He never signed the roster, but our security guard, Henry, swears he waved him in and out."

"I don't care, Anissa. Maybe he saw somebody lurking. Let's find him, talk to him."

"He doesn't work at the delicatessen anymore. Joe checked. The manager couldn't give a home address, phone number, or name. She called him 'The Kid.' "

"Okay, Cagney, that's our first step."

"What's our first step?"

"The restaurant manager." Maryl ladled her scrambled eggs onto a Wedgewood plate.

"You're bonkers. I just said—"

"Sometimes a person will tell a pregnant Sam Spade the stuff she won't mention to cops or lawyers. It's a starting point, and we don't have much time. You're due to testify before the Grand Jury."

"Maryl, at ten months pregnant you can't bounce around town sleuthing. Drew will kill me if anything happens to—"

"Nothing's going to happen." She swallowed the last of her toast and eggs, and reached for a bag of bagels. "I once told Delly I hated Cinderella because Cinderella never took control of her life. But Delly can't take control, she's too sick, so we'll have to play Fairy Godmothers."

"Jesus! First I'm Angie, then Cagney, now a Fairy God—"

"Interpret that Grand Jury thing for me, please."

"I'll try." Anissa heaved a deep sigh. "The magic words are 'probable cause.' The D.A.'s office brings evidence to the grand jury with the intention of seeking an indictment. That avoids the need for a preliminary hearing. Joe and Kathy preferred the grand jury since Delly wouldn't be taken into custody. But there's a big risk. I mean, they wouldn't convene unless the D.A. felt he had a convincing case. He submits the evidence. If the verdict is guilty, Delly will be arrested and tried inside a courtroom."

"Wait a minute. Slow down. The grand jury—"

"Is made up of citizens chosen by a judge. They hear the testimony in secret, then an indictment is drawn up if probable cause is determined."

"Have a bagel. Where's the cream cheese? How do they

determine probable cause?"

"I'm not sure I grasp the legal jargon. Joe tried to explain, but I ended up memorizing terms. On my soap, people get arrested for murder and suddenly they're spewing dialogue and wearing Nina Ricci prison garb. All I know is that arson is defined as 'the malicious burning of a dwelling house of another.' An arsonist is anyone who starts a fire or causes an explosion for the purpose of destroying another person's building or occupied structure."

"Go on," said Maryl, her voice muffled by her bagel.

"Maxine's death is classified as a felony murder. It could be murder in the first degree since the felony is one of a specified group—like arson, burglary, kidnapping, or rape."

"That doesn't sound good."

"Then we come to something called intent. The rationale is that criminal sanctions are not necessary for those who innocently cause harm. Oliver Wendal Holmes once said, 'Even a dog distinguishes between being stumbled over and being kicked.' "

"Do they think Delly kicked Maxine Graham?"

"It's more complicated than that. There's something called negligent homicide where a defendant didn't intend to bring about a particular result. A person who is acting as an automaton can't be guilty of a crime."

"An automaton? A human robot?"

"The classic illustration is an epileptic who strikes during seizure. Or a sleepwalker. Joe says there's a case that took place in 1879 that involved sleepwalking."

"Delly was drugged on tranquilizers and didn't know what she was doing, right?"

"Prove it. Anyway, there's a fine line between automatism, which is an involuntary act, and insanity. If it come to a guilty verdict, we'd rather have the automatism because a successful insanity defense subjects Delly to confinement. And anyway, insanity defenses are rarely successful."

Maryl shook her head. "I see, said the blind man."

Anissa bit into her bagel, chewed and swallowed. "A person who lacks the physical power to control an act has not committed a crime. But an automatist defendant might be just as dangerous as an insane one. Kathy said there was a case in 1955 where the defendant had been a model father until he struck his ten-year-old son on the head with a heavy mallet and threw him out the window. They found that Dad's behavior was caused by a cerebral tumor. Therefore, he was an automatist, not guilty, and he returned to his family."

"Good grief. Are you saying that if Delly had a cerebral tumor she'd be set free?"

"I don't know. I sat there in that Wong-Weiss office, listening as hard as I could, and I still got lost. The case sounds circumstantial to me. Delly just happened to be in the wrong place at the wrong time. Nobody saw her set the fire. She can't remember anything that happened after she entered the studio, except for her dream, and she can't really remember that."

"I still think the best idea is to find out who really set the fire. Jonah has my car. Is your Mustang working?"

"It could hit the starting gate at Santa Anita. Drew keeps that rubber-hoofed monster in perfect condition." Anissa belched, blushed, and patted her belly. "I'm curious, Maryl. How do Fairy Godmothers get pregnant?"

"They fuck Fairy Godfathers."

Chapter Twenty-Nine

The restaurant manager admired Maryl's blooming belly as she sat both women inside a red vinyl booth. There were three booths and two small tables since the deli did mostly take-out. On top of the faded linoleum floor was a wooden podium with cash register and telephone. A huge kitchen area, situated behind a rectangular window, completed the sparse decor.

"Call me Dawn," said the manager, who had comfortable curves and looked like Scarlett O'Hara's Mammy, minus the headgear.

"I can't help you," Dawn said, after Maryl had made her request. "We don't keep in touch with delivery kids. They come and go so fast."

"How about his social security number?"

"Nope."

"What do you mean, nope? Isn't that against the law?"

"Jake said he'd work as contracted labor, for tips. I needed him so I let it slide."

"Jake?"

"I told the cops I forgot his name 'cause I didn't want to get involved, but I guess I can tell you. It's Jake Smith."

"Oh, great. Why not John Smith?" Anissa eyeballed the vivid wall poster depicting a pastrami sandwich, gloppy potato salad, onion rings, and green pickle spears.

Maryl studied the same poster and licked her lips. "May we see Jake's job application, Dawn?"

"I threw it away."

"Are you sure?"

"Uh . . . yes, ma'am."

Maryl caught the slight hesitation and nodded toward Anissa. "My friend here works at the *Morning Star* studio. She's told me how the cast and crew members all call for your food. While we were parking the car, I noticed a brand new Greek deli about to open. But I guess most people won't change old habits, not unless someone suggests they try something different, like gyros. Do you have pita bread, Dawn? I love pita bread, it's so healthy." She smiled. "Are you absolutely certain Jake's application was trashed?"

"Maybe I kept it." Dawn returned Maryl's smile, but her eyes reflected the implied threat. "I never have time to clean my office, so it might be buried there."

"While you're searching, maybe your chef can make me a hot pastrami sandwich, double pickles."

"Maryl, you just ate breakfast," Anissa said. "Eggs, four pieces of toast, bagels, cream chee—"

"Joan's hungry."

When Dawn returned, Maryl was savoring the last of her seeded rye and spicy mustard. She moved the plate aside to study the wrinkled piece of paper, a standard form.

"Lord above," she exclaimed. "Jake gave his address as 77 Sunset Strip. There's no phone or previous employment. His birth date is 1947. I thought he was a kid."

"I call all my delivery people kids," Dawn said. "Well, that's one reason I hired Jake. He was older, more experienced."

"Under personal recommendations he listed a name. It's hard to read, looks like a doctor's prescription, but I think it says Elizabeth Crown."

"That's another reason I hired Jake," Dawn said, eagerly. "His reference was from a girl who used to work here. Now she waits tables at Tail O' The Cock. She said Jake was dependable."

"I guess our next stop is Tail O' The Cock. We should get there just in time for lunch." Rising, Maryl walked toward the cash register. As she fumbled inside her purse, she said, "I'm going to mention your heavenly food to my husband, Jonah Wiggins."

"Your hubby's Jonah Wiggins, the talk show host? Don't leave yet, Mrs. Wiggins." Dawn reached for the phone. Then she turned away, talked low, and hung up the receiver. "I didn't tell you everything, Mrs. Wiggins. That girl who knows Jake is my niece, Betsy Crown. She's an actress, and she's home right now if you want to pay her a call. No, no. Put your wallet away, Mrs. Wiggins. The pastrami's on the house."

Betsy Crown's house was in Glendale. Anissa maneuvered her Mustang through a maze of apartments, decorated with white pebbly exteriors and orange tile roofs. It was too chilly for swimming, but several women sunbathed next to a sparkling turquoise pool.

"You're Charl on *Morning Star,*" screeched Betsy as she opened her door. She gestured Maryl and Anissa inside, then turned toward Maryl. "I know you, too. The Rosebud girl. Except you look so different, so—"

"Pregnant. There's a new ingredient in Rosebud perfume. It's called Eau d' conception."

Betsy was young and slender. Her natural color would have filled the pool's sun worshippers with jealous hostility. She had just finished showering and her dark curls shined. A blue velour robe couldn't hide her curves. Like Dawn, she offered red vinyl, cleverly disguised as a leather couch. Then she pointed toward an open box of taffy. "Help yourself."

"No, thanks, we just ate," said Anissa, sitting and watching

Maryl stuff her mouth with candy.

Betsy's fingers twiddled her robe's sash. "Auntie Dawn says you're trying to find Jake Smith."

"That's . . . ummm . . . right," said Maryl, chewing.

"I wish I knew where he was. The police were no help at all."

"The police?" Maryl stopped chewing.

"Jake stole some stuff from me. But when I called the cops, this sergeant or somebody said they couldn't do anything 'cause Jake was a guest in my house. Ain't that a piece of shit? Pardon my French, but it just proves you can't tell the truth. I should have lied and said I was robbed by a stranger."

"Did Jake live with you?" Maryl swallowed her taffy.

"Yes, for a while. I should have known there was something fishy about him."

"Fishy?"

"I thought Jake was okay. Not that I couldn't get a dozen straight actors into my bed. I mean, life. For instance, the first year's rent on this place was a gift, paid for by an actor who, if I mentioned his name, you'd know him."

"Is Jake an actor?"

"I guess. We met outside the *Morning Star* studio when I interviewed for an under-five. Didn't get it." Betsy swiveled her face toward Anissa. "I wonder if you could put in a good word for me? I suppose you think I have nerve asking, but if you're not pushy in this friggin' town, pardon my French, you can't get anywhere."

"Sure, Betsy. I'll talk to Vance Booker, our casting agent."

"Thanks."

"You met Jake at the studio," Maryl prompted.

"Yeah. He sounded nice. I was sore because I didn't get hired so he bought me some drinks. Well, one thing led to another and I took him home with me. I was a little drunk and we fooled around. He was okay in that department, if you know what I mean. Anyway, he had just moved to California and was staying at some motel, so I let him bunk with me, off and on, and got him the job with my Auntie Dawn. Auntie didn't like him."

"Why?" Maryl reached for another piece of taffy.

"She said Jake was a strange one." By now, Betsy's sash had developed multiple knots.

Anissa's gaze traveled from Maryl's avid consumption of candy to Betsy's fluttering fingers. "Define strange."

"Aw, can't we talk about something else? I have a scrapbook with all my reviews."

"Was Jake abusive?"

"What do you mean?" Betsy shifted uncomfortably in her red vinyl armchair.

"You said he was 'okay' while you're so beautiful," Anissa clarified. "Why did you let him stay? Did he threaten you?"

Betsy hesitated. Then she said, "Jake was different. Nasty sometimes, and he'd do things that made me want . . . need more. He'd hurt me then say he was sorry. I guess he had me under a spell. I thought about him all day, even at work, all the time. I never met anyone like him before." Tears coursed down her cheeks. "I can't explain it . . . why I let Jake . . . he's sick . . . you want to hear something really dumb? I was dating this neat guy and I broke up with him. We're back together now, but if Jake came to the door, I . . . please excuse me."

Betsy raced toward the bathroom while Anissa whispered, "I've never understood that masochism thing."

Maryl nodded. "Betsy said it. Sick. I think I've finally lost my appetite."

When the girl returned, Maryl cut off her apologies. "What does Jake look like, Betsy?"

"Ordinary. Dark, thinning hair, but it could be dyed. I think his natural hair color was lighter, blond or brown. He's a couple of inches taller than me and he has big muscles. But I think he was once fat."

"Why?"

"He works out religiously and he always looked at himself in the mirror, you know, as if he couldn't believe he was thin."

"Does Jake belong to a health club?"

Betsy shook her head. "He worked out here. I have some exercise equipment." She pointed a slender, rosy-tipped finger toward a closed door.

"Does he have an accent?" Anissa asked. "A southern drawl? Foreign? Spanish? British?"

"Not really. Jake didn't come from California, but . . . oh, I don't know. Chicago, maybe? He sounded a little like Dan Ackroyd and John Beluchi in *The Blues Brothers.* Did you see that movie? It was a hoot. I tried out for the Carrie Fisher part, but I think it was pre-cast."

"What kind of car does Jake drive?" Maryl leaned forward, resting her hands and chin atop her belly bulge.

"A beat-up old Dodge. Black. He said he bought it from some junkie near the community college in Pacoina. We usually drove my car, a new Toyota. Cost a mint, not to mention the fuckin' insurance, pardon my French, but that's why I need a steady job, for instance a part on *Morning Star.* You won't forget to mention me, Charl, will you?"

"If you've already interviewed for an under-five, Vance will have your picture and résumé, unless they burned in the fire. I'll nudge him a little, refresh his memory."

"Jake probably has a California license plate," Maryl said. "You didn't happen to notice the letters or numbers on his plate, did you Betsy?"

"I can't remember my own numbers. Sorry."

"You said he stole some things. TV? Money?"

"No. I keep my tips in a cookie jar, and Jake knew it, but he took off with some clothes. And makeup."

"He stole your clothes?" Maryl raised one eyebrow.

"You sound like the cops. Look, I had some really nice stuff. For instance, a black jersey dress, mock turtleneck in front, plunging down the back, covered with sequins. I spent three hundred friggin' dollars on it, pardon my French. I put the dress on lay-away, and it took forever to make the pay—"

"Did Jake do that often? Dress up like a woman?"

"No, never. That was my bit. He'd have me wear a child's dress. Pink, short, with a bow tied in back. I think he had it sewed special. Oh, and a long platinum wig. That sure turned Jake on. He took all that stuff with him when he left."

"When did he leave?"

"After the fire at the *Morning Star* studio. He saw it in the paper. He said he made a food delivery to the lady who burned, just before the fire. Maybe he thought he'd be blamed."

"But the fire started *after* he left the studio."

Maryl's statement had been rhetorical and Betsy was in her own world. "I'm glad he's gone," she said. "Good riddance to bad rubbish. I wish he'd eat shit and die, pardon my French."

Outside, walking toward the car, Anissa said, "That dressing up like a little girl bit sounds like Topher Coombs, except Betsy's physical description doesn't fit."

"She's a tad dippy."

"Not that dippy, Maryl. Topher couldn't dye then un-dye his hair. He doesn't have muscles and never will, no matter how often he works out. And he has a beard. Betsy would remember a beard."

Both women climbed into the Mustang and adjusted their bellies. Anissa put the car in gear, turned the ignition key and yelled, "Popeye!"

Marl glanced around the parking lot. "Where?"

"Not where. Who."

"Okay. Who?"

"This may sound bonkers, Maryl, but a man named Popeye killed Randy's lover inside a Malibu beach house. Then he ran away. But what if he didn't? Suppose he waited, hid, saw me?"

"Did you witness the murder?"

"No."

"I'm confused. If this Popeye person killed a woman, why didn't the police arrest him?"

"Popeye didn't kill a woman. He killed a man named David. There was nothing in the papers, so I assumed the cops traced him through his fingerprints. But I don't know for sure."

"Why would Popeye set fire to your studio?"

"Before the fire started, I told Delly an overzealous fan was following me. Maybe Popeye wanted to get rid of me."

"Why, Anissa? You never saw him and couldn't identify—"

"He was crazy, Maryl. He stabbed David with an ice pick."

"Was Popeye once blond?"

"What? Oh, the dyed hair. I don't know. Randy mentioned muscles, so Betsy's description fits. And Randy said Popeye worked out. Or did he say Popeye liked to boat? Damn! I can't remember."

"Assuming Popeye's real name is Jake and he's bi rather than gay and he has this thing for little blonde girls, I still can't get a fix on his motive. You'd never be able to identify him, and you weren't inside the studio when it burned."

"That theory's way out in left field, huh?" Anissa started the engine. "What next, Fairy Godmother? Too bad Jake didn't leave behind a scorched slipper."

"Don't be such a smartass. You sound like my brother. Look, we've found out more in a few hours than the police or Weiss and Wong-Weiss found in a whole week."

"But where do we go from here? We've just eliminated Topher and Popeye, and for all we know Jake could have flown the coop. I can't even fathom how to track him down. He looks ordinary and he drives a black car. Terrific."

"Doesn't the criminal always return to the scene of the crime?"

"Who says Jake's a criminal? We know for a fact that the fire started after Henry saw him leave."

"I have an idea. Betsy said she met Jake outside the *Morning Star* studio, but she's not sure he's an actor. He could be a soap fan, maybe the one who's been following you. That makes sense. I mean, his quirky thing about blondes. Let's put a classified ad in the paper and suggest a meeting. We can sign it Charl. When he contacts you, we can ask him who was at the studio before the fire started. He's still our only lead."

"That's such a long shot, Maryl. This Jake has to be obsessed with Charl *and* read classified ads."

"Okay, let's assume Jake is obsessed. Can you signal him during the show?"

"No. The shows are taped ahead of time. Wait a sec. Tomorrow we're shooting live. Maxine had tomorrow's episode on the office telly when she died, and the tape burned. There's a scene with Cal. It's steamy, takes place in bed. With Max gone, I could probably adlib something and use the newspaper as a prop. I'll ask the guy who works the dolly to zoom in on the classifieds. Isn't jake a nineteen-twenties word for okay? That fits. After my thing with Cal, I'll say everything's jake. I'll say it twice. Most viewers won't catch it since they'll be looking at Drew's gorgeous body, but Jake . . ." She paused, shuddering. "If Jake's obsessed, he'll be watching me."

"Anissa, that's brilliant. Won't Drew be suspicious if you adlib?"

"Aren't we going to tell Drew and Jonah about today?"

"Yes. No. I don't know. Let's go home, call in the ad, then prepare a sumptuous feast for our men. How about lasagna?"

"Maryl, you just had breakfast, lunch, candy—"

"Lasagna dripping with *tons* of meat and cheese. Tomorrow, while you adlib, I'll nurse my indigestion. The next day you have that Grand Jury thing. While you're testifying, I'll visit the fire department."

"Why? To roast a Dalmatian?"

"Jonah once suggested I secure guest stars for his show. Wouldn't it be fun to have film director Irwin Allen appear with a rep from the fire department? Didn't Paul Newman star in *The Towering Inferno?* I'll track down Paul and see if his eyes are really that blue. Then, just for grins, I'll ask the Fire Chief how someone can start a fire when they're not even inside the frig-gin' building, pardon my French."

Chapter Thirty

Anissa glanced up at the Hall of Justice, a forbidding rococo Victorian monstrosity. Jutting granite blocks provided roosting places for pigeons and starlings.

"This building is so ugly it's beautiful," she told Drew, "like a Volkswagen Beetle."

"Or a gargoyle," he said.

Anissa recalled the sculpted stone gargoyles outside The Playground, and suddenly had an awful premonition that things were about to go—as Jacob might put it—kaput.

She traveled to the fifth floor and wrinkled her nose at the rank smell. The top floor had holding tanks for prisoners and several odors, including a strong disinfectant, drifted down to mingle with the smell of bird droppings.

"The Grand Jury is a mystery to most people," Joe had explained, "because nobody is permitted inside except the jury, prosecutor, and witnesses. The press is forbidden. Defense attorneys aren't even allowed to be present with their clients, which is one of the reasons we've decided Delly won't testify. There's a jury foreman but no judge. Due to its size and population, Los Angeles has a twenty-three man jury with fourteen votes needed to indict."

"You mean condemn, don't you?"

"Look, angel, the prosecutor's case is very weak. Benton obviously wants publicity for political reasons. The arson investigators believe the fire began with lighter fluid. Delly had lighter fluid inside her purse, but the perpetrator could have removed it while she napped. Her motive is allegedly revenge. Because she was fired from the show."

"Joe, her contract wasn't renewed. There's a big difference. Topher Coombs was fired, not Delly. Topher was furious. He threatened to 'cut off Maxine's balls.' "

"Nobody believes Delly meant to kill Maxine Graham, but that doesn't matter. It's the old example of a bank robber who exchanges gunfire with the police and kills an innocent bystander. The bank robber would be brought up on murder charges. In any case, nobody *saw* Delly set the fire. I don't think they'll indict."

"Condemn."

Cast members from *Morning Star* made up the bulk of the witnesses. A subpoena had also been issued to Henry.

"Delly was invited to appear, but she can't be subpoenaed," Kathy had said. "Under our system, a defendant or possible defendant is protected by the Constitution from being forced to testify against herself, or to be put in a position where she might inadvertently incriminate herself. Delly is feeling much better, physically. However, she doesn't remember the studio fire or the roof incident, and we won't allow buttons to be pushed where she might have another breakdown."

Although Drew was scheduled to testify at Monday's hearings, he insisted on accompanying Anissa. "I'll wait in the hallway, mingle with the newshounds," he said. "That will take the pressure off you and Bugs."

Outside the Grand Jury room, press members clustered. When Drew and Anissa arrived, reporters surrounded them, shouting questions.

"Hold it." Drew gave a shrill whistle while Anissa slipped through the crowd. "One at a time. You know I'm not allowed to talk about my testimony or my wife's testimony, but you can ask me anything else."

At the corridor's corner, Anissa bumped into a small, elderly lady dressed in an ankle-length, violet shirtwaist. Her white hair was tightly crimped around her scowling face. Her eyes hid behind harlequin eyeglasses with thick lenses. She had troweled pancake makeup onto her face, caulked the grooves from her nose to her mouth, then added red rouge and purple eye shadow. She didn't look grotesque enough to be pretty—in fact, thought Anissa, she looked rather pathetic.

"Well, I never," she huffed. "I'm an important witness and I was in the middle of a sentence when the reporters left me, just like that." The snap of her fingers sounded like the pop of a soggy breakfast cereal. "Not even a 'thank you, Mrs. Grady.' "

"Mrs. Grady?"

"DeLoras Grady. You're that soap actress, aren't you?"

"Yes, ma'am. I don't believe we've met. Are you an actress?"

"I was. Vaudeville. I danced with my late husband. We were called T.L.C. The T was for my late husband, Timothy, the L for his sister, Lucille."

"And the C?"

"That was me. They called me Carmen."

"Right. Carmen."

"I sang, too. The music is so loud today, don't you think? It shakes a body from head to toe. I had to stuff my ears with cotton when *she* had that band in her house."

"Who? Delly?"

"Played night and day, they did. A body couldn't get any rest. I thought my windows would shatter, and Jack Benny howled like he wanted to be one of 'em."

"Jack Benny?"

"My dog. He's my third Jack Benny, and very good company when he's not howling to beat the band. That's why I'm here."

"Because of your dog?"

"Yes, indeedy. I walk Jack Benny three times a day, past *her* house. I live down the street."

"Oh, I see," said Anissa. *I see, said the blind man.*

"They sent some nice gents from the D.A.'s office to talk to neighbors. It's lucky I remembered what I saw."

"And what was that, Mrs. Grady?"

"Call me DeLoras. *They* have this window. You can't help but look inside when Jack Benny waters their palm tree. What's a body to do? Watch a dog pee? Sometimes I look toward the house, not spying or anything, so I won't have to watch Jack Benny squirt pee."

"Of course."

"I saw *her* on the day of the fire. She looked crazy. Maybe the loud music drove her crazy."

"Go on, Mrs. Grady."

"Call me DeLoras. Or Carmen. I answer to both. *She* had a small ax, and I thought she might be planning to kill someone."

"You saw that from the street?"

"No, the window. I heard the piano, only it sounded funny, so I took myself a closer look. *She'd* hacked the piano to pieces and was hitting it with a doll. At first I thought the doll was a real baby, but then it's face broke. *She* glanced at the window, and I was so scared I just about fainted dead away. Her eyes looked like zombie eyes. I ducked down quick 'cause I never doubted for a minute that she'd hack Jack Benny and me—"

"Really, Mrs. Grady."

"To pieces. On TV Pandora looks so innocent but I'll let you in on a little secret. I peeked through a side window one morning, just after sunup, and she and her boyfriend were . . . well, I don't want to shock you, you being pregnant and all, so I won't go into details. But *she* was cussing and so was her parrot."

"Parrot? Oh, Samantha."

"Who?"

"Delly has a twin sister."

"It was *her,* missy. She cussed. The man told her to be quiet. 'I sing when I fuck,' she said. Maybe she sings when she sets buildings on fire and kills people. I'll have to remember that for the jury." Mrs. Grady made several stabbing motions as she sang "Sing."

Karen Carpenter she wasn't. Anissa suppressed a shudder.

"One day she cussed at me when Jack Benny peed on her new car," Mrs. Grady continued. "Sake's alive, it was only a tire. Tires run over shit so what's the diff—"

"Were you mad at Delly because she cussed at you?"

"Not mad, scared. She looked like she was about to sing, and we all know what happens then." Mrs. Grady sliced the air around her throat with her first finger.

"It's a shame Jack Benny can't testify and substantiate your ridiculous theory, DeLoras," Anissa said.

"Mrs. Grady to you. I saw what I saw, missy, and they're calling your name." This time the snap of her fingers sounded like the crackle of a well known breakfast cereal. "I guess it's time for you to go inside."

The Grand Jury room was immaculate and air conditioned. Anissa estimated the size to be fifty by thirty feet. Jury members sat on individual chairs behind long desks, arranged in rows, amphitheater style, facing what looked like a judge's bench and a witness stand. Prosecutor Russell Benton and his assistant sat behind the bench.

This is so unfair, thought Anissa. *Weiss and Wong-Weiss should be up there, too.*

"The jury members are sworn in by the court reporter," Joe had explained. "My educated guess is that the dialogue will go something like this. 'Name of possible defendant: Delilah Gold Diamond. Matters to be considered in connection with above named possible defendant: Alleged arson of property and the murder of Maxine Graham.' "

"Then the court reporter will briefly relate circumstances of the alleged crime," Kathy said, "and ask if any Grand Jury members have a 'state of mind which will prevent him from acting impartially and without prejudice.' If such a member exists, he'll be excused."

Unfair, Anissa thought again.

Placing her right hand on a black leather-bound Bible, she swore to tell the truth, the whole truth, and nothing but the truth.

"State your name."

"Anissa Flory."

"Mrs. Flory, can you tell us your occupation?" asked the district attorney.

"Yes."

"Yes?"

"I can tell you my occupation."

"Then do so, please."

Anissa faked a cough. Joe had told her not to be a smartass, and yet it was hard to resist. She stared at Benton. He wore red suspenders under an open suit jacket. His silver hair, once bright orange she had heard, was combed into a high pompadour. His blue eyes were small but piercing.

Benton's assistant had talked to Anissa on the *Morning Star* set, questioning her about Delly's behavior. She'd answered yes, no, I don't know, then excused herself for her next scene. Now the assistant smiled and winked. Anissa ignored him.

"My occupation is performer," she said, folding her hands in the lap of her black maternity dress. Joe's angel charm swung from its gold chain and her diamond birthday earrings felt too heavy. "I'm an actress on the daytime drama, *Morning Star.*"

"How long have you known the defendant?" Benton asked.

"I've known Delly for over a year."

"Do you believe she set fire to the studio, leading to the death of Maxine Graham?"

"No, sir. In fact, I'd swear to it."

"That isn't necessary, you're under oath," Benton said with a smile. "Were you at the studio on the day of the fire?"

"Yes. Not during the fire. Before."

"Did you see or talk to Miss Diamond?"

"Yes, sir. Delly was planning to pick up some things she'd left . . ." Anissa snapped her mouth shut. Joe and Kathy had told her to keep her answers short and not offer any unsolicited information.

Benton said, "What things?"

"Clothing and personal items."

"Is there any reason why Miss Diamond suddenly decided to retrieve her items on that particular day?"

"I assume it's because we don't tape the show on weekends."

"So she was aware that the studio would be deserted."

Anissa studied the jury members, all men. They were listening with interest—a real live soap opera.

"Mrs. Flory?"

"Sorry, I didn't realize that was a question. The studio is usually deserted on weekends. I assume Delly knew."

Benton snapped his red suspenders. "What role did Miss Diamond play on your show?"

"Pandora. My roommate."

"Your roommate in an apartment?"

"No, sir. A hospital."

"The mental ward of a hospital, correct?"

"Yes."

"Was Miss Diamond's character insane?"

"No. She has a mental breakdown. They didn't go into a lot of detail on the show. Pandora was a sounding board for Charl, my character, so the viewers would know what Charl was thinking."

"Is Miss Diamond a good actress?"

"In my opinion, Delly is an excellent actress."

"Yet she was fired from the show."

"No, sir."

"She wasn't fired?"

"Her option wasn't renewed. There's a difference."

"I'm not sure I understand. What's the difference?"

"My character recovered from her illness. Pandora wasn't needed as a sounding board so Delly's option was dropped. It happens on daytime drama all the time. Pandora knew that. And Delly was aware that her character might recur, come back." Anissa looked at the jury members. "Delly wouldn't torch the studio, knowing Pandora might return to the show."

Three jury members nodded.

Benton snapped his suspenders. "Mrs. Flory, you called Miss Diamond both Pandora and Delly."

"That's right. One's her TV name and—"

"Did she ever call herself Pandora?"

Joe and Kathy had both told Anissa not to underestimate Rusty Benton. "He's a snake," said Kathy, "hiding behind a pile of rocks, ready to strike, to rattle you. If you need time to think, have him repeat the question."

"Could you repeat the question, please?"

"Of course." Benton grinned at the jury. "Let me clarify. Did Delly Diamond ever call herself Pandora outside the *Morning Star* studios?"

"We all do that. I mean, we all call ourselves by our stage names . . ."

"Yes?"

"That's all."

"I'm not an actor, Mrs. Flory, but I don't go around calling myself F. Lee Bailey. Isn't that unusual?"

"No, sir. I've starred in two Tennessee Williams plays. Everyone, including me, called me by my stage names, Blanche and Laura, off stage and on, the whole run of the play. They were crazy, too."

"Who?"

"My stage characters. Laura wasn't crazy, more like naïve, but Blanche went bonkers. The end of the play has her heading for a mental institution. It doesn't mean I'm insane, just because I acted the role."

"Was I suggesting that Miss Diamond is insane?"

"You bet! I could see by your questions—"

"Did Miss Diamond act insane when she wasn't on the set?"

"No, sir."

"You're under oath, Mrs. Flory."

"Define insane. Delly sometimes retreated into her character. I've known many performers who do that."

Benton smiled. "I'll change my question. Did Miss Diamond act strange?"

"Not as strange as half the actors in this town."

"Did she sometimes suck her thumb like an infant?"

"I . . . yes."

"Did she call her rag doll her baby?"

"Yes."

"Did she refer to herself as Pandora, or Panda, in third person?"

"Yes, but—"

"That's not strange?"

"She didn't do it all the time. It's called 'staying in character.' By the way, I often call myself Charl and my husband refers to himself as Cal."

Benton snapped his suspenders. Aware that the gesture meant a change of subject, Anissa tensed.

"Mrs. Flory, please tell us how Miss Diamond felt about her producer, Maxine Graham."

"Delly respected Maxine. We all did. She was responsible for our high ratings and high salaries, for our jobs."

"She was also responsible for Miss Diamond's lack of a job and salary."

"That's one of the risks of playing a part on daytime drama, Mr. Benton. There's always a chance you'll be written out of the script. Contracts are renewed every thirteen weeks." Anissa sneaked a peek at the jury. Two men looked appalled, one sympathetic.

"I understand your writers liked Pandora very much," Benton said. "They even enlarged her role."

"Yes, that's true. Pandora was popular with the viewers."

"So Maxine Graham was directly responsible for dropping the role of Pandora."

Anissa slowly counted to ten. "That question calls for speculation on the part of the witness," she said.

Benton chuckled. "We're not in court, Mrs. Flory. I just wanted your opinion."

"I can't answer you, sir. I don't know what Maxine was thinking. If you do, you're Houdini."

Benton snapped his suspenders. "Another performer, a Miss Fitzgerald, says Delly Diamond was very vocal in her dislike of Maxine Graham."

"That's a lie!" *What the hell is Scottie doing in Hollywood?*

"I suppose Miss Diamond was vocal in her praise for the woman who had her fired," Benton said sarcastically.

"How many times do I have to tell you? Delly wasn't fired. Maxine made Delly nervous, all of us nervous, but if anybody hated Maxine, it was Christopher Coombs and Scottie Fitzgerald. They were washed up, not Delly."

Snap.

"Did you attend a dinner party the night before the murder?"

"Who said Maxine's death was murder?"

Benton laughed. "Objection sustained. Did you attend a party at the Sawmill restaurant the night before Maxine Graham died in a studio fire?"

"Yes."

"Other cast members were present at the event, a goodbye party for Miss Diamond." Benton paused. "That's a question," he added.

"Yes. Other cast members were present."

"Do you recall how Miss Diamond felt about Maxine Graham that night?"

"What do you mean?"

"Was she angry?"

"No. She was resigned, maybe a little sad."

"Some of the cast members recall her saying, 'I'll kill our Max off.' Does that sound like resigned and sad?"

"Delly didn't say that. In fact, another actress did. Echo Foster."

"Well, then, I apologize. I misunderstood. What did Miss Diamond say?"

"She said lots of things. We all did. It was a party."

"Wasn't there a discussion about murdering your producer, the same woman responsible for your astronomical salaries?"

"I didn't say astronomical."

"I suppose you get paid the same amount as a schoolteacher."

"No. Do you?" Anissa turned toward the jury members. "The district attorney's making a big deal over a joke, gentleman. We were all joking. Every person at our table talked about ways to murder Maxine Graham. Echo Foster said she'd sabotage Maxine's sound booth. Someone suggested strangling her with wires from the set. Someone else mentioned Topher cutting off her, uh, body parts. It got wilder, more and more inventive. We were drinking cham—"

"What was Miss Diamond's plan for Maxine Graham's demise?" Benton's voice cut across Anissa's plea.

"I'm not sure I remember."

"You're under oath, Mrs. Flory, and you've just demonstrated an excellent memory, even corrected my impression that it was Miss Diamond who wanted to 'kill our Max off.' What did Miss Diamond say that night?"

A snake. A fucking snake.

"We're waiting, Mrs. Flory. Do you need the question repeated?"

"No, sir. Maxine was a chain smoker. She lit one cigarette from another, never stopped."

"What did Delly Diamond say the night before your producer was murdered . . . sorry, before she burned to death in a studio fire?"

"We were drinking champagne and kidding around. Delly made the biggest joke of all. She wasn't serious. We laughed."

"The biggest joke of all," Benton repeated. "Murder is the biggest joke of all." He shook his head. "Go on, please."

"Maxine was a chain-smoker. Delly said . . . she didn't mean it, of course . . . she said Maxine should die by fire . . . go up in smoke. That a cigarette . . . the ash from her cigarette . . . should ignite her office and . . . don't you see? The others will tell you the same thing. It was a stupid joke. You can't pin a murder rap on someone who makes a stupid joke."

"Thank you, Mrs. Flory," Benton said. "That will be all."

"It was a joke," Anissa said, tossing the *L.A. Times* across the room. "If I told you guys I wanted to strangle our district attorney with his suspenders and then he choked to death, I'd be charged with first-degree murder."

"It's not your fault," Maryl soothed. "You didn't know what

Benton planned to ask. Anyway, you couldn't lie under oath."

"I got emotional and talked too much. That's one of the things Joe and Kathy warned me about. At the end I sounded as if I wanted to avoid answering. It made Delly seem twice as guilty. If I'd only answered Benton's question calmly, given the jury a shrug and a smile. Damn!"

"Easy," said Drew. "Think about Bugs. The baby will feel your stress."

"Really! You had a fine time with the reporters while I was getting grilled."

"Be fair, Anissa, that was our game plan."

"Fair, hah! How did those newshounds gather *secret* information about *secret* events inside the Grand Jury room? Isn't there a penalty for spilling the beans?"

"Sure. But the reporters aren't penalized. I imagine the leak came from Benton's office. Or it could have come from cast members. The newspapers said 'reliable source.' "

"The district attorney showed video tapes to the jury, Maryl. Tapes of Delly as Pandora setting the hospital fire on *Morning Star.*" Anissa gestured toward the spilled pages. "It's all there, in the paper, from another reliable source. And the paper said Benton had two witnesses who partied with Delly and Judith, and Delly quoted the ladybug jingle, you know, the one that goes 'your house on fire, your children will burn'? Both witnesses said Delly threatened to burn Maxine."

"I'm hungry," Maryl said.

"You're always hungry, Miss Scarlett," Drew said in a non-Southern, Clark Gable drawl. Then he turned on the TV and punctuated the remote with his thumb until he found Jonah's show.

Ushering Anissa toward the kitchen, Maryl said, "Need anything, Drew?"

"A beer. No hurry."

Maryl opened the refrigerator. "While you were having that horrible experience inside the jury room, I was sleuthing."

Seated at the kitchen table, Anissa patted her belly. "Drew's right. Bugs is stressed. But your kid's overfed."

"I can't stop myself," said Maryl, munching on rare roast beef. At the same time, she spread a slice of seeded rye with mayonnaise. "Just like I couldn't stop myself from questioning the darling Fire Chief. He was ever so helpful."

"Was he?" Anissa watched her sister-in-law add lettuce, tomato, cheese, and three sweet pickles to her sandwich. "What did he tell you?"

"Are you finished feeling sorry for yourself?"

"Yes, ma'am."

"Good. I'll skip the chief's marital problems. I won't bore you with the flaws in Irwin Allen's film. As far as I'm concerned, if a movie has Paul Newman, there are no flaws."

"Maryl!"

"The bottom line is that if gas or lighter fluid has been poured on the floor, the fumes would float toward any air space, say the cracks under a door. If someone put a lit cigarette into a box of matches and left that on the floor, fumes would eventually reach the matches. Are you following?"

"Absolutely."

"This is the way I picture it. You said that Delly had a box of matches from the Sawmill, and that she took tranquilizers. We know she fell asleep. Let's assume she left her purse on the floor. Our friendly arsonist finds the purse and steals the lighter fluid, her cigarettes and her matches. Then he lights a cigarette and props it inside the box of matches." Digging her fingers into a jar, Maryl fished for another pickle.

"Hey, don't stop now."

"Okay." Maryl wiped her fingers on a dish towel. "Our perpetrator hurries from the building. The cigarette burns slowly until it ignites the matches. Abracadabra. Studio fire."

"Holy smoke. And I don't mean that as a pun."

"Due to the delay, allowing fumes to drift under the door, and the time it took the cigarette to burn down to the matches, our clever arsonist could have been far away from the studio when the fire started."

"What the hell's going on?" Drew stood in the kitchen doorway.

"Hi, big brother. Would you like half my sandwich?"

"I'd like half your idiotic head. I caught the end of your story. Where did you get that information about fires?"

"From a 'reliable source.' I thought you were watching Jonah's show."

"Jonah's show has more commercials than show, so I decided to fetch my own beer. Would you like to explain what you've been doing in your spare time?"

"You can't intimidate me, Florentino. I've seen you run through the sprinkler, butt-naked, your tiny quick swinging in the breeze. Starve me, pull out my fingernails, I'll never tell."

"Yes, you will."

"What are you doing?"

"Calling Jonah's studio. I'll leave an urgent message, scare the shit out of him."

"That's not fair, Drew."

"Talk!"

"We drove to the deli, planning to track down the delivery kid," Maryl began. Then she related the details of their search for Jake Smith, ending with her classified ad idea.

Drew hit his head with the heel of his hand. "Yesterday Charl ad-libbed something about a classified ad. Then she said 'Everything's okay, Cal, it's jake.' Twice. I didn't mention it because I thought she was bird-brained from her pregnancy. I should have known better. She's never bird-brained."

"Thank you, honey." Anissa smiled.

"Don't 'thank you' me, you—"

"Fairy Godmother. Just call me Fairy Godmother. Betsy Crown said she met Jake outside the studio. On the off chance that he might be an actor, I checked with Vance. The file cabinet didn't burn in the fire, so he went through the 'S' drawer. But he couldn't find an application or photo and he didn't remember a Jake Smith. Don't you see, Drew? If this Jake is an obsessed fan, rather than an actor, he'll set up a meeting with Charl."

"That's a big if. On the other hand, he could be the one who set the fire."

"That's even better. Then we'll catch him and the whole mess will be over and Delly will be safe."

"What makes you think *you'd* be safe?"

In the silence that followed, they could all hear the TV. Tennis star Chris Evert's voice came through loud and clear. "Men playing women? I hope it never comes. Everyone knows that the number one woman can't beat the number thirty man. That would be the battle of the sexes, and everybody would become masculine."

Jonah's voice: "Do you have anything to add, Joe Kapp, before we say goodbye?"

"Well," replied the Minnesota Vikings quarterback, "I've always wondered, is it normal to wake up in the morning in a sweat because you can't wait to beat another human's guts out?"

"Tune in tomorrow," said Jonah. "We're planning a rematch between Pat Huxley and Samantha Gold. Talk about spilling one's guts."

Applause sounded.

Anissa gave a mock sigh. "Have you ever flirted from the neck up, Maryl?"

"I don't think I've ever flirted. Why?"

"Before she died, Maxine asked Judith to write a new plot treatment. Charl, already bored with marriage, has begun to flirt with Dr. Ron. But they're trying to hide my belly bulge, so I'll have to flirt from the neck up."

Drew said, "Are you bored with marriage, my love?"

"No, never!" She sped forward and buried her face against his chest.

"Has my brother named your breasts yet, Anissa?"

"What?"

"Drew likes to make mountains out of molehills," Maryl said. "For example, my breasts are named Gweneth and Heather."

During the teasing conversation that followed, no one mentioned the classified ad. Or Jake Smith.

Intermezzo

While he had been cruising the streets in his black Dodge, the maid had changed the sheets. The maid's name was Margarita, like the song.

He scribbled a note and placed it on top of the VCR.

Margarita. This is for you. Thanx.

Ordinarily he didn't give gifts, but he had laid the maid twice and he didn't need the VCR anymore. Soon he'd have the real Charl.

"Wasting away again in Cally-forny-ville, laid the maid—"

Abruptly, he stopped singing and glanced around the motel room.

His weights were in the trunk of the Dodge, and his hair dye, minus his fingerprints, had been trashed. He wasn't tall, but he looked like Drew Flory; muscles and dark, almost-black hair. She'd like that.

The Morning Star *tapes were packed, along with his clothes and bathroom junk. He hadn't stole a towel because he was a killer, not a thief.*

Well, he'd stolen from Betsy, but that didn't count. He'd taught Betsy a lot. Jesus would pay, too.

Only one piece of clothing hung inside the closet, his outfit for tomorrow, so there was nothing to link him to Jake Smith. He'd even handed the motel manager cash every week.

The perfect crime.

He could drive away and never get caught. Shit, he could fly anywhere, using his real name or his fake I.D.

Margarita had a cousin named Popeye, who'd forged a drivers license for "Jake Smith." Popeye bragged about how he'd once killed a man with an ice pick, and "Jake" had been royally pissed. Because it was "Jake," not Popeye, who'd committed the perfect crime. Two perfect crimes. He'd almost forgotten Jane Doe.

"How come you never got caught, huh Popeye?" he'd asked.

"I stole some stuff so's it would look like a robbery. Then I wiped away the blood and fingerprints. Then I stuffed David's body inside the trunk of his car and ditched the car in San Francisco."

Yeah. Sure. Popeye watched too much TV.

Speaking of TV, Jonah Wiggins was wrapping up his show. Jake aimed his gun at Wiggins and said, "Bang, bang, you asshole."

Thank God he hadn't pulled the trigger the night of the fire. Thank God the TV had cut in with a news bulletin.

Maxine Graham, deader than a doornail!

He remembered screwing Maxine's brains out. She had called the shots and he didn't like that, but she was a big shot so he had no choice. She'd even promised him the job of security guard. As a security guard, Charl would have to notice him. But the Graham bitch lied. She deserved to burn.

"Burn, baby, burn!"

He wished Betsy-Wetsy Crown was with him tonight. He had such a hard-on. But he could wait. He'd waited such a long, long time. Tomorrow he'd call Charl and visit the studio.

On the maid-made bed was a newspaper. Now he glanced down at his special message, right there in the classified-personals. She'd even paid to have it boxed so it would be easy to find.

Jake Smith. Know you're not to blame.
Miss you and want to talk. Our secret.
Call me. Love, Charl.

She missed him. She wanted him. She loved him.

Chapter Thirty-One

The *Morning Star* makeup room was embellished with several newspapers. A sleazy tabloid proclaimed: CRAZED PANDA SEEKS REVENGE. The *L.A. Times* stated that *Terms of Endearment* had won the New York Film Critics Circle award. On the same page, a smaller caption read: "Grand Jury to Determine Pandora's Fate."

Placing her soda can on top of CRAZED PANDA, Maryl studied her reflection in a dressing table mirror. "For the first time in my life I have breasts," she said. "I've named them Joan and Richard."

Anissa smiled. "So it's Richard if it's a boy, huh?"

"Yes. Jonah thinks Richard is for his father, but it's really for Gere. Richard Gere Wiggins."

"Your brother wants me to name my breasts Drew One and Drew Too. T-o-o."

Echo Foster stamped her foot. "This is, without doubt, the stupidest conversation I've ever overheard. And you both look . . . I don't know . . . jumpy . . . yeah, jumpy . . . as if you're waiting for a bomb to go off."

"There's a bomb inside Maryl's belly, Echo. She's ten months pregnant." Anissa zipped up her white maternity dress with its tatted lace collar, then glanced at her watch—5:03 P.M.

T.G.I.F. *Thank God it's Friday.* N.T.T. *No Taping Tomorrow.*

No Grand Jury, either. The decision would be handed down

next week, after Drew and a couple of other cast members had testified.

Strolling through the doorway, Echo stopped mid-stride. "Are you sure I shouldn't wait, Anissa? You and Maryl could join Peter and me at the Unicorn."

"No, thanks. Everybody has left for the day, including stagehands, so I plan to show Maryl the studio."

"If you see Delly, tell her I didn't say boo to that stupid Grand Jury. Tell her my tongue was butter-soft, not knife-sharp, and that I hope the district attorney's chest collapses from suspender-itis."

"I hope he chokes to death on his own venom." Anissa fisted her fingers. "Supercilious snake!"

"It was fun meeting you, Maryl. I used to sneak a peek at your steamy telegrams. They sounded like my favorite author, Edwinna Cartwright. Are you really Drew's sister?"

"That's what I've been told. It was fun meeting you too, Tabby Cat."

After Echo's footsteps had faded away, Maryl scooped up a handful of potato chips from a nearby bag and washed them down with Pepsi. The colors on the can matched her outfit; a red and white striped T-shirt and blue maternity slacks.

Anissa said, "All systems go?"

"Yes. I'm supposed to hide, with my tape recorder, behind that room divider screen next to the door. If anything goes wrong, I waddle like hell to a phone and call the cops."

"Drew had a meeting at Paramount or he'd never have let me enter the studio without his protective custody."

"I told him I planned to shop for layette items. I thrust my humongous belly under his nose. He patted my belly, gave me a timid guy-smile, and said have fun."

"Well, I guess we just twiddle our thumbs until Jake Smith arrives. I asked Henry to buzz." The wall phone buzzed. "Talk about a cue line. What a break. When Jake called this morning he said he'd be here around five-thirty. I'm glad he's early. I hate to wait and Bugs is squirming."

The phone buzzed again. Motioning Maryl behind the black lacquered screen, Anissa picked up the receiver. "Hi, Henry."

"Miss Anissa, there's a woman at the gate. She says her name is Monica Hoffman."

"I don't believe I know her, Henry."

"She says she's from Madison Wisconsin, the wife of someone named Bobby Hoffman, and she's got a message from your momma."

"What's the message?"

"She says it's personal."

"I'm expecting the food delivery man. Could you tell Mrs. Hoffman it's late and everyone's gone home? Ask her if she can come back tomorrow. No, wait, tomorrow's Saturday. How about Monday? Tell her she can watch us tape the show. That's why she's really here. I talked to my mother last night."

Anissa tried to keep her voice steady. Following Jacob's sudden stroke, Helene had retreated more and more into her dream world. Last night's call had been surreal. Mama had chastised *Charl,* warning her over and over again that she'd lose Cal's love if she continued her shenanigans. Anissa's pregnancy, carefully hidden during her Charl-scenes, hadn't even been mentioned.

"Hold on," said Henry. After a short silence, he returned to the line. "Mrs. Hoffman says she's flying home this weekend. Ordinarily I wouldn't try and change your mind, child, but she's all gussied up special."

"Okay. I'll talk to her. Please don't forget to signal when the delivery man gets here. Thanks, Henry." Anissa hung up the receiver. "I guess you can come out of hiding, Maryl. It's just some hometown lady with a so-called message from my mother.

All she probably wants is an autograph. She's married to a guy I grew up with, Bobby Hoffman. He was a hateful little shit, and I loathed him, but I can't blame her for that."

"I'm comfortable, curled up in this old stuffed armchair. You can chit-chat with your fan, Anissa, and I won't have to listen to all that aren't-you-the-Rosebud-girl crap."

"Okay. I'll sit at my dressing table, let Monica Hoffman think I'm taking off my makeup, anxious to leave." For a few minutes Anissa straightened clutter, discarding tissues, capping tubes and lipsticks. "I hear footsteps, Maryl. That was fast. I guess Mrs. Hoffman didn't stop to study our famous mural."

Turning, Anissa forced her lips into what she hoped was a sincere smile.

Screw the cops, thought Drew, as he watched his speedometer needle hover around eighty-five. Strange. Maryl was the one with premonitions. Hadn't she accurately forecast her *que serra?* "I have this strong feeling that something special will happen soon," she'd said.

Drew had a strong feeling that something awful would happen soon. Because he was too damn happy. Too damn lucky.

He wanted to get home faster than a speeding bullet, hug Anissa, make mad passionate love, christen her beautiful breasts with his tongue.

Monica Hoffman wore an expensive, high-necked black gown with three-quarter sleeves and overall sequins. Pretty in a small-featured way, her platinum hair fell to her shoulders. Her brown eyes were set close together, the lashes caked with thick mascara. A cupid's bow outlined her thin lips.

Then Anissa caught a glimpse of the woman's back in a wall mirror and heard the echo of Randy's voice: *You can't disguise a man's shoulders and back. It's a different shape than a woman's.*

Monica was short, muscular, and she was a man.

"Won't you s-sit d-down, Mrs. Hoffman?"

"No thanks, Nissa. Shit! You knew me right away, didn't you? I've been in California for months and you never saw me. You wouldn't even say hello at Jacob's fancy party. Then I wear a dress and you nail me."

"Why are you pretending to be your wife, Bobby?"

"The security guard would recognize the deli delivery boy."

"*You're* Jake Smith?"

"Think, Nissa. Jake Smith. J.S. Jacob Stern. I named myself for the senator."

"You're a first-rate mechanic, Bobby. Why on earth would you work as a delivery kid?"

"Because it got me inside your studio."

Turn on the tape recorder, Maryl, Anissa pleaded silently. *Then sit very still, like a model model.*

"Did you start the fire?" she asked.

"Yeah. But I didn't mean to hurt nobody. I seen you in this room, Nissa, combing your hair. Then I gave Maxine her sandwich. On my way out, I seen Pandora sleeping. Her purse had spilled stuff. Ciggies, matches, a can of lighter fluid. I stared at that can for a long time before it hit me. I'd set a fire, wait outside, then save you."

"Save me?"

"I lit a cigarette and put its end in the matchbox. I seen a guy do that on TV once."

"You started a fire so you could save me?"

"I figured you'd be grateful. On that TV show they hugged and kissed, but only after he saved her from the fire."

Anissa couldn't stifle her nervous giggle.

"Don't you laugh," Bobby said, stabbing the air with his index finger. "The last bitch who laughed at me is dead. I killed her."

"Maxine Graham?" Anissa heard an audible gasp from behind the screen. "I thought you didn't mean to hurt anyone," she said quickly, hoping she'd covered Maryl's breathy *whoosh.*

"Hurt Maxine? Shit, no. I killed a whore named Jane Doe. Before that I shot Moosie, my wife. At your party you brushed me off, wouldn't say nothin'. Moosie rubbed my nose in it, needled me for weeks. She died while hunting, an accident, shot through the head. No one suspected me. Why would Hoffman kill his wife? She didn't have no insurance and she wasn't sleeping around. Bobby loved Monica. 'Fact, Bobby mourned so much for his dead wife he had to leave Wisconsin. The perfect crime."

Maryl, we've collected enough evidence. He's looking at me, his back to the door. Waddle the hell out of here.

"I sold my business," he continued, "so there's lots of money socked away. I'm not some snot-nosed kid living off the senator's charity. A long time ago I told Jacob I wanted to marry you, but he laughed. Helene said it was all right with her. 'Things will work out,' she said. Well, things worked out great. I'm free as a bird. I've got money. And I still want you."

"What are you talking about, Bobby? I'm married to Drew Flory. I'm pregnant with his baby."

"So what? We'll tell Jacob it's ours."

Anissa shook her head. "Don't you understand? I'm *legally* married to—"

"Nah." Kicking off his high-heeled pumps, he wriggled toes clad in nylon. "You don't love Cal no more, Nissa. Anyways, he's chasing that new singer while you're making eyes at Dr. Ron."

"Dear God, Bobby, that's *pretend.*"

"If it bothers you, I mean being legally married and all, I'll get rid of Cal. You can make sure he comes to the studio. I'll knock him out and set another fire and they'll blame it on

Pandora again, like they did before. She's not in jail, so they'll think she wanted to finish what she started."

Anissa took a deep breath. "You'd better leave before I call the police."

"But on TV you said everything was Jake, and you wrote that newspaper message about how you missed me, wanted me, loved me."

"I didn't mean—"

"Liar! You were laughing at me."

"How could I laugh, Bobby? I didn't know Jake was you. I thought—"

"Why do you keep staring at that screen? What's behind the screen?"

"Run, Maryl!"

Bobby turned and sprinted toward the entrance. Diving, he caught Maryl's ankle.

She pitched forward.

At the same time, Anissa jumped on top of Bobby and grasped the first thing that came to hand—his platinum wig. Hairpins flew. Off balance, still clutching the wig, Anissa fell backwards.

Bobby crawled through the doorway, retrieved a blue gym bag, and pulled a small gun from its interior. He aimed it toward Maryl. "One false move, Nissa, and I'll shoot your friend."

Dropping the wig, Anissa lifted her hands. "Okay, Bobby. Will you let me see if she's hurt? Please?"

He nodded, then sat with his back against the wall, resting the gun on his drawn-up knees.

Anissa knelt next to Maryl. "Are you all right, love? You took a nasty spill. Folks probably heard the thud inside Dodger Stadium."

"Not . . . Dodger . . . Stadium. It's football season. The damn Raiders will sign me . . . fullback or fullbelly." Maryl sat up and took several deep breaths. She'd bumped her nose on the floor and blood trickled down to her mouth. "I should have tried to leave earlier," she said, "but . . . oh! Oh, shit!"

"What is it? What's wrong? You can't be . . . no!"

"Yes. 'Maryl Goes Into Labor During Crisis.' I'll have to remember details for Ed . . . Edwinna's next book. Damn! Jonah was planning to videotape Joan's birth."

"Your pains, are they far apart?"

"Just started. Water broke. I shouldn't have worn blue slacks. Next time I'll ask Jonah's fashion experts to design a maternity wardrobe the color of amniotic fluid."

Clad in a white bra and girdle, Pat Huxley searched through her closet. Without pause, she tossed every glitzy outfit she owned toward the bed.

Why had she agreed to guest-star with Samantha Gold on Jonah's show tonight?

The gigolo joke—*pay* it again, Sam—sounded stupid. And that Gold bitch could give as good as she got.

"So what'cha' say, Bootsie?" The naked man's voice, muffled by her sequined galaxy pantsuit, came from her bed.

"Shut up, Buzzy."

"I've never seen you so antsy, Python." He found the carpet with his toes, and lumbered toward the closet.

Ignoring Beeson, Pat discovered the perfect outfit. A black gown, complete with fur collar. To attach the collar, you pulled a fox's poofy tail through its open mouth. The garment had just been returned from the cleaners. DRY CLEAN ONLY read the tag.

Black was good. Black would make her look slim. Everyone would stare at her foxy gown.

Pat grabbed the quilted hanger and turned around.

Beeson lowered her to the floor.

"Wait a minute, my dress," she said, but he'd already pulled down her panty girdle.

His lips nuzzled her breasts. Then he penetrated, groaned, withdrew, and ejaculated all over her perfect black gown with its grinning fox-face collar.

"Bobby, Maryl's having her baby," said Anissa, striving to keep her voice calm. "Will you let her leave?"

"Do you think I'm nuts?"

"We can walk out of the building together and I'll drive with you wherever you want—"

"No!"

"Lock Maryl inside an office. When we're far away from the studio, we can call an ambulance."

"No. We're not leaving, Nissa. I have unfinished business from a Christmas Eve ten years ago, and we have to get Cal here so's we can take care of him. Where do you film the show?"

"Top floor."

"Ain't never delivered food there." Bobby glanced around the makeup room. "Does that phone on the wall have an outside line?"

"Yes."

"Is Cal home?"

"My husband's name is Drew."

"Call Cal and tell him to get over here. Don't say nothin' 'bout your friend's baby. Do you understand?"

"Yes, but—"

"If I hear one thing wrong I'll shoot your friend."

"Okay, Bobby, I promise. Wait. Drew and I tease each other. We call our baby Bugs Bunny, so please don't think I'm signaling. If I don't tease him back, he'll know something's wrong."

"The phone has a long cord. Bring the receiver near me so's I can hear you and him." Bobby stood up, his gun hand steady.

Please be home, please be home, Anissa prayed, then felt her knees weaken when Drew answered the phone.

"Hi, darling, are you all gassed up?" she asked, placing the receiver away from her ear so Bobby could hear.

"Where the hell are you?"

"I'm at the studio. Don't be mad. I fell asleep and I'm feeling poorly. Belly-ache. Could you pick me up here? I know you're busy—"

"Not that busy." Drew's voice was gruff. "Lie down and rest. How's Bugs?"

Nodding at Bobby, Anissa watched his chipped tooth flash in a tight smile of acknowledgment.

"Bugs is fine, Drew, buck-jumping. It reminds me of that Warner's cartoon, the one where the whole gang dressed up as Biblical characters. Bugs Bunny played Samson and I think Daffy Duck played Delilah. Wasn't Porky Pig the emperor Nero, fiddling while Rome burned?"

"Good casting," said Drew.

" 'Disney has the best casting. If he doesn't like an actor, he just tears him up.' Quote, unquote."

"Who said that?"

"Alfred Hitchcock. Your sister adores Hitchcock movies, especially the one about birds."

Bobby's gesture meant hang up the phone. He looked furious.

"Drew, I have to lie down now. I'm in the makeup room. I love you. Hurry."

"I'm on my way. I love you, too. Don't fret."

"I won't. 'Bye."

Bobby scowled. "What was all that shit about cartoons and cocks?"

"*Hitch*cock. I told you. Drew and I always make jokes over the phone." Anissa placed the receiver on its cradle.

Maryl moaned. "I think baby's in a hurry. Damn! It's not polite to arrive at a party early."

"Bobby, won't you please, please let Maryl leave?"

"Help her walk to the top floor."

"But Drew will look for me here, inside the makeup room."

"Move!"

Samantha scowled. Delly, the bane of her existence, had ruined everything with that stupid arson attempt. The publicity had even eclipsed Samantha Gold's TV debut. Delly-Dog strikes again. How could Samantha Vivian Gold strike back?

With a wicked smile, she walked toward Garrison. "Write me a song about fire, darling."

"It's already been done. Jerry Lee Lewis. Great balls—"

"Something country. Fire, desire—"

"*Inspire* me, Samantha."

She made a little moue, stuck out her tongue, then kept it stuck out as she fell to her knees and unzipped his fly.

With Bobby behind them, still pointing his gun, Maryl leaned against Anissa. "Birds?" she asked, her voice low and breathy. "I adore Hitchcock's movie about birds?"

"Speaking of birds, wait until we reach the top floor. The ceiling grid lights look like a flying flock. Everybody instinctively swerves the first time they see it. Bobby might hunch down, too. Should we try and rush him together?"

"I don't think I could rush a marshmallow right now. I'm trying to keep my sense of humor, but baby's awfully pushy."

"Hang on, Maryl, it'll be over soon," Anissa whispered. "I'm so glad we told Drew about Jake Smith. If he didn't get my 'Delilah' and 'Rome burning' hints, he'll snap to the Hitchcock allusion. He once told me about your loft shoot and the freaked-out parrot."

Crew members had left a few lights glowing but the studio was cloaked in gloom, as if carpenters had nailed together rooms, loaded them with furniture, and forgotten to add ceilings. It smelled like the new paint that covered the smoke-blackened walls from Delly's fire.

No, thought Anissa. *Bobby's* fire.

Gritting her teeth, she guided Maryl toward a bed on the Lady Nan set.

Susannah Benton sat in her husband's office and stared at the knife she'd ordered from a TV ad. They hadn't lied. Damn blade could slice anything. Pennies. Cable wire. Political aspirations.

Glancing at her watch, she sipped the last of her club soda, stood, walked over to a window, raised her arms high, and aimed the knife, Kamikaze style, toward her left breast.

Sunset spiked her husband's Jaguar. She heard Rusty's footsteps—right on time. He was never late for dinner, except tonight there'd be no dinner.

"What the hell!" His voice was sardonic and just a little bit alarmed. "Are you planning to audition for a role in *Madame Butterfly,* Suze?"

She lowered the knife. "I've already auditioned, darling, for *Morning Star.*"

"What?"

"You heard me. It was going to be a small part, what they call an under-five. But they loved the idea of Rusty Benton's wife performing on Delly Diamond's soap, so they contracted me on the spot. Thirteen weeks, Rusty, with a renewable option. We start taping Monday since they plan to cash in on all that delicious Grand Jury publicity. Guess what part I'm playing? Come on, guess. Aw, you're no fun. I'm the district attorney who prosecutes Hannah's murderer. They killed off this character named Hannah and blamed it on this chick named Tabby-Cat, so they need a D.A."

"Jesus, you must be drunk."

"No, darling, and that's the truth, the whole truth, and nothing but the truth." Walking forward, she severed his suspenders. "I haven't had any martoonies since the night you played Bruce the Shark. In Hollywood, America, a wife doesn't have to take her husband's abuse, not if she's sober."

"Why'd you cut my suspenders, Suze?"

"Because that's what they do to clowns. I saw it at the circus."

"The circus?"

"You're not usually so dense this early in the evening, Rusty. Haven't you been listening? I've been cast on a soap opera and you're gonna' be a clown."

"No way! I'll beat you black and—"

"Blue? I don't think so. This knife can slice more than suspenders."

"Are you threatening me?"

"You bet your life."

"But Suze, you can't appear on that soap opera. I'll be the laughing stock—"

"Leave me alone, Rusty. Prepare a brief or summation or something. I want to study my script. There are so many ways to perform the part. For instance, I considered Scaramouch, you know, that French buffoon? On the other hand, I could play her with more . . . shall we say dignity? Then you might not be such a laughing stock. Would you do me a small favor? Call my beauty salon and tell them to send over someone to dye my hair red?"

"Red?"

"There's this actor who plays Dr. Ron. He says he likes red hair and he looks a little like James Dean and he's already insinuated that we might 'get it on,' his words. But I swear to

God I won't cheat on you, Rusty, not if you toe the line."

Drenched with perspiration, Maryl hugged her stomach. "I want Jonah, I want Jonah," she kept repeating, her voice raspy.

Anissa dabbed at Maryl's bloody nose with the pillowcase, then reached out blindly and grasped the first thing her hand encountered—a green cloth. The cotton cloth covered a bird cage. Jon had given Samantha's parrot to Echo. Echo must have placed the parrot and cage on the Lady Nan set before she left, another one of her practical jokes. There was seed and water, so Echo's shtick was planned for Monday's taping. *Great! Just what Maryl needs. A parrot. Thanks a lot, Echo.*

Anissa readjusted Sinbad's cage cover and, instead, wove the bedspread through Maryl's fingers. "Pull on this when the pain gets too overwhelming, love."

"My body's not built for having babies. Should have stayed a virgin. Hope she looks like Jonah—without the quick. Damn quick got me into this mess."

Anissa felt like laughing and crying at the same time. "I'd tell you to scream your head off, Maryl, but I think it would drive Bobby even more bonkers and he might gag you. Listen, I know these sets better than he does. I'll think of something."

"What are you two whispering about? Get over here, Nissa. On second thought, find a cord and tie up your friend."

"No. I won't do that, Bobby. If I tie her up, she won't be able to move with her pain."

He shrugged, then ripped at his dress until it tore apart. The gown had a built-in bra stuffed with shredded foam rubber. Shifting the gun from hand to hand, Bobby wriggled out of his panty hose. Finally, he stood there, clad in his shorts. "Is there another bed, Nissa? Never mind. I like the nightclub better. It has more light. You know what? You look like a bride in that dress. A beautiful bride. Take it off."

"Go to hell!"

"Take off your dress. I'm not kidding. I'll make sure your friend can never have her baby if you don't. I want some fun before I kill Cal, and once you see what I can do, you won't care if he's dead."

"I know what you can do. I talked to Betsy Crown."

Bobby laughed. "Betsy-Wetsy? I taught her lots of things. Now I'm gonna' teach you. Take off that damn dress."

Judith Pendergraft walked toward her white Cadillac.

Directly in front of Delly's lawn stood a small, elderly woman and a large dog.

"Squirt pee, Jack Benny," the woman said. "Or better yet, squat and shit."

Crazy! Everyone in Hollywood was crazy, including Delly's boyfriend.

Judith had come calling, in person, to offer reinstatement. If Delly wasn't indicted, Judith would write her back into the show.

Jon Griffin had told Judith to get lost.

Mayella, Beverlee and Scottie were waiting in the car. Judith had suggested they to go easy on Delly during the Grand Jury investigation, but they'd ignored her advice. Was her control slipping? Maybe she should seriously consider the offer to produce that new east coast daytime drama, *Chantilly Lace.*

Anissa stepped from her dress.

Bobby grinned. "I couldn't see the baby so good when you were all covered up. There's a nice little bulge 'neath your panties, Nissa. Shit! Wish I had a camera. Jacob would love a picture of his grandson. Do you know how to work this stuff?"

"I guess so, if the cameras are loaded with film."

"What's this thing called?"

"A dolly. The cameraman can move around and shoot from different positions."

"Aim it toward the top of the bar. Does the jukebox work?"

"Yes. All you have to do is plug—"

"You plug it in, Nissa. I want music."

"What song?"

"Anything mushy."

The machine whirred into life. Doris Day. "Once I Had a Secret Love."

"Turn on the camera," Bobby said. "Hurry."

She fumbled at the dolly and camera. Bobby stood on the other side, watching.

Doris sang about how impatient she was to be free.

Free, thought Anissa. She would have to figure out how to free Maryl from this maniac.

"Okay, lie down on top of the bar," said Bobby. "This time Joe's not here to stop our fun."

"You're insane."

"If you say that again, I'll shoot."

"Shut up," squawked the parrot.

"Oh, no, help!" Maryl screamed. She had dropped the bedspread and reached for the green cage cloth.

"Lady Nan has great tits," Sinbad squawked.

Bobby instinctively glanced toward the parrot. Anissa ran around the dolly, grabbed Bobby's gun hand, lowered her mouth and bit his wrist. Despite his angry howls and Maryl's frightened screams, a thought flashed through her mind: Bobby Hoffman pinching a little girl until she cried.

This is for me and Maryl, Delly and Maxine, she thought, biting harder, tasting blood.

Jon Griffin stared at his computer screen.

He tried to concentrate, but all he could think about was the

Grand Jury. He had testified that Delly was resigned, not angry, and her jump-from-the-roof threat had been caused by personal stress. Then Benton had snapped his suspenders and sprung his trap, asking Jon about the hacked-up piano. How did Benton know about Samantha's goddamn piano?

Jon heard someone cry his name. Leaping to his feet, he raced toward the bedroom.

"Jonny! Oh my God! Jonny!"

"What is it, Delly?"

"I remember." Her green eyes blazed. "I fell asleep and dreamed about Samantha and Maxine and Southern Comfort."

"Yes. We know you dreamed."

"I opened my eyes for a minute and saw that guy who delivers sandwiches. I think he stole something from my purse."

"What did he steal, baby?"

"It wasn't my tongue," she said.

"Delly!"

"I'm not crazy, Jonny. That was a joke."

"Sorry. I'll call the cops and tell them about the delivery guy. First, do you remember the roof?"

"Yes. I tried to jump but Cal . . . Drew talked me out of it."

"Anything else?"

"I lost our baby," she said, and burst into tears.

"Okay, good, cry it all out." Jon pulled Delly into his lap and pressed her face against his chest.

"After you call the police, call Drew," she said, her breath catching on a sob. "I never thanked him."

"Drop your gun and freeze! Police are at the entrance and I have a rifle aimed at your head."

Anissa recognized Drew's voice, booming from Maxine's skybooth.

With his free hand, Bobby pulled Anissa's hair and slapped her face.

Like a bulldog, her teeth gripped harder.

Bobby dropped his gun.

Heels drummed the floor as two policemen ran toward them.

"Up against the wall," ordered one of the cops.

"I can't," Bobby yelped. "She won't let go."

Anissa felt Drew wrap his arms around her shaking body.

"It's over," he said.

Doris Day sang about how her secret love wasn't secret anymore.

Sudden silence.

Except for Bobby's anguished howls.

Anissa clenched her jaw and held on. Drew gently tugged at her shoulders. "Cut, that's a wrap," he said into her ear.

Releasing Bobby, Anissa shouted, "Maryl's in labor, Drew! The Lady Nan set."

"Maryl's here? At the studio?" Unbuttoning his shirt, he followed Anissa.

"Call an ambulance," she said to the cops, who were handcuffing Bobby's injured wrist.

Maryl lay on her back. She had knocked over the parrot cage and Sinbad fluttered, squawking obscenities.

Drew tossed Anissa his shirt. Then he sat on the edge of the bed and stroked his sister's perspiration-soaked hair. "Marilyn Monroe Bradley Florentino Wiggins," he crooned. "You're always so difficult. Why can't you have your baby on the back seat of a cab, like everyone else?"

"Oh, Drew. Thank God. Please make the pain go away."

"I guess it's time I learned how to deliver a baby. Listen, Miss Scarlett. Atlanta's burning and Sherman's marching through Georgia. The countryside's a mess but Tara's still standing. Take a deep breath. Rhett Butler Flory's here."

Maryl winced. "You sound like Clark Gable impersonating Clark Gable. Did I kill the parrot?"

"Just ruffled his feathers," said Anissa, swallowing a sob.

Approximately forty-five minutes later, Norma Jean Wiggins made her entrance. She received a standing ovation from one uncle, one aunt, and two paramedics.

"Norma Jean?" Anissa sat on the bed. "What happened to Joan of Arc Wiggins?"

"Norma Jean was Marilyn Monroe's real name. I must remember to tell Jonah that labor pains are like his commercials. Toward the end they're much longer and closer together."

"Jonah's on his way to the hospital. We'll join him there. How do you feel?"

"Sore. Like someone just pulled a bowling bowl through an opening big enough for a ping-pong ball." She patted her wet, tangled curls. "Rosebud hair products are supposed to withstand windstorms and humidity. But they never mention childbirth, clever bastards. Did you film the big event, Anissa?"

Both women glanced at the camera, whose red light blinked. During her struggle with Bobby, Anissa had swiveled the dolly toward Lady Nan's bedroom.

"Good show." Maryl smiled. "Norma Jean's first starring role. She's perfect, isn't she?"

"Yes." Anissa clasped her friend's hand. "Delly's innocent and you're safe. Oh Maryl, it's true. The morning stars sang together and all the sons *and daughters* of God shouted for joy."

With a grin, Drew handed his sister the baby. "Here's Joy."

"Jonah's Joy," said Maryl.

"Jeannie Joy," said Anissa. "Great stage name."

As if on cue, the baby began to cry. For joy.

Curtain Call

September 8, 1985

Propped against plump pillows, Delly could smell the roses outside her open window. Funny how New York always reminded her of roses, not California. It should be the other way around. Rose Bowl. Rose Bowl Parade. Happy New Year. Auld Lang Syne. Time for auld acquaintances to be forgot.

Especially one auld acquaintance. She'd missed Sunday night's sixty minutes with Judith Pendergraft.

During their first visit to the hospital, Anissa and Maryl had told Delly about the Volkswagen driver who'd been drunk as a skunk. Then there was the tourist from Tulsa, who kept screaming look-at-all-that-blood-is-she-dead until someone sat her down on the curb. Whereupon, she'd passed out and the ambulance personnel thought the woman from Tulsa was the accident victim.

Anissa said Delly had broken her leg—again!—and sustained a concussion. When she was released from the hospital she'd stay at the Flory residence, okay?

Okay. Drew and Anissa could support her. Why not? She always played the supporting role. The only leading role she'd ever successfully performed was *Duck Pond*'s Virginia.

From her pillowed perch atop a four-poster, Delly glanced around Anissa's guest room. Pale yellow curtains fluttered in the gentle breeze, a backdrop for the zebra-colored kitten who slept draped across the windowsill. Maybe Toto Too dreamed about the fish populating Long Island Sound. The other kittens, Dolf Too and Schatzi, were curled up under the bed. Late afternoon sunshine haloed Toto's dotted muzzle and quivering whiskers.

Against one wall, bookshelves were filled with haphazardly stacked paperbacks and scripts. A second wall showcased a photo collage of Anissa and Drew's little girl, Randi Theresa. In one photo Randi posed with Jeannie Joy, Maryl's fiery-haired toddler. Another photo flaunted Jeannie Joy's baby brother, Richard Gere Wiggins. Maryl had virtually given up her modeling career. Instead, she was churning out historical romances. Her third Civil War saga, *Charlotte's Reb,* had hit the *New York Times* bestseller list.

Anissa's refinished maple dresser sported a portable TV, turned down low. A local channel televised Jon's *Groundhog Murders,* the movie that had led to Drew's successful series, *Casey's Castle.* Jeff Casey, a New York detective, lived in his "castle"—a large boat anchored off the Sound. A toy company had recently issued Jeff Casey dolls and Jeff Casey boats.

Delly's gaze shifted so that she could enjoy the sight of Jon entering the room.

"How's my girl?" he said.

"In better shape than you, Tarz. You've lost so much weight. Cheetah the Monk could carry you with one arm while he swings through Hollywood and Vine."

"I look better than I did two weeks ago. What good is Tarzan without his crocodelly?"

"I'm sorry."

"No, I'm sorry." Jon turned off the TV, sat on the bed, and placed a large manila envelope near her pillow. "After the accident, during my flight to New York, I kept wondering if I'd lost the chance to apologize and tell you how much I love you. I once said that emotions should be up-front. I said if you were unhappy I'd cuddle and protect you."

"But you did. Pandora, the fire, you couldn't have been more supportive."

"When it was all over, I shut out your problems. You wanted another soap, but I was afraid the whole thing would start again, those damn character flip-flops. I couldn't deal with it, so I ignored your desperation. I even convinced Drew's agent to allow you time to recover. He's a busy man and you got lost in the shuffle. That was my biggest mistake."

"I had lunch with Judith on the day of the accident. We've both made mistakes, Jonny."

From another room came the sound of a radio. Samantha Gold. During the last two years, Sami had appeared briefly on *Morning Star,* then completed a whirlwind concert tour. She'd won a Grammy, and last month she had begun rehearsals for an Andrew Lloyd Webber musical, inspired by Joan of Arc. As Saint Joan, Samantha would die heroically in one of history's most famous bonfires.

Lucky I didn't burn to death in the studio fire, Delly thought, *since Sami will burn better.*

She waited until Sami's song ended. "What's inside the envelope, Jonny?"

"Photographs. I had a long talk with your mom. After she flew back to Chicago, she sent these. They were taken by your father." Jon opened the envelope and retrieved an enlargement.

Delly stared at the portrait of a little girl. Her chin rested on one hand while she gazed dreamily through a window. Reflected in the pane of glass, Sami's angry face looked distorted. "Is that really me? I don't remember Daddy taking it. Can . . . may I see the others?"

Jon handed her a second picture. It showed Delly, eight or nine years old, on her way down a slide, her face about to explode with laughter. At the bottom of the slide stood Sami, glaring at her sister.

"William titled this 'A Day at the Playground,' " Jon said.

Delly shivered as she recalled another Playground with rooms called Seesaw and Merry-Go-Round. Accepting the next enlargement from Jon's outstretched hand, she stared at herself again, tiny, wide-eyed, holding an earnest conversation with a giant panda, offering him "tea" from a miniature cup and saucer. In the background, Sami appeared both furious and miserable.

"I don't remember these pictures, Jonny. Mom had a bunch in frames with Sami and me posing together . . ." She paused. "What's your point?"

"Look at Sami's face. I've never seen anyone so jealous, so envious."

"Of me?"

"Yes. She's been in competition with you her whole life."

"No, Jonny, it was the other way around. Sami was always Daddy's favorite, his Gold star."

"Not true. Look at these pictures."

"But we were small children. I grew up a teenage mess while Sami was Princess Pretty."

"Sami worked at cultivating her beauty because you were naturally smart, talented and lovely."

"Bullshit! I was fat and had a crooked overbite."

Jon grinned. "Let's just say that you weren't as flashy as Samantha. She used her early physical maturity to get the parts you wanted in school plays and to mess around with popular boys, especially the boys you admired. Then you started to catch up. She married your prom date, had kids, worked on her singing, all things you hadn't done. But it wasn't enough. She wanted what you had, too. California, *Morning Star*—"

"And you."

"And me." Jon pulled Delly into his lap and settled her

injured leg on top of a pillow. "Will you marry me? Now that your sister's divorced from Jules *and* Garrison, will you at least think about it?"

"Sami's with Rattlesnake again, hinting to the gossip columnists about pending matrimony. Remember our Chinese Zodiac signs?"

"Is that a yes or no?"

Delly leaned back in Jon's arms. Should she say yes?

Her mind raced. *Morning Star*'s ratings had gone downhill—like an avalanche. They needed a new story line, a fresh plot treatment. Although Charl had been written out of the show, another actor played Cal. How about a relationship between Cal and Pandora? Wouldn't that be a ratings boost?

There was a new producer and a new head writer. Maybe Delly could convince them to try Pandora in a recurring role and evaluate viewer reaction. The public adored Panda.

No. The public felt sorry for Panda. Poor, poor Pandora Poe, maddest kid on the whole damn show. If Delly played Pandora, she'd be right back where she started. It took talent to act crazy, but it took even more talent to act sane.

What about Charl? They could resurrect Charl, couldn't they? Charl was pretty. And smart. And sane.

She could grow out her bangs and bleach her hair the same color as Anissa's.

Forget Judith Pendergraft! If Delly couldn't make it on her own, she didn't deserve success, and success would taste so much sweeter if she made it on her own.

Once she had baked a soufflé. It hadn't fallen, and it was the best meal she'd ever eaten in her whole life.

Because she'd made it all by herself.

Suddenly, she felt puffed-up, just like her perfect soufflé. She had Jon. And she had friends. Anissa. Maryl. Drew. Jonah. Joe Weiss. Kathy Wong-Weiss . . .

Love gave her strength, and friends gave her love.

Samantha's voice hummed around the corner. It was "Play It Again Sam Day" on the radio.

Delly stared into Jon's eyes. "I want . . ."

"What, honey?"

"I wish—no! Forget wishes, forget *Morning Star,* forget Pandora, forget Charl. I'll pull myself up from the ashes, hitch a ride to the ball, and organize my own cleaning service. For starters, I'll hire myself a chimney sweep."

"Chimney sweep?"

"A new agent, someone who believes in Delly Diamond. I just realized that if one is an ugly duckling on the inside, she's an ugly duckling on the outside. Hollywood loves to dine on duck, Jonny, especially sweet and sour duck, but they don't eat swans. Have you ever seen swan on a menu?"

"I think *cygne de coquilles* was our dinner special the night I met you, the night I fell in love with you."

"The night I fell in love with you," Delly amended.

Three, two, one.

ABOUT THE AUTHOR

Denise Dietz is the bestselling author of *Fifty Cents for Your Soul, The Landlord's Black-Eyed Daughter* (as Mary Ellen Dennis), and *Footprints in the Butter*—an Ingrid Beaumont Mystery co-starring Hitchcock the Dog. Denise met her husband, novelist Gordon Aalborg (*Dining with Devils*), on the Internet. They wed at a writers' conference and bought a heritage cottage on Vancouver Island. Denise's most recent books are *Eye of Newt,* starring reluctant witch Sydney St. Charles, and *Strangle a Loaf of Italian Bread,* fourth in the Ellie Bernstein/Lt. Peter Miller "diet club" mystery series. The first and second, *Throw Darts at a Cheesecake* and *Beat Up a Cookie,* are available in large print. Denise loves to hear from readers. You can contact her through her Web site: www.denisedietz.com.